PRAISE FOR

BLACK AND WHITE

WITHDRAWN

"In this complex tale, Kessler and Kittredge create a dark world where the narrow line between hero and vigilante is defined by corporate interests. . . . Jet and Iridium's multifaceted relationship will appeal to all who have come to want more from their superheroes than good vs. evil and mindless battles."
—*Publishers Weekly*

"A fast-paced and compelling take on superheroes."
—*Romantic Times* (4 stars)

"What could one possibly add to the superheroes' lore that hasn't already been done in comics? . . . Could *Black and White* offer something fresh to the genre? In one word: yes. . . . This is a story and a world that both pay tribute and make a parody of superheroes. It works and it is cool." —The Book Smugglers

"Not since *Good Omens* by Gaiman and Pratchett has a co-authored novel come across as seamless as *Black and White* does. . . . Ms. Kessler and Kittredge know their superhero comics [but] please don't just think that this is just a comic book in novel form. Kessler and Kittredge blend elements of romance and mystery into this well thought out story [and] fans of thrillers will end up satisfied as well. . . . 4 out of 4 stars!"
—Preternatural Reviews

"The gripping first volume of the Icarus Project series captures the reader's interest and holds it hostage until the very last page. . . . Full to the brim with action, emotional resonance, and humor, *Black and White* has something for everyone. The Icarus Project series sets a new standard for superhero novels, and this reviewer anxiously and avidly awaits the next installment." —Bitten by Books

"Kessler and Kittredge do an impressive job in laying the foundation and building their world of heroes and villains. . . . If you're not instantly caught up in the action, then the emotional aspect of *Black and White* is sure to capture your attention and hold you spellbound until the very end. Whether you love a good comic book, or just enjoy getting caught up in the fantasy of superheroes, this is one book that readers should have on this year's wish list." —Darque Reviews

"There are no words to properly describe how much I adored this book. . . . *Black and White* has action, suspense, mystery, and fantastic characterization. When I wasn't reading it, I was thinking about it and could not stop thinking about it! I was immersed, obsessed, and in love with this book for three days of nonstop reading. . . . Kessler and Kittredge are the ultimate writing duo and are sure to gain a huge following with this exciting new fantasy series." —Night Owl Romance (5 out of 5, Reviewer Top Pick)

"This is a must for comic book fans that like their heroes three-dimensional. I couldn't put it down. I'm panting for the sequel due next year." —*University City Review*

"*Black and White* is cover-to-cover superhero girl power awesomeness. . . . A wild, fun, irresistible ride. It's fast-paced enough to read in a day. Just don't plan on doing *anything* else until you're through." —Waiting for Fairies

"Besides being a terrific character study of two female superheroes in the early twenty-second century, I loved the pervasive duality of this novel. . . . I loved getting to know these two complex but wounded characters. . . . *Black and White* does an admirable job of making us care about Jet and Iridium and their friendship. . . . Superb character-driven storytelling with no prerequisite for comic book appreciation needed."
—SciFiGuy

"A stunning superhero story . . . The plot is fascinatingly layered, with the authors leaping between past and present to drop story seeds and watch them grow. There's so much happening, and it all ties together, making for a compelling exploration into the secrets at the heart of this society. There's something corrupt and dark hidden in the depths of the extrahuman world, and watching it all unfold changes the nature of things considerably. Toss in some well-executed action scenes, and you pretty much have an ideal comic book in novel format. It's going to be a long wait until the next installment of this series."
—The Green Man Review

"This complex story explores the good and evil in all of us, even superheroes. . . . Without taking itself too seriously, this Justice League–meets–Harry Potter novel offers some valuable insights into the nature of being human. . . . Kessler and Kittredge definitely filled a void for me by creating female superheroes who stand on their own and aren't connected to existing male superheroes. . . . I'm definitely looking forward to the next installment in this series." —SF Signal

Also by Jackie Kessler and Caitlin Kittredge

BLACK AND WHITE

SHADES
OF
GRAY

SHADES OF GRAY

JACKIE KESSLER
CAITLIN KITTREDGE

SPECTRA

BALLANTINE BOOKS
NEW YORK

FICTION

A Spectra Trade Paperback Original

Copyright © 2010 by Jacqueline H. Kessler and Caitlin Kittredge

Published in the United States by Spectra,
an imprint of The Random House Publishing Group,
a division of Random House, Inc., New York.

SPECTRA and the portrayal of a boxed "s" are trademarks
of Random House, Inc.

Library of Congress Cataloging-in-Publication Data
Kessler, Jackie (Jackie H.)
Shades of gray / Jackie Kessler, Caitlin Kittredge.
p. cm. — (Icarus Project ; bk. 2)
ISBN 978-0-553-38632-5 (pbk.)
1. Superheroes—Fiction. 2. Friendship—Fiction.
I. Kittredge, Caitlin. II. Title.
PS3611.E845S53 2009
813'.6—dc22
2010012662

Printed in the United States of America

www.ballantinebooks.com

2 4 6 8 9 7 5 3 1

The authors dedicate this book to their parents,
who bought us all those comic books
when we were kids.

Acknowledgments

JACKIE SAYS . . .

A huge thank-you to everyone who made this book possible—my co-author Caitlin Kittredge, without whom none of this would have happened; Miriam Kriss, the best literary agent in the world; the entire Ballantine Spectra team, most especially Anne Groell, our tireless and phenomenal editor; Heather Brewer and Renee Barr, for their support and humor; my mom and dad, for understanding the importance of comic books in a girl's formative years; my Precious Little Tax Deductions, Ryan and Mason, who watch the best cartoons; and my Loving Husband, Brett, the thief who stole my heart many years ago.

CAITLIN SAYS . . .

First and foremost, I have to thank my superb co-author, Jackie Kessler, for being endlessly patient and creative. This book is a true collaboration, and we couldn't have done it alone . . . only together. To my lovely agent, Rachel Vater, solver of problems and soother of nerves, and our wonderful editor at Spectra, Anne Groell. All of the readers who enjoy the Icarus Project around the world, my parents, Team Seattle, and Ed Brubaker, a fantastic guy who writes fantastic comics. Stan Lee, Jack Kirby, John Byrne, and Neil Gaiman—for me, they started it all.

What Has Come Before

It's a dark world out there. Whether it's from the ever-present pollution layer in the sky or from the power-hungry tentacles of corporate consolidation, none can truly say. It's a world of gangs and guns, of good people scurrying like rats and trying to avoid notice. It's a world where you have to be some sort of hero to change the way things are.

That's probably why the heroes—the powerful extrahumans in the Squadron—are all under strict control by the megalomaniacal global enterprise known as Corp-Co. But the heroes are too busy to notice, what with fighting crime and working for their corporate sponsors. (After all, heroes need to earn their keep when they're not off battling for justice.) Some members of the Squadron, like the Shadow-wielding Jet, resent that photo ops are just as important as keeping the streets safe. But there's no changing the system.

Then the day comes when Iridium, daughter of New Chicago's most infamous villain, and Taser, a vigilante, attack Corp through its Academy for extrahuman students. The duo's intention is to take down Ops, the high-tech operations system that links Corp to the Squadron. Iridium thinks this will simply leave the heroes without Corp eyes and ears.

Instead, it destroys the only mechanism that keeps the extrahumans—*all* Squadron extrahumans in the United and Canadian States of America—under Corp-Co's thumb. Once Ops goes down, the subtle brainwashing signal that had reined in the heroes is cut off.

And suddenly, hundreds of superpowered men and women realize they had been slaves. For years.

Most of them don't take the news very well.

SHADES
OF
GRAY

PROLOGUE

Channel Surfing

Nothing good on the tele anymore. Hey, thanks for the drink."

"No problem. You checked everything already?"

"Mostly. Pretty much everything's just more of the same. Depressing stuff. Here, see for yourself."

BLINK
[Mega Broadcasting System's Financial News, with Miles McCormick, already in progress]
MILES: . . . again, the Dow dropped more than eighteen hundred points today in the wake of what seems to be an unprecedented Squadron rebellion—
BLINK
[United and Canadian Broadcasting System's Evening News, with Gena Mead, already in progress]
GENA: . . . more reports of citizens being victimized by those they turned to only yesterday to protect them: the Squadron. Hospitals are filling beyond capacity—
BLINK
[The News Network's Spin Room, with Tom Carlin, already in progress]
TOM: . . . seriously, I want to know: who laced the extra-humans' food with *junk*? If this isn't an incredibly bad drug trip, then I don't know what the hell is happening in the Americas. Someone better tell the Super 'Roids we

ain't the bad guys. And for the love of Jehovah, can *someone* get more from Corp-Co Chairman Stan Kane than "No comment?" Really, Stanley, what the hell happened to your supersoldiers—

BLINK

[Transnational Broadcasting System's Evening News, *local edition, with Shannon Beverly, already in progress]*

SHANNON: . . . five Squadron heroes have smashed their way into Bank of Americas over on Lakeshore, destroying most of the building, terrorizing the bank staff, and taking off with more than e500,000 in digichips. Fifteen people, including eight police officers, were hurt—

BLINK

[The News Network's Headline News, *with M'Chelle M'bachu, already in progress]*

M'CHELLE: . . . Everyman Society Chairman Frank Wurtham is demanding immediate action against not just the Squadron but all extrahumans.

[CUT to FRANK WURTHAM in a press conference, outside Everyman headquarters in Boston]

WURTHAM: It's not just *unthinkable*, it's *un-American* for us to sit back and watch everything our fathers and their fathers and their fathers before them struggled to build, watch it all pounded to dust by a handful of genetic *freaks*. It's our duty to the Americas, and more than that— it's our Jehovah-given right as *normal, everyday citizens* to fight to protect ourselves and our country against these abominations of nature. All of us must rise up and—

"Jaysus, *please* shut him up."

"Sorry. He can be mesmerizing."

"You just have a thing for redheads."

"Mmm. Lucky for you."

BLINK

[American Public Television's The Captain and the Kid, *already in progress]*

. . . CAPTAIN COURAGEOUS puts a gloved hand on KID POWER's shoulder, stopping the youth from running into the dark cave that hides LADY EVIL and her captive.

"Deadly."
"Yeah, this is a good one. I saw it when it first aired . . ."
"Shhh."

CAP: Really, Kid, ya gotta . . . take a breath and think before ya go chargin' in headfirst like that.
KID: See, that's the problem, Cap. You think too much. While you're so busy exercising your graymatter, there's a *girl* in there—an innocent *girl*—who's terrified and alone and has no one to help her!
CAP: I know ya got . . . feelings . . . for the girl. But ya gotta use your head, Kid.
KID: I love her, Cap. And I'm not letting Lady Evil get away with her dastardly plan!
KID POWER shrugs out of CAPTAIN COURAGEOUS's grip and runs pell-mell into the cave.
CAP: Kid, wait!
From inside the black cave, a shout of surprise . . . and then a long, bloodcurdling scream.
CAP: Dang it, Kid.
CAPTAIN COURAGEOUS shakes his head. Then he clenches his jaw determinedly. With his cape billowing heroically, he marches toward—
[BLACK SCREEN]

"Hey . . ."
"You blinked."
"Not this time. Damn it, I like this one. Lady Evil's going to get the captain all horned up . . ."
"Hang on. Something's happening."

[American Public Television logo appears, followed by a close-up of APT Evening News *anchorwoman Randi Rose]*
RANDI: Good evening. At 7:13 P.M., President Kirby, in

an effort to contain the extrahuman revolt in New Chicago, New York, Toronto, Los Angeles, and other cities across the Americas, has invoked the Insurrection Act. That's right: he's sending in the troops to rein in the superheroes.

[CUT SHOT of PRESIDENT JOHN KIRBY in the Rose Garden, illuminated with plasbulbs and vidlights, standing at a podium with the presidential seal.]

KIRBY: My fellow Americans, we are in the midst of a crisis of epic proportions. The extrahumans, whom we've come to trust and depend on, have suddenly, tragically, turned against us. They are unleashing horrors in our cities, destroying property, harming innocents. While some of the Squadron have contacted us, and promised that they were doing everything they could to stop these so-called rabids, it's clear that we can no longer depend on extrahumans to protect their human cousins. Their acts of violence are nothing short of terrorism. And so it is with a heavy heart and a firm hand that I have invoked the Insurrection Act. I have authorized five hundred thousand members of the National Guard to join their brothers and sisters in the police force to do whatever it takes to once again bring order to the United and Canadian States of America.

[SCREEN SHOT of SCREAMER and THE ANGLE demolishing a building in the Downtown Grid, pre-Flood district; citizens watch in horror, and the police use their riot shields to keep the flying debris from pummeling them.]

[RANDI in a V.O.] For the past two days, it's been chaos in the streets and in the air, as Squadron members have unofficially declared war on standard human authority.

[CUT SHOT of COLOSSAL MAN, smashing the Old Millennium Park Field House with a giant booted foot.]

COLOSSAL MAN: You think we're still your *prisoners*? You think we're still your *dogs*? You can't command us anymore! We don't hear you anymore!

[RANDI's V.O. continues as additional footage of SCREAMER and THE ANGLE rampage through Old Downtown.]

RANDI: We still don't know what has caused these heroes to turn against the very society they have sworn to protect, or why they have come to blows with the men and women in the police force who have risked their very lives to maintain order. But it's clear that the president—

"Turn it off."

"Garth . . ."

"I said *turn it off.*"

BLINK

"Happy now?"

"No. Jaysus. I'm not happy. I . . ."

"Garth?"

"We have to call the Network."

". . . *Excuse* me?"

"We have to. Everything's falling apart. The Squadron's gone insane, the police can't handle it, now the troops are coming in . . ."

"Let Corp fix it. They always do."

"So why haven't they? No, something's wrong. It's all banjaxed. We have to help—"

"Have you gone totally daft? We *can't* help! You know what'll happen if we do."

"But what choice do we have?"

"Let Corp clean up its own mess."

"Julie . . ."

"Garth, I love you. But I swear to Jehovah above, if you pick up the phone and tell Terry to get the Network in place, you're doing it on your own."

". . . *Julie* . . ."

BLINK

[*American Public Television special emergency broadcast, already in progress*]

RANDI: . . . what this means for society at large, or us here in New Chicago, remains to be seen.

"Come on, Julie. Turn it off."

"You can damn well turn it off yourself, Garth McFarlane. While you're at it, you think long and hard before you do something that can't be undone."

A moment later, the door to the bedroom slams.

Garth McFarlane gets up and walks over to the plasiscreen and turns it off. In the dim living room, his eyes glow softly, almost thoughtfully.

Looking at Julie's unfinished drink sitting on the coffee table, Garth thinks, long and hard.

When he opens the bedroom door some time later, Julie turns to face him. The lights are off, but he sees her perfectly well—her halo of fuzzy blond hair, the shimmer of tears in her hazel eyes.

And he tells her what he's going to do.

NOW

CHAPTER 1

JET

The biggest question my brother has about the extra-humans is whether they are heroes because they are told they are heroes or because they believe they are heroes. My only question is how to control them before they realize they don't have to be heroes at all.

—From the journal of Martin Moore, entry #103

Jet was positive there was nothing in the *Squadron Policies and Procedures Manual* that covered how to take down rabid members of the Squadron itself. Even so, she'd looked. Twice.

In the past, she supposed as she fended off a blow from Slider, there might have been a subsection that covered such a topic. But once Corp-Co started brainwashing its elite extrahuman fighting force to be the good guys, there'd been no need for the manual to cover what to do when superheroes went insane. So Jet had to wing it.

Light, she hated improvising. But at least she'd caught a break in that Slider had lost it here in Grid 13, which was mostly deserted this early in the morning. Jet had been able to manipulate Slider into an alley. If the speedster had gone rabid in the downtown district of New Chicago, the casualty rate and property damage would have been horrific. And with Jet's luck, the mainstream media would have been televising the fight like some pay-per-view event. Ever since nearly all of the Squadron had effectively declared war against society two days ago, it seemed like the vids had been capturing every move she made, just in time for the evening news.

The world had gone mad, and the media was having an orgasm.

Slider spun around, her roundhouse kick in perfect form. But even at double speed, she'd telegraphed her move. Jet ducked beneath the woman's leather boot as it zoomed by.

"Come on, Slider," Jet said, letting two Shadow creepers fly. "You don't want to fight me."

The red-clad woman screeched as the black bands wrapped around her legs, pinning them together. "Want? *Want?* I want my life back, that's what I want!"

"And you can have it. Come on, this is me," Jet said, commanding the creepers to move up Slider's body and bind the woman's hands. "You can talk to me, Slider."

"You're one of them!" Slider snarled, her upper lip curling. "You're Corp's lapdog!"

"I was." The admission hurt, but Jet was honest. Her voice soft, she said, "But they can't tell us what to do anymore."

"Liar!" Slider struggled to free herself, even beginning to vibrate. But she wouldn't be able to move fast enough to escape her bonds. Once the Shadow had you, it didn't let you go.

Jet knew that all too well.

"Babe?" That was Meteorite, whispering in Jet's ear thanks to her comlink. "You all right? Your heartbeat just galloped past 130."

"I'm fine," Jet murmured.

"Just checking. And heads up: You've got a normal headed into your sector."

Terrific. The way things were going, it would probably be an Everyman looking to take down one of the extrahuman "freaks." Jet took a step toward the bound woman. "Listen to me . . ."

"Lucy," Meteorite supplied.

"Lucy." Meteorite had always worked well as Operations, providing Jet with much-needed information. Thank the Light that Frostbite had jury-rigged a closed-network version of Ops for Jet and the others to use. The earpieces no longer broadcast subliminal messages about serving Corp, but they did still work beautifully as communication devices.

Jet lifted her gauntleted hands into a soothing gesture, trying to calm Slider like she would a spooked horse. "It's going to be okay, Lucy. I know what you're going through. You can get past it."

"Liar!" Slider shrieked again, bucking. She overbalanced and crashed to the ground, then writhed on the broken pavement, slamming her head on the ground. Her cheerful red helmet cracked from the impact.

"Hey now," Jet said, kneeling. "Come on, Lucy. Don't hurt yourself." She reached over to comfort the fallen hero, then yanked her hand away as Slider tried to bite her.

Damn it to Darkness. Jet didn't want to blanket the woman in Shadow, not if she could help it. The last time she had done that, she'd nearly killed a man.

And the time before that, she *had* killed a woman.

It had been an accident during a life-or-death situation. Even so, Jet's vision blurred as she saw Lynda Kidder's still form lying in the filth of the sewers, the reporter's body monstrously warped from a serum she'd been forced to take . . .

Pain wrenched her out of the grim memory. Cursing, Jet pulled her gloved fingers free from Slider's clenched teeth.

"Sorry, Lucy," Jet said. Then she released a ball of Shadow. It unfolded as it hit Slider's face, wrapping its ends around the red-clad woman's head. Slider slammed her head on the ground once, twice . . . and then was still.

Sighing, Jet called the Shadow back into herself. It wasn't supposed to be like this.

Meteorite's voice: "Normal approaching in five, four, three . . ."

Jet pulled out a pair of stun-cuffs from her belt and slapped them onto Slider's wrists. Still kneeling, Jet turned her head to face the mouth of the alley. It took only a moment for her to blend into the shadows, making herself all but invisible.

A man lumbered into view, a black ski mask covering his face like a parody of the Shadow blanket Jet had just used on Slider. He sported a black bomber jacket over a slim frame, black jeans, and boots. And he toted an oversized, bulging sack in his gloved hands. He was too busy looking over his shoulder to notice that the alley was not deserted.

Behind her optiframes, Jet's eyes narrowed.

The man lurched to a stop and yanked off his cap, revealing sweat-plastered mousy hair and a very plain face. He grinned ecstatically as he opened the bag.

"I sincerely hope those are presents for the local orphanage," Jet said.

The man squawked, jerking around to see who'd spoken. His gaze slid right over where Jet crouched and fastened on Slider's unconscious form. His eyes widened, and his mouth worked like a landed fish. He stepped back, nearly tripping over his bag.

"Citizen," Jet said, standing slowly, calling back her power so that she no longer was one with the shadows, "what do you have in the bag? Stolen goods?"

The man squeaked, "Take it, it's yours! Please don't hurt me!"

A breeze whispered down the alley, bringing with it a hint of ozone. Jet's black cloak swirled around her legs and boots. She allowed herself a small smile. "Hurt you? Now, why ever would I do that, citizen?"

The man whimpered, cowering behind the large, swollen sack.

Just as Jet was about to launch into her standard Crime Doesn't Pay speech, Meteorite hissed, "Incoming!"

A crackle like lightning, followed by a thunderous boom.

Jet created a Shadowshield reflexively, protecting her, the criminal, and Slider as one of the alley walls crashed over them. The man screamed and started praying in a screechy voice, which didn't help Jet's concentration at all. Sweat trickling beneath her cowl, she pushed her shield forward, forcing the debris away.

The broken wall warped the shape of the alley, turning its opening lip into a sneer. There, backlit by the morning sun, stood two Squadron soldiers. One of them, a man with shaggy brown hair, Jet knew all too well. The other, a woman wearing enough spangles to blind a casual passerby, Jet knew mostly by reputation.

Were and White Hot. Former comrades in arms . . . and now, based on the glow of power around White Hot's gloves and the growl in Were's throat, rabids.

Some days, Jet thought, *it just doesn't pay to get out of bed.*

CHAPTER 2

IRIDIUM

Imagine a world without pain and suffering, a world without fear. Imagine your children growing up free of disease and the pain of age. Imagine your future. It could be so bright.

—Article by Dr. Matthew Icarus, submitted to
The New England Journal of Medicine (rejected)

Iridium almost let the kid get away with it.

The day had been too long already, tinged with smoke from the fires downtown and full of the wail of police sirens as their hovers crisscrossed Wreck City, searchlights cutting through the smoke and fog like the long fingers of a giant. So when Iridium turned the corner and saw the metal security door of the check-cashing branch bent inward, as if by a fist, and heard the alarm whooping, she almost walked right on by.

With New Chicago in its death throes, it wasn't her problem if some guy was ripping off another, equally crooked guy.

"Hey!"

The voice spun Iridium around. She was jumpy already from the rampant anarchy that had spilled out from the implosion of the Squadron, trickling down from extrahuman to criminal gang to street thug like a virus. "Yes?"

The owner of the voice lumbered forward—bald, tattooed, a ring through his nose and surgical horns atop his bald pate, all of which marked him as a Death's Head—and jabbed his finger at the check-cashing shop. "You gonna do something about that, Princess?"

Iridium narrowed her eyes. "How, exactly, is one of your friends lining his pockets my problem, *Princess*?"

The Death's Head turned and spat a wad of something noxious and bright green into the gutter. "Fucker ain't one of ours. He ain't local. Just some punk kid with powers who swooped in and said this was his street now."

"The Squadron doesn't leave their people with the best grip on reality," Iridium said, but she reconsidered that dented door. "He'll get over it."

"This is your fuckin' city, yeah?" the gangster demanded. "You run things, and you just let some dipshit with a cute costume stroll in?"

"Easy, Damien." Iridium held up a hand, feeling the light heat gather against her skin like a caress. The gangster backed up a step. He didn't get her joke—Damien, the devil child from the old flatfilm *The Omen*. No one in New Chicago could take a joke these days. Iridium frowned. "I run a tight ship. You know that."

"I don't want them here," Damien said, rubbing his forefinger against his thumb like the junkfreak he was. "I don't like the superfreaks. No offense."

Iridium was already halfway across the street. "None taken."

She felt the weight of fatigue press on her shoulders as she shoved the broken door aside, along with all of the various aches and pains. She could catalog the bruises—the set on her rib cage from Howler's sonic boom tossing her into a wall the day before last, the cut on her cheekbone from where she'd let Arachnia get too close with her stinger darts.

She'd dreamed about taking them on, everyone in the Squadron and the little voice inside their heads. The reality was proving a lot more painful and dirty and tiring than the dream.

The lights of the check-cashing shop flickered uselessly,

and Iridium set a strobe to float in the air above and behind her head, creating an arch of light. "Here, little superbrat," she lilted. "It's not polite to put your hands on things that aren't yours."

The kid was squat and stocky, clear optiframes strapped to his head and a shock of faded purple hair falling into his eyes. He looked like the type who should be sitting in front of a VR rig somewhere, playing an elf or an errant knight.

"Holy crap!" he exclaimed. "I mean, it's really you! Iridium!" He grabbed another handful of digichips and shoved them into a duffel bag from the New Chicago Hobby Emporium. "I'm Blockbuster," he said, puffing out his chest. "I have super-strength."

"Be still my heart." Iridium pointed at the bag. "Set it down and get on home to your mummy, child. I don't have time for you."

"But we're doing it!" Blockbuster cried. "We're taking the city apart, just like you wanted."

Iridium looked back out the doorway, at the skyline. It was painted with flame, like a crown marching across the horizon. "Who said this was what I wanted?"

"But . . ." Blockbuster's face crumpled. "But I don't have anybody! I'm a felon now. I can't go back to the way things were . . . Corp is still out there and they'll throw my ass in jail!"

Iridium sighed. "Look, kid, I don't have answers for every sad superbrat in this town. I suggest you go home and move on."

Blockbuster flushed, his jowly little face quivering. "I don't *have* a home!" he bellowed, grabbing more of the E's. "I'm an orphan, just like you!"

"Take it easy," Iridium warned. "You're not in the bush league anymore. Wreck City is mine. I can't have you tearing around like a chubby little tornado."

Blockbuster let out a snarl. It would have been comical, except he reached out and pushed her. Iridium felt herself lift and go back, crashing through the front counter and skidding to a stop in the lobby.

"Fine," she told the ceiling. "I tried."

Blockbuster leapt the broken counter, drawing back a pudgy fist as he landed on top of her. Iridium strobed him, hard, in the face. Blockbuster repeated her flight, in the opposite direction.

"You know what your problem is?" Iridium stood up and dusted herself off. "You kids today have no sense of history." She picked up the duffel bag and emptied it back into the safe, pocketing a few thousand E's for her trouble.

On the floor, Blockbuster let out a groan. He flopped a little, but a strobe in the face was a lot like a baseball bat. It made you reconsider turning to crime—or getting up again.

"Hey, you chose to play the villain," Iridium told him. "If you want to roll in the big leagues, this isn't anything. Wait until you meet a real hero."

"I thought you understood," Blockbuster whined. "I thought you were like me."

Iridium kicked the door aside and looked back at his hunched, miserable figure. "I'm not a villain, and I'm not a hero. You want to worship somebody, go to church." She shoved the packet of E's into her belt and pointed at Blockbuster. "Come to Wreck City again, and you'll be wearing my name across your forehead. As a third-degree burn."

As she left, Iridium threw a salute to Damien and his horned pals skulking in the shadows. Alone, she walked on toward her warehouse. As she approached, she let out a sigh. Iridium, once Public Enemy Number 1, now reduced to a superpower hall monitor for the scum of New Chicago.

Yeah. The reality definitely sucked.

CHAPTER 3

JET

Certain powers, like Earth, have taken to the conditioning better than others. Some powers, notably Light, have proven unpredictable.

—From the journal of Martin Moore, entry #74

Hey, Were," Jet said, nonchalant, her fists by her sides. She'd never worked with White Hot, but Jet and the shapeshifter went way back. What was more, Jet *knew* him—how he reacted, how he fought, what pushed him over the edge from man to animal. If he thought Jet was going to fight, he'd attack first. And if he thought Jet was acting weak, he'd attack first.

The trick, then, was to hold her ground with confidence, and never mind how exhausted she was from playing hero for two days without a break. *Duty first*, she thought sourly. *Always.* The Corp edict still held true, even if Corp itself had proven to be worse than any enemy the Squadron had ever faced.

"Babe," Were said, his voice a thick growl—damn, he was already halfway gone—"I didn't see you there."

She smiled. "What, under all the rubble? Imagine that."

"Jet," Meteorite hissed in her ear. "Were's stats are off the board. He's got less impulse control at the moment than a sugared-up two-year-old."

Without moving her lips, Jet whispered: "No kidding."

"Why are you wasting time talking to her?" That was White Hot, who hadn't called back her power. Her gloved hands were bright as suns, and they twitched either with nervous energy or madness. Or both. "She's one of the lapdogs."

Jet was getting tired of hearing the slur. "Was," she spat, not having to fake her disgust. "Light, how many times do I have to say it? I don't work for them anymore."

"You were their poster child," White Hot sneered. "Like you really could just turn off your adoration?"

"*You* don't know me." Jet pointed her chin at Were. "You do."

Were's nostrils flared. "I do," he agreed, and grinned hugely. "You still smell like you'd be a great lay. You try to send out these untouchable vibes, but under all that black leather you're practically begging to get fucked. Bet you're a screamer."

Light spare me. "My, you sure know how to sweet-talk a girl."

"I know how to do more than that," Were said, stepping forward, all gangly legs and hormones. "I know how to make you see Jehovah. I can do things with my tongue—"

"Shut it, perv." White Hot scowled as she flipped her dark hair over her shoulder. Probably didn't like not being the object of his attention. White Hot was arrogant, self-centered. Jet had seen the type before, mostly from Lighters. White Hot. Razzle Dazzle. Sunbeam. Dawnlighter.

Iridium.

"You know," Jet said, pushing away thoughts of Iri, "there was a time, Were, when you'd be cracking jokes along with making moves." She allowed herself a smile that hinted at "come hither." She wasn't a flirter by nature, not like Jezebel or Curves, but even Jet knew how to turn it on when necessary.

Were chuffed laughter, the sound dancing with the animal in his nature. "Oh, I'm thinking of *lots* of things that'll make me smile . . ."

Jet motioned to the debris at her feet. "Maybe first you'll apologize for bringing a wall down on me. That was just rude, wouldn't you say?" She shrugged her cloak off her shoulder, the motion calling attention to her breasts.

And . . . yes, Were's gaze slid down to her chest.

She allowed her smile to widen. A little more banter, a touch more innuendo, then Were's guard would be lowered enough for her to take him out with a kiss of Shadow. He was the more deadly of the two; he had to go down first, before White Hot knew what was happening. As for the Lighter, Jet would knock her out the old-fashioned way.

But of course, that was when the normal decided to bolt.

Screaming like his hair was on fire, the thief pushed past her and headed for the mouth of the alley. Before Jet could catch her balance, White Hot lit up—the millions of spangles that made up her skinsuit transformed into prisms of eye-bleeding color. She aimed low, blasting the ground beneath the man's feet.

With a squawk, the thief pinwheeled to the broken, smoking cement. White Hot planted a high-heeled boot on the man's back and threaded her gloved fingers through his hair.

"Baby," she crooned, "going so soon?"

"He's a thief," Jet said, her gaze locked on White Hot. She didn't like the sadistic smile on the woman's face, or the way the air still crackled with ozone. The Lighter wasn't still glowing, at least, but she hadn't tamped back her power. Not good. "I was going to deposit him with Commissioner Wagner."

White Hot didn't bother looking at Jet when she replied. "And why would we want to do such a thing?"

"He's a thief," Jet said slowly.

"Mmm. I do so like bad boys." White Hot yanked the man's head back, exposing his bare throat. "What do you think, Were?"

"Not my type," Were said. And then he pounced.

Jet rolled, but Were still tagged her, grabbing her shoulders and going down with her. *Fast,* she thought, *so damn fast.* She brought her legs between their bodies and kicked hard. Too late—she missed his kneecaps because he was already shifting. Calling up her power, she pummeled him with a Shadowbolt.

Were, half-human, flew off her and slammed snout first into the alley wall.

Protect the normal.

Jet launched herself at White Hot, who had already flipped the thief onto his back and was fumbling with his zipper. Propelled by Shadow, Jet built momentum and cocked her right fist back as her left leg came forward, bent at the knee. White Hot looked up just as Jet swiveled, the knuckles of her right hand aiming for the Lighter's pouty lips.

The meaty thud of her fist connecting was music to Jet's ears.

White Hot's head snapped back, and she spun drunkenly before crashing to the ground. She didn't get up again.

Wimp, Jet thought, shaking out her hand.

In Jet's ear, Meteorite screamed: "Down!"

Jet dropped hard to the cement, her hands and arms absorbing the impact. Her cloak pulled taut against her neck before the clasp let go. Jet didn't need to hear the snarls or the snapping of teeth to know that Were had completed his transformation to wolf. Fabric tore, and she winced.

"I liked that cloak," she muttered, sending her creepers into the black material. The folds rippled with Shadow, and the cowl reared back with a life of its own as the rest of the cloak wrapped itself around Were.

Jet pulled herself to her feet, swallowing thickly against the dizziness. She'd expelled too much power. She needed to rest.

Soon, she thought, feeling the beginning of a headache behind her eyes. *I'll take some time off soon. Right after things here get less insane.*

Whenever that would be.

She walked over to Were's bundled form, and she couldn't help but be impressed by how he was still struggling. Most people—humans and extrahumans alike—succumbed quickly to the numbing cold of the Shadow. "Hey," she said, prodding Were lightly with her boot. "Come on, Shaggy. Calm down."

Were roared and lashed out, swiping at her through the Shadow-covered cloak. It didn't matter that the sounds were muffled or that the claws were unable to pierce either the material or Jet's power. It still made Jet take an involuntary step backward.

"Traitor!" he howled, lunging for her.

Jet sidestepped. She watched the bundle sprawl to the broken concrete, feeling sad. Fighting with Were now was nothing like sparring with him back at the Academy. Then, all of his attacks were punctuated with dirty jokes and innuendo just shy of sexual harassment. Now it was deadly serious. If he tore his way free, he'd go for her throat.

But the Shadow held. Beneath the cowl and cloak, Were's form shuddered, then finally went still. The material shifted and rolled until a man's shape was clearly outlined under the black fabric.

Jet sighed, her heart feeling heavy, her shoulders sagging with exhaustion. "I'm not a traitor," she said softly. But after fighting her former colleagues—and now her former friends—she wondered if Were was right.

right right

Behind her optiframes, Jet's eyes widened. *No, no—Light, no.* It was too soon.

soon soon sweet girl sweet Shadow sweetness like bones crunching like dead leaves like

Gritting her teeth, Jet called back the Shadow, let it swim over her body and sink into her skin. The Shadow voices faded to whispers, which easily could have been the wind. But Jet knew better.

Not crazy yet, she told herself as she retrieved her cloak—torn and slobbered on. Groan. No, she hadn't given in to those voices. Not yet. *Not ever again,* she promised herself as she clasped the soiled cloak to her shoulders and tugged the cowl over her head.

She'd sooner kill herself.

Feeling much older than her twenty-two years, she slapped a pair of stun-cuffs on Were, and another on White Hot. For the human thief, she resorted to good ol' duct tape. He didn't fight her; he was too busy babbling the Twenty-third Psalm of David. At least his hands were already clasped together, so tying them was a cakewalk.

"Ops," she said.

Meteorite replied crisply, "Go ahead."

"Note that I'll need to carry more cuffs."

"Noted." A pause, then Meteorite asked, "You okay, babe?"

"Dandy," Jet said, looking at Were's pale form. "Just dandy."

Meteorite cleared her throat. "Okay. Enough mommying. The others are here. You may have forgotten, what with all the fighting, that there's a meeting in, oh, two minutes."

Crap. "I'll be there as soon as I drop these packages off at the Sixteenth. Out."

Jet tapped her comlink, replacing Meteorite's voice with the white noise of a waterfall. It wouldn't be enough to keep the Shadow voices at bay, not forever. But for now, it would do.

She summoned a floater of Shadow big enough to hold White Hot, Were, Slider, and the thief, then she called up one for herself. It took a moment to create a graymatter leash to connect the two floaters. It took a little longer for Jet to massage away the headache.

Dragging the unconscious rabids and gibbering human on the disc behind her, Jet flew to the Sixteenth precinct, just inside of Grid 16—what many people referred to as Wreck City.

Iridium's city.

Jet deposited the four people in front of the building, wondering if Iri was fighting against the madness infecting New Chicago and the rest of the Americas or reveling in it. Then again, Jet admitted to herself, she really didn't want to find out.

After leaving a note for Commissioner Wagner, Jet was going to take off to old Wrigley Field for the meeting—she was already late, and the last thing she wanted to deal with was Frostbite's grumbling. But after tucking the note into White Hot's shoulder strap, Jet noticed that she had an audience. Civilians, ranging from early twenties to late seventies, based on outward appearances. None of them looked hostile, which was something. A few seemed curious. And one or two actually looked relieved. And blissfully, there was no media.

"Hey," one of the civilians said—an auburn-haired man in sunglasses. "Littering's a crime, innit?"

She couldn't help it; she smiled. "Just dropping off a care package for Commissioner Wagner, citizen."

The man grinned. "You don't think he'd maybe prefer some freshly baked cookies next time?"

That actually made her laugh. "Next time," she said, "maybe someone will be as thoughtful for me."

And with that, Jet rocketed away.

CHAPTER 4

IRIDIUM

"I lost a daughter. My work, every second of my life, are geared toward making sure no other parent has to experience that void inside them."

—Interview with Matthew Icarus on *60 Minutes,*
January 19, 1970

Iridium's warehouse crouched back from the street, like a shy animal or a sleeping bum, grit and dirt and teeth on the outside hiding what lay within.

She hit the code for the door—an old-fashioned keypad that couldn't be sliced by any hack with a wireless rig. You had to get up close and personal to break in, and an equally ancient biometric scanner ensured that anyone besides Iridium or her assistant Boxer would get a healthy jolt from the city power grid.

Inside, Boxer sat with his back to the door, his shoes off, his feet in their mismatched socks propped on the shipping crate Iridium used as a table. A holo played on the wall, 3-D film explosions painting the wide, high space in sunset.

"Sitting on your ass is a good way to get a cap in it," Iridium said.

Boxer jumped up, knocking over his soda and redimeal. He cursed. "Sneaking up on me's a hobby for you, ain't it?"

"Your own fault, old man. You didn't used to be so sloppy." Iridium grabbed her own meal from the freezer and shoved it into the cooker before she sat opposite Boxer. They'd developed a routine since they'd made their agreement—Boxer worked for her instead of gang running, and Iridium provided food, shelter, and the occasional 3-D film night.

Boxer wasn't a brother, or an uncle—he was just Boxer, Academy washout, cranky old man, and the closest thing to a friend she had.

"I figure we ain't worried about the Squadron anymore." He shrugged. "Why do I need to guard the door?"

"Maybe because of the unmitigated chaos just beyond our doorstep?" Iridium got up again when the cooker chirped and pulled her meal out by the edges, peeling back the film and sticking a fork into the soy chicken. Real meat was a luxury, cloned on farms and sold in upscale markets. They'd eaten real meat at the Academy. "It's not safe out there, Boxer. This city has descended into hell."

"What's the song? 'Hell ain't a bad place to be'?"

"Christo, you really are old."

He threw his wadded napkin at her.

She ducked, grinning, then grabbed her can of Tab and popped the lid. The pink can shimmered as its malleable metal morphed into a cup. *A division of Corp-Co* appeared in pink script. Iridium turned the glass so she couldn't see the writing. "I saw your nephew on the vids today."

"Tyler? He commed me a few days ago. I didn't pick up."

Iridium chewed on her grainy chicken. "Why not?"

"Hell, what do the kid and I got to say to each other? I ditched out of the Academy when he was in diapers, and he spent most of his better years ready to arrest me on sight."

"Things are different now," Iridium said. "But hey, your family is your business." Christo knew, she didn't want anyone poking into the Bradford clan's dysfunction.

"Different, sure. Inmates are running the damn asylum," Boxer snorted, flipping the vids to the news. It was, if possible, even more violent than the action film he'd been watching. Iridium caught a flash of Shadow and saw Jet in fine form, kicking ass and taking names and still letting the camera find her good side.

Training was hard to shake.

On screen, the anchor announced, "And in other news, mounting tensions in the civilian sector as prison guards at the infamous Blackbird facility for supervillains go on strike." The anchor smiled perkily at the camera. "Cited causes are lack of pay and increased safety regulations for workers. Blackbird Prison is one of the few not disrupted by riots during this time, but we can only assume that will change. Here's Tom with your weather."

Boxer flipped the channel again, to a rerun of *Squad House*. "You know, my brother was short-listed for this. Before he got his bum leg."

Iridium heard him from a long way off. She was seeing the sterile corridors of Blackbird, the narrow doors marked with designations instead of names. The screams that echoed endlessly no matter how much Thorazine the medics pumped.

"Iri." Boxer nudged her with his toe. "You with me?"

Iridium shoved her dinner aside. "I have somewhere I need to be."

CHAPTER 5

JET

The conditioning will guarantee that the Squadron will always be defenders of the public good. And of Corp-Co's interests, of course. Can't bite the hand that feeds you.
—From the journal of Martin Moore, entry #68

The baseball field had long given way to age—the grassy field now nothing but dust, and the bleachers filled with junk and old ghosts. Jet tried to picture what it must have been like to see baseball outside, to watch a ball hit so hard that it flew over the stadium's edge until it was lost to the pollution layer. She thought that the notion of playing any professional sport outdoors was a joke, or maybe a whimsical dream. Baseball outside a dome? Impossible to imagine.

And yet, here was Wrigley Field—the original, dated all the way back to the early 1900s, not the covered astropark of the same name over in Grid 3. Jet soared over what had once been home plate, wondering what it would have been like to see Babe Ruth make his famous called shot.

"I'll take you to a baseball game," Sam had said, not even two weeks before he'd be killed in the line of duty. *"You and me, we'll*

get a weekend pass and we'll hit the Downtown Grid to catch one of
the Wrigley vids. You'll love it!"

Jet blinked back sudden tears. They'd never made it to that
game; third year had been insanely busy at the Academy, and
Jet had too much work on her plate to request a weekend pass.
And Samson hadn't pushed. Samson had never pushed.

Light, there were times she missed him so much that it hurt
to breathe.

Jet took a deep breath, then blew it out, cleared her
thoughts. She'd have time for sentimentality when she took
that fabled break. Hovering over the remains of home plate,
she whispered, "Watch my dust." Then she zoomed to the roof.

Flitting past the long-rusted bleachers and crumbling
bricks, ignoring the broken chairs and tabletops, Jet flew into
the abandoned rooftop clubhouse. At first glance, it looked like
any onetime pub: wooden-style bar and matching stools; clus-
ters of booths, their built-in seats waiting patiently to be filled;
and brick face over the plast walls, complete with a moldering
framed poster of an ancient baseball uniform. An old-fashioned
refrigerator—complete with a turn-of-the-century Coke logo—
lurked behind the bar, backlit and filled with water tabs, caffeine shots, and cold pizza.

On a closer look, one would see the telltale glow of computer screens peeking out from a section of the bar counter.
The constant hum of energy spoke of the power Meteorite and
Frostbite had piggybacked from New Chicago Light & Heat. It
wasn't stealing, Frostbite had argued; it was an exchange. He
and the others worked their asses off to rein in the rabids, and
the good city gave them the power they needed to juice their
computers. Jet and Steele hadn't liked it, but they'd been out-
voted four to two. Jet might be team leader in the field, but
when it came to operating decisions, that was all done by vote.

The linoleum floor had been recently swept and scrubbed,
and the windows gleamed with the morning sun. Meteorite's
work, Jet guessed. The former Weather power took clutter and
mess as a personal offense.

"Hey, the Jetster made it." Behind the bar, Meteorite
grinned as she tapped on a keyboard. She'd gotten soft in the

three years she'd been off active heroing; her gray jumpsuit strained around the middle, and her jaw was round where it used to be chiseled. While she had never been a classic beauty, the former Weather power still hinted at pretty, and that wasn't due to her stormy eyes or her white-streaked pale hair. Instead, Meteorite had a smile that made her glow like a Lighter and a laugh that was positively infectious. And a sense of humor that rivaled Were's. For someone who claimed to hate dirt, she had a positively filthy mind.

"About freaking time."

Jet didn't need to look at Frostbite behind the bar to know that he was sneering. She was too tired to argue, so she simply arched an eyebrow at him. Unfazed, Frostbite glared back at her, his face looking too old for his years. Like Meteorite, he was in a Corp-issued jumpsuit—the same one he'd been wearing for the past three days, based on the coffee stains. And the smell.

"Cut her some slack," Firebug said with a laugh, brushing bright orange hair away from her eyes. Her black leather trench coat creaked as she moved her arm—a nod to the chilly October weather outside. "Duty first, eh, Jet?"

"Not funny, Kai," Steele, even when not swathed in metallic bands, cut an imposing figure. Nearly two meters tall and quite muscular, she was more masculine than most male Squadron soldiers with extra helpings of testosterone. But right now, Steele's eyes were soft, and the small frown on her lips was distinctly feminine. "Jet's fighting the good fight. No need to make it unsavory."

"Christo, it was a joke, Harrie." Firebug placed her hand over Steele's. "You used to have a sense of humor."

"Things have been a little tense as of late," Frostbite said as he tapped on a computer next to Meteorite. "Maybe you haven't noticed."

"Sorry I'm late," Jet said, sliding onto a barstool. She nodded cautiously at the only one of the small group who hadn't acknowledged her.

Seated at the far end of the bar, Hornblower continued to ignore her. Hulking in the shadows, he flexed and unflexed his massive hands as if eager to crush walnuts. Just looking at his sheer bulk, one would guess he was an Earth power. He wasn't.

"No worries," Meteorite chirped. "We were about to get a game of bridge going while Frostbite manned the screens, but now that's been blown to hell. Can't play bridge with five people. So we might as well have our status meeting."

"Firebug," Frostbite said. "Kick it off."

The Fire power frowned. "The cleanup isn't going well. New rabids, old rabids, the gangs, the Families, the petty criminals . . . Christo, it's a fucking mess out there."

"Language," Steele chided.

Firebug shrugged by way of apology, and her coat creaked. "There's just too much to clean up. And the city's Finest aren't making our jobs any easier."

"That's for sure," Meteorite grumbled. "You should hear what they're saying on dispatch. Most of them don't buy that you four are still card-carrying good guys. Lee's pressuring Wagner to extend the warrants to include you."

Firebug rolled her eyes. "Lee's an ingrate."

Jet silently agreed. The mayor was quick to go whichever way the wind blew, especially in an election year. Hard to believe that not even two weeks ago, he'd been presenting Jet with an award for her service to New Chicago. But then, a lot had changed in two weeks.

"It's not his fault," Steele said softly. "How can any of them trust us? Hundreds of other Squadron soldiers are razing the Americas. Why should they think we're different?"

"Gee, maybe because you haven't tried to rip off their heads yet?" Frostbite scoffed. "Or destroy the city? Or declare war against the humans?" He punched in more keyboard commands, then scowled. "Colossal Man's not helping, what with his 'We're not your dogs' speech. That's still getting airtime, if you can believe it. Freaking drama king. The media loves him."

"We're lucky that more of the Squadron haven't gone completely rabid," Jet said.

"Lucky?" In the corner, Hornblower let out a bitter laugh. "Yeah, that's us. Real lucky."

Jet held her hands up, hoping to placate him. If anyone

loathed her more than Frostbite, it was Hornblower. "All I'm saying is it could be worse."

"Yeah, right." He glared at her, and she felt the heat of his rage rolling off him in violent waves. "You haven't had to go up against your own *family*. Oh, right," he said, snapping his fingers. "You don't *have* family, do you?"

Jet forced herself to unclench her fist. "Tyler . . ."

He slammed his palm against the table. "Don't you 'Tyler' me like we're buddies!"

"Sorry," she gritted. "Hornblower. I know that going against Lancer yesterday was hard, but you did the right thing."

"Hard?" The large man's snarl would have terrified a serial killer. "You don't know anything, you Shadow freak."

"Hey now," Meteorite said. "No call for getting nasty."

"I don't trust her," Hornblower said, his piercing gaze lancing Jet. "She's unstable. Always has been. She'll turn on us faster than Slider can run."

"Speaking of Slider," Jet said, casting one last look at Hornblower before pointedly turning away from him, "she's one of three I took down this morning."

"Rogue?" Firebug said. "Or rabid?"

It was a fine line between the two. But Jet and the others had agreed that the extrahumans who were merely lashing out at the system were rogues—wannabe anarchists, born-again criminals, petty terrorists who liked the attention. Dangerous, but manageable—possibly even convertible. The rabids, though, were the ones who had lost their minds when their brainwashing stopped. They were the ones Jet and the others had to rein in as quickly as possible.

"Rabid," Jet said. "Were and White Hot were borderline."

Frostbite blinked. "You went up against Were?"

She nodded.

He held her gaze for a moment, then said, "I'm sorry."

A sad smile flitted across her lips. For all that Derek hated her, part of him remembered that at one time, they'd been friends—her and Iri, and Samson and Were, and Frostbite and Red Lotus. "Thanks."

The others gave their reports, and Meteorite checked off

their list of active Squadron members in the Americas. Out of the 412 names, 36 had been marked as either "incarcerated" (for the rabids already delivered to the police) or "pursuing" (for the rogues whom they were trying to talk down from the ledge.) That just left 378 to go. And that didn't take into account any of the missing Academy extrahumans—the students who hadn't earned their hero status yet, or any of the Ops staff who still held their powers even though they were off fieldwork. That brought the number over a thousand.

Jet wanted to sob with frustration.

"There's more bad news," Meteorite said. "Everyman's been making the rounds again. Wurtham's all over the place, and the demonstrations are getting more popular. They're giving out badges now." She snorted. "*Badges.* The world has gone to shit, and Everyman is marketing."

"Language," Steele sighed.

"Everyman runs a tight campaign," Frostbite said. "Always has. Nothing like preaching fear to really capture the minds and hearts of the brainless masses."

"Everyman is nothing new," Steele said. "We can ignore them. The larger threat is the rabids. On top of that is how we're supposed to work with the police and now the National Guard when they don't trust us as far as they can spit."

"The Everyman Society is more dangerous than you know," Jet said tersely. "And that's because of a man named Martin Moore."

For the next five minutes, Jet recounted her failed attempt to save *New Chicago Tribune* reporter Lynda Kidder, and how one of Corp's techies, Martin Moore, had worked with the humans-first organization initially to kidnap, then inject, Kidder with an experimental serum—one that had mutated her into a monster.

She didn't mention how she'd killed Kidder in self-defense. That was still too raw.

"We know that our former masters were working with Everyman," Jet said through clenched teeth, ignoring how her head screamed even at the barest hint of slandering Corp-Co. "Whether they sanctioned Moore's work with Everyman remains unknown. And we suspect this serum is still out there. If so, it poses a real threat."

"Even if they spaz out and inject people with that sludge, it's just normals pretending to be extra." Hornblower snorted his derision. "What's the big?"

"The big, Tyler," Frostbite said, "is that the normals are innocent citizens. If they get juiced with this serum, we have to fight them."

"*We?* Oh, that's good. How long's it been since you've been out of your grays, Tinkerbell?"

"How long's it been since you actually thought before you opened your mouth, Tyler?"

"I don't even want to know what you put in your mouth, fairy."

"*Boys,*" Firebug hissed. "Come on now. Play nice, or Meteorite will take away our toys."

Meteorite held up her hands. "Don't look at me. No way am I getting caught in that pissing contest."

"We don't have time for this," Jet growled. "There's more than a thousand extrahumans unaccounted for. Let's finish our business and get back to work."

She was only a little surprised that both men actually listened to her.

"Just as high a priority as reining in the rabids," she said, "is finding Martin Moore."

"Working on it," Frostbite said. "I still have my personal back door to Corp's network. Meteorite and I've been downloading files."

"Which ones?"

He grinned. "All of them. Take now, sift through later. Once we're done with the transfer onto our local network, we'll start on decryption. That'll go a hell of a lot faster than the downloading, thanks to our built-in cooling system." He snapped his fingers, sending a smattering of icicles arcing through the air. "Among other things, we'll search for Moore's files. We'll find him, and maybe even Corp's role in this mutation serum."

"Good." Jet paused, considering her words. "Things are hitting a crisis point."

"Hitting?" Firebug laughed. "Jetster, where've you been?"

Jet spread her hands and looked at each of the heroes as she spoke, silently imploring them to listen. "Maybe it's time for us to reach out to the citizens of New Chicago, work with them. Build goodwill."

"Scorch me," Hornblower muttered, "she's freaking *branding.*"

"When do you propose we do that?" Firebug asked lightly. "Before or after we chase down the thousand or so extrahumans still unaccounted for?"

"Firebug's right," Steele said. "We've got our hands full just trying to do our jobs. We don't have the time or the resources to play Goodwill Ambassadors."

"Maybe we should make the time."

"Jet's got a point," Meteorite said. "Not that I'm into marketing, but the Squadron approval rating wasn't even at the 50 percent mark for the last three quarters. Why do you think Everyman's got such a huge audience?"

"Money," said Steele.

"Or fanatical followers with good messaging." Firebug shrugged. "Look, I'm just as happy as the next superhero to say that it's all about the citizens, but that doesn't mean we should go out of our way to improve our likability scores. Sponsorship's been sewered. We don't have Runners, or Corp backing, or any of the amenities."

"Hey," Meteorite said, affronted.

"Okay, or most of the amenities," Firebug said. "Now's not the time for us to be expanding our job scope. Let's concentrate on going after the rabids and the bad guys."

"Agreed," Steele said.

"You ladies are forgetting something," Frostbite said. "Corp-Co is responsible for everything that's happening now. We have to go public with how they manipulated us. "

"Take 'em down." Hornblower cracked his knuckles. "Hit 'em where it hurts: the public eye."

Frostbite nodded. "We're lucky that all they're doing now is saying 'no comment' and dodging the media. Public favor is going to be way down. Now's the time for us to move against them—loudly. If we do it right, we can get them delisted from the American Stock Exchange. We do it better, we can bankrupt them as well as bring them up on criminal charges. We do it perfect, and Corp-Co is a thing of the past."

"It'll never happen," Firebug said. "They're too big."

"No one's too big to fail. You really think the government will bail them out?"

"Corp's got governments in their pockets," Firebug insisted.

"You're giving them too much credit."

"And you're not giving them enough."

"What're you afraid of?" Hornblower asked, smirking. "Maybe you liked being their lapdog, huh? Maybe you'd rather go fetch?"

Firebug stood up, snarling, "Now listen, you oversized junk-freak—"

"What're you going to do?" Hornblower laughed. "Sic your girlfriend on me?"

"Stop it," Jet shouted, slamming her fist on the bar counter. "This isn't about . . . them." Damn it to Darkness, she still couldn't even say *Corp* without her head threatening to burst. "It's about the people of New Chicago, and the Americas!"

"You're all getting ahead of yourselves," Steele said calmly. "First and foremost, we have to stop the bad guys."

"Corp *is* the bad guy," Frostbite growled. "Don't you get that?"

"No, the hundreds of rabids out there are the bad guys!" Firebug glared at him. "I know you haven't been heroing in a while, Frostbite, but even grounded in Ops, you should be able to remember that!"

Ice licked over the bar and cracked over the chairs as Frostbite shouted, "They sliced my brain! They raped my mind! Don't you preach to me about remembering who the good guys are. Don't you dare!"

"Derek," Meteorite said, putting a hand on his shoulder. "Come on, man. Calm down."

He shrugged out of her grasp. "I'm calm, Sheila. I'm real fucking calm."

"Language, Derek," Steele said.

"Fuck off, Harriet."

And so it went: Frostbite and Hornblower insisted they concentrate their efforts on taking down Corp-Co. Steele and Firebug remained steadfast in their determination to first rein in the rabids and the other criminal elements in New Chicago and beyond. Meteorite tried to get everyone to stop shouting.

And Jet, meanwhile, sat on her barstool, one gauntleted hand pressed to her temple, willing her headache to disappear. The infighting among the six of them had to stop; otherwise, they'd be doomed to fail.

Just like she was doomed to go crazy, no matter how she fought it.

The Shadow voices giggled, and Jet pretended not to notice.

CHAPTER 6

IRIDIUM

I have no regrets. Scientific advancement never merits begging forgiveness.

—Matthew Icarus, diary entry dated September 20, 1986

Blackbird Prison sat under a freeway, a sprawl of complexes old enough that the buildings still had bars on the windows. There had been a prison on this spot since the nineteenth century, and Iridium could feel the tang in the air from the security grid that surrounded the place, lasers and bots and traps pocking the old grounds.

She shifted, her leg cramping. She'd been sitting on the struts of the overpass all night, watching the prison, learning the new routine. It was chaos, like everything else. The striking guards were massed out front. The prison was on lockdown. A snarl of news hovers blocked the access road.

Iridium had spent hours of her life thinking about how she'd break into the prison. She'd managed it, too. What she hadn't been able to do was break someone out, and that was what kept her up at night.

A garbage truck chugged down the access road and up the ramp to the rear of the prison. Whatever else was happening in the world, the garbage still needed to be shipped out.

Iridium swung herself down from the strut and joined the crowd milling in front of the prison. In her nondescript black outfit, she blended like any other gawker looking for a glimpse of superfreaks. A second garbage truck joined the first, and she waited until it slowed, the horn sounding from within. There was no driver—all of the garbage in New Chicago was bot-controlled, which made it easy for her to climb aboard.

There were no guards inside. There was a formidable security system, but no one to watch it.

If Iridium was ever going to beat Blackbird, the time was now. She crouched inside the empty bot, ankle-deep in watery slime, and shut her eyes, feeling the truck roll on under her.

Iridium hefted herself out of the bot, landing in a pile of refuse higher than her head. No one had loaded the bots in days. She looked up at the camera on the wall, the placidly blinking power light. No alarms. No guards running to stun her.

Iridium found her way to the main corridors. She'd walked them dozens of times as Dr. Sampson, a blond psychiatrist sent by Corp to minister to Arclight, the worst of the worst locked inside Blackbird.

Everything looked different now, sharper and clearer when her eyes weren't dulled by Dr. Sampson's purple contacts. The prison authorities thought that Arclight was a monster, the worst villain the city had seen in decades.

But Iridium knew that Lester Bradford was no monster. She paused in front of his cell door, looking up at the stark black letters painted over it. She reached out, touched cool steel. "Dad?" No answer. "Dad, it's me!"

There was a long moment, long enough for her heart to beat faster, before he answered. "Callie?"

Iridium felt like she could collapse right there in the hallway. "We need to go!"

"A fine idea, Callie, but the prison's on lockdown. Don't suppose you've developed the ability to walk through walls?"

"I'm not Slider," Iridium said, pressing both hands against the door. Heart hammering, palms sweating—prison was bad for her health. "But I'll go to the control room and open up your cell. Then we really need to move, Dad—the garbage bot leaves in ten minutes."

"You can't seriously expect me to ride out of here in a bloody garbage scow."

"Dad, you've been in lockup for twelve years. Now is not the time to get picky."

"Get to it, then." Lester's voice was clipped, as it always was when he issued her an order. It had made him a formidable field commander during his days with the Squadron. "And while you're at it, open up a few others for me."

"Dad, we don't have time . . ." Iridium started, but Lester never ceased to be Lester, commanding, controlled, and in charge at all times. Iridium would admire it if she wasn't already nearly tachycardic from the tension.

"Good folk," said Lester. "Mates. They deserve to be on the outside again, Callie. Would you deny unjust prisoners their freedom?"

"I . . . fine," Iridium said, her own voice taking on an edge. "Just give me their designations and be quick about it. Clock's ticking."

Lester's eyes appeared in the small window of his cell door and he put a finger against the glass for each name. "Nevermore. Kindle. Protean. Radar. Lionheart." He flashed her a grin. "And me, of course. I may be old, but I have my uses."

"Got it," Iridium said. What the Academy hadn't drilled into her, Lester had. Her recall was perfect.

Iridium turned and ran for the prison control room.

The computer panel was so old, it took her a moment to figure out the protocols to open the high-security cells. Old computers were harder to hack, she supposed. That, or Corp was just cheap enough to think that a bunch of overmedicated, overweight former villains weren't *really* a threat.

Why would they be, when the real psychopaths were wearing skinsuits in Corp colors?

Iridium was just about to send her command when cool steel kissed up against the base of her skull. Judging from the size and feel, it was a plasgun. A small one, but a bolt of hot plasma in your skull was all the same.

"Take your hands off that keyboard, young lady." The voice was male, high and soft.

Iridium's palms beaded with sweat as she called a strobe to her.

"And should you think you're faster than I, let me tell you that I was a trained solider before retiring to work for Corp-Co. I do not fear death. I will pull this trigger as my dying reflex and you will be less half a head. That situation does not suit either of us, so please do not insult me with your light display."

The gun didn't leave her skin.

Iridium lowered her hands. "All right, you've got the drop on me. Can I at least see who I'm talking to?"

"Very well. Turn around."

The gun lowered and Iridium moved, dropping and kicking back. She felt her boot impact with a kneecap, heard a grunt of pain, and threw a strobe without looking.

Carried back by the blast, the man slammed into the opposite wall, but he didn't let go of his gun. He also shot at her, leaving a smoking hole in the control-room door.

"That was a warning shot." He was bald, his face bright red, and he wore a nondescript gray suit and tie like a good lackey. His hands were massive—rough and scarred, hands made for beatings and breakings. "The next one will burn your heart out of your chest."

Iridium flared her nostrils as the scent of the plasma dissipated. "So, what? You want to lock me up in here too? I'm not real scared of death, myself. I'll burn you if you come any closer."

He smiled, all teeth. "Young lady, if I wanted you incarcerated, you would be. I am not here to apprehend you."

"Let me guess, then . . . dancing contest?"

He tucked the plasgun into his jacket and swiped a hand over his brow to clear the sweat. "My name is Gordon."

"That's nice. Germanic. You got a first name?"

"Just Gordon." He twitched his cuffs and fixed his tie. "I am authorized to offer you a deal, Ms. Bradford."

Iridium crossed her arms. "I'm listening." But only because she thought he'd probably gun her down if she made a break.

"The city cannot sustain this bedlam," he said. "The remaining Squadron are ineffective and too few, even if they could form a cohesive effort. We need goal-oriented men—and women. Those who are used to taking charge, who have the stomach for bloodshed, who can rip order from the screaming maw of Chaos."

"You like monologues, don't you?" Iridium said. "To blab or not to blab, that is the question . . ."

"Be quiet." Gordon's tone went from soft to slicing in an instant. "Your father and the five he mentioned—we will agree to their release."

Iridium felt her eyebrows rise of their own accord. "If?"

"If," Gordon said, rebuttoning his suit jacket over his gun, "they agree to bring New Chicago back under the control of Corp."

Interlude

All Garth wants to do is get home. More accurately, he wants to get off the streets. There's a tension in the air that makes the hair on his nape prickle. And his damned eyes are itching. Maybe it's from all the residual energy. These past couple days, power's been getting snapped about like wet towels at a sleep-away camp—everywhere you look, you see extrahumans practically crackling with the stuff.

And breaking stuff, no lie. This morning, the bodega on the corner got leveled by Bigfoot (or maybe by Red Sasquatch; Garth can never keep those two straight). He shakes his head. You think you're going out for morning coffee, and instead you're helping Jose dig out from all the rubble.

Good man, that Jose. Garth would like him even if he weren't part of the Network. And so what that Jose thinks Garth is a nutter for even suggesting that they try to stop the chaos in the city?

Garth hugs the cup of coffee closer to him. Jose had nuked up a cup of the instant sludge—best he could do in a pinch—by way of thanks for Garth lending his back. Not his blended beans, of course, but it'll do. As long as it's liquid caffeine, Julie will be happy. Last night hadn't gone well, and Garth frowns as he remembers the way Julie's tears had sparkled like crystalline jewels as she shouted at him for wanting to get involved.

No, last night hadn't gone well at all. His side of the bed had been cold, and lonely. *Well,* he thinks now, *a woman holds a grudge tighter than a miser holds money.* His da had told him that long and long ago, and it was Jehovah's own truth. Thus the coffee: the morning-after peace offering. Garth picks his way along Obama Road, ignoring the steady itching of his eyes.

Barely a block away from his flat, a mighty crash reverberates on the street, making him throw his arms out for balance. Coffee slops over the cup, but he doesn't feel the hot sting. His attention is riveted on the two figures who've tumbled to the ground in a lover's knot.

One's a woman—huge and metallic, but clearly feminine, based on the curves. The other's a wiry sort in black, complete with a death mask over his face. He's got a noose around the metal woman's neck, and she's scrabbling at the rope that's strangling the life out of her.

Garth recognizes them from the vids. Steele and the Hangman.

He senses other spectators cautiously gathering like him, watching the schoolyard fight of small gods. But Garth assumes that none of the other witnesses are extrahumans. Not that *he's* an extrahuman per se. If he had more of that *extra,* he wouldn't be living the life of a normal citizen, now, would he?

"We're not extrahumans," Terry, the de facto leader of the Latent Network, told Garth just last night. *"It's not our fight. We stay hidden."*

"How can you say that?" The frustration welled up in Garth, tingeing his words with the brogue of his childhood. *"The world is falling to shite, and you're telling me we're supposed to sit on our arses and do nothing?"*

"Just give thanks that you're not completely wired," Terry said, *"or you'd be out there with the rest of the superfreaks."*

"You have to get the Network involved."

"No."

His fist tightens around the coffee cup, as if in counterpoint to the noose tightening around Steele's throat.

Behind his sunglasses, Garth's eyes burn. And he thinks, *Fuck it.*

Garth strides up to the duo and hurls the steaming coffee into the Hangman's eyes. The man screeches—more surprise than pain, Garth decides; the mask had to have taken the brunt of the heat—and releases a hand to wipe the sludge from his eyes.

Steele places both her hands around the Hangman's wrist and squeezes. And the Hangman screams.

Yeah, Garth thinks, stepping back. *Now* that's *a cry of pain.*

Not even a minute later, the Hangman is trussed up with one of his own nooses, whimpering like a baby over his crushed wrist, and Steele is looking around for the man who'd stepped in to distract her opponent.

But Garth McFarlane is long gone.

THEN

CHAPTER 7
VIXEN

A human being will never be able to walk through walls or levitate above the ground. Not without certain improvements at the genetic level.

—Matthew Icarus, diary entry dated May 11, 1972

Valerie Vincent hated New Chicago. She hated the cold, the rain, and the constant waft of pollution that blocked the sun. She hated the way the cops treated her like she was no better than the criminals she apprehended. Most of all, she hated her teammates.

Squadron: New Chicago was nothing like Squadron: Orlando Basin. In Orlando, she hadn't had a real family, but she'd at least had friends. Here, she was the new kid.

Valerie hated being the new kid too.

She shivered inside her skinsuit. It was cut to reveal her midriff and a portion of each flank, a nod to growing up in a city where you could still see and feel the sun—a gleaming, glass city built on stilts over mile upon mile of waving green swamp and razor-sharp palmetto, reclaimed from the urban sprawl of Orlando Proper after Hurricane Axel had leveled most of central Florida.

She'd have to talk to Branding about creating a new costume. This one made it hard to move when it was cold, never mind fight. She didn't even have a cape to keep warm, like Angelica.

Valerie had been in New Chicago for two months, and none of the other Team Alpha members had so much as tried to speak to her at any length, other than in the field. The four of them had come up together in the Academy, just like Valerie and her classmates had back in Orlando Basin.

But that was all over now. One graduating class, one stupid twit who had powers that were more marketable than Valerie's, and Valerie found herself here, in the biggest, meanest, coldest city in North America. She supposed she was lucky—she could have been bumped to Team Beta in Orlando instead, and forced to stand around watching Sparkle-Brite or whatever her name was lord Valerie's old spot on the Squadron over her.

But at least she'd be warm.

She was also on patrol alone because Angelica was off with her sponsor, posing for the cameras.

To be fair, if Valerie was as petite and blond as Holly Owens, she'd probably be a good deal less shy. But she wasn't. Valerie was broad-shouldered and dark-haired, and taller than one of the *men* on the team. She was good-looking enough to make the Squadron, but nothing to stop hover traffic.

Just plain old Valerie Vincent, with her plain old superstrength. No glitz, no glitter, just a rock-solid arrest record and three villain takedowns to her credit, which apparently counted just enough to get her transferred to New Chicago.

She wasn't part of a matched pair, like Angelica and her Light comrade Luster, or Night and Blackout, brothers in Shadow. The press had been calling the four Black and White, Dark and Light.

Until Valerie ruined it by joining Team Alpha. She had never felt odd until she'd transferred to New Chicago. Now she felt nothing but, all day, every day.

The comm in her Corp hover pinged. It was an automated

alert, sent out when one of the Squadron spotted a high-priority target.

Valerie flicked on her speaker. "Ops, Vixen."

"Go, Vixen."

Valerie breathed a silent sigh of relief that Crush was working Ops today. The Earth power had landed in a wheelchair after Demolition Man had brought a building down on him, but he at least didn't treat Valerie as a second-class citizen.

"I got a ping. Something up in my sector?"

"Hold on." Keys clicked. Valerie watched the faceless gray city slide by under her feet. "Yup," Crush came back. "Looks like your boy Luster just engaged Professor Neutron."

The WANTED file popped on her screen. Neville Marsh, a.k.a. Professor Neutron. A physicist who'd lost his wife in a super-collider accident; unstable; able to alter atomic structure. He'd created a small black hole outside Des Moines, and now was on Corp's Most Wanted list. Ironically, he'd eschewed hero training and gone to work for them in R&D before his nervous breakdown. That had apparently not worked out so well.

And of course Luster had been the one to find him. Of course.

"Got it." Valerie sighed. "Guess I'm the cavalry."

"Luster can handle it," Crush said. "You go bag yourself a nice mugger or two, make the price we pay to keep the hovers fueled worth it."

"Squadron regs state that backup must be given priority one when confronting a supervillain," Vixen snapped.

"You know they'll just freeze you out more if you save their asses," Crush said quietly.

Valerie flipped over to GPS, locking on Luster's beacon. "Like I'm here to make friends. Vixen out."

The hover banked as she took it off autopilot, and she dove deep into a maze of half-built warehouses, their rusting girders long abandoned. Wreck City, this place was called, and it wasn't a stretch to see why.

She spotted Luster's white uniform and piloted down to join him. Lester Bradford turned at the sound of her hover, a smile playing around his face. It was a fine face, made for vids, with just enough insouciance in the smile to hint at danger. Luster had the total package—black hair, snapping eyes, heroic height, and a smile that could blind you if you weren't careful.

He was a package, all right—a package that, as far as Valerie could see, was full of crap. Bradford's smiles for the vids were fake as Cupida's breasts.

"You've got Neutron?" she said without any finessing. Luster thought of her just like the others—second-class all the way. Just because he wasn't overtly hostile . . . and looked like a 3-D film star . . .

"And a fine hello to you too." Bradford hadn't dropped his accent for Branding, and it worked in his favor, in a big way. "My, my—they let you out alone already? Someone upstairs thinks highly of you."

"More like they all think I'm a joke." Valerie bit back a curse. She'd said too much.

Lester grinned at her. "Do they? What's so terribly amusing about you? The fact that you can twist my head off barehanded, or the fact that with your body, I'd probably enjoy it?"

Valerie felt her eyebrows fly up of their own accord. He had cornered a supervillain . . . and he was *flirting* with her?

"I guess your mouth *is* the quickest thing on you," she shot back. He wasn't going to throw her off-balance and laugh about it with the Shadow boys later.

"Oh, by far," Luster agreed.

Valerie hadn't expected him to agree, and now she was off-balance despite everything. Damn it all. "Are we going after Neutron or not?"

Luster shrugged. "I could, I suppose. Flash a few Yuletide lights, give all reporters on the scene an orgasm. Or you could do it."

Valerie choked, "Me? You called it in. It's your collar. Protocol states the responding hero must . . ."

Bradford stepped closer to her, and her voice trailed off. His smile really was devastating. His eyes too. They were pale and bored into you like a diamond drill. Lit from within by his gaze, Valerie finally realized why citizens and news feeds loved Lester so much. He always looked like he was having fun.

"I haven't commed in. For all they know, Neutron beat me about the head and you flew to my rescue like a shining princess in armor." He brushed the back of one gloved hand down Valerie's cheek. "Would you? Rescue me?"

"I . . ." Valerie stopped talking when the warehouse behind them vibrated, bending inward with an ominous groan. She felt a tug deep in her gut, as if the entire world had just jerked sideways.

Lester glanced toward the structure. "Bollocks. He's creating another vortex."

Valerie felt her blood race, warming all of the exposed parts of her. "We need to hurry the hell up and collar him, then."

"Well?" Lester demanded. "Do you want point, or shall I swoop in and dazzle the city like I've done a dozen times before? I favor your lead. Dazzling is rather humdrum when you're as handsome, charming, and intelligent as me."

This close to him, Valerie felt a reckless part of herself that she rarely allowed off the leash break loose. Luster in real life was nothing like Luster in the vids or the briefing room at Squadron HQ. Here, he was relaxed. Funny, even.

She smiled at Luster and squared her shoulders. "I'll take him down. Call Night and Blackout for backup."

Lester snapped her a salute. "As you say. And Vixen?"

Valerie turned back as she started toward the warehouse. "Yes, Luster?"

"You look absolutely stunning in that outfit."

CHAPTER 8
ANGELICA

*Aaron still insists that Angelica should be classified as a
Mental power, not as a Light power. Frankly, I think he just
wants the excuse to study her in every way possible. I've
never understood his taste in women.*

— From the journal of Martin Moore, entry #7

Holly Owens pivoted to look over her shoulder, flouncing
her long, blond hair and billowing her white cape. She
gave the cameras a wry smile—one that she knew suggested humor and (according to Branding stats) sexual prowess. Lights
flashed and popped, and if she hadn't been a Light power, she
would have been momentarily blinded. But Holly loved the spotlight. Always had. It was a necessity if you were a superhero.

"Brilliant, love," the Glamique rep cooed. "You look delectable. A little more with the lips, please."

Of course—had to show off the latest lip color. "Mulberry
Mischief," it was called. Holly always read the names on the
sample tubes she was given as freebies during her photo shoots
for the cosmetics maker. She got a kick out of some of the
product names—"Razzle Dazzle" eye shadow, "Ghostly Blush"
foundation and matching powder; "Lay It On Thick" mascara.

Some Squadron soldiers got the shaft when it came to mandatory sponsorships, but not Holly Owens, code name Angelica. She'd scored big when Glamique Holdings had selected her during her fourth year at the Academy.

"Like that, love. Yes, perfect! That'll have the ladies scrambling to buy Number 601 like mad."

"Angelica," Jamie said, tapping his handheld. "You're supposed to join Vixen for patrol in five minutes."

The Glamique rep squawked, "Absolutely not! We've scheduled you for the next two and a half hours."

"Sir," Jamie said politely, "I'm afraid Angelica must fulfill her duties to the Squadron and the people of New Chicago . . ."

"She must also fulfill her duties to her corporate sponsor." The rep sniffed, looking down at the Runner. "Unless Angelica would prefer that Glamique cancel its contract with Corp-Co, I suggest that you remember which of her duties are a priority. There are a million other little superheroes flitting about this city of ours. Get one of them to do the dirty work."

That last bit annoyed Holly. Fighting for justice and the good of innocent normals wasn't something to scoff at. Patrol was boring, but it was a necessity. It wasn't like the bad guys advertised when they were about to strike. Usually.

Jamie, flustered, turned to Holly for help.

She smiled soothingly at him, *pushing* only a little bit of Light into it. As a rule, she didn't like to glam her Runners too much—they tended to get a bit dopey if she overdid it, and a dopey Runner did her no good. "It's okay, Jamie. Go ahead and comm in that Vixen should go ahead without me. If there's a dire emergency, of course, I'll come running. Okay?" she added, throwing a meaningful look at the Glamique rep—and this time, *pushing* significantly more.

"Oh, absolutely," the rep said happily. "If you're needed, you're needed. We at Glamique understand you have a responsibility to the city."

Holly grinned. "Well then. Let's finish up here so that I can get back to heroing."

Three hours later, Holly strolled into Squadron headquarters. She peeled off her cape and handed it to Jamie—not the same Jamie as before; another Runner, this one a girl—and said her hellos to the handful of other Squadron soldiers lounging about the rec room. She paused to watch Speed Demon go a round of Ping-Pong with Velocity until she nearly got whiplash, then she bantered with some of Team Delta. Nothing wrong with encouraging them. They got a little boost to their confidence, and Holly got to practice her social skills. Everybody won.

In the middle of a rather inane conversation with a rookie hero saddled with the unfortunate designation of Slimer, a pair of arms circled around her waist from behind.

"Holly," a man's voice purred. "You're looking sexy as ever."

Smiling, she turned to embrace Hal Gibbons, code-name Doctor Hypnotic. "And you're a sweet talker, as usual."

By Jehovah, he was so gorgeous, between his black, black eyes that you could drown in, his dark hair that was a bit too long, and his jaw that was chiseled enough you could cut your fingers if you tried to trace it. To say nothing of his physique. Some women didn't find muscular men attractive. Those women, Holly decided, were utterly insane.

He pressed his lips to hers, and they shared a slow, delicious kiss.

Slimer coughed and cleared his throat. "Um, we were in the middle of a conversation, Hypnotic."

Holly felt Hal's mouth shift into a smile, then he broke the kiss. "You're done now." He said it in a tone that Holly recognized all too well—he was using his Mental power.

Behind Holly, Slimer said, "Uh. Uh." Then, blankly: "We're done now."

"In fact, you shouldn't talk to Angelica at all."

"I shouldn't talk to Angelica at all."

"Now go back to your quarters and have a nice nap."

Holly didn't need to see Slimer to know he was already on his way to the residential wing of Squadron headquarters. She frowned up at Hal. "You shouldn't do that."

"Do what?" he said innocently.

"Mess with his mind." That she, too, messed with people's minds didn't bother her; pushing a bit of Light-inspired bliss wasn't the same thing as forcing people to see and remember things that weren't real.

"I'm not," Hal said. "I'm just giving him a picture of a different reality. Everyone can use a little escape from the craziness of the real world."

One that didn't include Slimer speaking to Angelica. Sometimes, Hal's possessive streak drove her a little crazy. "And what if I'd been talking with a group of people? Would you have given them all such an escape?"

"So that I could kiss you whenever I wanted? Oh yes." He did something with his fingers, and Holly's belly fluttered.

She shook her head, but couldn't help smiling. "You're a rogue, Doctor Hypnotic."

"And you're ravishing, Angelica." He bent down to whisper in her ear. "Care to come with me to my quarters?"

"Mmm. I think—"

"Excuse me, Angelica?" That was the female Jamie, standing in the doorway.

Still looking up at Hal, she said, "Yes?"

"You have a call, from the Academy."

Holly sighed, untangled herself from Hal's arms. "I'll come find you."

"Do that." He stroked her cheek, sending a shiver of anticipation down her back.

She squeezed his hand once, then followed Jamie to a phone bank. Sitting down at one of the stations, she tapped the screen. And bit back a groan when she saw the face of Dr. Aaron Moore appear.

"Angelica!" the doctor beamed. "I'm glad to have caught you."

She inclined her head politely. "Doctor. What can I do for you?"

"I wanted once again to implore you to reconsider my offer."

"Which offer would that be?" she said. "Oh, yes, that's right. The offer to slice open my brain and putter around in there. Forgive me, but once again I have to say no thank you."

"But Angelica, the tests wouldn't hurt you. And they would help with my research immensely."

Angelica smiled tightly and bit back her initial response, which was to tell him to go to hell. Dr. Moore, the head of Corp-Co's R&D division, was constantly looking into what made the extrahumans tick. It was no secret that Corp's Executive Committee fawned over him and gave him all the resources he requested—no matter how insulting or insane those requests might be. So all Squadron members, for example, had to put up with countless hours of so-called therapy, which involved being hooked up to various machines that supposedly monitored their heart rates, their emotional reactions, their brain waves. Angelica hated being attached to machines, and she hated the required therapy sessions. The notion that she might *volunteer* her time to Dr. Moore almost made her laugh. "Sorry," she said. "Not interested."

"I understand," the doctor said amiably. "But once again, I have to press my claim that your own power is more Mental in nature than Light."

"And once again, I have to tell you that's absurd. I'm a Lighter, same as my mother, same as her father."

"Angelica, if you would simply allow me to perform my tests, we would learn the truth about your power. That would be beneficial not only to you, but to all extrahumans in the service of the Squadron and Corp-Co."

"I hope they pay you every time you mention Corp's name," she said. "And the answer is still no."

"But Angelica—"

"No buts, Doctor. I won't agree to you invading my mind."

"But think of all the good it will do . . ."

"Good-bye, Doctor." She tapped off the connection before he could say another word. Christo, the man was positively galling. He just wouldn't quit.

She wondered how long it would be before Dr. Moore went

straight to the Executive Committee to demand that Angelica submit to those alleged power tests.

Suddenly chilled, she rubbed her arms.

She was still frowning at the blank screen when she heard a commotion down the hall. Curious, she left the phone bank to see what was making such a stir, and was rewarded with a scene of the conquering heroes returning victorious: Luster grinning hugely, one arm wrapped possessively around Vixen's waist—and didn't *that* make Holly blink—and the two brothers in Shadow, Night and Blackout, shining darkly in stark contrast to Luster's brilliance. Already, a crowd of other heroes and Runners had swarmed them.

"It was no contest," Luster was saying. "Professor Neutron didn't have a chance, not with Vixen here leading the charge."

"You're exaggerating," Vixen said, blushing madly and looking flustered. "We all played our parts, were all necessary to the operation . . ."

"She's being kind," Luster said. "We were backup, nothing more. Vixen had it all under control."

"He's right," Blackout said softly, and Holly smiled at him. She knew he had a small crush on her, and he was a nice guy. But he was also Hal's opposite in every way: where Hal was tall and muscular, Blackout—George Greene—was smaller and slighter, more of a jockey's build than a football player's. Hal was confident and charming; George was quiet and brooding.

Yes, Blackout was nice. Sweet, even. But he was no Doctor Hypnotic.

"She did the right thing," Night said, "calling for backup. But we weren't needed. It was all Vixen."

Holly called out, "Sounds like you've popped your cherry, Valerie!"

Vixen blushed even deeper, but Luster laughed richly. "She certainly has. About time that Team Alpha's newest member stole the spotlight."

That made Holly chuckle. Maybe now Valerie would finally unwind a little and not be so standoffish.

She was surprised to find herself excited about that possibility. She didn't have any close female friends. And anytime she tried to get close to a male friend, Hal would bristle. If Valerie was really coming out of her shell, then Holly would finally have someone she could talk to.

With that happy thought, Angelica joined the others in cheering Squadron New Chicago's most recent addition.

CHAPTER 9

LUSTER

Violence is no more a genetic predisposition than is a taste
for spicy food. Violence is in the mind. Violence does not
interest me.

—Matthew Icarus, unpublished lecture
to his genetics students at Yale University, 1974

Lester Bradford grinned at the man facing him, then punched him in the throat. Vanisher gurgled and fell to one knee, his opacity flickering from invisible to solid and back again as he flopped on the practice mat like a hooked mackerel. "Damn it, Bradford! What was that for?"

"You dropped your hands." Lester dropped his stance and offered his sparring partner a hand up.

"You're a fucking Light power. You're supposed to throw light. You don't sucker punch!"

"And you vanishing and tripping me was *so* sporting." Lester withdrew his hand. "Get over it, Mark. Extrahumans don't always use their powers, and villains don't always do what you expect."

Mark struggled to his feet, rubbing the bruise forming on his neck like a giant hickey. "You're a class-A dick, Bradford."

"I live to serve." Lester snatched his towel and bag and left the practice room. Of course, he didn't *have* to hit Mark Villanova in the neck, just like he didn't *have* to call major news stations in advance when he knew there was a major battle going on, and he didn't *have* to flirt with his cohero, Vixen.

All right, that last one he'd do even if he got no benefit at all. He'd thought her just this side of plain and a bit dull when she'd showed up, fresh from being muscled off Squadron Orlando in favor of some teenage moron who threw glitter, but after the fight with Neutron . . . He smiled. Still waters and all that.

The truth was, until Valerie joined Team Alpha, Lester had felt boredom threatening every hour of every day of his stifling Corp existence. News crews and spectacular battles made him a hero, but he had a niggling thought that the good he was doing was transparent at best and nonexistent at worst. He didn't miss that the Squadron protected Corp interests—Corp banks, Corp labs, and Corp employees—before they even pretended to care about places like the one where Lester had grown up.

The villains, at least, believed in something—even if that something was just greed. Lester hadn't had that since he'd been taken for training. And it was beginning to wear thin.

Which was why he had to be the perfect hero and stay far, far away from anyone with a Mental ability.

A small sigh caused him to whip around, his heart thudding and his skin heating as Light gathered around him. Lester hadn't experienced the sheltered childhood of a Corp extrahuman, and a few seconds in his neighborhood was often the difference between life and a bullet.

"Take a picture," George Greene muttered. "It'll last you longer." He looked dreadful, his skin pale and his nose leaking blood.

Lester set his bag down, slowly. You didn't make sudden moves around dangerous animals, or Shadow powers. His Light could burn, but it couldn't choke the life from you. Lester had a healthy respect for predators higher in the food chain.

With Shadows, you had to outsmart them, distract them. If you came at them head-on, you'd lose.

He said, "You try to take on Behemoth again? Not smart, mate."

"I was practicing." George sniffed and swiped at the blood on his face. "I want to use the Shadow to fly, like Night."

"Night's a freak of nature," Lester said. "Just be happy with what you have, is my advice."

"I can *do* it."

The snap in George's voice made Lester pause. George was mild-mannered to a fault, so mild that he wouldn't even speak up to Angelica and tell her that he fancied her to the point of pain. "All right, Georgie-boy." Lester clapped him on the shoulder. "If you want a Shadow sled, you'll have one. Out of curiosity, did the Shadow punch you in the gob as well?"

"I just . . . feel . . ." George's jaw twitched. "I'm fine."

"Maybe you should see a medic," Lester said. "You look like death, if you want my honesty."

"Well, I don't!" George shouted. "And if you tell anyone, if Corp finds out about this and throws me to Dr. Moore to experiment on, it'll be *your* fault, you Limey idiot!"

Lester blinked, but before George could continue his rant he swayed and fell over, his head cracking against the metal lockers in front of him.

"Bloody hell." Lester bent over George, while he bellowed toward the practice room: "We need a medic in here!"

George's eyeballs twitched under his lids. His pulse was racing like a hover engine when Lester pressed two fingers against his neck.

"Blackout. Blackout. *George.*" Lester shook him. "Come on, son. Wake up."

George's arm whipped out and caught Lester by the front of his shirt. His eyes were full of Shadow, black like someone had spilled ink across them. Lester felt his heart twitch in shock, but he let George hold on to him.

"Make them stop," George hissed. "I hear them and they never stop. I can't keep fighting, Les . . ."

A medic crew burst through the door and moved Lester to the side, working on George with smelling salts and a portable cauterizer for the cut in the back of his head.

"He lose consciousness?" one of the medics demanded.

"For a moment." Lester watched George's gaunt face. "He said he was . . ." He bit his tongue just in time. "He said he was feeling dizzy."

The lie rolled seamlessly out. Lester's father, a man obsessed with honesty to the point of lit cigarettes and leather straps, had impressed on him his need to be a superlative liar.

Of course Lester should report George's incident.

Make them stop. I hear them and they never stop. I can't keep fighting . . .

Of course George needed help if he was hearing voices.

But there was real fear in George's eyes, and Lester wouldn't be the one to condemn him to that barbarian Moore ripping out his brain, his innermost thoughts and secrets laid bare. Secrets were all somebody like George Greene had.

"Take care of yourself, yeah?" he told George. "And look on the bright side—maybe Holly will come and kiss you better."

"Screw you, man," George rasped, but his eyes were his own again, and he managed a weak smile.

Lester breathed a small sigh of relief. His teammate was going to be all right.

He had to be. Otherwise, Lester had just lied for a man who needed psychiatric help desperately, who could endanger the very people he was supposed to watch over, and Corp would bury them both.

CHAPTER 10

NIGHT

Aaron is fascinated by the Shadows. If it were up to me, we would lobotomize the both of them. They scare the hell out of me.

— From the journal of Martin Moore, entry #18

Night stormed down the hallway of Squadron headquarters, ignoring the pissants and lapdogs who tried to stop him with their tedious social obligations. He had no time to be bothered with "How are you?" or "Terrific collar" or "Who do you like for the series this year?"

Blackout was in the hospital wing.

Blackout, from the little that Luster had mentioned upon Night's return from battle, had lived up to his designation and blacked out. Just for a second or two, Bradford had insisted, playing up how quickly the medics had arrived and how strong Greene was and no worries, mate, he'll be back in black, tally ho.

Luster, for all his tactical brilliance, could be a fucking idiot.

No, Night allowed as he stomped down the last corridor. *Not an idiot.* Lester Bradford was many things—egocentric, proud enough to put peacocks to shame, and smart enough to do Corp to the letter whenever anyone was watching. But idiotic? Not Luster.

So when Night had returned from defeating Gold Digger and Luster had gamely by-the-byed Blackout's "episode," what Luster *hadn't* said had spoken volumes. Of course Bradford had tried to make light of it; that's what he did, in his sardonic way. But Night could almost smell Luster's apprehension, could nearly taste Bradford's unease. For all his bravado, Luster had been concerned—even scared.

Night's lips pulled into a quick, tight smile. If Luster ever saw the Shadow for what it really was, then he'd know what fear truly meant. Then he'd know what it was to fear the Dark.

But the Lighters never thought about the Dark, not really. They thought their little power could banish the Shadow and make the world safe and sound. Lighters, as a class, were a joke. At least Bradford was a genius, which made him interesting, and even a worthy teammate. Sometimes.

But whether Light or Earth or Water or Fire, or any other power, they were all weak before the Shadow. They would all crumple, gibbering their way to madness. No one was infallible—except for those born with the ability to handle, to master, the Shadow. Like Night.

Corp had no idea how lucky they were that Night was one of the good guys. They had no idea how easy it would be for him to scourge the world of fear and oppression once and for all.

Night smiled again, a knifelike flash of humor. Of course, he'd never be a villain.

He appreciated that Corp had rules. Good rules were part of good discipline. And as a Shadow power, Night intimately understood the importance of discipline. All that stood between him and the Shadow was his own willpower.

And that, ultimately, was why he was marching to his comrade's side right now.

Night strode through the hospital wing until he got to the room where they'd put Blackout. His brother in Shadow was lying on a cot, looking pale and somewhat bloody. Various tubes hung about him, dripping things into his veins through numerous IVs. His heart rate and blood pressure and other things were being monitored.

None of that mattered.

But then, as Night and Blackout were the only two living Shadow powers in Squadron: Americas, no one else on this side of the world knew what they really should be looking for. And that's where Night came in.

Night sat down on the edge of the cot, one hand behind his back, clenched tightly. He scanned Blackout's face. It was too thin, nearly gaunt. If he'd smiled in recent weeks, Night couldn't remember. "Blackout," he said softly. That was the first test: Did the man remember who he was?

Blackout stirred, and his eyes fluttered open. Brown eyes, bloodshot and haunted. But free of the telltale stain of Shadow.

Good. That was a start. Behind his back, Night's hand loosened, just a little.

Blackout's mouth moved, and he croaked, "Night. Christo, Night."

"We can talk freely," Night said. "I've put up a Shadownet. No sound will be recorded. We have privacy."

Blackout sighed, and his eyes closed. "Okay."

"Blackout," Night said, putting his other hand on the man's thin arm, launching into the second test. "Tell me. What happened?"

"Don't know."

Night's jaw tightened. Not good. Not good at all. "What do you mean?"

"It's a blank. There's nothing there." Blackout opened his eyes, implored Night to understand. "I was talking to Les, and then I woke up here." A shudder worked its way across his bony shoulders. "Dr. Moore was here when I woke up. Legitimate doctors too—but why him? Christo, Night . . . I think they cut me open."

Night silently agreed. "It's okay, man," he said, lying smoothly. Behind his back, his hand tightened.

Blackout rasped, "What did they do to me?"

"It doesn't matter," Night said, mostly to himself. "If they

were looking for something, either they found it or they didn't."
He looked at Blackout, searched the man's face. "Can you still
call the Shadow?"

Blackout paled visibly. "Rick . . . I'm scared."

Night bristled; he loathed it when he was called by his nondesignation name. But clearly, that added . . . *human* touch . . .
was what his teammate needed. "George," he said, "you have to
do it. You have to see if they took that away from you." If they'd
neutered him. This was the third, and final, test. "This will
prove whether Dr. Moore tampered with your brain."

Blackout sighed. Then his lips slowly turned blue, and his
breath frosted from his nose. From his left hand, a creeper of
Shadow inched out, hesitantly, as if tasting the air.

"Excellent," Night said, relieved. "Good job. It looks like
Moore didn't get inside your head after all."

Blackout hissed out a slow breath. "Then why can't I remember?"

"Trauma, most likely." Night clapped Blackout's shoulder
lightly. "You and I both know the real fight isn't against the supervillains, don't we?"

Blackout let out a weak laugh. It sounded like a scream.

Behind his back, Night released the Shadow knife, and it
unwound, slowly, and sank back inside of Night's flesh. Blackout had passed, though it had been a close thing.

But close only mattered, as the saying went, with grenades
and horseshoes.

Night smiled, pleased that he wouldn't be alone in the
Shadow. But as he talked with his power brother, he couldn't
help but wonder what, exactly, Dr. Moore had wanted with
Blackout.

Interlude

"This way," Julie says, lending a hand to old Mrs. Summers. "Sorry about the clutter."

"This is nothing." The old woman laughs. "You should see my place after my grandkids visit. Worse than Jehovah's scorched earth, it is. And you're a dear for letting us stay."

" 'Twasn't nothing," Garth says around an armful of boxes. "Glad to have you and the others."

"Safety in numbers," Julie adds cheerfully.

He can't help but send her a look. You'd think she'd be supportive of him trying to call up the Network, what with her praise of big numbers. But no—Julie, like the rest of the Latents he'd spoken with over the past few days, is flat-out opposed to the idea.

She smiles back at him, content as a cat with feathers poking from its mouth.

Mrs. Summers is chatting happily with the Brewers from across the street. Garth shakes his head as he hefts the cartons to the floor. Poor Heather and Paul, and their youngsters Alex and Jacob, all but thrown out of their apartment thanks to their landlord deciding that now is the perfect time not to pay Deke O'Connor.

Garth sneers as he thinks of that small-time crime lord—the sort whose idea of Irish pride was to tat Celtic symbols over every inch of his arms. Word is, ever since Iridium had paid him a call a couple weeks back at the Blarney Stone, Deke had gone looking to prove how far he could piss. Word is, Deke had explained to the Brewers' landlord just this morning that even with New Chicago festering worse than an unlanced boil on a leper's arse, it's no excuse not to make your weekly gambling payments.

Word is, Deke had explained it very succinctly with a fire-bomb to the landlord's apartment.

Say what you will about Deke O'Connor, Garth thinks as he ambles to the kitchen, *at least he did it when the kids were at school and the parents were at work.* The only one who'd been in the two-family house had been the landlord himself, sleeping the sleep of the dead after a particularly raucous night on the town. Now the man sleeps in the critical unit over at New Chicago General. The idiot.

"Anyone for pop?" he calls out.

The Brewer clan answers in the affirmative, and Mrs. Summers politely requests a spot of tea. Julie's in the kitchen with him now, setting up all the drinks on the counter as he putters by the faucet.

"I hear Screamer tossed about Kat's car," Julie murmurs, pouring. "Sent it slamming into one of the Squadron. You know, the still-good Squadron, not the junked Squadron. Kat says it's nothing but an accordion now."

"Kat's lucky she wasn't in said car when Screamer used it as a cudgel."

"Kat's got no way to get to work, not unless she takes a city hover."

"Shame," Garth says, waiting for it. Kat's one of Julie's closest friends, a teacher over at the Montessori. He puts the kettle on to boil and rummages about for the Twinings packets.

"I was thinking," Julie says. "I could drive her to and from the school. It's not safe to be walking the streets, or just waiting for a bus to show." She finishes doling out the pop, glances at him from over her shoulder to gauge his reaction. She frowns. "You should just nuke the water, have done with it."

"Bad luck to rush your tea," he says. "And how're you going to play chauffeur and still make it to the library on time? Your own job is worth less than hers, I guess?"

"I'll figure something out."

"Or you could come out and say, 'Garth my love, as you're a freelance writer with no set schedule, would you be a dear and chauffeur Kat to and from work until she's got herself an accordion-proof car?' "

Julie smiles, and even with his sunglasses on, it's positively radiant. "I was thinking I'd have to seduce you before I could ask such a thing."

"Smart lass."

He's about to say more, maybe even kick-start the seduction process, when the ground shakes. And then it groans and gives a violent heave, sending Julie into his arms. Husband and wife exchange a panicked look, then Garth's bolting into the main room. He doesn't have to glance behind to see Julie gripping the kitchen doorway, her knuckles white with worry; he knows his wife far too well.

"Drop to the ground," Garth bellows over the sound of the earthquake, "and get away from the windows! Alex, Jacob, under the table!"

The kids scamper like the Devil's on their heels, and their parents chase after them. Julie's calling out words that are meant to be encouraging, but her voice is too shrill. The walls are practically humming with energy, the old-fashioned 2-Ds shaking in their gilded frames. Things fall and splatter as Garth helps Mrs. Summers to the far corner of the room, the one away from the outside wall. He crouches over her as she hugs the floor, shielding her as best he can as he scans the room.

"Paul," he shouts, "the bookcase isn't bolted to the wall! Get closer to the door!"

Paul squawks and shuffles toward the front door. He makes it halfway before there's a deafening *THOOM!!!* and the door implodes. Paul dives to the side just as the metal door sails past, thundering to the ground like a dying elephant.

Garth's blood is pounding in his ears and the Brewer clan is shrieking and Mrs. Summers is praying loudly and Julie's telling him to look Garth look and so Garth looks.

On top of the fallen door, a thin man in blue is scrambling to his feet. He's battered worse than the door, all shaking limbs and torn fabric that's almost fashionable. He ignores Garth and the others as he faces the naked doorway, opens his mouth, and screams.

Earsplitting noise, the sort that makes your bones rattle. Garth clamps his hands over his ears and bows down low, doing his damnedest to think. Daring a glance, he blinks away tears to see a tall man in prison grays stepping through the ruins of his doorway, a wall of light shielding him. The man calls out words Garth can't hear, and a small, balding man slinks past him. Now the weasel-like man is throwing out his hand, and the screamer clutches his head.

Screamer, Garth realizes. The man in blue is Screamer, one of the Squadron-turned-rabids.

The noise cuts off, leaving Garth's ears ringing like mad. Screamer is on his knees now, gibbering and crying and shaking. The weasel is standing over him, a gleeful look on his narrow face. He reminds Garth of every serial killer he's ever seen on the vids.

"Enough," the tall man decrees. "Just cuff him already. No need to make a show of it."

Garth knows that voice—cultured, British, altogether commanding. He's heard it on interview shows and on the news. He thinks of the light shield and puts two and two together.

Arclight's busted out of Blackbird and is standing right here in his flat.

"Just one more minute," the weasel begs. "He tastes so good."

"Radar," Arclight says in that movie-star voice, "do I really have to repeat myself?"

The small man licks his lips once, twice, then reaches into the pouch on his belt and removes a set of stun-cuffs. Screamer's too busy bawling to notice that he's been captured.

I want to throw up, Garth thinks as he unfolds himself and stands tall. "Here now," he says, and his voice isn't even breaking, "you can't go barging into people's apartments to do your fighting."

Arclight turns to face him. His mouth is set in a bemused smile. "Seems like we already have."

"Fear," Radar whispers, crooning. "So very delicious."

Damn straight Garth is afraid. But that doesn't stop him. "There's kids here," he says quietly.

Arclight frowns, then darts his gaze about the place until it settles on the Brewer children, huddled beneath the dining-room table, clutching each other with desperate limbs. Something softens in the man's face, but when he speaks again, his voice is hard.

"Take Screamer outside," he commands. "Protean should have the Angle well in hand, but he may need some assistance."

Radar grins, and Garth once again thinks of evil things who live to kill all manner of creatures. Very slowly. And very painfully. The small man leads Screamer out of the apartment, humming "London Bridge."

Arclight watches the Brewer children for a moment, then takes in first their parents, then Julie, standing breathless in the kitchen doorway. He looks at Mrs. Summers, who's peeking out from behind Garth. Finally, his gaze lands on Garth.

"I apologize for the mess," Arclight says. "If these were different times, I'd put you in touch with the Squadron Claims division."

"If these were different times," Garth says slowly, "I'd think you'd still be in Blackbird and Screamer would still be a hero."

A grin touches Arclight's lips. "Touché." With that, the villain—former villain? Hell if Garth knows—spins on his heel and parades out of the apartment.

For a long moment, none of them say a thing. Then everyone talks at once. Alex and Jacob are going on about this being the best day *ever*. Heather and Paul are falling over themselves asking if the children are okay. Old Mrs. Summers insists that, in her day, even criminals respected innocent citizens' private lives and nothing like this ever used to happen.

Garth exchanges a look with Julie. "No," he says. "It surely didn't. Things change."

Julie gets his meaning. She lets out a sigh and leans against the doorway. "Some things shouldn't change," she says, but there's no fire to her words.

In the kitchen, the teakettle begins to sing.

NOW

CHAPTER 11

IRIDIUM

I have absolutely no doubt that this technique could have saved Miranda's life. I was too slow. Too slow by half. Never again. Nothing stands in the way of my work.
  —Matthew Icarus, diary entry dated June 16, 1976
    (the anniversary of Miranda Icarus's death from
      leukemia eight years earlier)

Iridium didn't hate people. Hate, Lester had taught her, was a useless emotion unless it was spined with anger or fired by ambition. Iridium didn't hate people just for being people. She didn't hate the doctors who'd worked on Frostbite; she didn't hate Night, who'd brainwashed Jet into a pale skeleton of her former self.

Iridium hated Corp. Corp was the machine that minted the doctors and the Nights, the true target of righteous rage, if you had any sense. Hating one part of a machine was like shooting the messenger—unsatisfying, and ultimately useless.

And if there was a living symbol of Corp, it was Gordon.

"You don't have a choice," the man said. It was a sick parody of when they'd met in the control room at Blackbird. He had the same gray suit and smarmy smile. The same gun.

Pointed at her face.

Iridium curled her hands. The air around her shimmered like an aurora borealis as the Light threatened to explode into the visible spectrum, searing Gordon's eyes from his skull, flaking skin like burned paper.

Christo, wouldn't that be nice.

No. Iridium couldn't afford to call down the remnants of Corp still obviously working in New Chicago, or the full force of Corp Headquarters, on her father and the other convicts. Couldn't afford to have Gordon and his smug grin rescind their pardons. Not yet.

"I suggest you get that thrice-damned gun out of my face before I shove it up your nose," she said. "Or someplace less comfortable."

Gordon flicked the barrel at the purse snatcher at Iridium's feet, then back at her, quick as a snake. He wasn't fast enough to be an extrahuman, but he had the quicksilver edge of a normal human who was just very, very good at what he did.

"You're off the reservation, Calista. This is not how Corp brings in a criminal."

The purse snatcher groaned, holding his broken nose. Iridium had eschewed her powers for shoving the sprinting thief in front of a robo-hauler. That had stopped him nicely, and it hadn't caused a scene that would have brought cops or worse, a flock of rabids, down on the block.

"This is how *I* do it," Iridium said. "You don't like it, I suggest you go cry in your beer and leave me alone."

Gordon raised a finger, wagged it. "You want to think about what comes out of that mouth, Calista."

"Call me that again, and I'm going to *feed* you that gun."

"Fine." He holstered it, straightened his tie, twitched his cuffs. "But I mean it when I suggest you think, instead of using that fine brain Jehovah gave you for pithy comebacks and cussing."

At Iridium's feet, the purse snatcher tried to jump and run. She stomped down on his hand. He crumpled again, moaning.

"Think about what?" she managed, even though the urge to strobe Gordon was overwhelming. This must be what Jet felt every day, felt when she'd nearly killed Taser.

"This world will not burn forever," he said. "Corp is negotiating with India to bring in their extrahumans to clean up the mess you've made."

Iridium felt her eyebrows go up. Squadron: India was like Squadron: Americas in name only. India was state-sponsored and served the people. They didn't go international. They were Switzerland, and the United and Canadian States was a war zone very much outside their jurisdiction.

"When they arrive," Gordon said, "order will tip back into balance. Where will you be then? Will you be a criminal, running for the rest of your days with your poor, dear father? Or will you be welcomed into the Squadron with open arms, the prodigal daughter returned to the light?"

"Squadron: India won't help you," Iridium said reflexively. "They don't answer to Corp."

"And yet, their funding is nearly half Corp's doing." Gordon smiled, like a lizard tasting the air. "I think perhaps they will reconsider their position of international neutrality in this case. And then the question remains—where will you be?"

Iridium looked into Gordon's soulless eyes, a gray that was nearly white. Corpse eyes. She knew with sudden, bell-like clarity that Corp couldn't be allowed to gain a foothold in the Americas again.

Her life and Lester's and even Jet's depended on it. If Corp came back to power, every extrahuman who'd escaped their grasp and exposed their skeletons was as good as dead.

When Squadron: India landed on American soil, there needed to be a compelling case to lock up the men and women responsible for the rabids vaporizing the city. Men like Gordon.

And to do that, they'd need evidence, from someone who'd been a Corp insider.

"Well?" Gordon frowned at her.

Iridium pulled the purse snatcher to his feet as two patrol hovers rounded the corner, waving them in to take custody.

"I'll be where I'm supposed to be."

Gordon smiled again. "Good girl."

Iridium smiled back, feeling ice crystals freeze the expression. "I try my best, sir."

CHAPTER 12

JET

*Aaron is positive that, without additional controls in place,
the extrahumans have only 1–4 years before their conditioning breaks down. I think that range is too conservative.*
— From the journal of Martin Moore, entry #51

Stop that," Jet said for the third time.

Nocturne, struggling against the stun-cuffs, tried to
slam her chin into Jet's face. The purple-clad woman missed,
then overbalanced and went crashing to the ground, landing
sloppily in the gutter. She was probably so used to phasing
through solid objects that she'd forgotten how to roll with a fall
or take the brunt on her shoulder.

Jet had little sympathy. Maybe next time, Nocturne would
rethink breaking into First National. Light, what *was* it with former heroes pretending to be villains? Had Nocturne really
thought all she had to do was phase inside the bank vaults and
that would be the end of it? As if the bank didn't come equipped
with both organic and inorganic matter sensors that automati-
cally triggered a silent alarm when they were tripped? *Please.*

Had Jet been the only one of her Academy class actually to pay attention in the Criminal Minds units?

Well, her and Iridium. And Iri, she was sure, had cheated in those units.

Jet helped the bigger woman to her feet. "Come on," she said to Nocturne. "You know the cuffs are messing with your balance. You're just going to get dizzy if you try to hit me." And if she tried to phase out of them, the cuffs would neutralize her. Painfully.

Nocturne suggested something anatomically impossible.

"You kiss your mother with that mouth?" Jet asked.

Nocturne spewed obscenities so blue that even Were would have blushed.

"Now that's just rude." Jet bound Nocturne with a graymatter leash, then summoned a floater to whisk them both to the Sixteenth precinct. Nocturne, not a flyer, shrieked. Loudly. And very, very long, the sound slowly fading to an echo of terror. The woman shuddered, inhaled, then let out another whoop of sheer panic, giving Screamer a run for his money.

It did nothing for Jet's headache. She hissed as Nocturne bleated, and she bit her lip to keep from crying out. The pain had begun when she'd stopped relying on physical training and skill against Nocturne and started tapping into her extrahuman power—a subtle thing, then, a stroke of discomfort as Jet had released a creeper of Shadow to startle her opponent. But as the fight had progressed, the stroking turned to knocking, then to pounding. And now her head felt stretched taut and her senses were as keyed up as a junkie's—colors too vivid, bleeding and raw; smells of pollution and ozone and sweat combating for domination. As Jet and Nocturne soared over Wreck City, Jet pressed her fingers against her temple, massaging, silently pleading for what was surely a migraine to vanish.

And maybe the Light was shining on her, because the other woman's voice finally gave out. When Nocturne fell silent, Jet breathed out a sigh of gratitude. Her head, though, continued to throb softly.

It's getting worse.

She knew it in her heart. The headaches were coming steadily now, in rolling waves of pain that lasted for hours. As much as she wanted to say it was due to sheer exhaustion—the last time she'd slept was two nights ago, and she'd already maxed out on caffeine patches for the day—Jet knew better.

Whatever else Corp's brainwashing had done over the years, at least it had kept the Shadow voices in check. Now, without whatever frequency they'd used to soothe that part of her mind, it was getting harder for her to ignore the Darkness that licked at her thoughts.

She was going to lose herself to the Shadow again.

As they flew, she peered down at the blurs of buildings, the cars and hovers that looked like children's toys, at the people marching antlike to their destinations. It would be so easy to step off the disc and let herself fall, until the ground came up to meet her.

She nodded, determined. If it came down to it—if the voices grew too strong—she would kill herself. Better that than to become something worse than rabid.

By the time they touched down in front of the Sixteenth precinct, Jet was feeling better. Her head still hurt worse than the scorched earth, but at least she felt in control, if exhausted. Nocturne had curled into a tight ball and wouldn't untangle her limbs even when on solid ground. Jet debated leaving the woman tucked in a fetal position right there by the commissioner's doorstep, but she decided against it. Wouldn't do her any good if the police or even Wagner himself tripped over Nocturne and wound up breaking an ankle.

As Jet hauled her captive up the precinct steps, a black limo pulled up to the curb, followed by a battalion of minihovers overloaded with screamingly bright news-channel logos.

Jet distinctly thought, *Fuck.* Then she prodded Nocturne harder, telling the woman to move. Peripherally, she saw a brute stuffed into an expensive suit climb out of the limo. Strictly bodyguard material. As he scanned the block, taking in both Jet and Nocturne, flashes and glares and pops from the newsies burst like localized fireworks.

Almost there, Jet thought, propelling Nocturne toward the

massive front doors. If she could escape inside the building, that would be the end of it; the media didn't make it a habit to set foot inside the police station, not since Wagner had nearly taken off a reporter's head for interrupting an interrogation by asking the prisoner to smile for the vids.

"Jet," a man's voice called out. "A moment of your time."

She turned to see the large man standing in front of the limo. Overhead, the cameras whirred and clicked.

"A moment, citizen," she agreed, despising that the conversation was being recorded and simulcast to the networks. Motioning to Nocturne's bound form, she said, "Then I must return to business."

"Understood." He opened the limo passenger door with a perfected flourish. The well-dressed man who emerged was small, fat, and wore enough cologne to fell Colossal Man at two hundred meters.

Mayor William Lee.

Behind her optiframes, Jet's eyes narrowed. Two weeks ago, this man was practically falling over himself to show Jet his gratitude for all the work she did as the official Hero of New Chicago. But then she'd offended him when she'd ditched an award ceremony (in her honor) to confront Iridium—at the time, still Public Enemy Number 1. Lee hadn't taken it well. In fact, he'd almost gotten her sponsorship with the City revoked.

So how to play this?

Jet wished she could get Ops online for advice, but there was no time—the mayor was approaching briskly, his face set in a scowl. Jet pushed aside her exhaustion and her worries, straightened her spine, and lifted her chin.

"Good day, sir," she said—not simpering, no, but borderline deferential. The cameras and vids caught every nuance.

The mayor glared at her, then at Nocturne. "Isn't littering a finable offense?"

She smiled tightly. "We're on our way inside to see Commissioner Wagner."

"Of course you are." He walked up closer until he was well within her personal space. "Nocturne saved my daughter's life last year."

Careful, she told herself. "Last year, Nocturne was a valuable member of the Squadron."

"And now?"

"I caught her breaking into First National, sir, then she fought me and tried to escape."

"And you prevailed. Miraculous," he said dryly. "So why is it that all of the Squadron goes insane except for New Chicago's own patented hero? Why is Corp refusing to comment? Can you give me any answers, Jet?"

If it were Hornblower here instead of Jet, he certainly would open his mouth and censure Corp-Co, damning them to the deepest Darkness. But the years of conditioning still held; if Jet tried to breathe a word against Corp, her brain would catch fire. She knew—she'd tried before.

So all she said was, "I wish I could, sir." And that was the Light's honest truth.

He held her gaze, and around them, the reporters salivated. Cameras flashed and vids gleamed in a dizzying array. Jet's optiframes irised, canceling out the blinding effects.

"Well, you have a long history of service to the city," he said loudly in his smooth politician's voice, smiling. He offered his hand, and as Jet took it, he leaned in close enough to kiss her. Lee whispered, soft enough that the vids wouldn't catch it: "One false step, and I'll have Wagner drop everything to haul your ass to Blackbird."

"I appreciate your words, sir," she said, her voice far too tight.

He shot her a look filled with venom, then released Jet's hand. "Dawson," he said, "take this burden off Jet's hands, would you?"

The bodyguard approached them, indifferent to the reporters, and hefted Nocturne over his shoulder in a fireman's carry. They disappeared inside the police station.

A long moment passed, and things unspoken hung in the air. Jet sensed the crowd of citizens that had gathered around the precinct steps, drawn in like moths to the light of the news vids. In her gauntlets, her hands were sweating. She hated being the center of attention.

"You go on with your heroing," Mayor Lee said. "I have an appointment with the commissioner."

She stretched her smile to its limit. "I'm surprised he didn't come to you." A tiny zing, one she shouldn't have let loose.

The mayor smiled in return, a nasty smile filled with promise. "He doesn't know we have an appointment yet." And then Lee straightened his lapel and walked up the remaining steps to the station.

As if on cue, the reporters swarmed her.

"Jet! How does it feel going after your own teammates?"

"Jet! Do you think you'll be going rabid too?"

"Jet, what assurances can you give the people of New Chicago that you won't put them in harm's way?"

"Jet! Over here, smile!"

"Jet! Give us a fierce look!"

She tried to get a word in, tried to think, but they kept coming at her, firing questions at her and flashing their lights, demanding. Insisting.

Enraging.

all of them all of them vultures suck them dry

Light, no. She wanted to cover her ears, but the vids would see her weakness and the reporters would never let her forget it. She had to get away before the Shadow grew too strong. She—

"Jet!"

The man's voice was loud, almost crystalline, easily carrying over the sounds of the reporters and paparazzi. And it came from above.

She looked up and saw a man swathed in black, his head covered in a ski mask fitted with goggles. His hover revved, and he extended a gloved hand.

Her heart skipped a beat.

"Sorry to break up the impromptu press conference, honey," Taser shouted, "but you're needed!"

Desperate, she smiled for the cameras. "My sincere apologies," she said brightly. "But duty calls." A spring of Shadow propelled her upward, and she grabbed Taser's outstretched hand. He pulled her onto the back of his hover with ease.

"Jet!" a reporter cried. "Is this your new boyfriend?"

She nearly gagged.

"Might want to hold on to my waist," Taser suggested. And then he gunned the engine and they took off.

Jet clutched onto him, hating him and thankful for him. As the wind whipped her cowl back and sent her cloak fluttering madly, the Shadow voices giggled and teased, whispering things that made her want to cry. Then they receded.

For now.

He said nothing as they rode, and neither did she, but there was an energy between them, dancing, suggestive. She gripped his waist and gritted her teeth, and in a charged silence Taser and Jet cut through the polluted skies.

When they landed on a rooftop somewhere in the Waterfront Grid, Jet nearly flew off the hoverbike.

"Usually, the damsel gives her savior a token of her affection," Taser said.

She clenched her fists, felt the Shadow pulsing around her curled fingers. "I'm so very grateful that you saved me from the evil press corps," she said curtly. "What do you want, Bruce?"

Under the mask, the outline of his mouth pulled into a grin. "You, of course. You're looking particularly sexy tonight in your skinsuit."

"Don't," she said quietly.

"That's right, you have no sense of humor. I remember that from your file."

"And I remember how you lied to me," she said, trying to keep her voice calm, "how you used me and seduced me, how you betrayed me and nearly got me killed!" She was shouting now, the words erupting from her mouth. "You're a bastard, Bruce Hunter!"

He watched her for a moment, then slowly brought his hand to his chin and lifted the mask. His face, pale against the black fabric and the dark mass of his hair, was still upsettingly handsome. Bruce Hunter smiled at her, but his blue eyes held regret.

"It wasn't personal, Joan," he said. "It was business."

"Right. Because mercs will sign on with anyone, for any

cause, as long as the money's good." Suddenly cold, she rubbed her arms. A small part of her had been hoping that the mercenary called Taser had lied to her, back when he'd captured her and Iri weeks ago, that he wasn't really the same man who had been her Runner.

The same man she had taken to her bed.

But the proof was right there in front of her. No, he hadn't lied—not then, and not now. Though she despised that she had been his assignment, she could appreciate his work ethic.

And damn it all to Darkness, she was still attracted to him. Stupid hormones.

"What do you want, Bruce?" she asked again, her voice flat.

"You and the others are in a bind," he said. "Too much chaos, not enough control."

"Your point?"

"I was a Runner," he said. "I can gather up the others, organize them into a cohesive unit."

"The others?"

"The other Runners. Think about it—a dedicated civilian group that would support you and the others."

She frowned. "You could do that?"

"Honey, I'm damn good at my job. When I was your Runner, I made sure to learn everything I could about the Runner network, how they operated, and what they did. How to contact others in a pinch." He grinned, and Jet's stomach fluttered. "They're running scared now, like sheep. All I have to do is herd them, and they'll be back in support mode in no time flat."

Light, how much easier things would be, having even a little help. They could work with Frostbite on sorting through the Corp data, decrypting it in their search for information on Martin Moore and his horrific serum. Meteorite would create their communications unit and start working the streets, countering the Everyman message and publicly reassuring the citizens of New Chicago and the world that, even in the face of madness, a handful of them still stood strong.

But . . . this was Bruce. And as tempting as his offer was, she couldn't bring herself to trust him. "What do you get out of it?"

"You mean other than the satisfaction of helping those on the side of justice?" He chuckled. "My standard rates apply."

Of course. Taser was a mercenary. He never did anything for free. Even when he'd seduced her, he'd gotten paid for it.

"I'll call for a meeting with the others," she said tightly. "I'll let you know what we agree to."

His sensuous lips pulled into a smirk. "You do that, honey. Not like there's a crisis or anything."

She opened her mouth to say something she'd certainly regret, but that was when Meteorite's voice hummed in her ear.

"Babe, you free?"

"Just slumming," Jet said, staring hard at Bruce.

"Slum later. A bomb went off in the Downtown Grid, on Third. I need you to help New Chicago's Bravest."

"On it." She paused, then said, "Firebug's busy?" The Fire power was a natural for such situations.

A longer pause from Meteorite. "She opted out of this one."

"Excuse me?"

"You heard."

A Squadron soldier choosing not to help firefighters? Unfathomable. Baffled, Jet asked, "Where'd the bomb go off?"

"The Everyman Society regional office."

Jet closed her eyes. Her head throbbed, and she was drained, and the thought of dealing with Everyman, even for something like this, made her heartsick.

"Jetster? You're going, right?" Meteorite sounded uncertain.

"On it," Jet said softly, then tapped her comlink to white noise.

"Duty calls, eh?" Bruce smiled at her. "Some things never change."

"And some things do." She wanted to tell him to drop dead. She wanted to ask him to come with her. And, horrifically, she wanted him to hold her, kiss her, run his fingers through her hair. She scowled.

He said, "You need any assistance on this?"

And there it was. Pride, or common sense?

Jet gave him her back, summoning a Shadow floater. The voices, thankfully, were still silent; maybe they were bemused by her reaction to Bruce. She said, "Gosh, I'm all out of milk money. I guess I've got this one all by myself."

"For you, Jet, I'm happy to throw in a freebie."

"Most men at least buy me dinner first. I'll get back to you about the Runner network."

"You know how to find me?"

She looked at him over her shoulder. "I'll just have another impromptu press conference. I'm sure you'll come running to save me."

The sound of his laughter followed her as she rocketed away.

CHAPTER 13

IRIDIUM

In vitro test subjects are risky. The incarcerated population provides an ample cross section of genetic material to test gene therapy on, and raises considerably fewer questions.
—Matthew Icarus, research notes, undated

There were times when Iridium wished she had a normal father. One who hadn't gone rabid. One who'd been around for birthdays and recitals.

At least one who wasn't so damn opinionated.

"We're at the end of this discussion, Callie. There's nothing more to debate." Lester and Iridium were crammed into her bedroom, while the rest of Gordon's escapees milled about the warehouse. They all had costumes now, thanks to Gordon. Except for Nevermore, they all seemed more interested in checking out her new tech than making a nuisance of themselves.

"You busted in on *civilians,* in their *home,*" Iridium gritted. "You could have killed someone, not to mention Radar torturing Screamer. That guy is a bad apple, Dad, and you know it."

Lester cut the air with his hand. "Enough. I'm in charge of my team, and I won't be questioned. Especially not by my own daughter."

"That's just it!" Iridium shouted. "You're not in charge. Corp is!"

Her father tensed like he wanted to hit her, and the radiant panels on Iridium's ceiling overloaded and sparked.

"You know I'm right, Dad," she said softly. "We can't trust Gordon. They're going to put us right back in prison when they finish with us and Corp sends in reinforcements to take back the city, if we aren't smart about this."

"I'm never going back," Lester replied, just as quietly. "And I would never let them put my little girl in prison." He gripped Callie's hands. "I'd die first, girl."

"I know, Dad," Iridium said. "I know. But can we at least get rid of Radar?"

"The team is for us and we're for the team," Lester said. "When we break free of Gordon's leash, we'll need every one of them. Including Radar."

Iridium opened the door a crack and looked out at the villains in her warehouse again. "You know, we'd have more firepower if I commed Jet and . . ."

"No, Callie." Lester's voice went harsh—and then it was Arclight who spoke. "Not Joan. She's not the answer to our problems."

"How do you know, Dad?" Iridium threw her hands up. "Jet didn't lose her mind like the others! She's still strong, and fighting the rabids, just like we are. We're going to need some friendlies if we plan to go up against Corp. Again. Need I remind you, that hasn't worked out so well for our family."

"Joan Greene is a ticking time bomb," said Lester. His mouth set, as if the truth hurt. "It's not a question of *if* she follows her father into madness. It's when."

"How can you say that!" Iridium's own power caused her 3-D unit to short. "Jet is a good person, Dad."

"I say it because I was there, Callie. I know what can happen when Shadow overwhelms a person."

A pause as Iridium digested his words. "The Squadron could be good allies."

"And how long would it be before our *allies* took issue with our methods and did Corp's job for them?" Lester sneered. "If you're crying over one destroyed flat, imagine those do-gooders' reactions to some of what we do when in the field."

"You're an impossible old man." Iridium left him alone, storming through the warehouse.

Protean, the huge Earth power, looked up from one of his old-fashioned paper books. "Are you okay, little girl?"

"I'm not anyone's little girl," Iridium snapped. "And it's none of your beeswax."

"Ooo . . . touchy." Nevermore, smirking, glided down from a balcony, her straight black hair, black eye makeup, black everything turning her into a porcelain doll.

Iridium summoned a strobe. "You do *not* want to start with me, Paleface."

"Children, children."

The voice slithered over Iridium's skin, low and soothing like a hypnotist's. She shivered as Radar came from the kitchen, holding a soy chicken meal. *Her* soy chicken meal. He was soft and round everywhere, with too-bright eyes that lingered too long on objects he desired. He reminded Iridium of Paul Collins, the rapist she'd killed during her final year in the Academy. Both Collins and Radar oozed covetousness from every pore, like a poison.

"Don't fight," Radar said. "Fighting never solved anything. You girls will get wrinkles if you keep frowning like that."

"Yeah, and I hear you prefer to kick people while they're down." Lionheart, the shapeshifter, snorted and moved away from Radar in disgust.

Radar grinned, showing all of his teeth. "You all should be careful how you speak to me. Everyone is afraid of something. Even heroes."

"Think you can suck me dry before I light you up?" Kindle's Irish accent reminded Iridium too much of her father's.

She had to get out of there.

"Dad! Your little sewing circle is fighting!" she hollered, then grabbed her jacket and hit the release for the front door. Behind her, she heard Lester's strident tones as he scolded his batch of pet villains, but Iridium didn't turn back to help.

She got on the first hover bus heading toward Wrigley Field.

CHAPTER 14

JET

Approached Everyman today. Mixed success. Will make second attempt tomorrow during meeting. Remain convinced Everyman is best source of funding and materials for Project Sunstroke.

— From the journal of Martin Moore, entry #273

The air over Third Street was choked with noxious fumes, acrid with black smoke and ash. Jet formed a Shadowmask over her nose and mouth to filter the worst of the pollution. As it settled onto her face, the Shadow voices whispered and giggled, as if stealing a kiss. She ignored them; people's lives were in jeopardy. She'd have to lose her mind later.

Throngs of people were crowded in the street, blocking traffic more effectively than a dam as they gawked at the furious blaze spilling out of the corner building. Between the firefighters combating the worst of the flames and the police barricading the pedestrians, things seemed to be well in hand.

Jet circled overhead, thinking that maybe she didn't have to step in at all. Besides, the newsies were already here, their lights and cameras working overtime. Good—she'd ask the fire chief if she could be of any assistance, and assuming the answer was no, she was out of there.

And then she could ponder Taser's offer without the man himself hovering over her.

"Freak!"

She stiffened. Even over the roar of the hoses and the rush of the fire, the word had carried.

Jet looked at the crowd, feigning dispassion, and she saw how people were pointing at her now, talking angrily, their voices lost to the background noise but their body language all too clear. She was used to being hated—even when she'd been the official Hero of New Chicago, she'd never made any inroads with the police, and Everyman despised her as much as she despised them—but the insults still stung. Only she was almost too tired to care.

Others were picking up the catcall now, creating a steady chant of "Freak! Freak! Freak!" Not the entire crowd, at least; some were noticeably arguing against the slur, and there were a few vain attempts to cheer her on. But those voices were easily dwarfed by the reality of too many extrahumans gone mad, of too much destruction and terror, of a lifelong trust not merely broken but shattered.

Jet closed her eyes. Light, it hurt. All she wanted to do was help people. And yet, they hated her. She'd never go so far as to say fear her—really, how could they? She was a hero. People didn't fear their heroes.

How many extrahumans would it take to rule the world? To crush humanity under their feet?

She shuddered, remembering Martin Moore's warbling old man's voice.

"Freak!" the crowd screamed at her now, their hatred staining the skies far worse than the smoke from the fire.

"You, Shadow Girl," a woman's voice rang out, as if she had a voice enhancer.

Jet opened her eyes and peered down. The woman calling to her looked like a melting lemon drop in her cheerfully yellow unisuit and matching yellow earrings. The red-backed sunburst badge over her ample bosom marked her as a higher-up in the Everyman Society, possibly even the regional chairwoman. Jet grimaced behind the Shadowmask over her nose and mouth as she floated to the ground to hover before the woman in yellow. "My designation is Jet, ma'am."

The woman jabbed a finger at her—Jet noted that the fingernail was tapered, and long, and exactly the same shade as the unisuit. She also noted how the chanting had stopped. Definitely the regional chairwoman. The woman declared, "This is your fault!"

Professional, Jet told herself. *Polite. Powerful.* The three P's of extrahuman civil servants—especially when the news was picking up every word. "What is, ma'am?"

"This!" The woman gestured broadly, taking in the burning building, the city block, the entirety of New Chicago itself. "The world has fallen apart because your kind has declared war on regular, everyday humans!"

"Ma'am," Jet said, her voice hinting on a growl, "I realize that things have gone mad, but not all extrahumans are causing such chaos. My colleagues and I—"

"Your *colleagues* have destroyed New Chicago, New York, central Texas!" the woman spat. "Your *colleagues* have proven to everyone what the Everyman Society has said all along! You freaks are dangerous, and should be put down like the rabid dogs you are."

The crowd, knowing a cue when it heard one, bleated "Freak! Freak! Freak!"

Jet took a deep breath, forced the anger back. "I've risked my life for you and the citizens of the Americas more times than I can count. And all you do is criticize and complain."

The woman's face purpled with righteous fury. "We don't want you! Go back to the labs you came from, you filthy Shadow freak!"

filthy filthy

"I take it back," Jet said, talking over the Shadow voices. "You don't just complain. You stir up the good citizens of New Chicago and get them to spew your hatred. At least my colleagues and I are trying to help everyone, human and extra-human alike. How are you and Everyman helping? How many times have *you* saved the world?"

The cameras whirred. Peripherally, Jet saw a teenage girl tentatively approach, then get shoved out of the way by a furious Everyman whose face was so flushed Jet thought he might have a heart attack.

In her smart yellow unisuit, the woman spluttered, "You . . . you . . . How *dare* you!"

"I dare a lot," Jet said. "Comes with the costume. Now, if you'll excuse me, I have to try to help save your headquarters."

She turned her back on the woman in yellow and allowed herself a small smile. If she were thinking clearly, she probably would have been horrified by how she'd just dressed down a citizen—even an Everyman—and on camera, no less.

But damn it all if it hadn't felt good.

The crowd had started up again with a rousing chorus of "Freak," but the insult slid off Jet. After all, it was just a word.

She approached a group of firefighters, shouted out to them, asking if she could be of assistance. One of the men—a captain, based on the bugles on his helmet—snarled at her to get back. When she tried to argue, he spat, "No, you can't freaking help. Let me do my job."

Jet glanced at the scattered police officers by the temporary barricades. A couple of them were glaring, their hatred searing her. The onlookers nearest them were screaming obscenities at her, about her, calling her filthy names. And the woman in yellow, the Everyman regional chairwoman, smiled nastily at Jet's dismissal.

"See that?" the woman said. "You're not wanted."

wants wants little Shadow wants to squeeze you crush you

Shut up, Jet thought, which made the voices giggle all the harder.

Gleeful, the woman added, "Go save the world somewhere else."

save her hold her make her scream

Over the whispering voices in her head, Jet heard a girl's voice call out: "Jet, wait!"

The teenage girl who'd tried to approach earlier ran up to Jet. She shoved something tiny into Jet's hand and whispered, "Oh cipio." Then she punched Jet in the mouth.

"Yeah, freak!" she shouted. "Go save the world *somewhere else!*"

The crowd roared its approval.

Jet clenched her fist around the object and ignored how her jaw throbbed. She frowned at the girl, whose desperate eyes belied her violent pose, then Jet turned to the Everyman regional chairwoman. "You may want to invest in some air filters," Jet said curtly. "Your headquarters will reek from the smoke. And other odors." She summoned a floater and took off before the woman could reply. Once in the air, she saw that the object the girl had slipped her was a key. She blinked, then tucked the key into one of her belt pouches. She was too angry, and too exhausted, to think about keys and whispered phrases.

It occurred to Jet, as she soared around the blaze, that she hadn't asked the fireman how many people had been injured or killed, or if anyone was still inside the building. Jet was horrified.

The voices giggled again.

She pulled up her goggles and rubbed her eyes. Light, she was tired. Obviously, she wasn't thinking straight. Allowing her Shadowmask to fade, Jet decided to go back to headquarters, curl up on a cot for a few hours. She needed some sleep. She . . .

. . . saw something gleaming on a rooftop below her.

Frowning, she pushed her optiframes back over her eyes and squinted, which kicked in the automatic zoom on her lenses. There on the rooftop not even five blocks from the fire was a naked woman.

Huh. You don't see that every day in New Chicago.

A closer zoom revealed that the woman wasn't nude, but rather her skinsuit was flesh-toned, leaving almost nothing to the imagination. White hair wrapped in metallic hair toys stood out in short spikes on her head. A white belt caressed her hips. She was staring in the direction of the fire, absently tossing something the size of an apple up and down . . . and doing something else with her other hand between her legs.

Yeah, Jet thought. *Absolutely nothing to the imagination. Ick.*

She recognized the woman as Bombshell, a long-time rabid with no powers to speak of—a normal who got off on playing dress-up and wreaking a little havoc. Jet had tussled with Bombshell before. That fight had lasted a whopping two minutes. The woman was all mouth, no might, especially once she was disarmed. Then she just got weepy. Jet thought the act probably worked better on the male members of the Squadron. Then, thinking of Frostbite, she amended that to *most* male members.

Bombs in her belt, extra fuses in her boots, Jet recalled. And there were the metalique hair toys, with about a thousand times more oomph than the exploding snaps children loved to throw to the ground.

After far too many days of battling extrahumans who had been her colleagues, Jet was actually relieved to be confronting a normal wannabe supervillain. It would be quick, and she'd just call in the capture to Commissioner Wagner, and then it would be off to headquarters. She missed her bed, but since the Squadron had lost its collective mind, her Corp-sponsored apartment had been compromised.

That thought—the loss of a comfort as simple as sleeping in her own bed—suddenly enraged her. Channeling that anger, she rocketed straight toward Bombshell.

The woman was so fixated on the burning building that she didn't notice Jet until it was too late: A Shadow band snaked around her torso and pulled tight, pinning her arms. Bombshell screeched, and the small lump dropped from her hand. But Jet had expected that; a cushion of gray matter was waiting, and the object landed on it with a soft *plop*.

Too easy. But then, Bombshell wasn't too smart.

Jet landed in front of the so-called villain and looked up at her. Even without Bombshell's stilettoed boots—Light, how did the woman walk without falling over?—she towered over Jet.

"Let me go!" the woman screeched.

"I don't think so." Jet retrieved the small item from the Shadow cushion. She would have recognized it as one of Bombshell's calling cards, even without the cursive B, utterly gaudy in neon pink. "I didn't take you for an Everyman hater, Bombshell."

The wannabe villain scowled for a moment, then shrugged. "The money was good."

Oh really? "Work for hire?" Jet said, arching a brow. "You're branching out."

"Got to pay the bills."

"Next time, try a job at the Quick Fix. Who's got you on the payroll?"

Bombshell shrugged again. "Haven't met him face-to-face."

"I'm not asking whether you'd date him. I want the name."

The white-haired woman lifted her chin. "My memory's sketchy. A couple hundred digichips might help me remember."

Jet was too tired to play this game. She constricted the Shadow band, and Bombshell gasped, her breath puffing out in a cloud, her lips turning blue with cold.

"The name," Jet repeated.

Bombshell looked down at her and snarled, "Get scorched. You're not like the rest of the freaks. You're still a good guy. You can't do shit to me, and you know it."

She was right. *Damn it to Darkness.*

Calling up her floater, Jet shoved Bombshell onto it, then stood next to her. "Maybe you'll feel more talkative when Commissioner Wagner asks you." Holding on to the Shadow band so her prisoner wouldn't fall, Jet directed the floater up and into the sky.

Halfway to the station, Ops chimed in: "Babe, you're not going to believe who I've got a fix on."

Jet sighed. All she wanted to do was curl up and sleep for a few years. She said, "Who?"

In front of her, Bombshell said, "Who what?"

Jet ignored her.

In her earpiece, Meteorite chuckled. "Iridium. Man, when it rains, it pours. You'll never guess where I found her."

There was no way Jet could take on another rabid now, not when a strong wind could topple her where she stood. And Light, this was Iri. She was probably falling over with laughter from the chaos she'd inadvertently caused when she'd broken into the Academy and taken down Ops . . . and fried the brainwashing signal that had turned the extrahumans into Corp's puppets.

Well, it couldn't hurt to check and see what Iri was up to. If the woman was looting, Jet would step in. For all she knew Callie was just getting a latte and enjoying the view of New Chicago burning.

"Where is she?" Jet asked.

CHAPTER 15

IRIDIUM

It was the most extraordinary thing I had ever seen. I now understand Einstein, Oppenheimer, Bell. I understand what it means to glimpse the face of God.

—Matthew Icarus, research notes pertaining to Test Subject 1102, code-named "Alpha"

Iridium looked down at Wrigley Field. The top deck was open to the air, unusual in a city bathed in smog and raining superpowered criminals from the sky.

Iridium had never seen a baseball game. Lester had told her sports were for simpletons. Lester had said a lot of things, like, *Trust me, girl, everything will be fine.* That had been as they'd walked out of Blackbird and into Gordon's waiting arms.

Callie sighed. She loved her father, and she knew he was brilliant, unshakable, brave, and had a razor-sharp sense of justice. But he was also an idiot if he thought that he controlled the situation with Gordon. As if he *could* control it, with only rabids at his side. If they were going to put Corp down for good, they needed real help.

And that was why she'd stormed out of her own warehouse, looking for superheroes.

A chill stole over Iridium's skin even though hot smoke from dozens of fires still singed the air. She snapped her head up and there was Jet, descending on a column of Shadow like a regular dark angel.

Iridium gave her a nod. "Nice entrance."

Jet stiffened. "Thanks," she said tightly. Her blond captive, wrapped in Shadow creepers, tumbled to the ground, as if Jet's concentration had slipped. "What are you up to, Iridium?"

Iridium sniffed. "Thought I'd catch a ball game."

Jet frowned at her as she reeled the prone figure, whom Iridium recognized as Bombshell—private name, "That crazy bitch, Bombshell"—back to her side. Jet said, "Really?"

Iridium smiled. "What, you'd rather I'd come to pick a fight?"

Jet's frown deepened. "I don't have time for this, Iridium. Enjoy your ball game."

"Aw, aren't you going to invite me to your secret clubhouse?" Iridium smiled when she saw Jet twitch.

"I don't know what you're talking about," the Shadow power said stiffly.

"You, Steele, Firebug, Hornblower, Frostbite, and Ops. New Ops. Not freaky brainwashing Ops. You guys set up shop here." Iridium took a step closer, risking a fight. If Jet knocked her on her ass, the mission was over and Iridium would have to deal with Gordon herself.

But Jet hesitated. She always did when things didn't go according to plan.

Iridium laughed softly. "I still know you."

Jet's optiframes irised, as if she were blinking.

"Look, Jettikins, are you going to invite me in or not? It smells up here."

"*How* do you know about Squadron HQ?"

Iridium crossed her arms and set grin to Smug. "Derek told me."

Far from being the flustered mess Iridium had expected, Jet let creepers explode from every plane of her body before snapping them back just as quickly.

Jet pushed up her optiframes and glared at Iridium. She snarled, "*Frostbite* compromised us to criminals?"

"Okay, first, I'm not a criminal anymore, as there's no Corp to have me convicted and the real law has bigger problems. And second, *Derek* and I are *friends*. We trust one another with basic information."

Well, *that* had shut her up. Iridium looked her former partner in the eye, saw the deep blue rings underneath. Saw bones under Jet's skinsuit and new lines around her mouth.

"How are you holding up, Joannie?"

"Do not use my name, Iridium. *We* are not friends."

Iridium shrugged. "Just making small talk."

Jet huffed, "I haven't slept in days, the city is falling apart, it's taking forever to rein in all the rabids, and to top things off, *this* silly wannabe—" she shook Bombshell—"firebombed the Everyman regional headquarters, and she won't tell me who put her up to it."

"Go to hell," Bombshell sneered. "I know you won't dirty your hands on me, Shadow Puppet."

Iridium snapped her hand out and grabbed Bombshell by the front of her costume. Sweaty and sooty. Great.

Jet's creepers retreated from the light-heat around her grip. Bombshell let out a yelp. "The hell! I have rights, yanno!"

"Not with me, you don't." Iridium used her superior height to walk the other woman backward, rapid time, until Bombshell's back was pressed against the railing of the upper deck.

"I'm not a hero," Iridium said. "I don't know or care why you did what you did. But Jet wants to know." She leaned close to Bombshell's face. "You have one chance to tell her."

"Iridium . . ." Jet said in a tone Iridium knew all too well. The *Can it before we get into trouble* tone.

"Fuck you, Snow White!" Bombshell spat. "I ain't going to say shit! I ain't—"

Iridium tipped her over the railing.

Bombshell let out a truly operatic shriek as she dangled, Iridium's hand knotted in her cheap plastic skinsuit the only thing keeping her from plunging seventy feet to the ground.

"You ain't what?" Iridium said pleasantly.

"You can't . . ." Bombshell panted, clawing at her hand. "You can't . . ."

"I can," Iridium said, and pitched her voice down. Her Lester voice. Her villain voice. "And I *will*."

"Martin Moore!" The name echoed off the right-field wall of the park. "Martin Moore paid me! Let me up, you fucking crazy bitch! I just did what he paid me to do!"

"Iri," Jet said, and there was pleading in her voice now.

Iridium held steady, her arm screaming but her face still as she let Bombshell twist in the wind. Literally.

"Iri," Jet said again. "Don't kill her."

Iridium let another second tick by, then she hauled Bombshell back over the railing. "If I *ever* see your tacky little poser ass in my orbit again, I'll end your criminal career and very probably your life."

Bombshell just sobbed and shook, slumped against the last row of seats. Iridium jerked her thumb. "Get lost."

Jet watched Bombshell run, then looked back at Iridium. "I suppose you think that's funny."

"Not really. She weighed a ton."

Jet rolled her eyes. "You let a criminal go."

"You want to go catch her? Be my guest."

Jet sighed, closed her eyes. "Another time." She sounded so tired.

Iridium massaged her shoulder. "Who's Martin Moore?"

For a split second, Jet's shoulders hunched and her cheeks flushed with what Iridium had to describe as shame. "He's a person of interest. Thank you for the help," she said brusquely.

Iridium could see the words grating out of her, shredding Jet's pride. "Hell. What else am I good for except trading on my terrifying reputation?"

Jet bit her lip for a moment, then said, "Indeed." She paused, then added, "Wrong Wrigley Field."

Iridium blinked. "Sorry?"

Jet's smile flickered, quick as clouds over sun. "The secret clubhouse. It's in the original, not the domed version. Come on, I'll take you there."

It wasn't much of a clubhouse—more like the dorm room of a computer-science student who was also a hermit. Iridium wrinkled her nose at the stale air.

"I'm back," Jet called out. A plump woman Iridium vaguely recognized from a few years ahead of her at the Academy stuck her head out from behind a Dietrich Systems command console that had to have been lifted directly from the Academy. It was enormous, the hum of its processors overtaking the room.

"And with company, I see."

Iridium threw a salute at the woman. "Weather Girl, right?"

"Meteorite." The name came out colder than sleet on the back of Iridium's neck.

"Right. Sorry." She needed their help—she'd have to call them whatever silly names they'd come up with.

A door slid open and Frostbite stepped out with a heaping plate of nachos and a Coke. He dropped both when he saw her.

"Callie!"

He bounded over and wrapped his lanky arms around her, and Callie hugged him back. She didn't have to pretend to get along with Frostbite, at least. "It's good to see you," she whispered. She'd stayed in touch with Derek after she'd escaped custody at the Academy, but they couldn't meet often for obvious reasons.

"You too, Miss Firefly," he whispered back. Derek was the only one besides her father who could call her that without getting a fist through the teeth or a strobe in the eyes.

Dad's decision is why you're here. Get to the point.

"Listen, Jet. Frostbite. Uh, Meteorite. I was hoping to talk to you . . ."

Her words were cut off by an obnoxious pinging from the console. Everyone snapped their attention to the computer.

She asked, "What's wrong?"

"It's a distress call," Meteorite said. "I'm putting it on speakers."

Frostbite grabbed a headset and slid into place next to Meteorite. "Triangulating location," he said, his fingers flying.

Iridium tilted her head toward Jet. "This happen a lot?"

"More and more every day," Jet said grimly.

"Firebug, Ops," a strained voice shouted through a haze of static.

"Ops, Firebug," Meteorite returned. "Go ahead."

"He's got her!" Firebug's voice held real terror. "Doctor Hypnotic's got Steele!"

Frostbite's fingers stopped moving. "Oh, she did *not* just say that."

"Hypnotic?" Jet ran over to the console. "*The* Doctor Hypnotic? He escaped?"

Iridium spread her hands. "Blackbird has a revolving door these days, even in the supermax wing. Wouldn't you escape if you were Hypnotic?"

Jet slapped a switch on the comm. "Jet, Firebug. Say again."

"Doctor Hypnotic has Steele!" The echoes against the mike made Iridium's head throb.

"She's in Looptown," said Frostbite. "An abandoned apartment building. Fixing now . . ." His screen shrieked an error at him. "Shit! The building has tilithium walls. It's messing with the imaging. I can't get a fix on Steele."

"Firebug," Meteorite said. "Do *not* engage. Wait for backup."

"Hornblower is in Joliet, dealing with a riot," Frostbite said quietly. "At least fifteen minutes ETA in a hover."

"If that's really Doctor Hypnotic," said Iridium, "Steele does not have fifteen minutes."

"I'm going," Jet said. "Firebug, wait for backup."

"No . . ." the hero's voice was frantic. "No, I hear her screaming . . ."

The comm cut out, and Frostbite cursed. "She went in after him. I lost her GPS beacon."

Jet was already booking for the door. "Download everything you can on that building to my wristlet."

"You can't go alone!" Frostbite shouted. "It took the entire New York Squadron and part of New Chicago Squadron to take out Hypnotic twenty years ago!" He ripped off his headset. "I'm coming with you. Sheila, cover Ops."

Meteorite, panicked, said, "Derek, no! I can't run the entire Squadron by myself—I need you here, doing Ops with me!"

"I'll go," Iridium said, holding up her hand.

"I don't need your help," Jet snapped. "I can take care of this."

"You can barely stand up," Iridium said. "And Derek's right. Hypnotic isn't some idiot in a dime-store rig. He's dangerous."

Jet considered for a moment. "Fine. You're under my orders, and you do what I say when I say it."

"Fine," Iridium returned. "Now can we please go save your friends' lives?"

"Fine," Jet said.

Hell, Iridium had wanted to get on the Squadron's good side, hadn't she? She just wished it wasn't via fighting a man that even Lester was afraid of.

And how the hell had Hypnotic broken out of Blackbird's maximum-security wing in the first place? Even with the situation in the regular prison, the supermax wing had roboguards, foot-thick walls, neural inhibitors . . . a thousand safeguards to keep the monsters in.

Iridium shuddered. Maybe she didn't want to know.

Aloft on Jet's Shadow floater, Iridium watched Wreck City slide by on their way to Looptown. Her grid actually looked clean in comparison to the chaos all around it.

Until she saw plasgun fire.

"Bollocks," she said softly, co-opting her father's favorite curse. "Jet, I can't."

"What?" Jet shouted over the wind.

"Someone's shooting up Wreck City. Set me down. I'll catch up."

It wasn't a lie. She'd dispatch whoever-it-was and get back to the real business. Deep in her gut, she *wanted* to fight Hypnotic. A *real* villain fight. The one she'd never gotten the chance to have before Corp had tried to ship her off to Blackbird all those years ago.

At least, not from the heroic side.

"Your funeral," Jet shouted, and the Shadow let go of Iridium, dumping her on a rooftop.

Iridium ran down the fire escape. It was over in three strobes—one for each of the gangsters robbing the liquor depot and one for good measure. They were sporting green and tats. Iridium cursed again and tapped her phone link.

"Oz, it's Iridium. Arrest Deke O'Connor. He's officially outstayed his welcome in Grid 16." See how a few years upstate mellowed that arrogant little Irish prick, thinking he could do as he pleased in *her* grid.

Someone tugged on Iridium's sleeve and she spun, a strobe growing.

The liquor depot's owner beamed at her. "*Thank* you," she said. "Those sons of whores would have taken everything I owned."

"That's all right, Mrs. . . ." Iridium spread her hands.

"Pak. Theresa Pak, and this is my husband, Benjamin."

Mrs. Pak's husband threw Iridium a salute. "We know what you do for us. Keeping the gangs out. Keeping innocent people out of harm's way." He squeezed Iridium's hand. "You keep doing it."

His wife handed him a broom and said something in Thai, pointing at the shattered plasglass of their front window. He sighed. "Duty calls."

"We're lucky to have a hero like you," Mrs. Pak said before she stepped back inside and flipped the holosign on their door to CLOSED.

Iridium stared for a long moment. Actual, honest-to-Jehovah citizens, thanking her for being . . . herself. Calling her a fucking *hero,* as if that weren't the joke of the century.

"Wonders never cease," she muttered. Jet would have a conniption when she told her, in that oh-so-polite Jet way.

Jet. Doctor Hypnotic.

Shit.

Iridium grabbed her phone again. "Boxer, bring your hoverbike and meet me by Pak's Liquors. I need a ride to Looptown."

CHAPTER 16

JET

Corp is debating whether to reclassify Mental powers as so-called Mind powers. They claim it's less derogatory. What they fail to understand is that calling a rattlesnake a flower doesn't change the fact that its bite is poisonous.
—From the journal of Martin Moore, entry #139

Jet landed in front of the condemned building in Grid 21, commonly known as Looptown, and stared grimly at the open front doors. No Firebug.

She tapped her comlink. "Jet, Ops."

Frostbite's voice: "Ops, Jet. Go."

"I don't suppose Firebug reported in, saying that she had Steele and they were on their way back, by any chance?"

"Nope."

Kai must have charged in without waiting for backup. Of course. Jet gritted her teeth. Now she had not just one hero to rescue but two.

Terrific. She sighed, lifted her goggles, and rubbed her eyes. Well, she'd have to fall over from exhaustion later.

Replacing the optiframes to fit snugly on her face, Jet thought about options. From everything she knew about Doctor

Hypnotic—thanks to all those classes back at the Academy—he was obscenely dangerous. Charging in would likely get her captured. Or killed. But she was too exhausted to risk a Shadowslide; that would put her at the mercy of the voices that came out in the dark.

She shuddered. No, sliding was right out.

What were her other options? Hornblower was otherwise engaged. Frostbite and Meteorite were grounded. Iridium was off being a criminal. Steele and Firebug were captured. That left Jet herself.

She snorted. No, it didn't. *This is the sound of my pride splattering on the pavement.* "Ops," she said, "link me over to the Merc line. Bruce Hunter's code."

"Connecting." If Frostbite had a comment about Jet wanting to speak to a mercenary, let alone her former Runner, he kept it to himself. Derek had always been smart.

On the other end of the connection, the click of someone tapping in. "Taser. Go."

"So it's not a press conference," Jet said, "but maybe you're still interested in helping. How do you feel about rescuing helpless superdamsels in distress?"

"I love it." He lowered his voice, the words pouring out syrupy thick. "Is Callie in trouble?"

Jet felt her forehead pound. Through clenched teeth, she said, "This isn't about Iridium. Firebug and Steele have been captured by Doctor Hypnotic."

Taser dropped the act. All business, he replied, "Give me your coordinates."

She did. Just as she was about to tell him she'd wait, a piercing scream filled the sky—coming from somewhere within the abandoned building. *Crap.* "I have to go in."

"Jet, wait. I'll be there in fifteen minutes. Don't go in alone."

"Whoever's screaming bloody murder may not *have* fifteen minutes."

It was probably Firebug screaming. Kai had a low threshold for pain; Jet recalled that from her fifth year at the Academy. An image danced behind her eyes—one of Firebug cradling her shattered arm as she was whisked away to the hospital wing, shrieking the whole way there. No, Kai would break if Hypnotic was torturing her.

Jet said, "I'll be careful. But come quickly."

"Joan, damn it, you haven't gone after Hypnotic before! Wait for me. I can—"

Another scream—one that cut off abruptly.

Jet switched her comlink to white noise, took a deep breath, then walked through the open front doors.

Analyze. She took in the details quickly: dark, but her optiframes took care of that. Smells of ash, of stale terror, of dust disturbed. The building's lobby was from circa early twenty-first century—a doorman station, abandoned; linoleum flooring, cracked and grimy; faux wooden trim, long since eroded by termites and time. Silent as the grave. Up ahead stood two figures, their backs to her. Firebug and Steele.

Battlescan. No signs of movement, either from her comrades or from Hypnotic, wherever he was. Clearly, a trap.

Confront. "Firebug," she called out. "Steele. I'm here to help you."

No response from them—then a burst of light erupted before her eyes. Her optiframes irised, negating any damage.

She whirled. Saw nothing.

"I'm here for my colleagues," she announced. "I'm not here to fight you." Too true; she was too damn tired for that.

"Do tell." The voice was from everywhere and nowhere; it surrounded her, enveloped her. "And what are you that you ignore my pretty Light?"

She turned again, keeping her frustration in check. Where was Hypnotic? In front of her? Behind? Impossible to tell. "I'm Jet. And I prefer Shadows to the pretty Light. What have you done to my colleagues?"

"They're fine," Hypnotic insisted, his voice echoing. "Content. You can be too. Just look at the Light."

Another flare in front of her face. She batted it aside. At least it wasn't a heat strobe, like Iridium's. *Enough talking.* She turned to her mesmerized friends and reached out, summoning a creeper of Shadow. It stretched from her hand, crawled over to Firebug and flowed up until it wrapped around her waist, then looped over to Steele and did the same. She tugged. Neither of the women moved; it was like they were rooted to the spot. Statues.

"A Shadow power," Hypnotic said, sounding pleased. "How wonderful! You must be Night's whelp."

Jet bristled. "He was my mentor." Why was she answering him? *Shut up, Joannie. Don't give him any ammunition.*

"Shadow is genetic. Your mother or father must have been a Shadow too, little girl."

More flares of light, so bright that she had to release her leash and shield her eyes.

"Tell me. Which of your parents is a Shadow?"

Despite herself, she said, "My father."

"Not Night?"

"Blackout."

The lights disappeared, along with the Darkness. From behind, Hypnotic said, "You're Angelica's girl?"

Jet spun, summoning Shadow.

"Stop that," Hypnotic said. "You're not here to fight, you said. So don't fight."

Jet found herself lowering her arm. *Damn it, get ahold of yourself, Joan!* She clenched her fist. "Let my friends go."

"What? Oh yes, certainly." He was staring at her, this tall man with his Earth-power physique beneath those prison grays, his dark hair peppered with white. "But first, tell me about your mother. How is she?"

"Dead," Jet gritted.

The man's eyes widened, and to Jet's surprise, she saw real grief in them. "I'm so sorry," he said, sounding sincere. "How did it happen?"

"Let my friends go, and I'll be happy to give you a family history."

The man peered at her, his gaze boring into hers. "Take off your cowl, those goggles. I want to see your face."

"Let my friends go," she repeated.

"Yes, yes. Of course." He snapped his fingers. Firebug and Steele crumpled to the floor. When Jet made to run to them to make sure they were all right, Hypnotic said, "They're fine.

Sleeping it off. Side effect," he said with a shrug. "Now then. Your turn."

Jet took a deep breath. *This,* she told herself, *is profoundly stupid.* But Taser was on his way, and more than that, Jet had this feeling that this man, Doctor Hypnotic, wouldn't hurt her. Not while she was of interest to him, at any rate.

She wondered, as she pushed back her cowl, if she were getting as arrogant as a Lighter.

"Golden hair," he said, smiling warmly. "Just like your mother's. Why do you keep it hidden?"

Surprised by the question, she replied, "Long hair isn't suitable for battle conditions."

"But a cape is?" Hypnotic snorted. "Braid it, then," he said, staring at her pinned-up hair. "So beautiful. You shouldn't keep it hidden away."

"I'll take it up with Branding," she said dryly.

"Your goggles," he said. "Please take them off, as you said you would."

Crap. Jet pushed her optiframes up until they rested on her brow.

He was staring at her, his face rapt. "Just like her," he breathed. "Except the eyes. You have your father's eyes." He reached over to her, as if he meant to stroke her cheek.

She stepped out of reach. This was bordering on creepy.

He murmured, "So tiny. Just like Holly."

Holly. That was her mother's name. Her just-between-Angelica-and-Blackout name.

"I'm Hal."

Just as she thought this confrontation couldn't get any odder, something else happened. She rolled with it. "Hi, Hal. I'm Joan."

"Joan," he said agreeably. "You lost your mother. But tell me, did you ever lose your true love?"

Thoughts of Samson flitted through her mind—his easy laugh, his strong, gentle hands. Jet swallowed thickly. "Yes."

Doctor Hypnotic paused, studying her. "Yes, you did, didn't you? How old were you?"

"Fourteen."

"I was twenty-two," he said sadly. "I lost her to someone else. I lost her to a Shadow."

"My love died," Jet said, sullen and suddenly angry. "He died on a training mission. He was fifteen years old, and he got killed by an Everyman."

"So much death," Doctor Hypnotic said, his voice full of regret. "And so young. I can give you a better world, Joan."

She let out a small laugh. "I appreciate the offer." More than she cared to admit. "But I'm duty-bound to *this* world." Before she could think better of it, she said, "You can be too. You can help make a difference."

Doctor Hypnotic smiled. "Why, Joan, what a marvelous idea. I'll have to think about that. Do you know how hypnosis works?"

Right. That was her cue. "Thank you for being a man of honor, Hal," she said quickly, taking another step toward her unconscious friends. "I'll just get out of your hair now . . ."

"It's simple, really. You need to distract the conscious mind so that it doesn't fight you when you whisper to the unconscious mind. Light works well as a distraction. But it's not necessary, depending on the mind I encounter." He grinned. "You're a Shadow power, Joan. You're practically conditioned to receive my suggestions. Just like your father was, during the so-called Siege of Manhattan."

"How nice," Jet said, taking another step.

"I've already hypnotized you, Joan. Don't you see? I've taken away the light."

"Of course you have," she said, and then she turned to her friends . . .

. . . but that was when the lights went out.

No! She reached for her optiframes to banish the Darkness, but it was gone. *Oh Light, no!*

yes yes little girl yes

She spun around, desperate to escape before the voices took over. But there was nowhere for her to go; the Shadow was all around her.

The Shadow was in her.

little Joan little Jet little lamb lost little lamb

She doubled over, screaming, clutching her head, pulling her hair. *No, not like this!*

like this you like this you like us little Joan don't fight

Her screaming faded to a whimper, and she wrapped her arms over her head, bowing in her despair. *Please, Light, not like this.*

don't fight don't fight don't

She didn't want to give in, but she wasn't strong enough to fight.

"Joan."

The voice was cool, calm, the epitome of reason in the face of madness.

"Joan, I can make the voices go away."

Light, please.

"Look at the light, Joan. Look at the Light and don't fight me."

don't fight

"Look at the Light."

Something bright, bright enough that she saw it through her squeezed eyelids. Desperate to believe, she opened her eyes.

The Light washed over her, and the Shadow cowered, retreated. The Light beckoned, easing her terror, soothing away her fear. Her body slowly relaxed.

"Joan. Look to your left."

She did.

"Do you see it, Joan? Do you see the Shadow?"

She did. It quivered as the Light noticed it, but though it hissed and spat, the Shadow didn't attack. It didn't try to seduce her again, but neither did it flee. It waited patiently for her to lower her guard.

"Look to your right, Joan. Do you see the door? It's reinforced tilithium. Nothing can get through it, Joan. Nothing can break it. Do you see it?"

She did.

"The door is open now. Do you see the tiny cell it hides?"

She did.

"There is nothing in the cell but wall and ceiling and floor. The door is the only way in. The door is the only way out. Do you see?"

She did.

"The Light is forcing the Shadow inside the cell."

At that, the Shadow bucked and screamed. It fought against the pulsing light, it launched itself at the Light, at Jet; it flowed up and down and scrabbled for purchase. But the Light caught it and redirected it, pushed it toward the cell.

The Shadow gathered itself, forming the shape of a woman, the shape of Jet herself, and with a delirious screech it launched itself at her.

Jet rolled with the Shadow, screaming, fighting back with everything she had. She punched at it, shouting her rage and fear, bellowing as she lashed out with brutal kicks. She fought it—and because she wasn't alone, this time, Jet was winning.

"Joan! The cell, Joan!"

With a defiant cry, she grabbed the Jet-Shadow and spun, throwing it toward the cell. The Light reached out and grabbed the Shadow's ankle and dragged it into the tiny room. The Shadow scrabbled and clawed, squealing and shrieking, but it didn't matter—the Light forced the Shadow into the prison cell. The door slammed shut with the finality of a coffin lid sliding home, sealing in the Light and the Shadow both.

Jet was swaying, now, shaking with fatigue, exhausted physically and mentally and emotionally. Tears of relief streamed down her face.

"The Shadow can't hurt you anymore," Doctor Hypnotic said. "By the way, I'm really sorry about this."

He grabbed her shoulders and spun her to the left . . . and then a bolt of electricity slammed into Jet.

Too stunned to scream, her limbs flailed and jittered. She didn't even register the pain.

She thought she heard Taser say, "Whoops."

When the Darkness reached for Jet, for the first time since she was a teenager, she didn't worry about the Shadow voices reaching for her. With a smile, she passed out cold.

CHAPTER 17

IRIDIUM

*I tried for days to make Subject 1102 replicate the effect,
but in the end I failed. An autopsy will probably tell me
more.*
  —Matthew Icarus, diary entry dated October 30, 1982

A figure lay on the ground outside the building, black and
black on the pitted asphalt. Iridium was off the bike before
Boxer had come close to stopping, sprinting for the smaller
body on the ground.

If I hadn't stopped if I hadn't waited if I'd stayed with her . . .

"If I'd been here . . ."

"You'd be out for the count too."

Iridium snapped her head up from Jet, who was breathing,
though not often or deeply. "You have a lot of fucking nerve
showing your face, Taser."

The mercenary chuckled behind his mask. "Not exactly."

Iridium rose, strobes blossoming all around her like a garden of poison flowers. "Give me a reason."

"To kiss me or kill me?"

"Hey," Boxer said, putting his hand on Iridium's shoulder as she started for the big man. "Your gal needs a hospital, stat. Her pulse is tachy and she's burned."

"Hypnotic." Taser scrubbed a hand across his goggles. "I got a call, and I saw Jet, then she wasn't Jet, she was . . . well. She was Doctor Hypnotic. I shocked her. I did it."

Only the befuddled pain in his tone kept Iridium from burning him to cinder on the spot. "There were two more. Firebug and Steele."

Taser waved his hand vaguely at the building. "He let us go. Why would he do that . . . ?"

Iridium snapped her fingers. "Boxer, help Jet." She started for the building. Taser grabbed her arm, Kevlar glove scratchy against her skin.

"No! What about me?"

Iridium cocked an eyebrow. "You? Roast in your own power, for all I care." She yanked herself free and ran into the building.

Steele and Firebug stood near a decrepit security desk. Steele looked worse for wear, leaning against the desk, holding her head. Firebug stood under her own power, but tear tracks made their way down her sweaty, grimy face.

"Harriet," she said. "Harrie, I'm so sorry. I didn't get here in time . . ."

"Forget it, Kai." Steele waved her away. "Nobody could have done anything against that maniac."

"He just . . . let us go." Firebug let out a shuddering breath. "Something's not right."

"Great. We're all members of the Something's Not Right Club," Iridium said. "Let's get you two out of here before old Googly-Eyes changes his mind."

Firebug gasped. "Iridium?"

Next to her, Steele said quietly, "We don't want any trouble with you."

"And I don't want to be babysitting heroes." She met Steele's glare for a moment, remembering that she favored her left in a hand-to-hand fight. She could beat Steele again if the bigger woman became a problem.

Stupid, bitchy, mistrustful heroes.

"Let's go," she said. "You and Jet both need a medic. Firebug needs to fix up her face. No future in hanging around here."

Steele stood, grimacing with the effort. "You walk first. Show us your back."

They didn't trust her. And they were smart not to.

Iridium sighed and walked ahead, making a show of turning her back on the two other women. "Satisfied? I'm not the boogeyman today."

"No," Firebug shivered. "No, you're not."

Outside, Taser had loaded Jet onto his hoverbike while Boxer stood by, glaring at the taller man with enough power to strip plastipaint off steel.

"Gramps here thinks I'm going to abscond with the princess." Taser's mask wrinkled as he grinned. All of the confusion and terror of before were gone, locked back inside his box. Iridium had a similar one, where she kept all emotion not immediately useful to the situation at hand.

That trick Corp had taught her, not Lester. It was the only thing of value she'd taken with her when she'd run—the ability to be heartless. Corp excelled at every level in that.

Taser loomed up next to her. "Powwow, chief."

Iridium glared at him. "What? If it's an apology, why don't you go throw it in the lake and jump after it?"

"We can't take Jet to a hospital." He flexed his gloves, armored plates creaking. "She's still got enough enemies to make it risky, plus a rabid could get to her while she's out."

Iridium glanced at Steele. "I know a place. Head for old Wrigley Field, top level. We'll meet you there."

Steele frowned hugely.

"Yes," Iridium snapped, "I know about your secret superhero club. Jet invited me. Can we trade meaningful looks after you and she have gotten some medical attention?"

"She's right, Harrie," Firebug said softly. "You need help."

"Fine." The look on Steele's face made it clear this conversation wasn't over, just postponed.

"Come on, ladies," Boxer said, patting the backseat of his hover. "There's room if we all get friendly."

Taser climbed onto his bike, making sure Jet was secure. "See you at the ball field." He gunned the engine, and a moment later, he and Jet were gone.

Iridium looked at Boxer. "Make room for one more."

"All right, but if my hover discs give out, you're paying."

"Oh, Jehovah." Meteorite leapt up from the console when Iridium, Taser, Boxer, and the motley assembly of heroes marched into the main room of Squadron headquarters. "What is this, the halfway house for supervillains?" Then she saw Steele's limp, and Jet in Taser's arms, sagging like a sack of cement, and hissed in a breath.

Iridium stood to the side and let the heroes fuss. Sooner or later, they'd get over this ridiculous reaction to seeing Iridium up close.

"What happened?" Frostbite had slipped off his earpiece and was helping Taser with Jet.

"Hypnotic got the drop on us," Steele said, sinking down into a booth. Firebug sat opposite her, rubbing her arms, her eyes wide and shocked. Whatever Hypnotic had made her see, she was having a hard time of it. Iridium vaguely recalled Firebug being a whiner at the Academy, crying whenever she'd get a skinned knee. Terrific—a thin-skinned superhero. Iridium checked herself from rolling her eyes.

Meteorite, by Frostbite's side, said, "Get Jet into the med room." As Frostbite carried the small woman around a corner and out of sight, Meteorite turned to Steele. "You okay?"

"Just need a moment," Steele muttered.

"More like you need a week's vacation," Iridium said. "Christo, when's the last time any of you got any sleep?"

Meteorite gave her a look that was pure venom. "Firebug, you can show our . . . guests . . . out."

"I ain't going anywhere until Jet's all right." Taser settled himself under a playoff pennant and crossed his arms.

"I stay if she stays," Boxer said, jerking his thumb at Iridium.

"Look," Meteorite said. "It's cute you have a little thug

entourage, Iridium, but this is a place for the Squadron. You're not needed."

"Christo, Sheila," Derek said, coming back into the room. "Just let her stay until Jet wakes up."

"I can't believe you trust her," Meteorite snapped at him. "She attacked me! She and him took down Ops," she shouted, pointing at Taser. "They caused all the chaos that's happening now!"

"Not on purpose," Iridium said quietly. "This isn't what I wanted."

"She's my friend," Frostbite said. "She can stay."

Meteorite stared at him, emotions playing on her face. "Maybe Therapy really did make holes in your brain."

Frostbite's gaze went sharp as a razor blade. "Think very, very hard about what you say next, Sheila," he said quietly. "None of us want a mess to clean up in here." Frostbite never raised his voice, but Iridium shivered at the words all the same.

Meteorite's face went red. "Fine. Just make sure they don't steal anything." She spun on her heel and marched around the corner. Taser followed her.

Iridium glanced at Boxer. "Stay here and make nice," she said, then went after Meteorite and Taser. Waking up and seeing Taser would probably be worse for Jet than getting her clock punched by Hypnotic in the first place.

If she woke up.

Stop that. Angry as she was at him, Lester's voice was the one she heard when she needed to keep her shit together. *She'll be fine. You've been through worse and you're fine.*

But Jet's not me.

The so-called med room had exactly one surgical table and a cabinet of meds that Meteorite was rifling through. Iridium noted the inventory: all drugstore stuff that she could buy on the street.

"This is your medic bay?" she said. "I'd hate to see what happened if one of you got a paper cut."

"Did I say you could come in here?" Meteorite grabbed a hypo of adrenaline and a swab. "Both of you, out."

Iridium turned on Taser. "You heard the lady."

He winked at her. "Only because you asked so nice, darlin'."

"Charming," Meteorite said. "You and your boyfriend make a lovely couple."

"If Taser were my boyfriend, Satan would be wearing a parka. How can I help?"

Meteorite muttered, "I've got it."

"You're a button-pusher, not a doctor. Your first-aid class was what, seven years ago?"

The temperature in the room dropped precipitously, and Iridium swore she heard thunder rumble in the distance. She'd thought that Meteorite was a former Weather power; maybe she needed to rethink the "former" part. "I may be a washed-up hero," Meteorite said, glaring at her, "but at least I didn't turn on my own."

"That makes two of us."

"You have some fucking nerve."

"Look, I didn't know what would happen when we took down Ops," Iridium said. "I didn't know about Corp's brain-washing everyone into being good guys. You can believe that or not. It doesn't make a bit of difference to me."

As Meteorite worked, stripping off Jet's skinsuit, checking her injuries, taking her vitals, Iridium walked over to the medical cabinet. "Jet mentioned she hadn't slept in something like a week."

"Who has?" Meteorite let out a bitter laugh. "We're all running on empty."

Next to the boxes of bandages and aspirin hypos were the heavy-duty painkillers, in labeled syringes. Knowing Derek, he'd gotten the meds and equipment from a gray-market supplier. Iridium said, "So you're just going to patch her up and get her right back out there, like a toy soldier?"

"There's no other choice." Meteorite sounded tired and mad and close to sobbing. "The police and even the National Guard can't rein in all the rogues and rabids."

Iridium said, "You know I'm not the bad guy here. Corp did this to her. To all of you."

"That doesn't change anything."

"It changes everything. She going to make it?"

"Yeah. Skinsuit absorbed the burn, but she's in shock. Probably more from exhaustion than from your boyfriend's love tap."

"He's not my boyfriend."

"Whatever. She'll be fine. She just needs some rest."

"She needs more than some rest, or she won't be good for anything except a body bag."

Meteorite grimaced, but she didn't argue the point.

So Iridium didn't feel at all guilty about injecting Jet with a sedative. "Sweet dreams, Joan. Beautiful ones, filled with light."

Meteorite, who'd seen the label on the hypo, frowned at Iridium. "That'll put her out for the whole day. Maybe more."

"She needs it."

Meteorite sighed, shaking her head. "Now that you've played nurse, get out of here, Iridium."

Iridium backed out of the med room, leaving Meteorite to pull a blanket over Jet.

Jet was going to be fine. Thank Jehovah for small favors.

Back in the main room, Iridium nearly smacked into a tall blond slab of hero. He'd grown and gotten some lines around his eyes, and he'd lost the arrogant sneer. But she'd know that blocky face anywhere.

"Hi, Tyler."

Hornblower's uniform was torn and spattered with some unidentifiable, sticky liquid, and he had a cut above his eyebrow rimmed with brick dust. Strong he might be, but he didn't heal any faster than a human.

"Holy shit. Derek wasn't yanking my chain about you flipping to the light side of the Force."

"Well . . ." Iridium started. "He might have overstated things."

"Doesn't mean I like you," Hornblower said. "Or trust you. Stay the fuck out of my way, Flashbulb."

He shoved her aside, and she let him. No need to pick a fight here at Hero Central, especially when she was supposed to be recruiting them to help her with her Corp problem. She watched as Hornblower stripped off his uniform jacket and tossed it onto a booth table. It was only then he noticed Boxer.

"Hey, kid," Boxer said. He pushed up his fedora and scratched at his hairline.

Hornblower swallowed, dropping his eyes. "Hi, Uncle Patrick."

"You look strong as an ox. These heroes keeping you busy?"

"Riot." Hornblower said. "Beating on some rent-a-cops. Had to step in and be the peacekeeper."

Boxer slapped him on the shoulder. "Good boy. Just like Warren taught you. He was always the upstanding brother."

"You, uh . . . You staying around?" Hornblower looked between Iridium and his uncle.

Boxer said, "Iri? Are we?"

She nodded. "For now." Until she got a few of them to help her.

"What about your guests?" Boxer raised his eyebrows.

"They can take care of themselves." She didn't want to go back to her warehouse, not when her home was overtaken by Lester and his pet villains. Not that she would say anything out loud. Last thing she needed was for the heroes to know she'd broken Arclight and Company out of Blackbird.

"I'm glad you're staying," Frostbite said. "We can really use you."

"I didn't say that I was helping," Iridium snapped. "I'm not strapping on a skinsuit. I know we're friends, Derek, but stop putting words in my mouth."

He glared at her, then sank behind his console, turning his chair so she was out of his line of sight.

Steele smiled gamely into the silence. "You helped me and Kai. Seems like you're helping, no matter what you say. And thank you, by the way."

"Forget it." Iridium sighed. "Just call it a freebie, and don't get all emotional."

Silence reigned for a long moment, drawn and strained.

The console shrieked in a sound that was becoming all too familiar.

"Bank robbery," Frostbite said. "The vault alarm at First Federal." He punched keys. "Looks like Satin, Kinetic Lad, and the feral twins, Tooth and Claw."

"That's a big job when we're a man down." Steele got to her feet with a weary sigh. "Iridium, could you?"

Iridium thought about Lester and Gordon, about Jet lying in the med room. She looked at Hornblower's glare and Steele's pleading gaze.

"Fine," she said. "Just don't expect me to make a habit out of this."

Interlude

"I can't believe you're watching the tele. Isn't life bleak enough?"

Garth smiles up at Julie, who closes the bedroom door behind her. In the main room, Garth hears the Brewer kids playing some game or another, even through the closed door. "After a long day of entertaining our guests and replacing the door, I'm ready for some escapism."

On screen, Gena Mead announces that doctors are reporting a new disorder that's running rampant in Looptown and its borders. "People are just staring into space, completely unresponsive to the world around them," Gena says grimly.

Julie snorts. "See, when I think escape, I think piña coladas, not new diseases on our doorstep." She frowns at the screen. "More Gena Mead? I swear, you've got the hots for her . . ."

"Hey now, you're the only one for me. Just wanted the news, is all."

"Oh goody. Then you won't mind if I make a switch."

Julie *blinks,* and Gena's serious face is replaced with that of Tom Carlin from the News Network's *Spin Room.* The pissed-off comedian-turned-commentator is railing about how the Squadron needs to get religion.

"Jaysus," Garth mutters. "Not him, *please.*"

"Aw, he's cute." Julie grins wolfishly. "And he's got red hair . . ."

Garth runs his fingers through his own auburn mop. At least, he assumes it's auburn; to him, his hair always looks brighter than it really is, even through his sunglasses. But then, to him, *everything* looks brighter.

He's mulling over colors when something Tom Carlin says catches his attention.

"And if you watched today's *Jack Goldwater Show,* you probably have your own Get Out of Confession Free card." Tom's eyes sparkle with humor. "Nothing like watching so-called holy men slinging mud. Better that than throwing stones, eh?"

The image cut to a clip from Goldwater—the host himself, seated across from a priest, a rabbi, and an imam on a sofa. *Sounds like the start of a bad joke,* Garth thinks. On the clip, Goldwater asks them if the extrahuman heroes' going insane is a sign that the End Times are here.

The rabbi, identified in scrolling text below as Rabbi Jonathan Cohn of the Third Temple, says, "Well, Jack, some of the signs of the end of everything include the truth being in short supply, wise people being scarce, and inflation soaring." He laughs. "If you go by that, the End Times have been approaching since, oh, the early twenty-first century."

"I think many people are understandably jumping to conclusions," says the priest. "What's happening now is certainly upsetting—"

"And dangerous," adds the imam.

"—but it's probably more likely to be the work of a supervillain, or even post-traumatic stress disorder, than a sign of Armageddon approaching."

"What's happening today is very sad indeed," says Rabbi Cohn. "But it's not like these heroes have declared themselves deities."

"Or Christo," says the priest.

"Or are trying to take over the world," adds Goldwater cheerfully. "Oh, wait. Some of them are. Whoops." The audience finds this quite funny.

"When deeds speak," the imam says over the laughter, "words are nothing. Whatever the cause, the effect is the same. The Squadron is dangerous."

The rabbi looks pained. "Something happened," he agrees, "but I have every faith that Corp-Co is working with the Squadron to fix it."

"Corp-Co?" Goldwater says. "You mean the same folks who run the superheroes in the first place? The same Corp-Co that's refusing to issue a statement other than 'no comment'? *That* Corp-Co?"

"The very same."

The imam waves a dismissive hand. "Some things are so broken, they cannot be fixed."

The rabbi insists, "The Squadron's not broken—"

"But they are," the priest says gently. "Something happened to the Squadron. And until it is resolved, we are all in grave danger. This isn't the End Times," he says to Goldwater, "but it is a very serious situation."

The clip ends, and Tom Carlin is shaking his head at the camera. " 'Serious,' he says. A root canal is serious. What's happening with the junked-up Squadron is a catastrophe! Corp-Co's not saying boo about it. Maybe their lawyers have counseled them to slink under a rock while they figure out legally how to make the Squadron's rampages not stick to them. Meanwhile, some people are talking about doing more than just talking about it."

Another clip, this one of Frank Wurtham, chairman of the Everyman Society, according to the text. Garth doesn't need the reminder of who the man is—besides, the text should ID him as "Raving Loon" instead of "Chairman." But whatever.

"We cannot depend on the authorities to take down these freaks of nature," Wurtham rants. "We must rise up, every man and woman and child, and we must fight back, with everything we have—"

A crash from the living room.

Over the sound of Wurtham's monologue, Garth calls out, "You folks all right?"

No answer.

Frowning, Julie opens the bedroom door and steps out. Beyond the bedroom door, she lets out a gasp that cuts off abruptly.

"Julie?"

She doesn't respond.

A creeper of ice stretches across Garth's spine, and his mouth is suddenly too dry. On screen, Frank Wurtham is spewing more venom about the evils of extrahumans.

Garth clicks off the tele and silently rises. He approaches Julie, his hand out for her to grab onto, but Julie doesn't move. He reaches out, turns her around.

Her eyes are white; her gaze is fixed on a spot he can't see.

"Julie," he whispers, stroking her cheek, his thoughts whirling about in a tempest of fear. A glance in the living room shows him that the Brewer clan and the old woman are lost in the same spell as Julie—the kids sprawled in front of their board game, Heather and Mrs. Summers on the sofa, Paul standing near the kitchen. By Paul's feet, a glass lies shattered, reflecting light like diamonds.

Garth tries to lead Julie back into the bedroom, but her feet don't cooperate. Snarling with frustration, he leaps toward his nightstand and grabs the phone, punches in nine-one-one.

And promptly gets a busy signal.

"Fuck!" He tries again. And again. He wants to go out into the living room, wants to run, wants to hit and hurt and scream. Instead he keeps trying the emergency line.

It's almost twenty minutes before he gets through.

It's nearly an hour after that before EMTs arrive. They're able to walk through the living room without turning into statues. When Garth, too, steps into the living room, he's fine. Either they are all immune, or whatever had happened had passed. But Julie and the others are still lost, their eyes solid white. The kids are smiling. Garth thinks that's a blessing; whatever they're seeing, they're happy.

"It's happening all over the grid," one of the men tells Garth as the team works to check Julie's vitals, to examine the Brewers and Mrs. Summers. Maybe he thinks he's comforting Garth by letting him know he's not alone. "People are just staring off," he says, "nonresponsive, like they're drugged. They're calling Looptown 'Zombietown.'"

The team loads the kids and the parents and the old woman onto their floating stretchers and hauls them out the door.

Garth is told pointedly not to come. "Too crowded," they tell him. "Patients only. Call for their status later." Julie and the others are whisked off to New Chicago Medical Center, and the door closes in Garth's face.

He is too stunned for it to register that he hadn't even kissed Julie good-bye.

THEN

CHAPTER 18
VIXEN

Adult subjects are unsuitable for replicating the research conducted on 1102. No money. No test subjects. Grants are thin on the ground for a study with only one verifiable instance of success. But I saw it. I heard him in my mind. I saw what he showed me. If going to the corporate sector means seeing that again . . . so be it.

—Matthew Icarus, diary entry dated 1985

Valerie propped herself on her elbow. "So what happened next?"

Lester folded his arms behind his head. Valerie didn't miss the taut muscles that swam beneath his skin, his head dappled with dark hair. "Why, then we followed the Chaos Brothers to their hideout, where we surveilled them."

"And that takes a while, right?" Valerie traced a finger over Lester's pectorals. She liked embellishing their cover story. It was like battle-scenario training back at her Academy.

"Oh, hours," he said. "Possibly even all through the night."

Valerie giggled, and Lester capitalized on the opportunity to pin her to the mattress and tickle her.

Valerie shrieked in delight, because no one could hear her. Not Ops, not Corp. She didn't know how Lester had found this apartment—if it could even charitably be called an apartment.

Peeling walls, stained ceiling, *radiators,* for Jehovah's sake. But what neighbors there were in the building kept to themselves.

Here, she didn't have to be Vixen. Here, she was Valerie. And he was Lester.

Of course, the story they'd give to Ops would include the Chaos Brothers.

"You think they're going to figure it out?" Valerie said when her breath came back. "We've been doing an awful lot of surveillance these past six months."

"Ops? Or the suits?"

"Either. Both."

"Luv, they can't find their arses with a GPS tracker." He tapped her on the nose. "You worry too much."

"Somebody has to worry for the both of us." Valerie sat up, suddenly cold. She wrapped the sheet around herself. "We are lying to Corp, Les. There are going to be consequences."

Lester's mouth turned down. "You don't like this? You'd rather we split up?"

"*No.* Damnit, Lester, I'm not saying that."

He shoved a hand through his hair. It was living ink in the faulty light, and Valerie resisted the urge to move it out of his eyes. He said, "Then what, luv?"

Valerie bit her lip. "I don't want to sneak around anymore. I love you, Les. I'm not worried about Corp."

Silence, and Valerie could feel her heart thudding. Men had told her they loved her, twice. She'd never said it back. She wasn't the honey that had bees swarming like Angelica was, not that she begrudged Holly the attention. She appreciated it when her friend took the brunt of the catcalls and press, really. Valerie would have taken some horny drunk's head off long since if she'd had to put up with Angelica's popularity.

The radiator clanked on, horribly loud in the still room.

Finally, Lester slid his arm around her shoulder and kissed her cheek. "All right, then," he said. "Tomorrow morning. We'll go to Extrahuman Resources and disclose our relationship. They'll probably throw us a press conference and all. We'll be terribly, terribly popular with the vids, me being so gorgeous and you being . . . well, you."

The doorbell rang, and Valerie jumped, glad for the distraction. "That's pizza." She grabbed Lester's undershirt and her own panties and dressed to get the door.

"Valentine." That was the name he'd made up for her, after their first night together. Right around Valentine's Day. She grinned from the memory. Only Lester could be that cheesy and get away with it.

"Yes, Les?"

"I love you too."

CHAPTER 19
ANGELICA

Blackout has shown signs of decay. I want to decommission him, but Aaron claims to have a better solution.

—From the journal of Martin Moore, entry #70

Angelica, get your mind out of the clouds!"

Holly blinked, then frowned at her console. An ambulance was blaring about five hundred meters behind her, coming up fast. Other hovers had skittered to the right, getting safely out of the way. Muttering, Holly punched in commands, and the patrol car zoomed to the right. It didn't matter that the ambulance could have jumped the currents over them; whether in the air or on the ground, there were road rules in effect. Sirens wailing? Move to the right. Fast.

"Jehovah, girl, where's your brain been lately?"

Holly sighed as she flipped on the autocruiser, then she spun in her seat to face Vixen. "Look," she said, "I'm sorry . . ."

"Button it." Valerie leaned forward, her dark eyes glittering with anger. "You've been going through the motions, and now you almost caused a collision with an emergency vehicle."

Holly bristled. "I said I'm *sorry*."

"And what happened before with Mnemonic? You forget how to turn off your power? Or maybe you like blissing out your teammates?"

"Christo, it was an *accident*. How many times do I have to say I'm sorry?"

"I'm *sorry*," Valerie said, mimicking her voice. "Sorry doesn't cut it, Angelica. Not on Team Alpha."

Holly bit back a scathing comment. Val was right. Damn it. She sighed, closed her eyes.

"Hols," her partner said, softening her voice. "What's wrong? You haven't been yourself in . . . well, in weeks."

How to tell Valerie that she'd been having trouble concentrating? *No,* she scolded herself, *be honest with yourself at least. It's worse than that.* She'd start thinking about something, but just as it would start to take shape, her mind would slip and she'd be distracted, then she couldn't remember what she'd been doing.

But if she said anything about it, she'd be sent to Dr. Moore for some of his unconventional therapy. And she'd be damned before she allowed that to happen. Her voice strained, she said, "It's nothing."

"Bullshit on toast. It's something, or you wouldn't be so off your game."

"Just not sleeping well." And that was the truth. Holly couldn't remember when the last time was she'd woken up feeling well rested.

"Everything okay with Hal?"

Hal.

Holly rolls over, a contented smile on her lips, and looks up at Hal. "That," she purrs, "was amazing."

He laughs softly, the sound doing incredible things to her way down low. "You were pretty amazing yourself."

"Mmmm." She stretches, working on a kink in her shoulder. The man was a fabulous lover, no question, but he could be a little rough in the heat of passion. Holly didn't mind. She loved passion. "I'd love to stay, but I have a 6:00 a.m. patrol with Vixen."

"It couldn't have worked tonight anyway. I've got an appoint-ment with Dr. Moore in about thirty. Have to get over to the Academy."

She rolls her eyes. *"I don't know how you can stand to work with the man. He's so pushy."*

"He's also my direct report."

Even more reason why she would never volunteer to let Moore perform his tests on her—if he proved that her power was Mental and not Light, she'd be answerable to him. And that would be over her dead body. She'd seen the look of naked hunger in the doctor's eyes more than once. It was the same look, she was sure, that had been in Frankenstein's eyes as he researched how to create his Monster.

"Thank Jehovah I'm not a Mental power," she mutters. *"The man won't get off my case about wanting to peek into my head and see what makes me tick."*

"He's driven," Hal says, stroking the curve of her waist. *"I admire that sort of dedication."*

"You're a good man, Hal Gibbons."

"I'm a horny man, Holly Owens." His hand dips lower, and Holly lets out an appreciative moan. *"Stay just a few more minutes?"*

"Mmm."

"I love it when you do that," he says. *"When you close your eyes and just go with how you're feeling. I want to etch your image in my mind."*

She laughs. *"You're such a romantic."*

"With you? Abso . . ." His voice trails off.

"Hal?" Holly opens her eyes and sees her lover staring off into space, his gaze unfocused. *"Hal? Are you okay?"*

He doesn't answer.

"Hal," she says again, firmly. When he doesn't respond, she reaches over to touch his shoulder. *"Hypnotic. What's wrong?"*

He blinks once, slowly, then turns his dark gaze to her. *"Sorry,"* he says, sounding strange and distracted, his voice creeping up Holly's naked back. *"Just lost in thought."*

Unconvinced, she says, *"You sure?"*

"Yes." He looks her up and down, and he smiles. *"I love touching*

your body," he says, moving his hand up over the swell of her
breast.

She arches into his touch, and her concern melts away.

There's a pinch on her arm, quick and then it's gone, replaced
with Hal's soft kisses along her arm, her shoulder, her neck. She
doesn't mind the pinch. Hal gets rough sometimes—pinching,
biting, slapping. That's what he needs, and Holly lets him be rough
with her because she loves him.

His hands are on her again, moving rhythmically, soothingly,
and Holly sighs, feeling warm and sleepy, and she lets her eyes drift
closed.

She wakes up in her own bed the next morning, when Vixen is
threatening to pour water over her head if she doesn't get up to
patrol with her. Holly moves at half speed, feels almost drunk. Va-
lerie, laughing, shoves coffee under Holly's nose. "Christo, if sleeping
with Doctor Hypnotic is that good, maybe he should change his
name to Doctor Love."

Holly grins, still feeling dopey and rubber-limbed. Yeah, it was
going to suck for her on patrol today. But after last night? Worth it.

"Hal's good," Holly said to Valerie.

"You didn't get into a fight with him or anything?"

"No." She forced herself to smile. "Really, I'm just not sleeping well."

And since that last night with Hal, she'd been plagued with
bad dreams, nightmare images that scattered when she tried to
focus on them. What had it been, a week? Two? She didn't
know.

"Maybe you should get yourself checked out," Valerie said
skeptically.

Holly shuddered. Sure, she could go visit the Medical wing
of the Squadron. But if this was something else, something psy-
chological, Corp would force her to go to the Academy for an
evaluation in the Mental wing. And that was something Holly
would avoid at all costs. She would never be Dr. Moore's play-
thing. Never.

"I'm fine," she said, turning back to the console and taking
the hover out of autodrive. "I just need a good night of sleep."

"Maybe make an appointment with Hypnotic," Valerie joked. "A night with him, you'll be sleeping like a baby."

"Yeah," Holly said, and was surprised to feel her stomach lurch at the thought of being with Hal again. "Sure."

Holly blinked, then looked over at Jamie. He was standing in front of her, his eyepiece projecting a green-tinged list in front of his face. Holly was seated at the vanity table in her room. She had a moment of dizziness, and she wondered why she'd been thinking of Dr. Moore, of all people. "Sorry," she said to Jamie. "Were you saying something?"

Her Runner was frowning at her, worry lines on his face. "I was reviewing today's schedule with you, and you just drifted off," he said, sounding concerned. "You okay?"

She rubbed her head. "Yes, sorry. I'm just tired. Not sleeping well."

Jamie nodded, understanding. "Maybe you should cut back on your late nights."

She stared at him, waiting for the rest of the joke.

"What?" he said, a nervous smile playing on his face. "You've been going out every night. I have seen it."

Her head started to pound, and she felt the blood drain from her face. "Oh," she said, her voice sounding queer and strained. "Yes, I suppose I should."

Jamie went over the day's events—Glamique photo op at ten, a lunch event with New Chicago's Grandes Dames at one, training exercises at four—and then he left her alone so that Holly could grab a shower before heading uptown to her sponsor's headquarters.

Holly stayed in her chair.

Something's wrong with me, she thought. *Sleepwalking, now, on top of the bad dreams?*

Shivering, she rubbed her arms and debated what to do. She knew she should suck it up and go to Mental, get checked out. But the thought of getting examined by Dr. Moore made her sick.

One more night, she told herself. If she woke up tomorrow still feeling distracted and exhausted, she'd call Moore. Getting up to start her day, Holly Owens sincerely hoped that she'd sleep well tonight.

Holly didn't know where she was.

She stood ramrod straight, her mind cartwheeling, as she tried to analyze her situation. There was a man standing in front of her, but his features were blurred, as if her eyes couldn't focus properly. He was a smear of color against a backdrop of white.

Had she been captured? Why couldn't she remember—

"Yes," a man's voice said. "It's time for you to take an interest in Blackout. He fancies you, and we need to keep him happy. You'll do nicely, Angelica."

Holly's eyes widened.

Behind her, Dr. Aaron Moore continued, "You'll have to make the first move, of course. He's so painfully shy around you. You can do that, Angelica, can't you? Kiss him, let him know you find him attractive, and let nature take its course?"

She spun to face him. "What the hell are you talking about? Where am I?"

His eyebrows raised in surprise. "Oh, awake, are we? Interesting. Hal, would you, please?"

Hands pinned her arms by her sides.

She glared at Moore and reached inside herself to *push* Light into him, enough to turn his mind to putty . . .

. . . and then she screamed as every nerve ending lit in agony.

"Well, the conditioning works," another man said. Holly heard that, even through the pain. "That's good."

"Indeed," Moore replied. "That was the first command, even before the Corp branding. Self-preservation, little brother."

"You're only two minutes older."

Corp? Holly thought, or tried to think, but then her brain caught fire.

Eventually, the pain ebbed, and Holly slumped in her captor's arms. When she could speak, she whispered, "What have you done to me?"

A hand lifted her chin. Dr. Moore was peering into her eyes.

"Hmm? Oh, we've been doing all sorts of things, Angelica. My brother and I are turning you into the perfect Squadron soldier. You'll be completely dedicated to Corp. And to me, of course."

"There's got to be a way to do this without relying on Hypnotic's power," the other man said. "And without tech. Something we can distill, distribute widely . . ."

"One thing at a time, Martin." Dr. Moore smiled a toothy smile. "The tech is just the first step. Well, second step, now that we have both Hypnotic and Angelica under control."

Angelica struggled, but the man holding her was huge, and Earth-power strong. "When I get out of here, I'll tell the Executive Committee what you're doing!"

Dr. Moore let out a tittering laugh. "Even if you did, they'd never believe you. I'm their dedicated chief scientist. Besides, you won't remember any of this, so don't worry your pretty little head."

"You're insane!"

"No need for insults. Martin, since she's up, let's give the earpiece a trial run, shall we?"

Holly stomped on her captor's foot, and was rewarded with a masculine grunt of pain.

"Stop that, Angelica. Don't take your frustration out on poor Hal," Moore said. "It's not his fault you woke up. You're a stubborn thing, aren't you?"

Hal?

"Ah, thank you, Martin."

"If this works," the other man, Martin, said, "you think Corp will give us a raise, based on all the money they'll save not having the Runners lacing their food?"

"One can only hope. Hal, if you would? Give the lady a kiss, there's a good boy."

Holly was spun around, and yes, there was Hal, in sweats

and a T-shirt, looking completely blank, as if he were sleeping with his eyes open. Still pinning Holly's arms, he leaned down and kissed her.

It was only a moment—Holly, desperately trying to understand what was happening, had been so stunned by Hal's action that for a moment, she stood still as he kissed her.

And that moment was all it took. Something was placed snugly into her left ear.

And then Holly Owens went away.

"I'm telling you," Holly said, "I'm feeling fine."

"Huh." Valerie shook her head. "If you define *fine* as looking like utter shit, then yeah, you're more than fine. How long since you've slept well?"

"Awhile," she admitted. "Just having the weirdest dreams."

They walked down the hallway, headed toward the Squadron lounge. Their bootheels tapped alarmingly loud on the polished floor, as if the entire headquarters had stilled to listen to their conversation.

"Hols," Valerie said quietly. "It's been going on for weeks now. You need to talk to Medical."

"I know." Holly sighed, rubbed her eyes. "I know. I just hate doctors."

Valerie laughed. "Don't tell that to Doctor Hypnotic."

"Yeah," Holly said. "About that. I don't think . . ."

She was going to tell Valerie that she didn't think she was going to keep seeing Hal—lately, whenever she would think about Hal, she found herself cringing, as if afraid of his touch. She didn't know why, but not only was she no longer attracted to Doctor Hypnotic, she was afraid of him.

But that was when they arrived at the lounge, and Holly saw Blackout seated in one of the plush chairs, an old-fashioned paperback novel in his hands. And her feet stopped moving as she watched him read, saw the smooth lines of his face, the dark intelligence in his eyes. The sensual curve of his lips.

She had to know what those lips felt like.

Valerie said something to her, but she didn't listen. Holly was too busy sauntering over to George Greene, planting herself in his lap and locking her lips onto his.

He let out a surprised squawk . . . and then wrapped his arms around her and thoroughly kissed her back.

When the kiss ended, she smiled at him. "I've been thinking about you." And she was surprised to realize that was exactly right—she *had* been thinking about George, about how he was so dark and aloof and so mysterious. And so very, very attractive.

He was smiling at her, but it was cautious, guarded. "But . . . what about Doctor Hypnotic?"

"Who?" she said. And then she kissed Blackout again.

A week later, they disclosed their relationship to Extrahuman Resources. As a result, they were moved into joint quarters, a place big enough to accommodate both of them.

The press loved it—Blackout and Angelica were the newest It Couple, and their faces plastered New Chicago. Corp loved that the press loved it.

And Doctor Hypnotic, strangely, didn't seem bothered by it in the least. He'd even wished them well.

Holly was relieved. Hal would find someone wonderful, she knew, just as she'd found George.

Just as good as living with the man she loved, and fighting by his side? Holly Owens, finally, was sleeping well again, safe in Blackout's arms.

CHAPTER 20
LUSTER

I don't mind this life as much as I thought. And people ask very few questions when you're giving them what they want most in the world.

—Matthew Icarus, diary entry dated 1988, the day after the opening of his fertility clinic

Luster squinted into the strobes of the vids. Even a Light power had limits, and more and more often, as they grew more and more prevalent, he found the swarms of press suffocating.

That was a laugh. Him, Luster, darling of the cameras, averse to the very thing that gave him his popularity. His power.

"Luster! Luster, tell us about you and Vixen."

"She's standing right here, mate. Ask her yourself."

Valerie stood to his left, her hand locked around the elbow of Jumper, a teleporting bank robber. Jumper was currently wearing stun-cuffs and a crop of bruises, courtesy of Luster's girlfriend.

He grinned to himself. A woman like Vixen was useful to

have around. Not to mention smart, beautiful, capable . . . pick your adjective, the woman was it.

Valerie threw him a wink, and for a moment he lost himself, the sounds of the press on the steps of Squadron HQ fading out. There had been a lot of women before Valerie, but none remotely as interesting. Luster, usually bored after a night or a handful of nights, had found himself unable to think about much except Valerie after being with her for only one night. And here it was, eight months since that first night together, and he was still happy. Wonders never ceased.

"Enough simpering for the cameras," said a voice in his radio. "Get Jumper to a holding cell. I'm waiting to interrogate him."

Lester rolled his eyes. "Right away, your lordship." Ever since his promotion to Team Alpha, Hal had been even more of a pillock than usual. Which was at least ten times as much as anyone else Luster knew.

"Don't take that tone with me, Luster. I'm still leading this op."

"Get stuffed, Hypnotic." Lester dialed his comm off and jerked his head at Valerie. "Time to wrap up. That's all for tonight, ladies and gents." He tipped them a salute, and in the cacophony of light and questions, the three extrahumans backed through the doors of headquarters.

"Man, they love you two," Jumper said, blinking the strobes from his eyes. "You're like, bigger celebrities than Hollywoodland. It's kinda awesome."

"You just tried to teleport an entire vault out of Chicago Trust," Valerie said, giving him a shake. "You don't get to talk."

"Hey, just making conversation." Jumper slumped down the corridor to the interrogation bay.

Hypnotic stood up like a jackknife when Valerie and Lester buzzed through the door. "Took you fucking long enough."

Valerie stopped short and even Lester paused. Hal didn't swear. He and Night were so Hero-Code Approved it was nearly sickening.

Lester revised that statement in his head as Valerie apologized, giving Hal one of those melting smiles that had first made Lester stop and look at her. She wasn't delicate, not by a long shot, but she was beautiful. Even Hal had to see that.

But Hal wasn't around much these days. These days, Hypnotic held the reins. Sure, he smiled and clowned when Angelica and Blackout were in evidence, but Lester saw the hardness in Hal's eyes, the stone of resentment when it was just Lester.

Hal wasn't over Angelica. And he wasn't fine, no matter what he said about it. When Blackout's back was turned, Hal had a look that Lester knew well, one he'd seen on Donnie Bradford's face, his father's face, too often.

Hal wanted to hurt someone.

"Leave," Hal snapped. "I'll handle this since you're so busy posing."

"That one's a bit musty, don't you think?" Lester said. "At least pick a slag that hasn't got dust all over it, Harold. Like, 'I'll handle this since you're so madly in love with Vixen' or 'I'll handle this, since you're so much better-looking and should be the one posing for the vids.' "

"*Leave*," Hal roared, and Lester, never the fool, beat a hasty retreat.

Valerie kissed him on the cheek when they were back in the corridor. "I'm going to check in with Ops and file my report. Don't let him get you too riled, all right?"

"I don't get riled, luv. I just get even." He watched Valerie walk away until she turned the corner, then he slipped into the viewing room off the bay.

"Come to watch feeding time at the zoo?"

Lester jumped at the sound of Blackout's voice. "Christo on the cross, George. Don't sneak up on a bloke."

Blackout shrugged. "Sorry. Sometimes I forget. I just . . . blend in. With the Dark."

In the interrogation bay, Hal stood behind Jumper, and put his hands on the man's shoulders. Jumper shuddered as Hal talked, painting a picture with his power, sending the thief into his own world, plucking out his secrets.

Lester shivered right along with the amiable bank robber. One of his recurring nightmares was being trapped in the

Mental wing, listening to the drone of Hal's voice. Hal's voice became his father's, became Hal's—an endless cacophony in his head until Valerie finally shook him awake.

Thank Jehovah for Valerie.

"Our boy's in fine form," he said to distract himself. Nightmares weren't real. He was a grown man now, and he knew that.

"It must be awful," Blackout said. "To have a voice in your head that's a stranger's."

"Voice in your head, period," Lester said. "Creepy."

"Oh, it's not so bad," George murmured, and Lester got the distinct feeling Blackout wasn't talking to him. "If it's a friendly voice. A familiar voice . . ." He shook himself and stopped talking.

"What the bloody hell are you on about, George?" Lester demanded. After a moment, "George?"

But Blackout had vanished, whether out the door or into Shadow, Lester didn't know.

The close little room was hot, but Luster couldn't shake his chill.

CHAPTER 21

NIGHT

Going to roll out the comlink today. Could be the answer to everything, if it works the way it should.
—From the journal of Martin Moore, entry #73

Rick."

Night froze. Then he lost count of his reps, so he started over. A scowl on his face, he pushed up. And again.

"I didn't mean to interrupt your workout, mate," Luster said, all bullshit charm and smarm. The man hunkered down on his haunches as Night did his push-ups. "Need a spotter?"

"For push-ups? Not likely."

"For the barbell."

"No need."

"You haven't done your free weights yet," Luster said, with that I-Know-Everything tone in his voice. "You're like clockwork, you are, and more regular than an old lady on her fiber pills. First you put in your run, then floor work, and last is free weights. And then you do some sparring, if anyone's feeling particularly like getting pulped into next week."

"You want something, Luster?"

"Right you are," he agreed after a pause. Pitching his voice low, he said, "I want your thoughts on our brother-in-arms."

Night arched an eyebrow.

"More to the point, on *your* brother in Shadow."

Midpush, Night paused. "What about him?"

"That episode he had, a while back? You know, the one that sent him to Medical for a few days?" Luster lowered his voice even more. "He didn't just get dizzy, mate. He'd been raging. Ranting like an insane man. You should've seen him. In that moment, he wasn't our Georgie-boy."

"So what?" Night said, his voice a verbal shrug even as his mind was whirling. He had to play this carefully. Night knew that behind Luster's brilliant smile were shark's teeth. "We all get enraged now and then."

"If it was just that, I'd shrug it off as an adrenaline surge." Now Luster paused, as if considering his words.

Night pushed up to a seated position and waited, schooling his face to blandness.

"His eyes, man. You should have seen his eyes." Bradford's voice was whisper soft, and full of the terror known by small children who wait in the dark for the monsters to steal out of their closets. "They were full of Shadows."

Silently, Night cursed.

"He said things too. He begged me to make them stop. Said he always hears them. That he can't keep fighting." Luster stared hard at Night, his gaze penetrating. "What the hell was he talking about?"

Night shook his head. "I don't know," he said, modulating his voice for the perfect blend of honesty and concern. "Did you . . . did you tell Dr. Moore?"

"George warned me not to spill the beans." Luster snorted. "Like I'd say anything to Moore. Bloody mad-scientist wannabe. But don't you get it? That was our Georgie, threatening me. And just today, he was commenting about voices in his head."

Night blew out a breath. He hadn't known Blackout had succumbed to the Shadow in front of Luster. Damn it. It was a saving grace that Bradford had been so distracted with seducing

Vixen that he hadn't focused on Blackout before now. Clearly, that free pass had expired.

He ran a hand through his hair, raking it away from his face. How to play this? Anything that he said about Blackout, Luster would obviously wonder whether Night, too, was walking a razor's edge.

And that was scrutiny Night couldn't allow.

Part of him wished he could. In his own way, Night respected Luster, and he admired the man for being concerned about a teammate. But there was no way on Jehovah's scorched earth that he was going to tell Bradford, or anyone, the truth about the Shadow. Not about the voices he constantly kept at bay.

Not about the struggle to hold on to his sanity.

So he made himself believe his own words as he said, "It sounds like it was a combination of exertion and stress, making his power twitchy. He had time off after that incident, if I recall. And then he was fine, right? That's probably all he needed: a bit of rest."

"Probably," Luster said slowly. "You're not convinced?"

"Mostly. But just in case there's something more here . . . well. You and I, we'll keep our eye on him. We'll make sure he's in full control of his power. He has been, before and after that one time. I'm sure George is fine, but it's good for all of us if we're diligent." He smiled grimly. "I'm glad you mentioned this. Try not to worry. As I said, I'm sure he's fine."

Luster nodded. "Rick, if he's not . . . then is George a danger? To himself? To Holly?"

"As much as any extrahuman would be a danger." Then Night chuckled, and even clapped Luster on the shoulder. "You see yourself blinding Vixen on your off days?"

Bradford laughed. "Right. The woman would hand me my own arse if I even tried to lay a hand on her in violence."

"There you go. We'll watch, just in case." Night smiled again, and this time, it touched his eyes. "I'm sure he's fine."

They were all assembled in the main assembly of Squadron headquarters, Teams Alpha through Epsilon, standing at ease as

Corp's latest suit assigned to the extrahumans explained what the latest technological marvel was, how it was guaranteed to make their jobs and lives that much easier. The New Chicago branch should be proud, they were told, because they'd been selected to beta-test the new gadget. That it only made sense for New Chicago—home of Corp global headquarters and R&D—to field-test it wasn't brought up.

Night stood stoically, counting the seconds until the meeting was over. He was itching to go on patrol, to wrap Shadows around criminals intent on preying on the innocent.

It was a rush whenever he used Shadow in battle.

"So you see," the suit said happily, "the comlink will put you in touch directly with Operations, in real time. Completely wireless, each with its own unique frequency so that you won't get stuck on a party line, nor will you have to wait your turn to speak to a free Ops controller. You won't be reliant on your hover consoles, or on handheld devices that aren't always conducive to battle conditions. Hard to throw a punch when you're trying to connect to Ops."

A few laughs from that comment. Night didn't roll his eyes, but it was a close call.

Next to the suit, a Runner was displaying a white earpiece that looked distinctly like a slug.

The suit went on with the hard sell. "Designed to fit snugly in your ear canal, you'll have a constant stream of data from Ops."

"Sounds like it'll be an overload of information," one of the heroes called out.

"You'll be able to moderate it, of course." The suit laughed. "You'll be the one requesting information from Ops, and Ops will get you the data you need directly—whether you're requesting new equipment or a Runner to be dispatched, or if you need eyes and ears for an upcoming situation."

"Where is this Ops controller going to be?"

"Ops will be centered in the Academy, right here in New Chicago. Close to your headquarters, close to the Executive Committee, and readily available and in service to all heroes. Over the next few years, Ops will be for all of the United and Canadian States Squadron. But for now, it's all yours."

"I don't fancy having someone yammering at me all the time." That was Luster. "How'm I supposed to think if there's a little voice in my head, telling me what to do?"

Night's lips twitched in amusement.

"Of course, it will take some adjustment," the suit said. "But once you're used to having Ops at your beck and call, you'll wonder how you did your jobs before. Corp wouldn't have sponsored this technology, let alone given its seal of approval, if we didn't believe this would be a powerful tool in your arsenal. Try it," he said like a parent coaxing a toddler to eat. "You might like it."

"Just what we need," Blackout murmured. "More voices."

In a rare burst of humor, Night said, "But this is the *good* kind of crazy." And he and Blackout chuckled.

One by one, Runners handed out the comlinks to the extra-human heroes. Night and the others fiddled with the devices, getting them to sit in their ears just so.

"One of the best things about the comlinks," said the suit, "is when you're not tapped into Ops, the device remains on in a default white-noise setting. Completely unobtrusive, and designed to be both a concentration aid and, when you're not out in the field, something to help you relax." He tittered laughter. "It's come to our attention that some of you are a tad high-strung."

More laughter from the heroes.

"Go ahead," the suit said happily. "Turn them on. Tap once for white noise, twice to link into Ops."

Sighing in resignation, Night tapped his device and heard the comforting rush of a waterfall.

In the back of his mind, the place where the Shadow constantly clawed and whispered and giggled, things . . . quieted.

Night's eyes widened, and he let out a soft gasp.

Next to him, Blackout trembled. "Rick? Do you hear it? The silence?"

Elated, Night nodded. A smile bloomed on his face as he listened to the joyous sounds of Shadow-free white noise. And he thought that maybe, just maybe, the comlink was the answer to prayers he'd long since forgotten.

CHAPTER 22

VIXEN

We put safeguards in place to monitor the children. Puberty is often the trigger, although sometimes the abilities manifest earlier. My silent partners are very interested.

—Matthew Icarus, diary entry, undated

Luv?" Lester knocked on the bathroom door, which just made Valerie's head hurt more. "Luv, what's the matter?"

Valerie reached up from her hunched position and waved a hand in front of the flush sensor for the toilet. "I'm fine," she croaked. "I must've eaten something bad at that City Hall banquet last night."

"That, or you took Mayor Fujikawa's speech to heart." The door rolled back, revealing Lester in torn jeans and a T-shirt for some obscure twentieth-century band called The Who. "I swear, I've never met such a man for banging on about absolutely nothing."

"That's your sponsor you're slagging off." After a year of living with Lester, Valerie's American English was peppered with Britishisms, much to the dismay of Corp and her sponsor.

The thought of her sponsor made her stomach buck again

and she lunged for the toilet. "Oh, Jehovah . . ." Her voice cut off as a fresh wave of vomit spewed out.

"My sponsor can take a fast hoverbike to hell," Lester said quietly, holding her hair out of the way. "Luv, really. Do you need to visit Medical?"

"No," Valerie insisted. "It's either food poisoning, or PMS. I get nausea sometimes at this part of the month . . ."

Though she hadn't last month . . . oh.

Oh boy.

"Les?" she said, as he dabbed a cool washcloth on the back of her neck. She found herself incapable of looking anywhere except the white and blue tile floor of her and Lester's shared quarters. That had been a media coup—the darlings of New Chicago, shacking up.

"What's wrong, Vals?" His face furrowed with concern. "You going to keel over? Feeling dizzy?"

"I, uh." Valerie straightened her spine. She'd faced worse situations than this. Though probably not more awkward.

"Les, I don't think it was something I ate," she said. "I just realized it's been two months."

"You've been nauseous for two months? Don't tell me it's my company, darling."

"No, Les. It's been two months since I last got my period."

Lester's eyes went wide, like he'd just spotted a hoverbike about to fall on his head.

Jehovah, why me? Valerie thought. Angelica and Blackout should be the ones about to embrace parenthood. Not her, awkward too-tall Valerie Vincent, who was still Valerie Vincent, for Christo's sake, and not even Valerie Bradford. Her mother would have dropped dead on the spot.

"You're pregnant?" Lester's touch became warm as his power surged from emotional backdraft.

"Well, I'd have to get a test and make sure I counted right and go talk to a doctor in Medical and . . ." Valerie realized she was babbling and bit her lip. "Yes. I don't see what else it could be."

She'd never had to have the bun-in-the-food-unit talk with a man before, so she wasn't sure what she expected. Maybe yelling, or accusations of cheating, or cold denial. For herself, she felt strangely calm. *I'm pregnant.* No panic at that. *I'm pregnant with Lester's child.* Valerie felt herself smile a bit, hiding her face because she knew Lester was about to explode, get angry, ruin this moment of perfect peace . . .

Lester grabbed her and held her so tightly her air whistled out. "Valerie," he whispered against her hair. "Valerie, Valerie. Valentine. You've made me the happiest bloke on the bloody earth."

"Really?" Valerie said. It came out more like "Krumph," muffled as she was against Lester's chest.

"We'll be a real family," Lester said. "The three of us. And it'll be a girl, so I can spoil her rotten."

Valerie put her arms around him—carefully, because her own powers were feeling a little unstable with the swell of emotion in her chest. "Or a boy, who'll be just as big a pain in my ass as you."

"Quite." She felt him smile. "Of course, now I'm going to have to marry you properly. Care to guess what our wedding photos will bring in?"

"Lester Bradford, are you proposing to me? Here? Now?"

"Bloody right." He helped her up and sat her on the lip of the tub, then knelt down before her. "Valerie Edwina Vincent . . ."

"You wanker. You know I hate my middle name."

"Valerie *EDWINA* Vincent, light of my life, mother of my child. Marry me."

Valerie had to smile. Lester looked so serious, kneeling on the bath rug with his arm spread theatrically.

"Well?" he said, winking at her.

She nudged him with her toe. "Like you even have to ask."

Once the initial thrill wore off, pregnancy, Valerie found, was the most boring condition on Jehovah's scorched earth. At least she'd stopped puking once she'd hit her second trimester.

She watched Lester suit up from her position on the chaise, with a pillow under her feet, swelled to roughly twice their normal size. To think she had at least three more months of this. "I wish I was coming with you."

"Yes, dazzle them with your pregnant tummy. That'd do wonders."

Valerie threw a shoe at her husband. He ducked it. "Seriously, Les. I'm so bored I could chew the plastipaint off the walls. All I have to look forward to today is another exam, then a birth class. Me, Krakatoa, and Prismatic. All pregnant. In a class run by a suit."

Lester shuddered. "Suddenly, taking on Mildew and his Rotting Crew doesn't seem so bad . . ."

Valerie sighed. "You're terrible."

Lester checked himself in the mirror, his eye mask the only dark spot on his snowy costume. "Damn, I am a handsome devil." He came and kissed Valerie on the forehead and started for the door.

"Your earpiece!" She held it out.

"Not likely. I hate that bloody thing."

"Les." Valerie sat up, with a little effort. Her stomach made it awkward for her to move, even with her superstrength. "You know what Corp said after last time. Wear it, or you're on suspension."

"One, I can't think with that thing in my head and two, I'd like to see them try." He grinned at her. "I'm the Hero of New Chicago, luv. I make the rules, not them."

"Les . . ." But he was out the door. "Be safe," Valerie finished, to no one but herself.

CHAPTER 23

ANGELICA

All Mentalists continue to resist comlink control. Results discouraging. May have to decommission the entire Mental power.

—From the journal of Martin Moore, entry #109

You look so gorgeous," Holly Greene said wistfully, gazing at Valerie's swollen belly. Every day she visited, Valerie got bigger and more beautiful, almost glowing with her pregnancy.

Her friend chortled, nearly spilling her water. "You mean for a bloated cow of an extrahuman, right? Thanks, Hols. Honestly, I can't wait for the baby to decide to get out of my nice warm womb and into the cold cruel world with the rest of us. Christo, to have a solid night when I don't have to get up to pee . . ."

"But won't you have to get up to feed the baby?"

"Don't make me kill you. I'd feel guilty for minutes afterward."

Holly smiled and sipped her ginger ale.

"Three weeks to go. Thank Jehovah. So," Valerie said,

settling back into her recliner and setting her glass on her belly, "tell me how you and the others put away the Torrent Brothers."

Holly rolled her eyes. "Come on, I know Les told you all about this."

With a Vixen-appropriate purr in her throat, Valerie said, "A man's version leaves something to be desired."

"It really wasn't that big a deal . . ."

"Come on, I'm bored out of my skull being stuck on bed rest. If I watch any more daytime soaps, I'll go rabid and destroy all the furniture. Let me live vicariously. Tell me about the fight."

So Holly told her all about the collar, emphasizing Les's role for Valerie's benefit. In truth, Luster had called the shots, but it had been Blackout and Night doing all the heavy lifting.

As for her part, Angelica had been on the sidelines, trying not to throw up. Remembering her own weakness, Holly bit back a disgruntled snort. She knew that lots of the Squadron would have sympathized with her moment of nausea—fighting extrahumans whose internals were decidedly on the external side of things made even the staunchest hero queasy. And using their own intestines for ropes? Utterly pukeworthy. So she didn't tell Valerie about how she'd been sequestered behind a Dumpster, fervently praying that the contents of her stomach behaved.

And she hoped to Jehovah above that Les had opted for discretion when he'd told Valerie about the day's events, let alone when he'd made his official report to Corp and the PR spinners. The last thing Holly needed was for rumors to fly about how Angelica had tossed her cookies after one look at the inside-out Torrent Brothers.

"You guys," Valerie said with a sigh. "So lucky, getting to get out there and beat the snot out of supervillains. Me, I'm just getting fatter."

"You're not fat. You're pregnant."

"You're not allowed to say anything about my not being fat, Miss Size Two." Valerie shifted her weight. "I have about another minute before my twenty-fifth bathroom break. How's all with you and George? Still experiencing newlywed bliss?"

Holly laughed. "Whenever we have a moment alone, sure. Our schedules have been insane lately. I think the last time I saw George out of costume was a month ago." Actually, it was five weeks ago—thirty-seven days, if you wanted to get technical. Holly knew. She'd gone back and counted.

"But it's all good?"

"Yeah." Holly smiled, thinking of George's hands, of his serious eyes and sensual mouth. "He's charming and funny and loving and just wonderful."

"Good," Valerie said, toying with her glass. "I'm glad the two of you work so well. I've heard . . . well, you know, Runners talk. One of your Jamies mentioned in passing to my Reggie that Blackout had another . . . you know." She made a vague circling motion with her hand. "A thing."

"If you mean that George lost his temper," Holly said primly, "yes, that happened. But so what? He's only extrahuman. He's allowed to get mad."

"In front of a reporter?" Valerie asked, arching an eyebrow. "Hols, you know that the press eats that shit up. And the way Reggie said it, it was less getting mad and more of Blackout seething in rage. He threatened to make the reporter afraid of the Dark."

"The reporter had gotten too personal," Holly said. "Wanted to know about our sex life. George isn't the sort of Squadron hero to tell such intimate things to the reporters." A not-so-subtle dig, that. The sex tape of Luster and Vixen had made the digital rounds and back again. Both Valerie and Lester had laughed about it, with Les going so far as to track his favorability ratings for the month after the scandal hit the vids. Of course, his ratings had soared through the roof, and he'd been nominated as Sexiest Hero of the Year. Valerie had gotten a cover story on *Extrahuman Weekly*. Holly wondered which of the two of them had leaked the tape. Probably both.

"You don't want to go threatening the media, Hols. Bad press is more dangerous than the most powerful rabid."

"Look, it was one time," Holly said, exasperated. "George is a quiet man. He doesn't get angry." Often. Sure, he had his moments when a black fury would possess him, and he'd rant and say horrific things. And do some horrible things. But the moods would pass, then he was sweet, funny, loving George again. As long as Holly was there to temper him with her Light power during those moments, everything would continue to be just fine. Her power soothed his savage beast.

The thought made her smile. Her man loved her so much that she could quiet his rages, hold him as he walked in the Dark. She knew about his fear of the Shadow—there was little about George Greene that she didn't know—and as long as she could help him, they both agreed there was no reason for them to report his outbursts to Dr. Moore or any of his staff of Therapists—men and women hand-trained by Moore to work with Mental powers and . . . troubled . . . extrahumans.

Neither of them wanted that.

"Hey," Valerie said, "I didn't mean to get you upset."

"I'm not. It's just sometimes, it's like people expect the worst from George, just because he's a Shadow power." Holly sighed. "He's a good man, Val. I wish more people remembered that when they saw him."

"People have a healthy fear of the Dark. It's normal. Well," she said cheerfully, "off to my favorite room in the suite."

"I should go. I've got to be at the Academy by four."

"Teaching?"

"No. Visiting Hal." Her voice grew sad. "Dr. Moore says he does much better after I see him."

"That's just terrible," Valerie said, shaking her head. "Even when the other Mental powers started slipping, I thought Hal would stay strong."

Started slipping. That was Valerie's diplomatic way of saying *Losing their minds.* Right after Corp had given out the Ops comlinks, the three Mental powers in the New Chicago Squadron—and, rumor had it, all twenty Mental powers Americas-wide—had to be permanently restrained. And that was a diplomatic way of saying *Pumped full of drugs.*

Dr. Moore had quickly assured the Squadron and Corp that it was a power feedback specific to those with Mental abilities.

The doctor was confident that they'd isolate the source of the feedback soon, then the Mental powers would be back on active duty.

No one blamed Dr. Moore for the Mental powers, perhaps appropriately, going mental.

Sometimes, Holly would wonder about that. And sometimes, she'd think about how Blackout, too, had grown unpredictable since he started wearing the earpiece. But then she'd think about something else, and the notion that Dr. Moore's comlinks had caused the Mental powers' or Blackout's instability would scatter like raindrops.

Holly looked down at her hands, telling herself that at least Hal wasn't as bad as the others. He hadn't tried to kill himself, or to kill others. That counted. Hal was by far the best off. And Holly still thought there was hope for him. Every time she pushed Light into him when she visited him in his cell, he seemed to come back to himself. "Hal *is* strong," she said. "And I'm sure he'll bounce back."

"Me too." Valerie hoisted herself out of the chair and walked heavily to the bathroom. "Ugh, my bladder. Be glad this isn't you, Hols."

Holly smiled, touching her own flat belly. Way, way too soon for her to feel anything, let alone show. Barely five weeks. She and George had both agreed that they should wait until they heard the heartbeat before sharing their news with Valerie and the others.

She just knew that once George was a father, he'd have a constant anchor to help him stand fast against the Shadow. Between Angelica and the baby, Blackout would never again lose himself in the dark. And then, finally, his rages would stop.

Yes, what she couldn't do alone, she and the baby would do together.

And then everything would be perfect.

CHAPTER 24

NIGHT

Unexpected result of comlink: Traits have become ampli-
fied. The Lighters have, as a class, become more arrogant.
The Earthers have become more stubborn. The Shadows—
is it possible for the Shadows to have grown darker?
                        —From the journal of Martin Moore, entry #77

Night didn't choke the life out of Angelica, though he dearly
wanted to. Instead, he stood impassively as she put the
ridiculous paper hat on his head.

"Pink's your color." She chuckled, tucking the elastic under
his chin.

"The things I do for Team Alpha," he muttered, which made
her chuckle all the harder.

"You're having a good time and you know it. And just think
of this as practice for when it's mine and George's turn." She
pecked him on the cheek, then blew a kiss to Blackout. A radiant
smile on her face, Angelica glided over to a group of other guests,
whom she accosted with tiny pink hats. None would escape.

"Just breathe," Blackout intoned, either to Night or to
himself. Like Night, he was wearing a Little Girl Pink paper hat.
"It'll be over soon, then they'll all leave."

"You're being extraordinarily positive," Night said dryly. "I think we'll be stuck here until the better part of next week."

With the crush of people in the rented hall with them at the New Chicago Museum of Art, he probably wasn't exaggerating. The Runners had done a spectacular job planning Vixen's baby shower, making sure all heroes not currently on engagements were in attendance, as well as key members of the government—all standing around, hobnobbing and gossiping, acting like idiots. And with so many civilian celebrities, you'd think it was an awards ceremony. Even Corp made an appearance—three female suits, all wearing identical smiles and sporting identical haircuts (complete with the pink paper hats), all parroting the corporate party line and letting Vixen and Luster know how pleased Corp-Co was that a new generation of Bradfords would soon be joining the Squadron.

Night wanted to vomit all over their identical expensive shoes.

The whole thing was ludicrous. Vixen and Luster, having a baby. And now Blackout and Angelica, doing the same. The world had gone mad when he hadn't been looking. They didn't have the time, the luxury, to have babies. Heroes, raising children? Were they going to be changing nappies instead of fighting crime? Cleaning up spit-up instead of the streets of New Chicago?

It made him want to scream. *Babies,* for Jehovah's sake. He smiled blandly as a reporter made an inane comment about superhero true love. Silently, Night raged. It no longer mattered that Luster was the official Hero of New Chicago. No, now Luster was the official Expecting Daddy of New Chicago.

And Luster clearly loved it.

Obviously, Night was the only one of Team Alpha who still gave a rat's ass about actually heroing. Hadn't he been going above and beyond, not only following procedure down to the letter but also pulling extra patrol shifts, to make up for Vixen's bed rest and Angelica's morning sickness? Yes—because Night didn't just care. Night was a *hero.* It was in his blood, his bones, his thoughts. Duty first, they'd been taught at the Academy, and over this past year, Night had made that his personal mantra. Duty first. Always.

Night lifted his chin proudly. Even with all his voluntary extra patrols, he hadn't overlooked his Corp requirements. In fact, he'd been extremely accessible to the New Chicago Metro and Transit Authority, standing for photo op after photo op, all to get his serious face plastered on the sides of all city buses, hovers, and trains, just like his corporate sponsor had insisted. It didn't matter that he was barely catching five hours of sleep every other night.

He was the picture-perfect superhero.

And yet, here Night stood in a rented room at a museum, wearing a ridiculous pink paper hat, forced to pretend he wanted to be here, celebrating and wasting time.

Smile for the cameras; there's a good extrahuman.

It was so . . . fucking . . . humiliating. Him in his stupid pink paper cap, standing near the table with the buttercream cake and thermoses of coffee. Colorful streamers and balloons littered the walls, as did an obscenely large banner declaring that GLAMIQUE CELEBRATES VIXEN'S BABY!!! Complete with three exclamation points, to show they were really *really* celebrating, even though they sponsored Vixen's partner and not the lady herself.

He hated them all.

He hated wasting his time here, wearing this stupid pink cap. He hated Vixen for spreading her legs, hated Luster for knocking her up. He loathed Blackout and Angelica for doing the same. It wasn't any rabid or even any normal human criminal that would be the end of Team Alpha. It was his own teammates and their primal urges to have fucking *babies*.

"Vixen!" one of the newsies screeched. "Have you picked out names?"

Sitting on a plush chair, acting like a Junoesque queen on her throne, Vixen laughed. "We have, but my husband would kill me if we shared them."

"It's bad luck, you know," Luster said, grinning easily as the cameras ate him up. "Don't want to go naming babies before they're born. Besides, we have to have some secrets. You already know our identities."

Of course, everyone broke up over the stereotypical joke.

Secret identities, how very droll. Their canned laughter thundered through the large room. The more they showed how much they loved Vixen and Luster, the more likely one of them would grant an exclusive—if not today, then another day. Reporters lived for the possibility of the story. Any story.

Night's head throbbed, and his eyeballs felt like they were bleeding. In the back of his mind, in the darkest corners, he heard the whispers, the giggles, taunting him, telling him he was a good doggie, that he knew how to roll over and beg.

Telling him how easy it would be to show everyone in this miserable room what power really was.

By his sides, his fists trembled. All he had to do was listen to the Shadow and let it free. Let it embrace the guest of honor and crush the life out of her. That would give the reporters a story, all right.

No.

Fighting back a snarl, Night turned up the volume of his earpiece. The background noise of running water calmed him, and he let out a breath through his clenched teeth. See what events like this did? They forced him to daydream of the Dark, just to give him something to fight. It was that, or die from sheer tedium.

Really. *Babies.* Night shook his head. The things he did for Team Alpha . . .

"Well," Blackout said glumly, "maybe we'll get lucky and a supervillain will attack the museum."

Night's eyes widened as Blackout's words registered.

Yes. *Yes.* By all that was holy, *yes.*

The problem with Team Alpha wasn't the need to procreate. It was how easy victory came to them. They were New Chicago's living legends, the celebrities of celebrities. They always won.

They needed a villain worthy of their skills—one that would force them to drop all other commitments and once again work together to defeat.

And Night knew the perfect candidate for the job.

"Hey," Blackout said. "What's with the smile?"

"It's nothing," Night replied. "Just thinking of the future."

CHAPTER 25
LUSTER

*The treatment is proven to work, now. Miranda, if only you
could see. All you went through was worth something,
finally. Now hundreds of children will never be sick or
weak. They'll never be you.*

— Matthew Icarus, diary entry dated 1989

Lester thought the old cliché of men sitting in a waiting
room, smoking, while they waited on a baby to be born was
a fiction, but he would have strobed someone's eyes out for a
fag at that moment.

George was reading an age-old vidmag and Night was pacing. Back and forth, back and forth.

"Will you cut that out, mate?" Lester finally snapped. Medical wouldn't allow him to be in the room when the baby was
born. Vixen might lash out with her powers, and the Hero of
New Chicago couldn't afford a crushed rib cage because his
wife forgot her Lamaze breathing.

Lester thought that was bollocks, and he'd said so, but
Valerie had ordered him out before he got suspended.

"I should be there," Lester muttered, cracking his knuckles
like rifle shots, *pop-pop-pop*.

"There are procedures," Night said, standing stock-still now. Well, looming was better than pacing.

"I'm glad it's in place," George said. "I don't think I could handle it. All of that screaming."

"I'm so glad I got shoved out here with the Nancy Brigade," Lester muttered, putting his head in his hands. Honestly, between Night's line-by-line reading of procedure and George practically taking up pom-poms for Corp at every opportunity, it was a wonder he hadn't gone rabid.

"Childbirth isn't something you need taking your head out of the game," Night quoted at him. "It's for the women to worry about."

"Keeps one-half of the couple sharp while the other's indisposed," George agreed.

Just as Lester was about to either scream or strobe the living daylights out of something, a nurse in a Corp-branded white uniform came into the waiting room.

"Luster?"

He snapped up, faster than Speed Demon. "Is it . . . is she . . . is Valerie . . ."

"*Vixen* is resting, sir." The nurse took in his haggard countenance and her face softened. "Why don't you come with me? The nursery is just down here."

She led Lester past a series of delivery rooms, doors all shut and locked. The nursery was a sterile place, cots with blue or pink blankets holding the only life. Only three babies were in residence. Only one blanket was pink.

"Congratulations, Luster," said the nurse, leading him to the cot. "This is your baby girl."

Lester reached out, more carefully than he'd done anything in his life, and took the small body into his hands. The baby opened her eyes. They were bright ocean blue, paler around the edges, hinting they'd fade to something closer to his own gray.

"She's . . . mine," he said.

The nurse touched his arm. "I'm only supposed to give you five minutes, but you stay as long as you like. You're the Hero of New Chicago, after all."

For the first time in nearly a year, Lester was grateful to the damned sponsorship. He curled his daughter in the crook of his elbow, like he'd seen his mother do to his younger brothers. Before she'd passed, of course. After, the only touch in the Bradford flat was fist to face and boot to gut.

"Hello, Calista," he said.

The baby stared at him. She blinked, once.

"Let's get one thing straight," he said. "I had a shite father, and I've no experience myself, but I'll do my best for you." He walked, because his mother'd told him babies liked to move, slow careful steps around the near-empty nursery. "I'd do anything for you, girl. You're mine."

Straighten up, fly right, wear the bloody earpiece. He'd do it all with a song for his family. For the first time in . . . well, *ever*, if he were being honest, Lester didn't chafe at the thought of Corp and sponsorships. He had something else now, something that was only his. A wife and a daughter.

A family.

Lester felt a small ragged hole inside him close. For once in his life, he was something near to complete.

CHAPTER 26

NIGHT

Hypnotic no longer salvageable. Extremely disappointed. Will begin decommission paperwork. Once approved, he'll go to Therapy.

—From the journal of Martin Moore, entry #120

Night's footfalls echoed as he walked down the hallway of the Mental wing, sequestered deep within the Academy. He pointedly ignored the sounds from behind the tilithium-reinforced doors of individual cells. It was easy; here, the extrahumans' Mental powers had been all but negated thanks to drugs, and Night had survived his entire life by shutting out the voices he didn't want to hear.

He approached room 6002 and tapped in the code he'd been given by the Containment captain outside the wing. The door slid open, and he marched inside, his black cape billowing almost regally as he entered.

Doctor Hypnotic sat in the corner, his legs crossed and his arms bound mercilessly in a straitjacket. His dark hair hung in greasy strands over his eyes, and his jaw was covered by an uneven beard. He didn't look up as Night walked inside the cell—

he'd just been medicated, Containment had told Night, which was the only reason that he'd been allowed to come here without an escort.

Apparently, Hypnotic had been causing some problems. Night had always appreciated the man's sheer willpower.

Night squatted in front of the former hero. "Doctor Hypnotic," he said mildly. "Anyone home?"

Dark eyes rolled to peer at him—dulled, yes, but that didn't dilute the intensity of that gaze.

Well and good. If the man had been too doped up, it would have wasted Night's time. He cast a Shadownet: an invisible, soundproof bubble of Shadow. No one would overhear what he had to say to his former colleague. "I only have three minutes, so I'll keep this brief. It's not a social call. Actually, it's an offer."

Hypnotic stared at him.

"Do you want to spend the rest of your life tucked away in Mental? You'd be safe from the world if you stay. And the world, I suppose, would be safe from you. And from what I hear, every Tuesday, Angelica comes to visit. Very loving of her, no?"

Hypnotic's eyes narrowed.

"Or," Night said, "you could go out into the world. No more drugs to dull your wits and steal your power. No more Dr. Moore and his Therapists telling you what you should be thinking and why you're safer in your padded room and jacket without arm movement. And," he added, his voice like velvet, "I'm sure that Angelica would love to see you free."

Hypnotic frowned.

"I know, you're probably thinking that she went and married Blackout and is now carrying his whelp inside of her. But you should see her eyes whenever she speaks of you." He smiled. "Blackout might own her body, but there's no question who owns her heart."

Now Hypnotic's frown deepened, as if he were considering Night's well-rehearsed words.

Night pitched his voice as low as the shadows. "You *do* know it was Corp that insisted she leave you for Blackout, don't you?"

Hypnotic closed his eyes. Night saw a fine tremble work its

way over the man's massive shoulders. Good. It had been a cal-
culated lie—but it had struck home. He had no idea why the
vapid woman had left Hypnotic for Blackout, nor did he care.

"So you can stay here," Night said, "safe from the world. Or
you can go out there and use your power. Make the world the
way it should be." He stood, taking care to flare his cloak
enough to mask the sudden movement of his hand. He dropped
the tiny square, which landed on Hypnotic's bent knee.

"Put it on your tongue. It'll dissolve quickly. And within
twenty-four hours, it'll scrub your system of the drugs they've
pumped inside of you. And then . . ." Night smiled. "Well, I
leave that to your imagination."

Before he turned his back, he saw Hypnotic bend over double. When he straightened, the square had disappeared.

"Be seeing you," Night called over his shoulder as he
dropped the Shadownet. And then he marched out of Hypnotic's cell and locked up behind him.

If the Shadow whispered to him that day, he didn't notice.
Night was too busy thinking of what tomorrow would bring.

Interlude

Garth holds Julie's hand as he sings to her. He knows she can't hear him; she's lost somewhere his voice can't reach her. But he sings anyway, and he squeezes her hand, and he pretends that everything is going to be right as rain.

He knows he's lucky Julie got a hospital bed. The place is overflowing with victims of this so-called zombie plague. Seven other people share the room with Julie, and they each have at least one person holding vigil. Garth doesn't care about the tight quarters. Truth be told, he doesn't even notice.

Garth holds his wife's hand, and he sings softly in Gaelic. And he prays to a god he's sure isn't listening that Julie will wake up again.

NOW

CHAPTER 27

JET

Wurtham cut off all funding today, claiming 'questionable background.' Thinks he's untouchable. Hired a freelancer to show my displeasure. City Hall too; good distraction. Phase 3 of Project Sunstroke delayed indefinitely.
—From the journal of Martin Moore, final entry

She knows she's dreaming because Sam is with her, one hand sliding around her waist.

"Nothing is going to happen today," he murmurs in her ear. "It's a good day."

"You're lying." She says it like a sigh. Her heart is heavy, and her eyes sting with tears. "You're going to get killed, and all I'll have left is the Shadow."

"Jet," he says, "I promise you, I'm still here." He embraces her, and looks her in the eye, promising, "I'm not leaving you."

"You're lying."

"No, Joannie. I'm not. I have to go away for a little bit. But I swear to you, I'm coming back."

"I want to believe you," she whispers. "But Sam, you're going to break my heart again."

"I promise you, Joannie Greene, I'm coming back. I love you."

She throws her arms around him and he bends down to kiss her. Their lips meet, and Jet allows herself to believe Samson's promise. And for that little piece of forever, everything is perfect.

The kiss lasts a long, long time.

Jet's eyelids fluttered as she swam up to consciousness. Three things hit her immediately: one, she was wearing only her bra and panties. Two, she had no idea where she was. And three, if she didn't get to a bathroom right now, she was going to burst.

She sat up, blinking as she looked around. After a moment, it clicked: She was in one of the headquarters' back rooms they'd been using as sleeping quarters. Pennants and jerseys littered the walls, brushed with the dust of glories past. Okay, that meant the bathroom was down the hall, headed toward the main barroom. Progress.

Grabbing the blanket that had covered her, she pushed off the cot and tested the strength of her legs. She was a little dizzy, but that could be from low blood sugar. She wrapped the starchy blanket around her, making an impromptu toga, and padded out of the small room. In the hallway, she got her bearings and soon found the women's room and did her business.

She eyed the shower longingly, but instead she headed out to the main room, modesty be damned.

A glance showed her Meteorite hovering by the main console, absently polishing the bar top with a rag as she watched a multiscreen vid of what looked like rioting and newsies commenting and police holding back protesters and—

"Light," Jet breathed, "is that City Hall on fire?"

Meteorite squawked as she jumped, her rag balled in her fist. Blushing furiously, she let out a shaky breath. "Christo, don't sneak up on a person like that! How're you feeling?"

"Fine," Jet answered. It was true: She was feeling clear-headed and, unbelievably, well rested. "Hungry."

Meteorite chuckled. "I bet."

"What's happening at City Hall?"

"More protesters. Some got creative. Firebug's already on her way to help the city's Bravest and to try to do some PR damage control."

"Good." Jet stared at the screens for a moment, thinking about how the mayor would take his office getting crisped. Probably about as well as Everyman had taken it when their HQ had been bombed. At least this time, Kai was doing her duty.

. . . *save the world* . . .

Something nagged at Jet, something about . . . Everyman? No, that wasn't quite right. But she had more important things to think about. Gripping her blanket tightly, she said, "How'd I get here? Where are the others? Are they all right?" A pause. "And why am I naked?"

That last bothered Jet immensely. She remembered the sound of Bruce's laughter, the feeling of his hands on her body. She gritted her teeth. Her hormones were going to be the death of her.

"Slow down," Meteorite said, holding up her hands in surrender. "The others are out, doing what they can. You're naked because I had to get your outfit off you before I could see the extent of your injuries."

Injuries? She'd been hurt?

Before Jet could ask about that, Meteorite said, "What do you remember?"

Jet frowned, thinking. "I'd gone after Firebug and Steele, then I confronted Hypnotic . . ." She blanked. She had the impression of talking to him, of his touching her face, his eyes shining in wonder. "He told me his name is Hal."

"Harold Gibbons, code name Doctor Hypnotic. What happened when you were in there?"

"I'm not sure. We talked, I know that much. But . . ." Her frown deepened. Part of her was insisting that Hypnotic had helped her with . . . something . . . but it was like chasing smoke. "I can't remember."

"That's not a surprise," Meteorite said slowly. "All things considered, you and the others got off lucky."

Jet's eyes widened. "The others. Steele, Firebug. And Taser, I'd called him in for assistance. Are they all right?"

"Kai's a little worse for the wear, but getting back into the thick of things has done wonders for her. And you know Harriet," Meteorite said with a chuckle. "Steele's unbendable."

"And Bruce?" Jet asked softly.

"*Taser,* Iridium, and Boxer got you and the others out. They brought you here, and I've been checking on you while you recuperated."

Iridium had shown up after all—and with backup? Jet's mind whirled as she tore at her memories, trying to remember what had happened when she'd gone into Hypnotic's lair. "I was hurt?"

"Yeah."

"Hypnotic?"

"Actually, Bruce." Meteorite smirked, then shrugged as if to say What Did You Expect? "He'd been aiming for Hypnotic, but got you instead."

Her jaw dropped. "*Bruce* zapped me?"

"Yeah. But you weren't burned, which was good, and your eyes were clear, which was even better. If you were under Hypnotic's influence, they'd have been milky white." Meteorite motioned to one of her assorted computers. "I've been reading up on Hypnotic. And based on everything I've been reading, we're in a hoverload of trouble."

"Okay." Bruce had almost electrocuted her. Light. Clutching her blanket, Jet said, "Download everything you've found about Hypnotic to my wristlet and tell me where I'm needed." She spun on her heel to head back to the so-called guest room. "And where's my skinsuit?"

"Where you're needed is the shower."

Jet paused, then looked over her shoulder at Meteorite. "Excuse me?"

"Joan," the other woman said gently. "You'd been fighting for two days without a break, then you were down for the count for two more days. Not to put too fine a point on it, you reek. And a shower will get you more focused for what you need to do."

"I was unconscious for *two days?*" Jet thought she sounded fairly calm, all things considered.

"Yeah." Meteorite sighed. "Courtesy of Iridium. She doped you so you'd finally get some sleep."

"Iridium *drugged me?*" Okay, maybe that wasn't so calm. Maybe she'd actually shouted that last part.

"Get over it, babe. Go on and shower."

"I don't have time to shower," Jet growled. She was going to kill Bruce and Callie. Slowly. And very painfully. "From what I see, everything's hit the roof."

"Joan Greene, you turn your ass around and look at me."

Clenching her teeth, Jet turned.

Meteorite had crossed her arms beneath her ample bosom, and there were thunderstorms in her eyes. "Yes, the shit has hit the fan, even with the overall violence lessening. Hypnotic's influence is spreading in a growing radius around his lair in Looptown." Jet must have looked puzzled, because Meteorite explained, "People, both norms and extrahumans, are just staring off into space. Falling under his spell, just like when he first went rabid."

Jet recalled studying the Siege of Manhattan during Fourth Year tactics training at the Academy. About twenty years ago, Hypnotic had parted ways with the Squadron—violently—and had controlled a small area in New York City. It had taken the Squadron five days to push through his henchmen, then confront Doctor Hypnotic directly. The casualty rate had been horrific. "We can't let that happen again," Jet said quietly.

"But it's already started. The hospitals are overloaded with cases of what the media's calling 'zombie plague.' Total number's hard to come by, but 212 cases have been confirmed."

Oh Light.

Duty first, Jet thought bleakly. All those people, lost in their own minds . . . waiting for Hypnotic to command them. She had to stop Hal, convince him that what he was doing was wrong.

"So far, none of the affected civilians, or extrahumans," Meteorite emphasized, "have done anything other than go blank."

Jet frowned. "He got some of the rabids?"

"From what I've been picking up, yeah. Thirteen of the zombies were ID'd as extrahuman." Meteorite listed them all, ending with a name Jet knew all too well from her Academy years: Dawnlighter. "Maybe we should recruit him," Meteorite said with a tight laugh. "He's doing some of our work for us."

"You can help make a difference," she says to Hal.

"Why, Joan," he replies, "what a marvelous idea. I'll have to think about that."

Jet cursed.

"And that wacky media has also just announced to everyone and their sister that rumor has it that Hypnotic has broken out of Blackbird, so now people are more scared than they were before." Meteorite snorted. "Which is saying something."

"This is all the more reason I have to go after him now, before his influence spreads."

"Will you shut it? I'm not done." Meteorite glared at her. "The brass hasn't pinpointed Hypnotic's lair yet. Derek and I are guessing Hypnotic's cloaked it somehow. If not for Kai's distress call two days ago, we wouldn't have found him, either." Meteorite frowned. "Just as well. The National Guard would probably bomb him to hell and back rather than go against him directly."

"Not with all the innocents caught in the crossfire, they wouldn't."

"Of course they would. Acceptable losses, and all that."

"So I *have* to go after him," Jet said impatiently. "We can't give this to the police. It's too dangerous for them."

Meteorite shouted, "Scorch it, don't you see? He's *too fucking strong.*"

Her words hung in the air between them.

Jet knew that Meteorite was right. Hal was much too strong. But what other option was there?

"Hypnotic's just the frosting on the shit cake." Meteorite ticked off points on her fingers as she said, "We still have groups of former Squadron soldiers venting throughout New Chicago, not to mention the rest of the Americas. There are more citizen protests like what's happening at City Hall, and even more zealous speeches from Everyman. Citywide curfew is in effect. Just to make it more fun, there are rumors of a mass breakout from Blackbird."

Jet felt dizzy. "Please tell me that really is just a rumor."

"We don't know," Meteorite said with a heavy sigh. "We can't get a solid answer from Blackbird thanks to the guards striking, let alone the police. And from the little I've picked up, Lee is poised to label all extrahumans terrorists, so we're not getting a lot of love from any of the brass."

Terrorists. Light.

"To top it off, we still don't have a beat on the missing Academy students or staff."

A lump formed in Jet's throat, and she swallowed thickly. The students had to be safe somewhere. Ops at the Academy might have been washed-up heroes, but most of them had still held on to their extrahuman abilities. What was more, they hadn't worn the earpieces that had brainwashed the Squadron into being Corp yes men. They had to have led the kids to safety.

"At least it's not all doom and gloom," Meteorite said lightly. "Your best buddy's been working with us on and off these past two days. She's been a big help. So's Taser."

Bruce and Callie, hand in hand. How fitting. "Iri's really one of the good guys?"

"For now. You know Iridium. With her, it's always about her own interests first."

"Indeed." She remembered Iri telling her to drop her off in Wreck City, instead of going with her to confront Hypnotic. "Taser as well."

Meteorite shook her head ruefully. "Don't be too hard on him just because he fried your circuits by accident. We're sort of screwed here, Jetster. Don't go looking gift horses in the mouth."

"I don't plan on doing anything with Taser's mouth," Jet replied, her voice clipped. Her stomach ruined her indignation as it let out a woeful grumble.

"I'm sure Taser's mouth is very disappointed. I'll scare up some food for you. While you shower," Meteorite added pointedly.

Jet glared at her. "Sheila . . ."

"Don't you 'Sheila' me, Joan Greene. Get your ass into that

shower." Meteorite smiled sweetly. "And then I'll tell you where I've hidden your skinsuit. Which, by the way, is now clean. Unlike you."

Jet stared at the Ops controller long and hard. Finally, she said, "You're incorrigible."

"And allergic to dirt. Go get clean." The smile melted off Meteorite's face. "Because Jehovah knows, you'll be getting dirty again."

CHAPTER 28

IRIDIUM

These parents have no conception of what their children could become. This isn't merely science . . . this is evolution.

—Matthew Icarus, undated research notes

Why, Iridium wondered, did packs of villains always travel in threes? A love of prime numbers? Or simply to annoy her? Iridium bet on the latter.

These three—Feedback, Blackwasp, and Duster—had to be the sorriest bunch of superpowered punks New Chicago had ever seen. All young, all barely out of the Academy, with probably three months of field training among them and a love of clashing colors on their skinsuits.

Still, they'd managed to take out an armored transport hover and tie up traffic for kilometers in both directions.

Iridium threw herself behind one of the hover's tilithium doors as Feedback's sonic scream ricocheted off the buildings all around. Glass rained down, and Feedback raised his hands like he was conducting opera.

Until ten thousand volts to the back of his neck laid him out flat. Taser shook his head, batting at his ears. "Damn it, that stings."

"Your left!" Iridium said sharply, as a dirt crawler controlled by Duster reared out of the pavement. Taser dove left, and the crawler took out the front window of a 3-D rental shop.

That left just Blackwasp unaccounted for. Iridium spun in time to duck a slash from the toxic stingers in his forearms.

"There you are, kiddo," she said. "My memory might be going, but haven't I kicked your ass once before?"

"That was then," Blackwasp panted. "This is now."

"Oh, well." Iridium called a strobe. "Two for two is better than one." She threw the strobe into Blackwasp's buggy face, and it left sunburn across his nose and cheeks.

He didn't flinch, even when his bug-eyed goggles steamed from the heat.

"Polarized glass." He giggled. "Old school. I'm smarter this time."

"But sadly, not prettier." Iridium let her power die down and curled her fists. Blackwasp wasn't that big, and all he had going were the stingers.

"Sweep the leg, Iri!" Taser called from where he had Duster down on his stomach, strapped into stun-cuffs.

"Get bent," she shouted back.

Blackwasp used her moment of distraction to strike, and one of the stingers scraped across her cheek—not deep enough to release its venom, but plenty deep enough to hurt.

"Christo," Iridium hissed. She caught Blackwasp's arm on the backswing, twisted, and snapped the stinger off.

Blackwasp howled as bluish ichor dribbled from his wound. "You *bitch*."

Iridium kicked him in the back of the knee and took him to ground in a police hold. "And don't you forget it."

She held a hand out to Taser. "Cuffs."

"So hot when you say it like that." Taser dropped the stun-cuffs into her palm.

"Put a sock in it, *Bruce*." Working with Taser was almost as bad as taking down junior supervillains. If he hadn't been so

damn competent, she probably would have strobed him by
now.

Iridium cuffed Blackwasp, who'd reduced himself to
snuffling invective against her looks, her parentage, and her
fighting skills. She looked up at the merc. "If Bruce is even your
name."

"Yup," he said. "Bruce Hunter. I never lied to you, Callie. I
just omitted."

Iridium hauled Blackwasp to his feet. "You don't get to use
that name."

Bruce's face crinkled under his mask. "Who does?"

"People I trust."

A cop hover pulled up, Oz's unmarked just behind it. The
patrolmen came over with their hands on their shock pistols,
and Iridium stepped back, raising her hands. "All yours, Officers."

Oz touched the lead patrolman on the shoulder. "It's all
right, Dennehy. Iridium here isn't like the others."

Dennehy took in the villains and Iridium, and the mess
they'd made of Lower Wabash. "Thanks, I guess." He handed
Feedback off to his partner and took Blackwasp and Duster
himself.

"You crippled me!" Blackwasp shouted at Iridium. "I'm
gonna sue!"

"Watch your head," Dennehy said, and banged Blackwasp
face-first into the roof of his hover cruiser.

Iridium smiled at Oz. "I like that guy."

"Bright future, that kid," Oz agreed. "Probably be the commissioner in five years, the way things are going."

Citizens had started to creep back outside, cleaning up glass
and brick, and picking up overturned possessions. A bum reclaimed his shopping cart and gave Iridium a toothless grin.
The owner of the rental store came over and held out her hand.
"You did a good thing," she said. "Thank you."

Iridium looked at the woman's extended appendage, non-
plussed, but Taser grabbed it and pumped it. "Just doing our
job, ma'am."

Even the dealer on the corner—one of the Russians, judging by his tattoos—tipped Iridium a salute before he skulked away from Oz and his gold detective's badge.

"I've been held up three times this year," the woman said to Iridium and Taser. "This is the first time I've seen uniformed cops in Wreck City in . . . well . . . years."

"New Chicago PD is making some changes, ma'am," Oz said. "Our influence is no longer mitigated by . . . outside parties."

"You show up next time I trip the silent alarm because some punk has a plasgun in my face, I might believe that," the woman huffed, then stomped back into her shop.

Iridium chuckled. "Not your biggest fan, Oz."

"And the NCPD isn't yours, Iridium, but here in Wreck City, we take help where we can get it." He patted her shoulder. "Fight the good fight, kid."

Taser watched Oz leave and cracked his knuckles. "As far as first dates go, this was pretty good, wouldn't you say?"

She glared at him. "How long will it take for you to realize those lines don't work on me?"

"The lady doth protest too much."

Iridium ignored him, electing instead to put a comlink in her ear. After they'd foiled the bank robbery two days ago, Steele had insisted she take an earpiece and be given an Ops channel. Just in case.

So far, Iridium had answered every time they'd called. She didn't really want to go home, and Boxer seemed content to stay at Wrigley Field with Hornblower, so . . . why not keep her grid from devolving into an urban slice of hell?

"What does work?" Taser said.

Iridium frowned at him, considering what worked—and if she should tell him. Jet had clearly marked her territory when he was her Runner.

But Jet wasn't here.

Finally, she said, "Try taking off your mask, for starters. And I don't mean that stocking over your face." She motioned to him. "I mean this. *Taser*. You haven't shown me one ounce of who you really are."

"You're a hard nut to crack, doll."

"You want easy, go for Jet. Oh wait. You already did."

Taser flinched, and Iridium was gratified to see that bringing up her former friend seemed to shut the merc up. He was good in a fight, but he was obnoxious, arrogant, and a champion-caliber liar. The sort of person Lester would have strobed without a thought.

She wasn't jealous that Bruce had chosen Joan to seduce instead of her. It meant she was smart and Jet was gullible. That was all.

Feeling inexplicable tension grow in her shoulders and neck, she turned away from him and tapped the Ops frequency. "Ops, Iridium."

"Go," Meteorite snapped. The washed-up hero still carried her grudge, which Iridium had to admire her for. The rest of the good-guy brigade had practically thrown her a parade. Even Hornblower, once he'd seen that Iridium was sticking around, had stopped looking like he wanted to twist her head off.

"Trouble's over in Wreck City. Cops took the Dork Trio to lockup. Taser and I are headed back."

"Confirmed," Meteorite said. "I'll tell Boxer and—"

An enormous crash, then a cascade of crumbling brick and rebar cut off Meteorite's next words.

Iridium spun, choking on dust as the storefront at the street's end shuddered and collapsed.

From the wreckage, a huge shadow emerged into the dust.

"What is that?" Taser shouted. "Bomb?"

"No . . ." Iridium could barely breathe, and she snatched a hazomask from her belt and slapped it over her nose and mouth. Her watering, stinging eyes she was just going to have to deal with. Maybe she should consider goggles, like Taser or Jet. "No, not a bomb." Lester's teaching, Lester's voice feeding her information on urban bombing. "Too little debris."

The thing in the shadow challenged them with a roar. Iridium was momentarily rooted to the spot.

The man—it *had* to be a man—was enormous, all vein and muscle, with a deformed face and hands the size of meat platters. He had jagged teeth and a mightily pissed-off expression in his eyes.

"I might be wrong," Taser said quietly, "but I think that dude wants to kill us."

"He came up out of the *ground*," Iridium marveled, her voice steady even though inside she was screaming. "Tore that shop right off its foundations."

"Callie." Taser gripped her arm as the thing roared again. "Run."

Iridium spun, only to see at least a dozen more enormous, bloated, twisted figures appearing out of the dust. They circled her and Taser. Some giggled, or smacked their lips.

"Either this is a bad trip from breathing in all of that asbestos," Taser said, "or we're in serious trouble."

The lead creature roared, and the others returned it. Thirteen pairs of eyes focused on Iridium.

"We're in trouble," she decided.

CHAPTER 29

JET

Phase 1 of Project Sunstroke has begun. Thirteen volunteers eager to become as powerful as the Squadron. We'll put the extrahumans down like the rabid dogs they are.
— From the journal of Martin Moore, entry #294

I'll do a sweep over Grids 3 through 6," Jet said as she strapped on her cloak. She kept the cowl off, though. Instead, she'd braided her long hair and wrapped it in a bun at the nape of her neck. Not too heavy, and the lack of cowl made it easier for her to turn her head.

Meteorite handed her another protein bar, which Jet took gratefully. "Curfew's about to go into effect," said the Ops controller, "so at least that'll get most of the civvies out of harm's way."

"Small favors." Jet tore open the wrapper and all but inhaled the pseudochocolate bar. It wasn't grilled chicken, let alone a beef taco, but it would do. Chewing, she glanced at Meteorite's list of Who's Left To Capture. Out of the 412 active Squadron members who'd gone rogue or rabid across the Americas, 27 had been incarcerated, and almost 30 were being pursued—they hadn't converted from rogue yet, but at least they'd stopped breaking things.

They were finally making a dent at home. Maybe in a few days, they could spread out, chase down rabids in other cities, and leave the normal criminals to the cops and the soldiers.

"I'll check in with you every thirty," Jet said, "unless something comes up. And you'll keep me posted?"

"Of course."

Jet summoned a Shadow floater, and was vaguely pleased at how the voices didn't whisper—how the power didn't try to either fight her or seduce her. While creating floaters had never been hard, this was the first time that it was . . . easy. She stepped onto the black disc. "I'll start with Grid 6, maybe see if I can pick up Colossal Man's trail."

Grid 6: the Old Chicago district.

Oh cipio.

Jet paused on the Shadow floater, remembering a teenage girl standing outside of Everyman headquarters, shouting at her to go save the world somewhere else. But before the shouting, the girl had pressed something into Jet's hand, and she'd whispered . . .

Not "oh cipio," Jet realized with a start. O.C.P.O. The Old Chicago Post Office, in Grid 6.

That was when the pinging sounded—a distress call. Jet hovered in the air as Meteorite grabbed headphones. "Triangulating location," the Ops controller said, sliding the headset in place. "Speakers on. Ops. Go."

Over a burst of static, Iridium's voice, high-pitched, on the verge of panic. "Hey, heroes," Iri shouted, "we're in a situation here. We need backup, like, right now!"

"Iridium," Jet said, "stay calm. What's happening?"

"Hey, Jettikins is awake!" Iri let out a strained laugh. "You remember the thing you fought in the sewer? Well, apparently a dozen of its closest friends and family have all gone the sewer-mutant route, because they're right here!"

Jet's stomach knotted as she remembered the feeling of Lynda Kidder's malformed fist slamming into her, how the monstrous creature had nearly killed her . . . and how she'd accidentally killed Kidder in self-defense.

And that had been one mutant. Now Iri was facing a *dozen* of them? She shouted, "Retreat! Callie, get out of there!"

Iridium, desperate: "Sort of surrounded here. Taser's and my light show's holding them back, sort of, but I don't know how long!"

"Can you get in the air? Get out of range?"

"His hover's on the other side of the mutants, and last I checked, neither of us can fly!"

"Got them," Meteorite said, and gave Jet the coordinates. Barely five minutes as the crow flew. Jet would be there in two. Already soaring toward the door, she shouted, "On my way!"

"Bring the fucking cavalry with you!" There might have been more, but Jet was already out of hearing range.

Zooming over old Wrigley Field, Jet tapped on her earpiece for Ops. "Call in everyone. We need all of us on this."

"But Hornblower's taking down Jezebel, and Steele's—"

"Meteorite," Jet snapped, "pull them out! This is bigger than chasing after rogues and rabids."

"But—"

"Sheila," Jet said over the rush of wind, "they're *civilians.* They've been injected with Moore's Everyman serum, probably under duress. We need everyone on this. Now."

Meteorite cursed, colorfully and loudly. Then she said, "On it. Go."

Jet went.

Air stung Jet as she flew faster than ever before. Her face was raw from windburn as she crouched on her floater, practically hugging the Shadow to lower wind resistance. She had to get to Iri and Taser, fast.

Before the dying started.

She heard the shouting before she saw Iri. The other woman's clear voice was raised in a defiant battle cry that would have impressed Screamer. But the Lighter herself was lost amid a closing circle of hulking monstrosities—vaguely humanoid creatures stuffed into tattered business suits and jeans and the remnants of shirts and jackets, all of the monsters reaching out with massive hands.

In the center, Iridium and Taser stood back-to-back, their hands alight—hers with Light strobes, his with electricity. Iri launched more strobes, hitting three creatures square in their chests . . . but all that did was make the things stagger back. It didn't burn them, didn't seem to even hurt them. Ditto Taser's electric blasts. He hammered two more mutants, but if getting shocked did anything more than push them back a pace or two, it was impossible to tell.

Jet zoomed down, her arms extended. Concentrating furiously, she sent a portion of her power under the rogue's and merc's feet, pooling beneath them to form a new floater. "Iridium, Taser! Hold on to each other!"

"Fuck, that's cold!" Iridium sent out a flurry of strobes, then extinguished the light over her hands and grabbed onto Taser's waist. He let loose a burst of power, illuminating the air in front of him with white-blue light and heat as he planted his feet wide and bent his knees for balance.

Bracing herself against her own floater, Jet called the other Shadow disc to her. It trembled, then with a mighty heave it launched upward. Iri and Taser scrambled to keep their footing as Jet lifted them out of reach of the mutants. Once the three of them were on the roof, she released the Shadow, calling it back inside herself. She didn't feel its cold touch as it seeped beneath her skin—she was too busy taking stock of the situation streetside. The creatures, cheated of their prey, were attacking one another. Maybe they'd catch a break and they'd all beat themselves senseless . . .

"*You're* the cavalry?" Iri barked out a laugh. "And here I thought they'd be sending the entire Mod Squad."

"We did," Jet murmured, silently counting the monsters far below. Thirteen. Light, thirteen of those . . . things. "The others are on their way."

"Great. Get Firebug to charbroil them," Iri said, shaking out her hands and wincing.

"Can't do that," Jet said, tapping her comlink. "They're civilians."

"Those are *civvies*?" Behind his black mask, Taser's mouth pulled into a surprised O. "Remind me never to egg their houses on Halloween . . ."

Jet tuned him out. "Jet, Ops."

Meteorite's voice in her ear: "Oh good, you're not dead."

"Iridium, Taser, and I are clear for the moment, but we have to restrain the mutants without harming them."

"And you'll do that how?"

"Working on it," Jet said tersely. "ETA of the others?"

A pause, during which Iri and Taser exchanged heated words—and unless Jet was wrong, threw each other a few meaningful looks. If Jet had been less stressed, it would have bothered her more. Then Meteorite said, "Hornblower due to arrive in three minutes. Steele and Firebug are a little farther behind. And—"

"Wa-*hoo*!" Iri shouted. "*Now* the cavalry's showing!"

Jet looked up to see Frostbite approaching fast on an expanding bridge of ice. But this wasn't the man who'd been hollowed out in Therapy as a boy, then shoved behind a desk in Ops for years. This Frostbite, with his clean Ops gray unisuit and thick-soled boots and a wicked grin on his lined face, was a teenager again, his spiky blue hair gusting in the wind as he landed roofside.

This Frostbite was a hero.

"Look at you," Iri said, rushing over to him and greeting him with a hug. "Getting all superhero on us."

"Derek," Jet said carefully, "are you sure you want to be here?" He'd been out of the field . . . well, since forever. The last mission he'd run had been during a Third Year exercise under strict Academy supervision.

But that didn't mean he'd never been tested. Light knew, he'd been tested. And blooded. And he'd survived . . . at least, until the Therapists had taken him.

Frostbite disentangled himself from Iri's embrace, shooting Jet a glare that should have made her hair catch fire. "From what I heard, you told Meteorite to pull everyone out, *Joan*. I'm part of everyone." The look in his eye dared Jet to argue with him.

A smile flitted across her lips. "Welcome back, Frostbite."

"Yeah, we'll get cozy over a latte later. What's the situation?"

"A rough dozen sewer mutants tried to eat me and Taser," Iri said, pointing to the street below. "Now they're bashing each other's brains in."

"Fabulous," said Taser. "Problem solved. Who's buying?"

"They're not sewer mutants," Jet said, casting Iridium a long look.

Iri blinked at her. "What? I've seen it on *Mysterious Chicago*."

"They're normals," Jet stressed, looking at the others one by one.

"Those are the least normal normals I've ever seen," Frostbite said, staring down at the street. "Moore's sludge at work?"

"I'm positive," Jet said.

"What sludge?" Iridium looked from Frostbite to Jet. "Who's Moore? And don't give me that 'person of interest' cowcrap, Jet," she added when Jet opened her mouth.

"Hey, those quote-unquote normals almost crushed me," Taser said. "I'm definitely a person of interest."

Jet walked over to the edge of the roof and looked down. In the street, the monsters danced with fists and fury. At least the citizens here had abided by curfew. *Small favors*, Jet told herself again. "You remember when we met in the Rat Network?" Jet said, not looking back at Taser or Iri.

"You mean when you broke my nose?" Iri said sweetly.

"When I'd gone up against one of them." Jet's throat tightened, and she swallowed thickly, remembering the overwhelming stench of her own sweat and fear, her rising panic of the Dark and of the thing that had loomed over her, wearing a string of pearls and a look of pure madness. "That creature had been the reporter, Lynda Kidder. She'd been injected with a serum created by a man named Martin Moore."

She remembered the sound of Lynda Kidder howling in rage as a blanket of Shadow covered her. Squeezed her.

Killed her.

"He's working with Everyman, or a fringe group connected

with Everyman. So was C—" Jet's words ended on a choked gasp as a knife sliced through her brain.

A hand on her shoulder. She looked up, blinking away tears, to see Iri frowning at her. "Joannie," she said softly. "You okay?"

"No." Jet shrugged off Iri's hand, grimacing through the echoes of pain. "Whatever their brainwashing was, it . . ." She took a shuddering breath. "I can't say their name, not if I'm speaking against them."

Iri stared at her, her gaze unreadable. "You have to tell the world the truth."

"Amen," said Frostbite.

"Don't you get it? I *can't.* I literally can't say anything about it!" She clenched her fist, and Shadows seeped between her fingers.

"Why not?" Frostbite asked. "I can, and they screwed with my mind more than anyone's." He shouted, "Corp sucks ass! Corp can blow me! Fuck Corp!" Then he grinned at Jet. "See?"

Iridium said, "Maybe it has to do with your Shadow power?"

"This is pointless," Jet snarled. "So what that I can't say the name? You know who I mean. Moore was a mole. Night had leaked code-black files to Moore for Light only knows how long, and Moore took that information and went to Everyman."

"Hey," Taser said. He was looking down at the street below.

Jet ignored him. "And with Everyman, Moore helped develop or maybe even created this serum that he believes will level the field between human and extrahuman. He hates us. He thinks we're all time bombs set to explode."

"He might've been right about that," Iri said. When Jet glared at her, she shrugged. "Maybe he was right, and we're just damaged goods."

"Hey," Taser said again.

"No," Jet growled. "I refuse to believe that all extrahumans are just wired wrong." She knew she was doomed to go insane, but the others? No. *No.* She couldn't believe that.

Iridium said, "You notice what's been happening with extrahumans lately?"

"That's because after years, decades, of brainwashing, we were finally free!" Realizing she was shouting, Jet forced herself to take a breath and lower her voice. "It's finding out you've been a slave only after the collar's come off. This madness will die down," she said firmly.

"Joannie," Iri said slowly, "have you stopped to think about why Corp bothered with the brainwashing in the first place?"

That hit Jet like a punch to the gut.

Frostbite rolled his eyes. "You mean other than them being evil overlords?"

Iridium kept looking at Jet, riddling her with that ice-blue gaze. "Maybe Corp knew we were all screwed up, so they made sure that we'd never turn on them."

"That backs my evil-overlord theory," Frostbite said.

Jet barely heard him. In her mind, Martin Moore was whispering to her.

You're ticking time bombs. The lot of you. Some are just wired to blow before others.

She remembered Dawnlighter during Second Year at the Academy, her eyes and ears leaking blood as she tried to destroy Jet and anyone else in her way.

She thought of Slider, of Nocturne and the other Squadron soldiers who'd gone rabid within hours of Corp's conditioning shutting down.

Some are wired to blow—

Suddenly cold, Jet rubbed her arms. Martin Moore had been given access to code-black Corp files, to records that had been expunged. He'd leaked a portion of those files to Kidder, and after her Pulitzer Prize-winning "Origins" series on extrahumans had concluded, he'd expressed his gratitude by having her kidnapped and used as a guinea pig for the Everyman serum.

wired to—

What else had been in those files? What had caused him to say that the extrahumans were time bombs?

Jet thought of an article she'd found hidden in Lynda Kidder's apartment—a file that the reporter had never published in the *New Chicago Tribune*, even though it was marked as the last in her series. The article tenuously linked Corp-Co to the Icarus fertility clinic in the late 1980s, as well as to disease-control facilities in Hong Kong and Mumbai. In her last article, Kidder suggested that Corp hadn't merely bought Icarus Biological at the turn of the twenty-first century, but instead had played a larger role.

Martin Moore's warbling old man's voice: *It's reasonable to assume that Corp-Co sponsored the fertility project . . .*

Just how much did Corp have to do with extrahuman origins?

What did Corp know about the extrahumans that they themselves did not?

She remembered the teenage girl outside of Everyman headquarters, shoving a key into her hand, telling her to go save the world somewhere else . . .

"Hey!"

Jet blinked, looked over at Taser, who was pointing to the street.

"Sorry to interrupt," he said, "but the rest of the cavalry's arrived. And they're going after the sewer-mutant norms."

Jet raced over to the edge and looked down. Sure enough, there was Hornblower, peeling off a sonic blast that leveled two of the creatures. Firebug's flaming shield had some of them flinching back, protecting their eyes. Steele took the direct approach: She pummeled any mutant that got in her path.

"Ops," Jet shouted, "tell them to stop, that they're civilians!"

Meteorite's reply left Jet cold: "I already did."

"They're not hurting the mutants," Iri commented. "Maybe that's even on purpose."

"Come on." Jet grabbed Iri's wrist as she summoned a Shadow floater. "Frostbite, take Taser down."

"Plan?" Iri asked as the two of them flew over the roof's edge.

"Help them push the creatures back," Jet called over her shoulder. "Knock them out or otherwise restrain them. We'll figure out the logistics after." She dropped the floater down in a free fall.

"Brilliant!" shouted Iri, holding on to Jet's waist for dear life. "Tell the heroes to stop beating up on the innocent, murderous, insanely dangerous sewer-mutant wannabes. I love this plan!"

Frostbite and Taser slid down an ice ramp as Jet and Iri touched down. "Don't hurt them," Jet shouted.

"Don't get killed," Iri countered before she dove into the thick of it.

Jet rushed forward, slamming the nearest mutant with a Shadow bolt that knocked it off its oversized feet. She turned to the next creature, this one a woman, and hit her just as hard as the first. The woman-thing stumbled backward and into a third, which turned its rage upon her with a vicious blow to the head.

"Herd them!" That was Steele. "Get them contained!"

"Open to suggestions," Iridium shouted, releasing strobe after strobe. Jet caught it peripherally as she blasted the first mutant again, and a third time. It still came for her, its meaty fists promising to crush her. She stepped back, and back again, and barely spun away from the second creature's attack.

Someone let out a cry of pain.

Do it, Jet told herself. It will be different this time. *Blanket him.*

But she saw Lynda Kidder's prone body, a husk discarded by the Shadow. She couldn't do it. Snarling, she battered the creature again, and again. All it did was hold the man-thing back for the moment.

Fire arced overhead; ice crackled below. Her ears throbbed as Hornblower released his sonic cry, leveling it like a battering ram.

Do it!

She couldn't.

Now someone was screaming—not fear, not battlelust. Agony—so raw and brutal it turned his voice into a weapon.

Hornblower.

"Oh, Christo, his leg!" Frostbite, in panic. "Callie, oh Christo, Callie you've got to cauterize it—"

"On it," she shouted. "Keep them off me!"

Jet doubled down, slamming the two mutants on her with everything she had, Shadowboxing them until they collapsed like dead trees. She pivoted and saw Iri squatting by Hornblower, clutching his right leg . . .

. . . which had been torn off above the knee.

Jet froze, staring at Tyler Taft as blood pooled beneath him and Iridium, watching him convulse with pain and shock.

Iri, stabbed by an Everyman in Third Year.

Sam, slain by an Everyman, shot in the back.

Jet screamed as she let the Shadow fly, blanketing the creatures around her. Two, three, four of the monstrosities, were swathed in Shadow, struggling to free themselves from the deathly cold. Jet squeezed, and in that moment she felt their light, their life, so sweet and thick and good, and she held her arms up, her face tilted to the moonlit sky, basking as she drank them down.

She felt them fall, one by one. And still she squeezed. When all four finally succumbed to the Shadow's touch, she unwrapped the blanket, let them sprawl on the ground, unconscious but alive.

Energy sang in her, danced along her limbs. With a cry she hurled the Shadow over two more of the warped creatures, wrapping them tight. Squeezing them in the darkest of embraces. They, too, fell before the power of the Dark.

"Jet!"

She turned, smiling to see Taser there—Bruce Hunter, her onetime lover, who was stepping backward, his arms up in surrender. She remembered what it had been like to blanket him in Shadow, to slowly drain the light from his body . . . remembered how good it had felt . . .

"Joan," he said, "whoa there! Good guy, remember?"

She stared at him, at the blank slate of his masked face, his eyes hidden by goggles, his sardonic smile obscured by fabric. And she thought about how easy it would be to kill him.

And then she realized what she was thinking.

Shuddering, she called the Shadow back to her, all of it. Creepers washed over her, tracing her curves in a seductive caress before they melted into her.

"Yeah," Taser said, "okay, hi there, welcome back from the Land of Crazy."

Ashamed and angry, she turned away.

Littering the ground were the bodies of the mutants—many

of them bloody and pulpy messes of flesh. All of them unconscious. Three of them were scrimmed with ice.

"Hypothermic shock," Frostbite said when she glanced at
him. "Not fatal. I was careful." He was also shaking, leaning on
Steele for support.

Off to the side, Iridium was crouched over Hornblower. Jet
hadn't imagined it: The man's leg was missing just above the
knee. Iri's hands were on the shortened limb, and trapped between her flesh and his was a blinding light.

Oh Light. Tyler.

"It's sealed," Iri said, her voice tired and strained. "But he
needs a hospital two minutes ago. Derek . . . ?"

"On it," Frostbite said weakly, pulling himself away from
Steele, but then he staggered, and she caught him before he
could fall.

Jet strode over to Iridium, knelt to touch Hornblower's
shoulder. He was out cold, either from shock or pain. "I've got
him."

Iri crab-crawled out of the way as Jet created a Shadow
stretcher and lifted the unconscious man. Rising on another
floater, she tapped Ops. "Nearest hospital?"

A pause, then Meteorite said, "Cook County."

"Make sure they're expecting me."

"On it."

One hand on Tyler's shoulder, her tears hidden by her optiframes, Jet rushed to the hospital, praying to whoever was listening that she got there in time to save Tyler's life.

CHAPTER 30

IRIDIUM

Subject 3224, the child in question, is in our care. His parents are dead. The president of the board tells me it was a car accident. Natural causes. I ask myself do I care that he's lying? I'm afraid the answer is no.
—Matthew Icarus, diary entry dated March 3, 1991

Iridium felt heavy. She sat quietly in a corner of the super-secret clubhouse, watching the real heroes move to and fro. They were all slow, all weighted with fatigue and the knowledge of what had happened to Tyler.

That poor kid. Ass or not, Tyler wasn't any older or wiser than she was, and he'd gotten himself crippled trying to help her.

Derek sat next to her after a time. "I'm sure he'll make it."

"Hope so." Iridium massaged her forehead. A truly epic migraine was brewing.

"It wasn't your fault," Derek supplied.

"Fuck, Derek, I *know* that!" Her shout brought the room to a stop, Firebug and Steele and Meteorite all gawping at her.

Iridium didn't care anymore. After what had happened, she almost welcomed it. Their scorn and fear was familiar.

Their pity was what she couldn't stand.

"What?" she demanded. "You still think that if I have a bad day, I'm going to vaporize the lot of you and go knock over a bank?"

Meteorite put her arms out, placating. "Iridium, calm down . . ."

Snarling, Iridium grabbed Meteorite's headset and threw it as hard as she could. It snapped in two against the far wall. "Haven't I *proven* myself to you people? What do you *want* from me?"

"To stop yelling, probably," Taser said mildly.

She whirled to face him, ready for a fight.

Except he didn't want to fight. He was looking at her, his face stripped of its ski mask, his blue eyes sad and knowing. "We've all had it rough today. It's never easy to lose one of your own."

"Hey, man," Frostbite growled. "Don't talk about Tyler like you two are drinking buddies. You don't know him."

"And we didn't lose him," Iridium said. "He's going to live." She slumped back down, screwing up her face into her worst Villainess glare.

It was better than crying.

"It doesn't change the fact that Hornblower lost his leg because we were outgunned," Taser said, looking at each of them. "We need support, and more important, we need to have our heads in the game when we're out there. We can't do that if we're worrying about who left the coffeepot on back at HQ."

Meteorite frowned at him. "What are you talking about?"

"I was a Runner for over a year before I was assigned to Jet," Taser said. "I could contact the other Runners. They could give you the hero support you really need."

"Yes, because what will save New Chicago from rabid extrahumans and crazy scientists is a well-made sandwich and a shoulder rub," Frostbite said. His voice cracked with ice.

"Hey." Taser shrugged. "You can stay here and push buttons, Frostbite, or you can get back into the field. You seemed pretty natural out there today."

Frostbite went quiet at that. Iridium knew that he'd wanted

a real shot at heroing since he'd gotten sent away before graduation.

"Suppose we do," Meteorite said. "How can we trust these people? Half of them were reporting to Corp Executive Committee directly, reporting all our actions, our conversations. They weren't real Runners, like Derek and I. They were fucking spies and you all know it."

Steele looked shocked.

Iridium couldn't help it; she laughed. "So the rose-colored optiframes come off at last. Yes, your beloved Corp-Co had its hooks deep in you, in more ways than one."

"They wouldn't," Steele said, sounding hurt.

"They would." Firebug took her hand. "We *know* that, Harrie. They would."

"I only befriended Runners free of Corp meddling," Taser said, looking at Steele. "I'll get you good people. Scout's honor."

Steele sighed tiredly. "Fine. Do it."

Firebug removed her hand. "You don't get to decide for everyone, Harrie. Maybe I *like* fixing my own coffee."

"Jet's not here, and when Jet's not here I'm team leader," Steele said quietly, looking hard at Firebug, then at the others. "I'm making an executive decision. Anyone have a problem?"

Firebug huffed, her short, shocking orange hair puffing around her face. "No, no problem. That doesn't change the fact we're grossly outnumbered by rabids on the street. Or that regular people are suddenly turning into the Incredible Hulk with PMS."

"Agreed," Taser said. "Your first priority has *got* to be bringing in Martin Moore. Before he creates any more of these things."

"We can bug Everyman," Meteorite said, "since he's their pet dog."

"Not anymore," Iridium said, shaking her head. "He bombed their headquarters. I'd say that's a pretty clear *I'm just not that into you* message." She relayed how the interrogation with Bombshell went, leaving out the part that she'd let the wannabe go hobbling home to momma.

"Great," Frostbite muttered. "So we can't go leaning on Everyman."

"No big." Iridium leaned her head back against the wall, the cool metal of the team cafe doing little to soothe her muddle of thoughts. "Moore is just the lunatic fringe. Rabids are the immediate threat. Let Squadron: India deal with Moore and his sewer mutants."

Frostbite eyed her sharply. "Squadron: India is coming here?"

Fuck. She hadn't meant to let that slip. She still hadn't approached the others about Gordon, let alone about how she'd busted her father and five other villains out of Blackbird. If they found out now, there went all the goodwill she'd built up over the past two days, goodwill and trust she needed to get those same Corp hooks out of the Bradford family for good. Damn it, she had to pull it together. Iridium shrugged, making light of it. "That's the rumor."

Firebug blinked at her, disbelief etched on her face. "And where'd you hear that? The supervillain-talk-show broadcast?"

"I have my ear to the ground," Iridium retorted. "I hear things."

"Let it go," Steele said, shooting her partner a warning glance. "We have another matter to discuss."

Firebug glowered at Iridium, but she held her tongue. Iridium smiled sweetly. Lester said it confused people.

"Specifically, Doctor Hypnotic," Steele said. "It will only be a matter of time before thousands are under his control. What's our strategy?"

"Police," said Meteorite. "Raid his lair and take him back to Blackbird."

"Are you serious?" Iridium jerked up, feeling like someone was tugging her strings. "Human police? Like the humans Hypnotic is turning into zombies? Yeah, that'd work out great."

Meteorite's eyes frosted to gray. "You have a better idea?"

"I do," Iridium said. "Kill him."

Silence sat heavy for a moment. "Just like that," Frostbite said. "Kill him, full stop?"

"It's the only way to be sure," Iridium said. "Because you can't beat him, and sooner or later, Looptown is going to be another Siege of Manhattan. You can lose a thousand lives or one. Kill Hypnotic."

"The Squadron doesn't kill," Steele said crisply.

Iridium fixed the larger woman with her gaze. "Right. I'd forgotten about that little rule."

Jet wraps the grotesque in Shadow until the woman—if it is a woman—screams, then whimpers, then goes still. Leaching the warmth out of her deformed body. Leaching the life.

The Squadron did kill people. When Lynda Kidder had attacked Jet in the sewer, after Jet and Iridium had both gotten too close to Martin Moore's disgusting experiment, Jet hadn't even hesitated. She'd let the Shadow overwhelm Kidder, and almost herself as well.

The Squadron didn't kill. Bullshit. The memory triggered gooseflesh up and down Iridium's arms.

"Supposing we could," Taser said, facing Iridium. He, at least, was being reasonable. "How would we get close enough?"

"Get our own Mind power to jam Hypnotic," Iridium said. "Get close enough, and put two in his head."

"Just like that," Steele said. "I won't listen to this."

"Then maybe you should walk away, Harrie," Iridium said coldly. "You want to finish this thing with Hypnotic? Do it the way that makes sure he's really finished."

Steele said nothing for a moment as her dark gaze bored into Iridium. When she finally spoke, her words were scathingly soft. "You may play the hero, Iridium, but you're no better than your father."

Iridium got to her feet. The Squadron's casual treatment of her as a second-class extrahuman she'd stomach, but not this.

A hand clamped down on her shoulder. "Iri," Frostbite said. "Don't. Walk away. Get some air."

"All right," she said. "You've heard how to take care of your little supervillain problem. If you don't listen, then I can't help you."

They had already gone back to arguing when Iridium got her gear and stormed out.

————

Iridium ignored greetings from Protean and Lionheart, a sneer from Nevermore, and an indifferent "Where ya been, girl?" from Kindle before she found her father in her office.

With Gordon.

"*What* is *he* doing here?" she demanded.

Gordon had the nerve to smirk. "Just paying a social call on your dear father. It seems he's misplaced something."

"Oh?" Iridium rounded on Lester, who grimaced.

"Radar's done a bunk. Haven't seen him since yesterday morning."

Iridium's stomach dropped. "You let the deranged telepath out of the pen? Dad, are you *nuts*?"

"They're not children," Lester said icily. "I don't keep them under lock and key."

Iridium's headache returned with a vengeance. "Fine. I'll deal with Radar, like I should have done before. Instead of letting your pet villains sit around, why don't you have them patrol the grid?"

"You don't give the orders here," Gordon said. "Arclight does."

"Like hell. We're a team," Iridium snapped.

Gordon's lips twitched. "Not in the least. Not unless you want me to ask where you've been for two days."

Lester's eyes narrowed as he looked between Gordon and Iridium.

"What's he on about, girl?"

"*Nothing.*" Iridium had never wanted to wring the neck of anyone like she wanted to wring Gordon's now. The smarmy bastard was actually blackmailing her. In front of her own father.

"As I was saying," Gordon purred, "all of the team's resources should be devoted to finding Radar. We cannot allow him to run unsupervised about the city."

"He's not a child," Lester growled.

"I'm sorry, Mr. Bradford. Perhaps you preferred your cell and your Thorazine cocktail to the free air you're currently breathing?" Gordon folded his arms.

Lester's power snapped, all of the lights in the warehouse

flickering. For a moment, he was Arclight in all his villainous glory. Then he got himself under control. Iridium was grossly disappointed. "Fine," he said, holding out his hands. "We find Radar."

"Where is he likely to have gone?" Gordon asked. "He is a wretched little man with no friends or family."

"Hypnotic." Lester sighed, shaking his head. "Bloke's obsessed with Hypnotic. Likely he went searching for the zombies to gawk at the lair of the man himself."

"If that's true, Radar could be under Hypnotic's sway by now," Iridium said. "Dad, if Hypnotic controlled another Mental power, especially one like Radar . . ."

Lester was already reaching for his comm and belt. "You don't have to tell me what a disaster that would be." He looked at his daughter, and she saw real fear in his eyes. "I know full well, girl. I was there when it happened the first time."

Interlude

Alone in his apartment, Garth sits on his sofa, staring at nothing. One might think he, too, has fallen victim to the zombie plague. But Garth McFarlane isn't lost in a virtual paradise. Behind his sunglasses, his eyes are burning.

He thinks about what the EMT had told him when he'd taken Julie to the hospital two days ago.

It's like they're drugged.

No, they weren't suddenly drugged. More like they were in a trance.

On his lap, Garth's hands clench into fists.

Someone had done this. Someone put his wife in the hospital, had disrupted the lives of too many people to count. Who?

Garth reviews all the known Mind supervillains, and then all the Mind superheroes. The list is staggering.

He remembers, two days gone, hearing Frank Wurtham on the tele. The man's words tease Garth like a fickle lover: *We cannot depend on the authorities to take down these freaks of nature.*

No, he surely cannot.

A growl in his throat, Garth lunges for the phone and calls Terry. This time, Garth won't take no for an answer.

The Latent Network must be raised, before all of New Chicago falls into madness.

THEN

CHAPTER 31

VIXEN

3224 exceeds every expectation. What 1102 showed me was but a shadow of what this child can do. Such wonderful things he shows me. Even corporate is pleased.

—Matthew Icarus,
observation notes of Subject 3224, aged 7

Valerie had never gotten any lullabies as a child—she'd been training for the Squadron since she was five years old, and they fell asleep to learning audios, not singing.

But she tried, often making it up as she went along, and Callie nuzzled against her stuffed toys when Valerie laid her into the crib.

The door to the nursery swished open as she was tucking a blanket around Callie, and Valerie pressed her finger to her lips. "She just went down, Les."

Belatedly, she saw he was in his costume and his face was drawn sharp and hard. "Les," she said, going to him. "What is it?"

"Hal escaped the Mental wing about twenty-four hours ago," Lester murmured, mindful of the baby. He gripped Valerie's hands, pressing them between his palms. "He went to

New York . . . they're overwhelmed . . . there are hundreds of people hurt . . ." Lester dropped his forehead to his chest. "I have to go."

"I'll come with you." The words flew from her mouth before Valerie had a chance to consider them. "I'll call a Runner for Callie . . ."

"No," Lester said. "Val, you know what he's like. Since he . . . since he lost his mind."

"I do," Valerie said. She could still hear the screaming from the day Hal Gibbons had snapped. Nobody knew exactly why yet—Lester thought it had something to do with the comlinks Corp made them wear. Valerie thought, privately, that Hal had always been crazy and just stopped trying to hide it. "That's why I'm not leaving you alone."

"Luv," he said quietly, "you're still on maternity leave. They won't let you."

Of course. They. Corp. Corp, who thought it was perfectly fine to leave her a single mother as long as it looked good to the public face to have the Hero of New Chicago swooping to the rescue.

"If he hurts you," she whispered, "I am going to kill him. Whatever it takes."

Lester pressed his lips to her forehead. "I'll be back before you know it." He left the nursery, and Valerie pressed her hands over her face. In her crib, Callie woke up and began to cry.

CHAPTER 32

ANGELICA

Still trying to determine whether the Mental breakdowns were caused by the comlink, or if the earpiece simply sped up their inherent decay.

—From the journal of Martin Moore, entry #111

New York City might have once been the epicenter of the Americas, the place to be if you were anyone worth being, but that had been a long time ago. Way before the Manhattan Quarantine.

"He's taken over the Tompkins Square Projects," Major Victory shouted through the comm. "Ten buildings on the block, all low-income residential."

"Civvies, got it." Blackout grinned over at Angelica. "I love saving civilians."

"I still can't believe Hal's doing this," she said, feeling like she was underwater and trying to break through to the surface. Since they heard about Hal's escape from the Mental wing at the Academy, everything had felt dreamlike, unreal. And then word came he'd burrowed himself somewhere in New York City . . . and the casualty count had begun. Just thinking about those poor people made Holly feel sick. She wished Valerie were with them instead of home with the baby. "He's not well."

"Angelica, the mistress of understatement," said Luster, snorting. "He's acting like a textbook psychopathic megalomaniac on a bender. What's the count up to?"

"Fifty-three confirmed dead," Night said, his voice flat. "More than four hundred hospitalized."

Holly squeezed her eyes closed. *Oh, Hal. Why?*

"Come in via the police station on C and Eighth," Victory instructed, his voice breaking up with bursts of static. "Roof's equipped for hover and cruiser landings."

"On it."

Holly grimaced; Blackout sounded like he was loving this. In that crystalline moment, hearing the excitement in her husband's voice as they prepared to capture her former love, she hated George, hated having his baby inside of her. She gripped her armrests tightly as the cruiser dropped in free fall.

Another screech of static, then Victory said, "Lady Liberty's waiting for you. She'll brief you. Victory out."

"Bloody hell," Luster muttered. "Took New York hours before they decided to swallow their pride and let New Chicago in. Now they're going to fucking chaperone us while we rein in one of ours gone bad?"

"He's not bad," Holly said. "He's off his meds, that's all . . ." She shut her mouth when Luster shot her a disgusted look.

"He's killed fifty-three people, Angelica," Luster said coldly. "Made them play in traffic, or take knives to their wrists, or put guns to their mouths. And those are the ones who got off lucky. If that's not bad, I don't know what is."

She bit back a sob and said nothing.

Team Alpha rode in silence until the cruiser landed. As soon as the door opened, Blackout vaulted out, followed quickly by Luster and Night.

Holly Owens Greene closed her eyes and whispered a prayer that, somehow, they could stop Hal without hurting him. Then Angelica opened her eyes and joined her teammates.

Lady Liberty was, shock, another Lighter, using a fake torch as a power focus. She looked ridiculous in her long toga and pointed crown. And if she was going sleeveless, Angelica decided, she really needed to shave her pits. If Vixen were here, she probably would have said the same thing. Aloud.

Liberty didn't bother with introductions. "Police evacuated all of Alphabet City, and most people actually left, which is something. We've got Hypnotic pinpointed in the Projects, but we can't ferret him out to see which of the ten buildings he's calling home. His henchmen are making it all but impossible for us to get any reconnaissance."

"Henchmen?" Angelica asked, blinking.

"Innocents he's brainwashed into doing his bidding," Liberty said. "Hundreds of them."

Oh Christo.

"Why don't you gas them out?" Luster said.

Liberty rolled her eyes. "Gosh, thank you so much for the suggestion. We never would have thought of that, or already pushed through the request to have it sit on the mayor's desk for hours while he reviews the P&L of matériel and man-hours versus nonconstituent lives saved."

"Squatters?" said Night.

"Some. Mostly those who have better things to do on Election Day than vote." Liberty sniffed. "They got the 'unwashed masses' right, I'll give them that much. You ask me, we should let Hypnotic have them, just get us the hell out of this shit-hole island. But the governor will pitch a fit if we don't end this thing, immediately."

Angelica wanted to *push* her, bliss her out until she was a zombie, then shove her off the roof. She thought she showed remarkable restraint.

Less so, her husband. "So why're we wasting time with you?" Blackout flexed his fists. "Point the way, Libby, and then get out of the way."

Liberty narrowed her eyes. "Listen, you Shadow freak—"

"Children," Luster growled. "Behave."

The woman glowered at them all. "One block up Eighth will

bring you right to Tompkins Square. Try not to get killed." She stormed off, yanking open the roof door and letting it slam behind her.

"Start spreadin' the news," Blackout sang, rubbing his hands gleefully. "We're leavin' today."

"Christo, shut it." Night spread his arms wide, threw back his head as if trying to catch the sun's rays. Angelica's breath frosted, and she wrapped her cloak around herself. A river of black pooled beneath him, spreading out into a wide circle. "Hop on."

Angelica held on to Blackout's waist, and Luster put a hand on Night's shoulder. The four of them zoomed down, almost too fast for Angelica to take in the burned smell of the air, the thickness that threatened to suffocate.

"Black and White, back in action," Blackout said happily.

Night growled, "Please. Shut up."

Tompkins Square Projects loomed before them, concrete slabs that spoke of misery and abandoned dreams. "Blackout," Luster shouted over the rush of wind, "do your ghosting and report. Ignore the civilians. Hell, ignore the New York Squadron. Just go in, find Hypnotic, and report back."

The gleeful look on Blackout's face made Angelica's stomach pitch.

Blackout used the technique Night had coined Shadowsliding: He effectively transformed into a ghost, temporarily becoming part of the Shadow. As he ghosted into one of the buildings, Angelica and the others ushered off the civilian casualties—the entranced humans who were like movable dolls. The heroes loaded up person after person onto ambulance stretchers, and Blackout went into a second building, Shadowsliding, intangible, hunting for Doctor Hypnotic.

And then a third building. And a fourth.

Before he moved into the fifth, Angelica stopped him. "George, you're bleeding."

Blackout grinned at her as he wiped the trickle of blood from his nose. "Just greasing the works. It's nothing."

"It's hurting you," she said. "Stop. Rest. One of us can—"

"Can what?" he snarled. "Walk through walls? Be invisible? Not even our precious Night can do that, now can he?"

One of the others said something, but she tuned him out. Smiling to offset Blackout's coming rage, she put her hands up in surrender. "You're right." She *pushed*, just a smidge, to blunt his anger.

His eyes widened, glazing, and his mouth opened in a surprised O.

Someone spun her around roughly. Night. She stammered, "What're you—"

"Stop it," he hissed. "He can't touch the Shadow if you dope him."

"I'm not *doping* him, you idiot. I'm *calming* him."

"We don't need him calm. We need him to Shadowslide. Which he can't do if he's seeing visions of Light, or whatever your bullshit power is."

Behind her, Blackout said, "It's okay. I'm fine."

Angelica turned, but too late. Her husband was already gone.

Four minutes later, they all heard the scream from somewhere inside—an agonized scream that cut off abruptly.

CHAPTER 33

LUSTER

I know they'll ask me if I knew they were making these children into weapons. I know they'll ask about the missing parents, the experiments, the in vitro fertilization. I know someday, somebody will drag this into the light and they'll ask. I guess I'll lie.

—Matthew Icarus, diary entry dated 1991

Luster strobed the door to bits, and Night and Angelica went through the hole, colliding with dozens of Hypnotic's victims. It was like an old zombie movie, Lester thought, and didn't have time to think again before he started throwing strobes.

They had very little effect, and Angelica did little better. "This isn't working!" she screamed. "Do something!"

A slither of Shadow wrapped the nearest group of people in black, and after a few muffled screams, they went to ground.

"As always," Night said, his voice colder than his power against Luster's skin, "I will take care of this." He snapped another trio of creepers out at the crowd. "You two keep them off me."

Luster went back to strobing, aiming them at the floor rather than the people, throwing up a cloud of dust and concrete chunks that kept a radius between the heroes and Hal's victims.

Damn Hal to hell. How could he go so wrong, so quickly? Luster heard his own heartbeat in his ears, but he could also hear Hal's screaming the day they dragged him away.

He should have known then that Hal wouldn't just go away, fade into a shadow of himself as Moore and the Therapists ripped his mind out.

Luster should have known this day was coming. But he hadn't. And now . . .

"Hostiles!" Angelica screamed. Luster whipped his gaze to where she pointed and saw a trio of costumed heroes coming toward them—or flying, in one case. The New York Squadron, eyes white on white.

Night's breath was sawing in and out behind his mask. "I thought everyone in the NYC Squadron was down."

"Down but not out—duck!" Luster dropped as the leader shot a bolt of electricity at him. Night rolled the other way and Angelica darted around the man and strobed the largest of the three, a woman who had a good head and a half and two stone on Luster.

The woman shook off the strobe and slammed a punch into Angelica's gut. Angelica let out a cry before she retaliated by snapping the woman's wrist.

Just for a moment, Luster felt the unnerving hum in his head fade, and the members of the New York Squadron blinked as their eyes returned to normal.

Then it returned, making Luster grind his teeth. "Angelica!" he shouted. "Call to him!"

"What?" she screamed.

"Hal!" Luster shouted. "He heard you! Call him!"

Angelica just stared at him as the New York Squadron closed in again.

CHAPTER 34

ANGELICA

If Icarus had known how dangerous these creatures were, he'd have aborted them in their mother's wombs and destroyed his research.

—From the journal of Martin Moore, entry #127

He heard you," Luster shouted again, then ducked to avoid a muscleman's oversized fist. "When you cried out before, Hypnotic heard you! He'll hear you again. Call him!"

Angelica delivered a roundhouse kick to a woman in green. "How's he supposed to hear me in all this?" It was so loud with all the fighting, she could barely hear herself think.

"He's a nutter, but he's still mad about you! Do it!"

Angelica thought Luster was certifiable, but she did as her teammate commanded. "Hal," she cried out, her voice muted by the sounds of battle around her. "It's me, Holly! Let me talk to you!"

The attacking Squadron halted, suddenly turned off.

Okay. That's creepy. She, Luster, and Night fell into a holding pattern: loose circle, back-to-back-to-back, arms and legs in ready positions. She breathed heavily through her nose, forced her heartbeat to slow. Around them, seven of the New York Squadron stood immobile.

"Holly." Hal's voice echoed all around, from everywhere and nowhere. Points for Holly that she didn't flinch. "How lovely of you to visit."

"Hypnotic!" Luster shouted. "Quit pissing around and get your arse down here! You've a lot to answer for—"

A flash of light, blinding and brilliant. Angelica, her back to Luster and Night, caught it only peripherally. She threw her arm over her eyes, pivoted away. Waited a heartbeat, two, three.

Realized that Luster was no longer shouting.

She lowered her arm and slowly turned to face the others. Luster and Night both were standing utterly still, their arms hanging loosely by their sides.

Oh Christo.

"That's better," Hal said. "He's always had a mouth on him, hasn't he?"

She swallowed thickly, told herself not to be afraid. This was Hal. Hal wouldn't hurt her.

A small voice wormed inside her brain, saying, *But Doctor Hypnotic killed more than fifty people. He hurt your husband. He just took down your teammates without even blinking.*

So she'd have to appeal to Hal, not to Hypnotic.

"Hal," she said, her voice surprisingly clear, "what have you done with Blackout?"

"Is that the only reason you came to see me? To get your husband back?" He clucked his tongue. "Holly. I'm hurt."

"No you're not."

"You're right," he murmured in her ear. "I'm lonely."

She stiffened, refused to turn around. "There are better ways to make friends and influence people, Hal."

His hands on her shoulders. "Oh, I don't know. I think I'm pretty good at influencing people."

"You've been hurting innocents."

"Mmm. Yes. Killing them too." His lips on her neck.

"Do you hear the words you're saying, Hal? Do you understand what you've done?"

"Not really my fault, the killing part. I've just been so depressed. I guess I've been projecting." His tongue darted between his lips, licking. Stroking her wetly.

She clenched her teeth to keep from reacting. "Hal, you have to stop. Turn yourself in before you hurt anyone else." Like George—where was George?

Laughter peppered against her skin. "Who should I turn myself in to, Holly? Corp?"

"Of course. Dr. Moore will help you, make you well again—"

"Who do you think hurt me the most?" Another kiss, feather soft. "Who do you think took you away from me?"

"No one took me away, Hal. I fell in love. It just happened."

More laughter, bitter now. "It's what he told you to do."

A pause, as Holly felt the world stop. She choked out, "What are you—"

His fingers dug inside her left ear, pulled out her comlink. He held it in front of her face.

"This, Holly. This has been controlling you, you and everyone else, ever since they put it in your ear." His fingers opened, and the device fell to the ground. She heard him stomp on it, grind it to junk.

She swallowed thickly. "Hal . . . I fell in love with George before Corp gave out the comlinks."

"Holly, you don't remember what they did to you. But I do. They controlled me, forced me to bring you to them. And then they cut open your mind."

Holly wanted to faint. She wanted to scream at him to shut up, that he was lying to her, but . . .

. . . but a tiny voice whispered that he was telling the truth.

"They made you his sex toy, and all I could do was watch. And now they made you his broodmare. You've got his whelp inside of you, all because they decided a child would distract Blackout, would let them better control him. *His* child," Hal growled, "growing in you, all on the whim of Dr. Moore."

Holly couldn't breathe.

"Even before they took you, they were controlling you, controlling us. All of us, with Dr. Moore's drugs. The Runners put them everywhere. In your food. In your drink. They were in you whenever we made love."

Too much. It was all too much. He had to be lying to her. Because if he was telling the truth, her entire life was a sham. "Stop it, Hal."

"I killed Dr. Moore first. Slowly. I made him see just how evil he really was. He dug out his own eyes."

"Stop it!"

"Don't you see, Holly? He made you stop loving me. He made you go to the Shadow."

George.

"The world is a better place without him. I'm just sorry his brother escaped. I had something special planned for little Martin." He chuckled wetly.

Fear on her tongue, now, thick and sour. "Please. Hal. Where's George?"

Both hands back on her shoulders, pressing lightly. "We talked."

She whispered, "What did you do to him?"

A pause, then the massaging continued. "He's just sleeping, Holly. If I'd killed him, that would have hurt you. I'd never hurt you. I love you."

Holly closed her eyes, made the decision that would haunt her for the rest of her days. "Hal," she said, a small purr in her voice. "I knew you'd save me." Then she turned around, pulled his face down to hers, and kissed him deeply, allowed herself to remember just how much she once had loved being with him, how he'd made her feel.

He responded, opening wide.

When the kiss ended, she looked up into his dark eyes and smiled. "I love you too."

Doctor Hypnotic let out an ecstatic roar, then he embraced the woman he loved.

Holly kissed him again, memorizing the feel of him on her lips, taking in his scent until she felt giddy.

And then she kneed him in the balls.

CHAPTER 35

NIGHT

One common trait in Mental powers: Too much exposure
leaves the recipient fragmented—sometimes, permanently.
—From the journal of Martin Moore, entry #8

Night blinked, then blinked again. He'd been in a world of darkness—a world of the Dark—and he had been worshipped as a god. No sun; no spotlight; no heroes or villains or humans begging to be saved from themselves. Just Night, and the strongest—the most worthy—of the extrahumans.

And the Shadow, of course. Everything belonged to the Shadow.

That hadn't been real.

But, oh Jehovah, how he wanted it to be real. Even now, he could hear the whispers, the Shadow voices urging him to make it real, to turn that delectable vision into a window of the world. A better world. A dark world.

It wasn't real.

But it could be.

He shook his head to clear it. And then he saw Luster next to him, rubbing his head and . . . blushing?

"I'm going to kill that bastard," Bradford muttered.

Who . . . ?

Hypnotic.

Night spun to the left, and there was Angelica . . .

. . . kissing Hypnotic? Madness. She had to be under his control.

Night snarled and summoned the Shadow, ready to take them both down if necessary—but then Angelica slammed her knee into Hypnotic's crotch. And she hit him again, and again: balls and chin and gut, slamming her fists and her knees and her feet into him, again and again. She was screaming like a madwoman every time her skin connected with his.

And Hypnotic let her. He didn't raise a hand to stop her. Didn't use his Mental power to mesmerize her.

Hypnotic loved her, Night realized. And it was love that betrayed him and defeated him.

Poetic. And that was also why Night never allowed himself to fall in love; inevitably, it would end poorly, either in tears or blood or both. Better to be alone and be certain than to be in love and risk everything.

"What . . . ?" That was Blackout, pulling himself up from the floor. "Holly?"

As Blackout ran over to his shrieking wife, Night took a quick count of the people in the room, most of them snapping out of Hypnotic's spell. The extrahumans—their New York compatriots—were coming around, but most of the civilians whom Hypnotic had used were still down for the count from when Night had smothered them in Shadow. At least they were still alive.

Night frowned, thinking of all the men and women who'd lost their lives to Hypnotic's insanity. Thinking of how he himself was responsible for those deaths.

Thinking that he didn't really care.

Night clenched his fist. He *had* to care. He was supposed to save humans, not allow them to be used as pawns, to be caught in the extrahuman cross fire.

Fifty-three people. That was how many Hypnotic had killed.

That was how many people Night had sent to their deaths when he whispered a lie to Hypnotic and gave him the medicine that would help him go free.

Fifty-three dead. And he couldn't bring himself to care.

Christo, he didn't care.

Someone was screaming.

No, *people* were screaming. Angelica, who was now wrapped in Blackout's loving arms. The New Yorker strongman, Major Victory, who was punching through the walls. Another New Yorker, Bonfire, who was clawing at his eyes and bleeding fire.

And Night himself. He was screaming to prove that he cared, screaming to drown out the Shadow voices whispering in his mind, telling him that they would help him bring the darkness to the world.

A hand on his shoulder. "Night," said Luster. "Rick. Come on, Rick. It's done now. Our girl's taken him down. It's all right now."

"No," Night whispered, his voice raw. "It's not."

That was when Bonfire lit up like a dying sun, shrieking to the heavens as he burned away his flesh.

"Look out," one of the New Yorkers yelled, "he's going nova!"

Major Victory slammed his fists through another section of wall just as Bonfire went critical. The building groaned, and the walls seemed to tilt—and in a scream of metal and concrete, the whole place came down.

They all would have died if not for the New Yorker called Barricade. Her force field shielded them as the building crashed on top of them.

They made it out, and they tried to save the people—those normals whom Hypnotic had entranced—who'd been buried in the rubble. A handful got out. Most didn't.

It was a long, silent ride home. Night stared out the window, his thoughts dark. If he noticed the Shadow licking at his eyes, he ignored it. When everything was dark, one Shadow was no more noticeable than another.

Back in New Chicago, Corp debriefed them. Angelica spoke for them, because Luster, Night, and Blackout claimed they didn't remember much after they'd gone in after Hypnotic. Night wondered if they were lying. He could remember.

Even now, he could see that dark, dark world, and him as its god.

Angelica told a story of how they'd all fought bravely and how Hypnotic, defeated, played his last card: He controlled Bonfire's mind and forced the man to blow up the building in a firebomb.

Corp bought it. Then they set up the press conference. This time, it was Luster who lied smoothly for the vids. The story had a happy ending: The traitorous villain, Doctor Hypnotic, would be tried by jury, and, assuming he was found guilty, he would be as Luster put it, "abso-bloody-lutely sentenced to life in Blackbird, medicated to the point of coma." The media loved them.

Luster went home to his wife and child. Blackout and Angelica went home to console each other between the sheets.

Night learned the names of everyone who died in what the press had dubbed the Siege of Manhattan. The number was far greater than fifty-three. For a little while, he pretended that he cared about those deaths. And then the day came when he stopped pretending.

If anyone noticed the deeper chill in his voice, or the dark cast of his gaze, they didn't say anything.

CHAPTER 36
TEAM ALPHA

Blackout showing renewed signs of decay. Decommission-
ing out of the question; Corp-Co too invested in its Siege of
Manhattan celebrities. May require Therapy. Will con-
tinue observation.

—From the journal of Martin Moore, entry #170

The most innocent of things can lead to the most damning of consequences.

This particular game of telephone didn't actually use phones or communicators or comlinks. It began a month after the Siege of Manhattan.

. . . Angelica, still horrified over what her old love had become, told Vixen what Doctor Hypnotic had confided to her—that Corp had forced her to fall in love with Blackout, and that the earpieces were tools to control their minds. Sheer lunacy, of course, but there were times when Angelica would catch herself thinking "What if . . . ?" Vixen patted her hand and told Angelica that between the stress and the pregnancy, Angelica was not thinking too clearly, and everything would be better once she had the baby.

Six weeks go by.

. . . Vixen, exhausted after yet another sleepless night (damned colic) mentioned to Luster that Hypnotic had accused Corp of raping Angelica's mind and enslaving her to Blackout. That led to a heated discussion about Hypnotic, whom Luster thoroughly despised, and *that* led to Vixen distracting him with a kiss. She didn't mention the bit about the comlinks brainwashing extrahumans; frankly, she thought that was complete cowcrap, and Lester was in no mood for such nonsense.

Eighteen months come and go.

. . . Luster, patrolling with Blackout, was horribly shorttempered because Vixen had had a miscarriage yesterday and Luster had spent the whole night holding her and telling her he loved her and everything was going to be okay, so when Blackout made a bad joke about Vixen getting her girlish figure back, Luster snapped that Blackout would be better off focusing on his own wife even if their marriage was a sham—that everyone knew the only reason Angelica was with Blackout was because Corp made her do it. Luster apologized immediately, and sheepishly told Blackout about the miscarriage and said he hadn't meant it about Angelica, and Blackout said he completely understood and was so very sorry for their loss . . . but then he became strangely quiet and said nothing for a very, very long time. Luster, who was grieving, was too upset to notice.

One day passes.

. . . Night, sparring with Blackout, commented that the other Shadow power was fighting poorly, and he asked what was wrong. Blackout wondered aloud if Angelica truly loved him. Night, who didn't care about such things, merely shrugged and suggested they continue sparring. He noticed splotches of Shadow staining Blackout's eyes as they fought, but Night decided that was simply from the physical exertion.

The very next night, Blackout hit Angelica for the first time.

Interlude

So," Jose says after a long sip of coffee. "Any word from the hospital?"

Garth manages not to slam his fist through the table. "None. Julie's like everyone else that's been brought in: catatonic."

It's enough to drive a person mad. No help from the nurses at the hospital, and even less from the doctors. No one knows anything, other than the hospitals are overflowing with zombies.

A hand claps him on the shoulder. "Hang tough, mate," Terry says. "She'll pull through. She's no porcelain doll."

Garth wants to punch in Terry's dentures. If the man had agreed to have the Latent Network up and running, maybe Julie would be sitting by Garth's side even now. But no—lashing out at the leader of their ragtag group wouldn't help matters, especially since now, at least, Terry was willing to hear him out.

Although punching Terry would make Garth feel a hell of a lot better.

The five of them take up the small card table in Jose's back room: wiry Jose, beanpole Luke, broad Terry, hardened Claire, and Garth himself, each with a minor power that keeps them safely off Corp's radar. As if old Terry with his minor control of levitation could be Squadron material, or scar-faced Claire with her ability to sharpen knives. Jose could whisk away dust with a thought. Luke's cast-iron stomach and unbreakable teeth let him bite through and eat anything, which was a plus whenever he'd tackled Julie's cooking.

Ah, Julie.

Garth grimaces, pushes away her image. *She'll be all right. She has to be all right.*

He'd just finished telling the others about what had happened over the past few days, from the fights in the street to Arclight's crashing into his apartment to Julie and the others falling victim to the so-called zombie plague. And now he's waiting for Terry to tell him that yes, the Latent Network will become active, and to hell with Corp and being discovered.

But time passes as Garth and the others sip coffee and half listen to the newscast in the background as the tele blares. And Terry doesn't say shite about it.

Garth drains his coffee and slams down his cup. "So what's it going to be? We going to sit here and watch the world burn? Or are we going to do something about it?"

Silence from his friends. In the background, the newsie blathers about Mayor Lee condemning extrahuman activity— possibly even those who have been helping the police and National Guard. "They cannot be trusted," the mayor rants. His voice sounds tinny and ineffective.

"Do what?" Terry finally says. His voice is old and strong, his tone is thoughtful. "Tell me how we're supposed to stop this insanity and I'll happily listen."

"Just get out there," Garth replies, pointing toward the door and beyond that, to the city. "Do the little we can do. Something's got to be better than nothing."

"We're not real extrahumans," Jose says with a shrug. "Barely any *extra* there. We'd get killed."

"Something's better than nothing," Garth repeats, his voice a growl. "We call up the whole Network, get everyone to come out. Yeah, there are hundreds of Squadron members gone bad, but we've got a *thousand* tucked away."

"A thousand wannabes," Claire grumbled. "None of them battle trained." She, of course, could hold her own—the woman had been in more knife fights than Garth could count.

"And all living normal lives," Jose says. "Paying bills. Avoiding Corp. We get involved now, we can't go back to that."

"There may not be anything to go back *to*," Luke says quietly, and Garth could kiss him for having his back. "The city's in ruins, and Corp's still not saying anything about it.

And it's not just New Chicago. The Americas are dying, man. The Squadron's gone mad, and they're destroying everything."

"What're you supposed to do?" Jose asks. "Eat the country to safety?"

Claire stiffens in her seat. "Guys."

Luke snarls, "Now look—"

"Boys," Terry sighs, "come on, this won't help . . ."

"Help what?" Garth demands. "We're not helping *anything*."

"Guys! Shut it, will you?" Claire points to the tele. "Listen to this."

Garth pivots in his seat, and he sees on screen a text banner declaring DOCTOR HYPNOTIC AT LARGE. The anchor, the lovely Gena Mead, looks appropriately serious as she tells the world, "It's been confirmed that the supervillain Doctor Hypnotic has in fact escaped from Blackbird and is at large."

A clip appears: Commissioner Wagner, looking haggard. "Harold Gibbons, known to the world as Doctor Hypnotic, has escaped Blackbird Prison. Citizens are strongly encouraged to stay off the streets until he, along with the other former Squadron members, have been captured."

Right, Garth thinks. *Just stop our lives for the next who knows how long. Just stay cowering in our holes while the gods duke it out.*

Wagner is bombarded with questions, but one stands out: "Commissioner, does Doctor Hypnotic's mind control have any bearing on the zombie plague infesting New Chicago?"

"Too soon to be determined," he says grimly.

"However," Gena breaks in, "some are already pointing to Hypnotic as the cause of what's being called the zombie plague. Specifically, the few Squadron members who haven't, as they call it, gone rabid."

The image shifts to a black screen, and a woman's voice is heard as the text appears along with the spoken words: "Not all Squadron members have gone rabid. There are a handful of us still sworn to protect the citizens of New Chicago and all of the Americas, and we're doing everything we can. Our top priority is bringing in Doctor Hypnotic and curtailing the effects of his mind control." The speech is attributed to the strongwoman Steele.

"That message from Steele was delivered to Commissioner Wagner earlier today," Gena says. "Whether that will sway Mayor Lee, who is still contemplating whether to ban all things extrahuman, remains to be seen."

Her coanchor dives into another story—the stock market has continued its swan dive—and Jose clicks off the tele.

None of them speak.

Doctor Hypnotic. Garth's mind is churning so fast, he can barely think. A Mind power in a long line of Mind powers with the same name. He'd flipped two decades ago and gone rabid. When he'd tried to take over New York, thousands of people had lost their minds. Hundreds had died. Garth had been a teenager at the time, but he still recalled the despair in the streets, the palpable sense of fear and loss that had filled the air. Until Hypnotic had been captured, no one had been safe.

He thinks of all the people already in the hospitals, their minds captured.

"You still think we should sit around," Garth says softly, "and wait until we succumb to the zombie plague?"

All of them agree that they can't just wait to be ensnared.

"But what do we do?" Jose asks, sounding like a man going under for the third time.

Terry shakes his head. "I don't know. But one thing's clear." He eyes Garth, and when he speaks again he doesn't sound anywhere close to seventy. "We're calling in the Network."

NOW

CHAPTER 37

JET

Project Sunstroke proceeds. Good news: No rats died in the transformation.

—From the journal of Martin Moore, entry #295

Jet hated hospital waiting rooms.

Meteorite had worked her magic, because when Jet had arrived with Hornblower she was met immediately by the trauma team, who quickly shunted her out of the way and fell on Hornblower like lions on an antelope. When Jet refused to leave, she was ushered to a private room by an ER nurse, who told Jet in no uncertain terms that she was to wait there. "In case we need you," the nurse said. Jet knew it was to get her far away from the public, whose patience with extrahumans was coming to a crashing end.

So she'd settled down in an uncomfortable chair. And she waited. She owed Hornblower that much. If she hadn't frozen—if she would have blanketed the mutants sooner—then Tyler would still have both legs.

It was very straightforward, all cause and effect. Hornblower was being operated on right now because she hadn't reacted soon enough. She knew this. She might have felt it, too, except she was numb on the inside. Cold.

Shadowed.

She replayed the fight in her mind, again and again. She saw herself freeze instead of blanket the mutants immediately.

She heard Hornblower's agonized scream.

I did that, she told herself. *I didn't act appropriately and I cost him his leg. Maybe his life.*

It was the fourth time she replayed the battle that she realized she'd nearly attacked Taser . . . and that the Shadow voices had been silent all the while. She'd danced on the edge of madness, and this time there was only herself to blame.

It should have made her feel angry, or terrified. It should have made her feel something other than this empty chill, this almost clinical detachment.

She wondered if you knew when you were going crazy.

As she sat alone in the small spartan room, she tapped into Ops periodically to get status reports: The group had deposited the mutants at Illinois State Prison without a hitch (at least something had gone right, she thought); Taser was rounding up the Runner network (he'd probably want some sort of payment after); Iridium had reported there was a rumor that Squadron: India would be entering the arena (maybe they'd all live to see that day happen). Tail-chasing conversations about how to stop Hypnotic. Iridium storming out instead of turning on Steele.

Jet leaned her head back against the wall and closed her eyes. Something had to go their way. They couldn't keep on at this pace—even if the Runners did come back to help them, there were only a handful of extrahumans doing the job of hundreds.

She never thought she'd feel so old at twenty-two.

"Jet?"

She opened her eyes, sat forward. Her neck complained hugely, and her teeth had grown fuzzy. Blinking away the dregs of sleep, she looked up at the duty nurse. "Yes?"

"I wanted to tell you," the nurse said, a tired smile on her face. "He's going to pull through."

Midnight—the witching hour. Jet allowed herself a tiny smile as she glanced down at her city. Backlit by the full moon, she hovered in the air like some darkling angel, Shadows playing on her face as she beheld her charge.

From up on high, New Chicago didn't look like a city under siege. But maybe that was because the pollution layer made it difficult to see the numerous fires still going—the remnants of local battle zones—or smell the telltale stench of ozone. In the sky, the problems of the ground seemed storybookish and faint, whispers of barely remembered dreams.

She could only just make out the National Guard patrolling the streets and air, riding the currents like khaki fish. At this time, most citizens were safely tucked in their beds, even before Mayor Lee's curfew had come into effect—but she'd seen some in the streets, unmoving, unblinking, the latest victims of the so-called zombie plague. The few she'd spied had been in Grid 21. Looptown.

Hypnotic's grid.

She'd called those cases into Ops, and either Meteorite or Frostbite had taken it the next step and got EMTs on the scene. Jet had hovered in the shadows, holding vigil until the entranced citizens had been safely removed, packed into ambulances like boards.

Troubled, Jet had taken to the sky, as if she could seek answers in the weak starlight. But if there were portents written in the stars, she couldn't read them.

Hal's voice, thick with promise: *I can give you a better world, Joan.*

They had to deal with Hal, with Doctor Hypnotic, and soon. But how? How did they convince a Mind power to stop pulling people out of their everyday lives and into a better place, deep within their minds?

How did they take him down without hurting the ones in their way—or falling under his power as well? Could they gas him out? That wouldn't harm any hostages he might have, and it would be a bloodless win—unless someone had an adverse reaction to the gas. And then there was the question of getting close enough to gas him without succumbing to his power, let alone where they'd be able to get the gas. Maybe beg the military . . .

She hadn't intended to linger, but Ops must have registered her position because soon Meteorite was speaking in her ear: "Babe. Where are you?"

Jet cast one more look at the stars. "Taking in the view before I patrol."

"You should get some sleep."

"I've been sleeping for two days," she said tersely. "I can go a little longer."

"Tomorrow's going to be a big day," Meteorite scolded. "Taser's been working overtime to pull in Runners. He swears tomorrow we'll have our own elves helping us once more."

"I'm sure he'll bill us appropriately."

"Don't get snarky. You know we need this."

Yes, they did. Jet closed her eyes, pictured Bruce's sensual lips pulled into a bemused smile. Damn him to Darkness.

"Derek and I are going to have our hands full tomorrow, if Taser's true to his word. Even if he only manages to bring in a quarter of the bodies he's promising, the two of us will have to train them on the network, and then we'll have to assign schedules and administrative duties, and start the PR machine, and . . ." Her voice trailed off, and Jet pictured Meteorite's eyes clouding over from all the things she needed to tackle.

"I can't think of anyone else better equipped to handle it," Jet said.

The other woman chuckled. "You're so full of shit, Jetster, but thanks. My point is, we're going to be stretched thin tomorrow, which means we're going to need you and the others to help us. So make it a fast patrol, then come back to get some sleep." A pause. "Running yourself to exhaustion won't help Tyler."

"Don't," Jet said softly.

"Whatever. Unless there's a situation, I'll expect you here in twenty. Even the rogues and rabids have to sleep sometime." Ops clicked off.

Jet flew down until she was streetside, skimming the road on her floater as she glanced up and down the blocks, scanned storefronts, checked alleyways. Even the rats in the sewers were silent tonight. Maybe, after a week of nearly incessant violence, the city was finally catching its breath.

No—there, around that corner was a man on his hands and knees, shaking his head as if to clear it. Surrounding him in a loose ring were three figures, youths from the size of them, toughened by their leathers and steel. Grendels, based on their clothing. One of them kicked the man in the ribs, the sound of impact slightly louder than the man's grunt of pain.

A week ago, Jet would have announced her intentions, given the gang members a chance to surrender peacefully. Tonight, she wasn't in the mood to play by the book. Gliding over on her floater, she reached out with her power, wrapping all three teens in Shadow. No more hesitation, not after what had happened with Tyler. By the time she was at the man's side, all three Grendels had stopped struggling. She released the Shadow, the ghost of their light clinging to her power like a desperate lover. Jet shuddered as the blackness sank into her body.

Light . . . it was so *good*.

"Citizen," she said crisply, offering the doubled-over man a hand, "do you need an ambulance?"

"I'm fine" was the reply, more grunts than actual words.

"You shouldn't be out after curfew," she remarked, making ready to leave. "Sometimes, bad things happen in the dark."

"And you would know, eh, Jet?" The man pushed himself up, and Jet was surprised to see it was Commissioner Wagner. "Thanks for your help."

"You're welcome, sir." She steadied him as he wobbled. Light, he looked horrible—in the moonlight, the Shadows around his eyes stood out like a raccoon's mask. "What happened?"

"My fault," he answered gruffly, shaking off her help. "Too busy thinking, not busy watching my back. It's been a long week. Didn't even get my gun out," he said with a bitter laugh. "Maybe I'm getting too old."

"You just need some rest," she said, fully aware that if

Meteorite was listening, she'd be getting an earful when she re-turned to Squadron HQ.

"Don't we all." He lowered his head, perhaps to regain his composure. Just as she was about to inquire if he needed help, he said quietly, "I like you, Jet. I have only respect for you. You should know that."

Her cheeks flushed. Embarrassed, she said, "Thank you, sir."

"Don't. Because unless something changes in the next two days, Lee's going to officially declare all extrahumans terror-ists." He looked up at her then, meeting her gaze. "All of them. No exceptions."

She tried to school her face to impassivity. Meteorite hadn't been exaggerating. Damn it. "Thank you for the warning, Commissioner."

"You won't thank me if I'm the one leading the chase to throw you into Blackbird." He let out a tired sigh, then gri-maced as he rubbed his side. "If you can stop this madness, you better do it soon."

"Understood," she said softly. "May I drop you off at home, sir?"

A smile flitted across his lips, there and then gone. "I can manage." He motioned to the unconscious thugs. "I'll call this in, stay until they're carted off to a holding cell. And then I'll catch a ride. You should go."

Translation: Others in New Chicago's Finest wouldn't ap-preciate Jet's company. "Understood," she said again, but this time the word tasted bitter on her tongue. No matter what she did, it would never be enough.

Miserable, Jet soared away. If the commissioner said any-thing else to her, it was left far behind on the dark, dark street.

CHAPTER 38

IRIDIUM

*I thought about leaving once. Corporate put me in a room
with a child who can see thoughts, lies. They made it clear
I wasn't going anywhere. I wasn't really going to do it, but
now I know how important my work is to them. Miranda,
I'm so sorry.*

— Matthew Icarus, diary entry dated 1993

Hypnotic's lair was as Iridium remembered it, except for
the people gathered around it in twos and threes, staring
at nothing, not even blinking.

They were mostly the homeless kids who huddled in the
lost corners of Looptown, or prostitutes and panhandlers. The
people who had no one to take them away to a hospital, to help
them when Hypnotic stole their consciousness. Her people.

Protean waved his hand in front of one of the bum's faces.
"You have to wonder what he's seeing."

"Something a sight better than this city, I hope," Kindle
muttered.

"Quiet," Arclight hissed. "Unless you *want* the madman
turning this city into zombies to know we're coming."

"Check comms," Iridium said, trying not to let her father's
tension spill over to her own feelings. "That's the only thing

that might save you if you get too close to Hypnotic. Listen to your comms, not his voice. If *anyone* starts to feel funny, get out. Don't wait, just go."

"Arclight," her father said into his mouthpiece. Iridium deliberately kept a distance between them.

"Protean on comms," said Protean. Then he added to Arclight, "Do you think Radar is really in there?"

"Hard to say," said Lester. "But I can't think of anywhere else he'd go running to."

"Lionheart on comms." The big shapeshifter hunched and slid into his namesake, a male lion at least twice the size of the actual beast.

"Kindle here," Kindle said, snapping flame to life on his palms.

Well, if she had to go into battle against Hypnotic, Iridium supposed she could have a worse team behind her. Even if they were criminals. After all, so was she.

The front door of the building rolled back of its own accord. Iridium smirked. Parlor tricks. In a way they made her feel better—if Hypnotic was trying to scare them, his hold on the city might not be as disastrous as she'd thought.

"Looks like the madman knows we're here," Lionheart growled, the human words sounding bestial from his lion's throat. He made as if to leap through the open door.

"Wait." Lester glanced up. "Nevermore, what's the status from up above? Are we clear?"

He clicked his earpiece when only static answered. "Nevermore? Where are you, girl?"

Iridium darted her eyes skyward, no inkblot shape soared above. "Dad. She's gone."

Lester cursed and ripped his earpiece out, storming ahead into the building. "Hal, damn you! Give me back my people!"

Before she could stop him, calm him down, Lester abandoned his stance, face white, nostrils flaring. "Not again," he muttered. "Not this time."

"Dad, wait!" Iridium shouted, lunging for him.

Lester shook her off and rushed into Hypnotic's lair.

Iridium turned back to the three villains peering nervously

into the building. "What are you waiting for, Santa Claus and his merry elves?" she shouted. "Get moving! Find Radar and Nevermore!"

She didn't wait to see if they listened to her—she had to catch up to her father. "Dad. *Dad.* Get back here!"

The layout was nothing like she remembered it from finding Jet sprawled unconscious on the floor. Now there were corridors, walls, endless labyrinthine passages that twisted back on themselves like a snake . . .

Iridium grabbed her forehead and shut her eyes. *A trick. Just a trick. A trick of the light.* Hypnotic was trying to confuse her, frighten her. Iridium fixed the real building layout in her mind, kept the orderly blueprint as a floodgate against her terror and opened her eyes again. "Dad!"

From behind her, Lionheart groaned. He'd lain down, massive head on his paws, and his eyes fluttered closed.

"Oh, bollocks," Kindle whispered. His face was sheet-white as he stared at the massive lion slumbering on the ground.

"We have to retreat," Protean said sharply. He extended his hand to Iridium. "Come on, girl."

Iridium shook her head. "I'm not leaving!"

"You can't save your father if you're captured."

From deeper within the warehouse came an anguished scream. Lester's scream. Iridium jerked free of Protean's grip.

"Run," he whispered.

"Come on, girlie," Kindle shouted. "You haven't a Mental power. You can't resist him!"

"He's got my dad!" She headed down the corridor, determined to find Arclight.

Behind her, she heard Kindle's scathing curse. "Don't you fade on me, you big lug! Protean! Greg?" Kindle's voice was small. "Ah, bollocks, man. What's he making you see? Don't cry . . ."

Gritting her teeth, Iridium kept moving.

"Girlie," Kindle shouted. "Save yourself . . ." And then he started to scream.

Iridium turned to see blue fire blossoming all around, a wall of heat far worse than her own strobes.

"Get away," Kindle screamed, thrashing his arms. "Get away from me!"

Iridium didn't need any more encouragement. She ran deeper into Hypnotic's lair. Everything faded but the single thought: She had to save her father.

Bruce looked up when she came through the door. His sleeves were rolled up and he had a dish towel slung over his shoulder. "You're out of breath, darlin'. Where's the fire?"

Iridium froze against the door, her heart thudding against her ribs. "What in Christo's name?"

"Sweetie, are you okay?" Bruce waved his hand at the sensor to shut off the water and turned to look at her. Frowning, he approached.

Iridium summoned a strobe. She had a vertiginous, nauseous churning in her guts, like she was on a hover in free fall. It wasn't right, wasn't safe . . . "Stay the *fuck* away from me, Taser."

"Callie, you can't be freaking out," Bruce said gently. "You know that reporter from the *Tribune* is in the living room."

"You're not real." Iridium batted at him when he tried to reach out and stroke her face. "None of this is real!"

"Callie," Bruce sighed. "I know you're under a lot of stress with your dad being sick, but it's going to be okay. I'm here for you."

"My dad's fine," Iridium whispered. She ducked Taser's arm and grabbed a butcher knife from the sink. "You're not real. You're Hypnotic."

Bruce's face flickered with concern. "You don't know what you're saying."

Iridium shoved the butcher knife against his neck. "I'm not one of those brainwashed superheroes, *Hal*. I didn't get Corp programming in my head to make me nice and malleable. I know you're just showing me what you think I want to see, but you're a bad guesser."

Black rolled over Iridium's vision.

"But is it Hypnotic?" a voice purred. "Or is it much closer to home?" A rough, stubby hand caressed her face. "Open your eyes, Calista. See what's right in front of you."

When she opened her eyes, she was back in the old apartment building. Radar was staring back at her, his eyes gleaming. Iridium tried to jerk away, but the little man was far stronger than he looked.

"You?" Iridium said. "Not Hypnotic? This is all your doing?"

Black again, and Radar was gone, replaced by a tall, dark figure, a man in prison grays and eyes the color of tilithium.

"Or perhaps it's all the same," Hypnotic said. "You're so pretty, Calista. You look so much like your father. Are you as vain as him too? Because Luster was always the first to say he was a handsome devil."

Iridium's legs folded, and she saw the apartment, light and bright and airy—*your home, with your husband Bruce*—around the corners of her vision.

"There is no Radar," she gritted. "It was you. It was always you."

"And you're smart as your father." Hypnotic offered his hand. "So a happy life isn't what you want—fine. I can give you what you want . . . I can make it go away. The hate and derision on the hero's faces. The fear of the citizens and the police. A father in prison and a life of loneliness."

She squeezed her eyes closed, tried not to listen. Her hand crept up, pressed the distress beacon on her earpiece. "Mayday," she said, her voice shaking. "Hypnotic's got us, took us down one by one. Backup, backup—"

Lips brushed her other ear, the one without the comlink, and her words died on her tongue.

"I can make it stop," Hypnotic whispered.

And Iridium listened.

A crowd spread out before her, the sea of faces below the courthouse steps as the mayor shook her hand. "The Hero of New Chicago," he said proudly. "Iridium!"

Iridium's costume wasn't her normal unikilt. It was a white skinsuit, with a starburst insignia spread across her chest. Her mask shielded her eyes from the worst of the glare from the vids. Her cape billowed in the crisp breeze.

"Smile, darlin'," Bruce whispered in her ear. "This is what you always wanted."

Iridium turned to the crowd, smiling as they cheered for her. And their roars of approval swept her away.

CHAPTER 39

JET

Therapy is the answer to the Extrahuman Question. Now all we have to do is sell it to the Executive Committee.
— From the journal of Martin Moore, entry #61

Jet yawned around her cup of coffee. "You're sure there's nothing?" she called out.

"Nothing," Meteorite replied, after a glance at one of her monitors. "All's quiet. Finally."

"Stop worrying," Firebug said around her croissant. She flipped her damp, bright orange hair away from her eyes, then winked. "They need us, they know where to find us."

They meaning the Runners on surveillance—five groups of four civilian men and women walking the streets. Patrolling, but reconnaissance only. More of the Runners were here at HQ, learning the ins and outs of the network from Meteorite, or poring through mounds of data with Frostbite. Still more of those normals dedicated to supporting extrahuman heroes would be arriving later that day, according to a message left by Taser.

Jet had woken to the smell of freshly brewed coffee, which

had all but yanked her off her cot. She hadn't had a decent cup of liquid caffeine since . . . well, since before New Chicago had imploded. Following her nose, she staggered into the kitchenette. And then she'd nearly attacked the four strangers standing there.

Okay, so she hadn't exactly been expecting the Runners to be at Squadron HQ already. Whoops.

After making her apologies, she tried to help them clean up—one of the four had dropped a tray of muffins (muffins!) in her surprise—but the Runners wouldn't hear of it. One of them, a lanky man who introduced himself as Lowell, ushered her out of the tiny kitchen and promised that breakfast would be ready in ten minutes.

Indulging in a second cup of coffee, Jet realized just how much she'd missed it. She picked at the remaining fruit on her plate, nibbled a strawberry. When she'd asked where the credit had come from to pay for all the extravagance, Meteorite had smiled sweetly at her.

"Courtesy of Corp," she'd replied. "Did I mention that we'd finished downloading all the files? Wouldn't you know that one of the first ones we decrypted were charge codes? Oh, don't look at me like that," she added in a huff. "As far as I'm concerned, Corp owes us all. The least they can do is buy us breakfast."

Jet had wanted to argue, but the coffee overpowered her sense of right and wrong. At least she had insisted on a status report before she'd allowed herself to be seduced by carbs and caffeine. The numbers of rogues and rabids at large hadn't changed, but so far this morning, there had been no extrahuman sightings, no in-progress crimes reported—*nothing* out of the ordinary, according to Meteorite. The lull was startling, to say the least.

But look: *doughnuts*.

Curled in one of the numerous booths of the main room, Jet held the porcelain cup close to her and enjoyed the feeling of warmth against her fingers. Sometimes, she forgot how cold her hands were when she didn't wear her gauntlets.

She sipped, marveling over how relaxed she felt. She hadn't

even finished getting battle-ready yet: Though she was in her skinsuit, boots, and belt, her gauntlets were on the table, her hair snaked down her back in a loose tail, and her optiframes rested high on her forehead. Her cloak was in one of the back rooms, draped over her cot. It almost felt like she was on vacation.

The back of her neck tingled, and Jet stiffened abruptly before she cast a glance over her shoulder. Frostbite was looking at her oddly, his mouth pulled into a lopsided smile, his gaze on her but also somewhere else. She quirked a brow, and he let out a rueful chuckle.

"Flashback to Second Year," he said. "You and Iri, and me and Samson, overdosing on coffee during midyear exams."

A startled laugh escaped her as she remembered Sam, so big and so strong, jittering like a junked-up cat after he'd downed his fourth cup. "We'd run out of milk," she remembered, "and the kitchen was closed because it was three in the morning."

"So from that point on, we took our coffee black," he finished.

They shared an easy laugh, and he raised his cup to her in salute. She did the same. Turning back in her seat, the smile stayed on her lips as she swirled the coffee in her cup. Thinking of Sam hadn't hurt for the first time in . . . well, forever. It was a bittersweet memory, to be sure, but it didn't dig a hole in her chest and threaten to scoop out her heart.

Maybe she was finally letting him go.

She ate another berry. "Still nothing?" she called out.

"Christo," Firebug muttered. "Someone put junk in your coffee? Calm down, Joannie. If we're needed, she'll tell us."

Jet knew that. But after a week of threat upon threat, she didn't trust this sudden lack of crime.

A trio of Runners marched in, carrying an assortment of boxes. "Personal goods from the Complex," one of them announced with a grin. "Not much, but it's the best we could do on short notice."

"And we had to wait until there was a security guard we trusted," said another, laughing. "Still had to pretend we were looters."

The Complex: Corp-sponsored housing for all Squadron soldiers when they were off duty. When everything had imploded,
Jet and the others had found out the hard way that their homes
had been compromised. Jet grimaced, remembering Bigfoot
crashing through her front door in the middle of the night,
screaming about bugs and trying to stomp Jet to death.

"A collection of 3-D films for Steele," said the first, holding
up a handful of memory sticks. "Hot off the remains of her vid
rack from her apartment."

"Deadly." Firebug grinned, motioning that she'd take the
lot. "Harriet's going to be thrilled to see those again."

"For Jet." The third Runner approached Jet's booth and set
down a short stack of old-fashioned paperback romances. "It
was a grab and dash from your apartment. Hope these are
okay."

"Oh," she breathed, dusting her fingertips over the well-
worn covers. "Thank you so much. Really, these are marvelous." Maybe she didn't have her favorite rocker, but the
books would do—would more than do. Ah, to allow herself the
luxury of fiction, of happy endings. She smiled, felt something
loosen between her shoulders. And as she relaxed, she heard a
teenage girl whisper urgently, remembered the feeling of
something pressing into her hand.

"Say," Jet said, "would one of you mind running an errand?"

"Of course we don't mind," the second Runner said, laughing. "It's in the job description."

Jet took out a key from her belt pouch—the key that the girl
outside of the burning Everyman headquarters had given her.
"Could you go to the Old Chicago Post Office and see what's in
this PO box?" Worst case: Jet was wrong about what "oh cipio"
really was, and she wasted a Runner's time. Best case: Jet was
right, and the package that waited in the post office box
wouldn't literally blow up in Jet's face when she opened it.

"Sure thing," said the first Runner, taking the key and heading for the door. "Back soon."

More goods were distributed. Between the food and the
presents, it was like Christmas had come to the Squadron.

Of course, even Christmas comes to an end.

"Damn it, who turned this off?" Meteorite punched keys, then glared at the handful of Runners she'd been teaching. "A monitor does no good if it's off, people!"

Jet went cold. The doughnut she'd eaten settled like a rock in her stomach. "What happened?"

"One of our newbies turned off our distress-call monitor!" Another heated glare that should have melted the brick face on the wall.

"I was trying to adjust the volume," one of the Runners said meekly, looking like she wanted to faint. "I'm sorry . . ."

Meteorite waved her off as she peered at the machine on the other side of the bar top. She read the information, and Jet saw the horror in the woman's eyes. "Oh Jehovah."

Frostbite was already by her side, looking at the information on her screen. Jet saw the blood drain from his face.

She stood, demanding, "What is it?"

"A distress call," Frostbite said, his voice grave. "From Iridium, in Grid 21."

Hypnotic's grid.

Oh no.

"She and a group of others had gone after Hypnotic, and he took them down, one by one." Frostbite cursed. "The call came in at seven this morning."

More than two hours ago. As Jet had been taking her time over her first cup of coffee, Iri had been entering Hypnotic's lair.

"I'm sorry!" the Runner wailed.

"Firebug, come on," Jet said, sliding her optiframes in place as she marched to the door. Forget her cloak—there was no time. To Meteorite she said, "Contact Taser and Steele, have them meet us outside his lair."

"Joannie." Firebug's voice was a tortured whisper. "I can't."

Jet paused midstride. She didn't look back when she said, "Excuse me?"

"You don't know what he did to me," Kai pleaded. "What he made me see. I can't go back there, Joannie. I'm sorry."

"Save it," Frostbite said, brushing past Jet. "Sheila, we'll stay in full contact. If either of us stops responding when you call, assume the worst."

"Understood." A pause, and then, "What happens in that case?"

"We'll be dead or enslaved," Jet said crisply. "If no one's left to fight, you tell Wagner what happened." He'd tell Lee, and the mayor would have the hard decision of whether to risk inno- cent lives to go after Hypnotic. And Wagner would listen. He was a policeman, dedicated to saving lives and upholding the peace—but he also followed orders. If Lee told him and the Na- tional Guard to bomb Hypnotic for the greater good, he'd do it.

Duty first, she thought grimly.

"I'm sorry," Firebug said again, sobbing. Or maybe that was the Runner who'd scorched everything by pressing the wrong button.

"Come on, Joan," Derek said, his eyes blazing. "Let's go haul Callie's ass out of the fire."

Jet didn't bother trying to talk him out of it. Light knew, they needed all the help they could get.

They bolted, leaving Firebug's sobs far behind.

Interlude

O kay, Mr. McFarlane. Let's do this again."
    Garth sighs. He's glad for his sunglasses; if the detectives see him rolling his eyes, it would probably go poorly. "We've already done this twice."

"Third time's the charm," says the Good Cop, a large man who looks like he wrestles bears in his downtime.

The prissy detective, the Bad Cop wearing a unisuit that probably costs more than Garth's rent, glances at his notes. "So you were walking down Third, just minding your own business."

"Right." Garth tries not to sound too put out. *But Jaysus, how many times does a man have to say the same thing?* And really, it's not like he's about to tell them that he had to walk out for some air, because sitting in the apartment arguing with Terry and the others about how to fight Hypnotic was enough to make a man do something desperate. "Just getting some coffee from a local shop—"

"Jose's Deli and Grill."

"Just so. Best brew in the city. So yeah, I was walking down Third, and as I'm passing by a resi, I hear someone crying. A woman. So I stop and listen to where it's coming from, and when I figure it's by the side entrance of the building, I head over to see if I can help."

"Because you're a Good Samaritan." This he says like it's a sexually transmitted disease.

"Come on, Joe," says Good Cop. "Let him tell it."

"Fine," Joe the Bad Cop grumbles.

"My wife's one of the zombie victims." Garth's voice is soft, tentative, laced with tenderness and rage. "I can't help her. But if I can help someone else's wife . . ." He shrugs. Sexist, maybe, but he has a soft spot for women in distress. He won't apologize for it.

"I'm sorry," says the Good Cop.

"Thanks." Garth says a silent prayer for Julie, then continues. "So I walk around to the side. And there I see a man laying into a woman. Girl, really. Looked to be all of sixteen. He's hitting her, and maybe getting ready to do worse. So I go up to him and tap him on the shoulder. And when he turns to me, I punch his face in."

"Don't you think maybe that was a little aggressive, Mr. McFarlane?"

He eyes Joe the Bad Cop. "Maybe I should've waited for him to blacken her other eye, yeah?"

Good Cop says, "You understand, sir, that the problem is Ms. Lang is saying that Mr. Jordan wasn't beating her."

"So I guess she accidentally fell face-first onto his fist. Jaysus!" Garth wants to spit. He manages to only scowl.

"You're lucky that Mr. Jordan isn't pressing charges."

"That's me," Garth says bitterly. "Mister Lucky."

"Let's talk about your . . . condition," says Bad Cop.

Here we go again. "Sure."

Joe scans his notes. "You're not in the data banks as a known extrahuman."

"That would be because I'm not an extrahuman." More like a sortaextrahuman. But whatever. It's always been enough to keep him off Corp-Co's radar.

"But your eyes glow, Mr. McFarlane."

"They do. It's a neat party trick. I'm sure it says in my medical records that I was given a high dosage of Praxical when I was three. My folks were rather desperate about me not being so sensitive to light," he says, shrugging. "You see all the good it's done me."

"You really expect us to believe that?"

"Sir, I've been sitting here for three hours, all for doing what I thought was a good deed. I don't really care what you believe. Are you arresting me, or what?"

"You should drop the attitude."

"Come on, Joe," says Good Cop. "He's been through enough."

He's let go with a stern warning to leave the policing to the police. Good Cop actually walks him to the precinct door.

"Everyone's temper's up," he says by way of apology. "Lunatic superheroes, rioting citizens. It's enough to give a cop a case of the nerves."

"I can see that," says Garth.

The detective shakes his hand. "For what it's worth, I think you did good. It's probably wasted, though. She's the sort who'll defend her man up until she wakes up dead one day, thanks to his not-beating her."

Garth leaves.

The big problem with vigilantism, he muses, isn't the swollen knuckles or the loose teeth. It's all the time eaten up when cooling one's heels at the local police station.

Maybe he should wear a costume. That seems to make people impervious to getting hauled in for questioning. Garth decides to raid his closet once he gets home; maybe he can find something in basic black.

When he walks into the apartment—still with the temporary wooden panel serving as a front door—he wishes so much for Julie to be there that he almost hears her puttering about in the kitchen, asking him if he wants a drink. Even if he says no, she'll bring him one anyway, overflowing with cubes, and he'll thank her, and they'll find something deadly on the tele and settle down for a cuddle and some mindless fun . . .

But it's not Julie. It's Terry, or one of the others, helping themselves to his food and drink.

Garth sighs, the sound like a sob. *She'll be okay,* he tells himself. Because really, what else can he tell himself? Julie was strong. She wouldn't stay a vegetable. A zombie.

She'll come home to him.

Silently, he kisses the memory of his wife. And now it's time to move on to other things, to get the report of how many Latents have responded to the emergency calls. To see if anyone has come up with a brilliant plan to help the remaining Squadron stop Hypnotic.

He's sure Julie would call him three kinds of fool.

"Well," he calls out, shutting the makeshift door behind him, "I'm back."

THEN

CHAPTER 40
LUSTER

"This is the world I wanted. But there is still pain, and fear, and suffering. I guess at least now we have a chance to fight back. Against evil. Against evolution."
—Matthew Icarus, unpublished commencement speech to MIT, class of 1990

Lester Bradford rarely felt nervous, but he did at this moment, walking down the endless corridors of Blackbird Prison. There were the usual sounds—shouts, screams, crying. The smell of sweat and urine and stale air.

A cell door *clanged*, and Lester flinched. He didn't like prisons. The long hallways and the flickering light tubes and the close, hopeless quiet reminded him too much of the tower block in East London where he'd grown up. Sleeping in the stairwells when his dad had too much to drink. Watching the world go by through stained, impenetrable glass.

"Thank you for coming," said the warden. Post, his name was. He was bald and a head shorter than Lester, built like a bulldog and the personality of a rabid ferret.

"Think nothing of it, mate," Lester murmured.

"He's been asking—well, screaming—for you for the last six

hours," said the warden. "Sedatives aren't putting a dent in him, so . . . talking is a last resort."

Lester followed the warden as he turned and trundled along the corridor, deeper and deeper into the heart chambers of Blackbird Prison. "You were on his Alpha team," said the warden. "Any idea what triggered this outburst?"

Of course Lester knew. It was the six-year anniversary of when they'd put Hal in here in the first place. Six years since the Siege of Manhattan ended. Hal did this every year on this day.

But the warden could get stuffed. "No idea, sir," Lester said. "None whatsoever."

The regular security wing of the prison ended abruptly at a black wall—tilithium-laced ceramic, indestructible, heatproof, and impervious to sonic interference.

Lester had helped design the security protocols for the man who'd been screaming his name. He'd known what was coming.

A guard collected all of his superfluous objects—belt, cape, and fasteners, gloves, even his boots. Post, also stripping down to the basics, grimaced as he snapped on paper booties. "So undignified. But better than the freak hanging himself with my shoelaces, eh?"

"Oh, Hal's never been the type to kill himself," Lester said as he twisted his wedding ring free and dropped it into the bin. "More likely, he'd choke you unconscious and use you as a human shield for escape."

That was why, when the two men buzzed through the containment scanner and out the other side, only faceless robo-guards greeted them. The roboguards rolled on twin tracks and had guns and laser targeting systems mounted to their fronts.

There was only one cell in the maxi wing of Blackbird Prison.

There was only one man who warranted one.

Post let the door scan his biometrics and keyed in his code. Lester stepped in and the door hissed shut behind him.

After a moment, a robotic voice announced. "Inmate walking. Gibbons, Harold Wyatt. Code name Doctor Hypnotic."

A door rolled up and two roboguards deposited their cargo in the visitor's cell. On the other side of thick plas-proof glass, Hal Gibbons smiled at Lester.

Lester sat down and waved his hand at the PA sensor to activate it. "Hello, Doctor."

"Please. At least call me by my right name."

"Doctor Hypnotic, then."

The other man sighed. "Still bitter, I take it?"

"You lost any right you had to a human name when you killed those people in New York, *Doctor.*"

"Don't be so sanctimonious, Bradford. You know it could have been any of us. Little Georgie Porgie." He smiled. "Your beautiful wife."

Lester felt a twitch develop in his jaw. "You're on thin bloody ice, my friend. Make a point or I'm out."

"Would you hurt me, Lester?" Hypnotic leaned toward the glass. He was thinner, and his eyes were the glassy beads particular to heavy sedation, but he still made Lester jump when he banged one palm flat against the glass. "Would you burn me up, like New York Squadron tried to do?"

"For my family?" Lester knew he was being recorded, but still thought, *Sod it.* "Abso-bloody-lutely."

Hypnotic sat back with a grin.

Lester rubbed his forehead. "Is this what you were so desperate to talk about?"

"No." Hypnotic trailed his fingers through the air.

The man was high as a bloody kite and still managed to keep Lester off-balance. Lester didn't like it one bit.

"No," Hypnotic repeated. "I wanted to talk about truth, Les. Truth and justice and the Squadron way . . ." He dissolved into giggles.

Lester stood up. "I don't have time for this. My daughter has a school play this evening, and I won't miss it to watch your one-man fuckwit show." He turned his back on Hypnotic.

"How is the little girl?" From behind, Hypnotic's voice was chilling as it had ever been. "Calypso?"

"Calista." Lester turned around and sat back down, carefully, carefully, so he wouldn't simply melt the glass and wrap his bare hands around Hypnotic's throat, burn that smirk off his face and call it done.

"Do you think little Calista has any future in this world? This world where men like us are leashed like dogs?"

Lester breathed, in and out, relaxation techniques designed to keep you calm in life or death situations. And this was life or death. For Gibbons. "I won't discuss my family with you."

"Then talk to me about truth." Something almost pleading made its way into Hypnotic's eyes, Hal's eyes, swam there under the surface scum of drugs and hopelessness. "I know you aren't a hero," Hal whispered. "Not really. I know what you think about when you hope no one is watching. How you chafe under Corp's controls and how you look at your little girl and pray that her life isn't this world, this terrible, gleaming world of profit shares and sponsors and corporate heroics."

Lester started. "You read my mind?"

Hal tapped his temple. "Every day. Before. All of you. Except her." He slumped. "Does she hate me, Les?"

"She does, mate. You shattered her only hope that her life wasn't always going to be the nightmare it is now."

Hal put his face in his hands, as much as he could move in his stun-cuffs. "Nightmare, yes. It is a nightmare, what happens in that house."

Lester felt his heart skid to a stop. "What did you hear?"

"I know," Hal purred. "I know exactly what they did to her, and I know what he's doing to her now. Blackout." The name came out like a curse.

"What?" Lester's voice sounded foreign, deadened. Valerie hadn't told him anything was wrong with Holly when she visited. "What exactly was said, Hal?"

"He was the worst of us, you know," Hal murmured. "Scared of his own Shadow . . ." He dissolved into giggles again. "An abusive maniac, with a pretty distraction to keep him sane so the Squadron can use him. Until he breaks her, and they make him a new one. I know, Lester. I was there."

"You could be lying to me," said Lester. "And I'm going now. Home to my wife and child." His pulse was back now, and throbbing. Not because he thought Hal was lying—because the cold, dreamy harshness in the man's voice couldn't be anything but true.

"You really care about your family," Hal said, his voice muffled by his hands. "Corp won't stand for that. Love doesn't generate revenue. Loyalty doesn't grab headlines."

He pressed his palm against the glass. "You were the best of us, Les. Get out while you still can."

"Time's up," the robot voice echoed. "Stand and prepare for containment."

"Watch the Shadows!" Hal cried as he stumbled away in the grasp of the roboguards. "Watch the Darkness. Break away, Les . . . do what I couldn't do!"

His screams cut off when the door shut, and Lester was alone with his own reflection in the glass. It was like Hal Gibbons had ceased to exist.

CHAPTER 41
VIXEN

These special children will receive education tailored specifically to their unique needs. They will be cared for, tutored, and taught to use their abilities for the benefit of all mankind.

—Mission statement of Corp-Co's Academy
for Extraordinary Youngsters, 2018

More wine?" Holly held out the bottle, but Valerie covered her glass.

"No thanks, hon."

Holly shrugged and filled her own glass to the rim, killing the bottle. Jamie, one of Holly's two creepy Runners, swooped in and took it away.

Valerie nibbled on the last of her breadstick, keeping one eye on Callie where she sat on the floor playing dolls with Joan, Holly's daughter. Everything was going fine until Joan decided she wanted Callie's Baby Be Mine, and yanked it away.

Callie burst into tears, and a light panel nearby shorted.

"No, sweetie!" Valerie jumped up and separated the two girls. "We don't use our powers on other people, remember?"

Callie pointed at the doll. "That's mine!"

"I know," Valerie soothed. "And I know Joan is going to give it back. Right, Joan?"

Joan clutched the doll to her chest. "I want the dolly!"

Valerie heaved a sigh, slinging her sobbing daughter onto her hip. "A little help, Holly?"

"George and I will buy you a new one." Holly drained her wineglass. "Just let Joan have it. She'll throw a fit otherwise."

Valerie massaged her temple with her free hand to quell the throb of what she'd named Mother's Little Migraine. "Callie, sweetie, you need to *stop crying* for mommy, okay?"

She sat back down and let Callie play with Holly's silver-plated tableware. "Holly. Les and I don't let Callie have a lot of toys. You know that."

"So when Joan's down for a nap, I'll weasel it out of her grasp and send Jamie or Jamie your way with it. You'll get the damn doll back."

Valerie frowned at the curse. Holly was working on a drunk. Again. "You have to set limits. Kids act out because they want limits."

"I know how to raise my child," Holly snapped.

"Of course you do. But you and George—"

"George is busy," Holly said crisply. "I make the calls with Joan. It's my job to oversee things here at home."

"You're also a person who has a job!" Valerie said. "Get a nanny to help you."

Holly sighed, pushing a hand through her hair. She looked much older than she had when Valerie met her. Or maybe that was because her Glamique contract had been canceled.

"I can't," Holly said. "George won't hear of it."

"Then maybe George needs to get his hearing checked."

Holly smiled nervously. "He has a lot of pressure. You know that. Les must be the same way."

"Sure, there's pressure. But Les is home at night," Valerie said gently. "When's the last time George was here when you went to bed?"

Her friend flinched. "I don't know what you're driving at, Valerie Bradford, but you stop it right now. George is just busy."

Valerie fussed with Callie's braid, which refused to stay neat. "So are you, Hols."

"It's not the same," Holly insisted. "He's constantly fighting, fighting all the time. He's so *stressed.* So I have to be here for him when he needs me, where he expects me."

"Holly, you're a superhero. No one *expects* you to sit home and bake cookies and do laundry all day."

"George does."

Something in her friend's tone made Valerie sit up and really look at her. Holly fiddled with her hair, her wedding ring, looking anywhere but Valerie's face.

"Hols," she said, frowning. "Are you okay?"

"He just gets . . . so angry sometimes," Holly whispered. "I know it's not him during those times. I know he's not the George I married. That George doesn't care if I accidentally burn supper."

"Holly," Valerie said, letting Callie squirm off her lap so she could reach across the table and take her friend's hand. "Has he done something?"

"Of course not. We just have our disagreements sometimes, that's all. Every marriage has some disagreements. Even you and Lester have some, don't you? That doesn't mean anything's rocky or—" Her breath hitched.

Valerie turned Holly's face toward her. "Is he *hitting* you?"

"No!" Holly's eyes flamed with panic. "He's a good man!"

The lie was all too clear. "Holly . . ."

"And if he did, anything that happened would be an accident," she said too fast.

"Hols," Valerie said softly, "George has a problem."

Holly's eyes took on a sinister cast. "At least he's not a loose cannon like Lester!"

"Oh, so *my* husband is the problem now?" Valerie stood up, her chair scraping back. "I have news for you, Holly, news that's been a long time coming. Your precious George is a whack job."

"How *dare* you . . ."

"For Christo's sake, girl, he's hitting you! If you can't think of yourself, think of Joan! What is she going to remember when she's grown?"

Holly stood as well, and there was a moment when Valerie saw the old Holly, the firecracker, the one who could smile and laugh as she took down a villain as easily as when posing for the camera.

"You have no right," she quavered. "No right at all."

"You're my friend, Hols," Valerie said softly. "And I'm saying this as your friend. George might be going the way of Hypnotic."

Holly shuddered, twin tears working down her face. "Get. Out," she gritted. "Get out *now!*"

"Okay," Valerie said. "I'm gone." She gathered up Callie and went into the kitchen to grab her purse. There she saw the cheerful red Panic Button, next to the combox on the wall.

Seeing it calmed her. If there were a problem, a true problem, Holly would hit the button and the cavalry would come running.

Tomorrow she'd talk some sense into Holly. She just needed to calm down and sober up, and then they could talk reasonably.

Tomorrow.

CHAPTER 42
ANGELICA

In retrospect, we were fortunate that Angelica lasted as long as she did.
    —From the journal of Martin Moore, entry #185

She had the dream again.

Holly sat up in bed, shivering, wishing that George were there to comfort her. But he wasn't in the bedroom.

She wrapped her arms around herself, told herself that it was just a dream, that Hal was still in Blackbird. That he couldn't hurt anyone ever again.

That what he'd told her during the Siege of Manhattan had been a desperate lie.

Shaking, she pulled herself out of bed and dragged on her robe. She tied the belt and tucked her feet into slippers. Padding out of the dark bedroom, she first checked on Joannie—safe in bed, sleeping the sleep of an exhausted five-year-old after a long day of play. Joan had had fun with Callie, even if Holly and Valerie had nearly come to blows.

No. She wasn't going to think about that now. And Valerie Bradford could go to hell.

Closing her daughter's bedroom door, Holly walked quietly down the hallway, noting the closed office door. George was up, doing . . . well, whatever it was he did in there. Holly had long ago learned that when the office door was closed, she mustn't interrupt.

Her shoulder still had the small, circular scar from when George had first taught her that lesson.

Holly entered the small kitchen and put on the kettle for tea. She stood there, motionless, as the water heated. When the kettle whistled, she shook herself out of her stupor and killed the sound before George could hear it.

She fixed herself a cup of chamomile and took it to the kitchen table. She carefully pulled out the chair so that it wouldn't scrape, then sat.

Holly sipped her tea and didn't taste it.

When Blackout came into the kitchen for something to eat, she didn't notice him—her back was to the hallway, and she was thinking about her dream—the same dream she'd had, on and off, for six years.

If she felt her husband's cold gaze on her back, she dismissed it as a chill and took another small sip of tea.

They stayed like that for twenty minutes: Holly thinking about another man as she took miniscule sips of tea, and her husband standing in the archway, gazing at his wife with his Shadow-filled eyes.

In Holly's dream, it's the end of the Siege of Manhattan, just as Hal has told her that she'd been used, that she'd been forced to leave him and love Blackout. Angelica has just played her last, desperate card: She kissed Doctor Hypnotic.

But in her dream, she never stops kissing Hal. There is no betrayal, no look of defeat and sorrow in Hal's eyes. There is only her and Hal.

Holly didn't know she was crying. She still felt the tingle on her lips from six years gone, and she knew it was false, that it had been just a dream. But it didn't matter. The feelings were still there—the passion, then the terror.

In her dream, Hal seduces her, or she seduces him, and the two of them ride the world in a wave of blood. When she gives birth to her daughter, she sacrifices the baby to the Shadow, deep at the base of the world at the boundary of hell. But it's not enough—the Shadow rises up, hungry.

And it comes for her.

"Sweetheart. What're you doing up?"

Holly jumped in her chair. Tea slopped over the side of her cup, splashing her fingers. Holly turned to see George—no, Blackout; he was still garbed in his work clothes—standing over her.

The darkness swimming in his eyes had to be a trick of the light.

"Couldn't sleep," she said, smiling at her own foolishness. When he said nothing, she talked, to fill the space between them. Surely, she wasn't babbling out of nerves. "Didn't like lying in bed in the dark."

He smiled at her—that had to be a smile and not a leer. "Why, sweetheart, you should know by now there's nothing to be afraid of. There's nothing in the dark that isn't already there in the light."

She smiled at him in turn, pretending she didn't hear the lie in his words.

Pretending she wasn't afraid of the man she loved.

CHAPTER 43

NIGHT

It's fascinating to watch the difference in Night and Blackout. The one thrives while the other deteriorates. Why does the Shadow spare one and condemn the other? Genetics? Statistics? Luck?

—From the journal of Martin Moore, entry #22

After the reporters turned away and the ambulance and police finally left, Night grabbed Blackout by his shoulder and spun him around. Though his brother in Shadow was smaller and slighter than he was, Night found it difficult to make Blackout move, as if the Shadow had given the smaller man additional strength.

"What was that?" Night hissed.

Blackout stared at him, his eyes hooded. "A press conference detailing how we defeated Calendar Man." He laughed suddenly, the sound high-pitched and girlish. "I loathe, I loathe, I loathe my little Calendar Man," he sang off-key, "every day, every day, of the year!"

Night darted a look behind them—no, none of the others had heard. Growling, he shoved Blackout into the alley between buildings. "Shut it! You want them to think you're on junk?"

Blackout brayed laughter, spittle flying.

"For Christo's sake, man, quit it!"

That made Blackout bend over, helpless with mirth, slapping his thighs as he guffawed.

Night gnashed his teeth, wondering how long to let this go. Blackout's mental stability had declined steadily over the past few years. Small things at first—memory loss, mood swings. But lately, Blackout had increased bouts of rage and was prone to wild bursts of laughter at inopportune times. And whispering, as if talking to himself.

Night, of course, knew better. If Blackout had merely been talking to himself, Night wouldn't be concerned. Schizophrenia could be managed.

But this wasn't schizophrenia.

Night had said nothing about Blackout's increasing instability. As long as his power brother could still handle the Shadow, there was nothing to discuss. Anything that he needed to do to keep his ability under control was acceptable . . . to a point.

Standing there, listening to Blackout's hiccuping giggles, Night wondered if that point had finally come.

He'd glimpsed Angelica this morning, when he'd come by to pick up Blackout for patrol. The woman was clever with her makeup, but she'd missed a spot beneath her eye. Night had stared at that purplish-green smudge, and he saw then just how red the eye itself was, how swollen the lid appeared, even with its cosmetic camouflage. She'd noticed his reaction and tittered stupidly, covering the eye lightly with shaking fingers. Allergic reaction, she'd said, her lips trembling as they held a smile.

Yes, her eye would be allergic to Blackout's fist, no doubt.

Night had seen the naked desperation in her gaze—how she was silently begging him to hold his tongue. Whether that was out of love or fear of Blackout, Night couldn't guess.

He might have said something to her then, or even to Blackout—Night frowned on domestic violence, as did Corp-Co—but that was when the little girl ran into the living room and attacked Night with a bear hug.

"Nigh!" she cried happily, squeezing. "Hi, Nigh!" The rhyme

sent her on a fit of giggles, as it always did. It had been her pet name for him ever since she was two.

He'd smiled—he had no patience for babies, who tended to be loud, and smelly, and overall quite unpleasant, but he had to admit a certain fondness for the little Shadow—and he'd allowed himself to be distracted by the child's glee and her attempts to make Shadow puppets. By the time he remembered Angelica's black eye, he and his partner were already out the door, Blackout raving in his excitement to try a new Shadow technique. The two had talked shop during most of their patrol. And over the course of the day, Night had forgotten about Angelica.

But now he remembered the raw pain he'd seen etched on Angelica's face. Snarling, he punched Blackout in the jaw.

The other man's head rocked back, and even after Night followed through on the punch and drew back his fist, Blackout remained with his head twisted to the side, his jaw already swelling. He slowly rubbed the side of his mouth, laughing softly.

"You broke Calendar Man's back," Night said, his voice a dangerous growl. "Last week, you used Shadow to almost crush Succuba to death."

"Grenades and horseshoes," Blackout said, lips pulled into a parody of a grin.

"You're just as bad as the criminals are."

"And I suppose you just gave me a love tap?"

"I'm trying to knock some sense into you!" Night realized he was shouting. Lowering his voice, he said, "Get it together, *George*. You can't go around crippling the bad guys."

"Less likely to face a repeat performance if you hobble them."

"And more likely to get yourself hauled off to Therapy for evaluation." He looked deep into Blackout's eyes and saw the Shadow staring back at him. "Bursts of violence are one thing, but you've taken it to an unacceptable level. It stops *now*, George."

Blackout chuckled softly. "Isn't that the pot calling the Shadow black?"

"It stops now," Night said again. "And keep your hands off your wife."

"Hey now," Blackout said, affronted. "We're thinking of Shadowling Number Two. Hard to do that if I don't touch her."

"Keep it up, and she'll be sponsored by the National Coalition Against Domestic Violence."

Blackout froze, his grin looking like a trapped scream.

When Night spoke again, his voice was colder than the Shadow he controlled. "And if I even suspect you're hurting the little one, I'll forget you're a friend."

Shadows swam in Blackout's eyes, seeped out of his pores, crawled over his flesh. Then the man drew in a shuddering breath, and the Shadows sank back into his body.

"Oh Christo," he whispered, squeezing his eyes shut. "Sometimes I don't know who I am anymore."

"You're a hero," Night said, clamping a hand on his partner's shoulder. "You can remember that."

"I can," Blackout said, sounding unconvinced but nodding all the same. "I can."

"You have to."

"Rick," Blackout pleaded, "please don't say anything."

Night made a sound that could have been agreement, or could have meant he'd think about it.

The two men returned to Squadron HQ, and they both pretended everything was fine. And then Night made the mistake that would change everything forever: He didn't report Blackout's behavior.

And for the next week, everything was fine.

CHAPTER 44

VIXEN

It's odd hearing my name on television. They call me a genius, on a par with the greatest in history. When they're not calling for my death, for trying to play God.

—Matthew Icarus, diary entry dated 1994

"Vixen! One more please!"

The flashes kept going off, but Lester's Runner Yuriko stepped in, spreading her arms. "Sorry, folks. Superheroes need rest too."

The press grumbled but retreated from the steps of the HQ. As soon as they were through the door, Les let his smile drop.

Valerie massaged her neck. "Tank Girl is aptly named. She was ten tons of fun."

Les grunted but didn't say anything as they walked through the silent hallway. It was Sunday afternoon, and Callie was out with Reggie, Valerie's Runner, catching a movie.

"Sweetie, what's wrong?"

"What makes you think something's wrong?"

"You always laugh at my jokes."

"Just tired," Les said, rubbing his temples. "Tired, worn-out, and fucking sore."

"I'll get a heat pack," Yuriko said instantly, darting off for Medical.

"Honey." Valerie stopped Les with a tug. "I know it's not that." Her husband had been moody and distant for weeks. Even Callie had stopped trying to get him to play their usual game of Space Invader, wherein Les put a box over his head and pretended to be an evil robot, or to be the voice for her boy dolls while she played with her dollhouse.

"It's nothing."

"Just tell me, please?" She put a finger under Lester's chin. "If we don't talk, we're just another . . . well. Supercouple."

"What were you going to say?"

Valerie blinked and chewed on her lip, looking away from her husband's sharp gaze.

Les shifted away from her, his posture sagging. "You were going to say something else."

Another Blackout and Angelica.

"I wasn't," she lied. What her friend—former friend, she guessed, since Angelica hadn't spoken to her since the Luncheon Incident—did in her marriage wasn't any of Valerie's business.

Angelica was no fool. She was a strong, competent hero.

Who lets her husband use her for a punching bag when he so much as stubs his toe?

"I'm worried about them too." Lester wrapped his arms around her, squeezed her.

Valerie started, then returned his embrace. "Are you okay, Les?"

"I am," he said against her hair. "But the team isn't. He's going to hurt someone, Valentine."

Valerie pulled back and regarded her husband. Her tall, beautiful husband, with his wicked gaze and smile that could render her speechless. He was the opposite of Blackout in every way—loving, a good listener, a good father. A hero. But there were shadows under his eyes and new lines around his mouth. After years of living together, Valerie knew the signs. "It's more than that."

"What? No. Don't be daft. I'm just worried about George and Holly."

"No," Valerie insisted. "You've barely been sleeping. You get up in the night and pace, your head isn't in the game in the field. Not that I blame you. We have to be so careful now because of that family suing Blackout . . ."

"He did break their father and husband's back," Les muttered. "Valerie, I just . . . I couldn't stand it if we became like that. Little puppets, with little strings, controlled by little men who know nothing about what it takes to do this job."

Valerie leaned up and kissed him on his cheek. There was stubble there—the Hero of New Chicago had even been forgetting to shave for the vids. "We will never be like them," she whispered.

"How do you know?" Les said glumly. "Our lives aren't our own, Valentine. They're just not."

"I know because you're a good man, Lester Bradford," Valerie said, meeting his eyes, "and George Greene is not. You could never hurt me and Callie, Les. No matter what Corp did to you. It's just not in your blood."

"But it's in Blackout's." He sighed. "He's changed, Val. You didn't really know him before. He used to be a good man. A great hero."

"I'm sorry I never knew him. But this isn't about him, Les. It's about Holly and Joan." Valerie bit her lip. "Do you think he's going to hurt them?"

A long pause before he said, "I do."

She curled her fists inside her gloves. "Then tomorrow, when the administrative offices are open, we do what needs to be done."

Les nodded, and there was a steel in his eyes that Valerie had never seen. Gone was the laughing, smiling Luster. The man staring back at her was hard, tempered with sorrow.

But Valerie wasn't afraid of those eyes. They were still her husband's.

And she felt a similar hardness growing around her own gaze and around her heart.

For Holly's own good, they'd have to turn in the man she loved.

CHAPTER 45

ANGELICA

I could have pulled Angelica and the girl out at any time. I could have pushed through the paperwork for Blackout's Therapy. I could have done either of those things, and others. All I did was watch. And record.

—From the journal of Martin Moore, entry #186

The last afternoon the family was together started out so well. George had been more loving and tender than he'd been in years, even talking seriously about their trying for another baby, something Holly desperately wanted. And now he was playing Bad Guys with Joannie, pretending to be the wolfish Big Bad and running around on all fours, laughing as he chased the giggling girl around the living room.

Holly was humming as she dolloped out more cookie-dough batter onto the baking sheet. She'd already made two batches, the cookies on cooling racks now, their smell filling the kitchen and making their apartment truly feel like a home. She'd even pretended not to notice when Joannie snuck a cookie. Smiling to herself, Holly shook her head. It was a good thing her little girl would be trained to be a hero; she had no natural ability to be a thief.

Yes, it was good.

Holly mopped her brow and eyeballed the remaining batter. Not enough for another batch after this; she'd just have to make it all fit. She rearranged the blobs of dough on the tray.

Joannie came charging through the kitchen, shrieking laughter.

"Stop running in socks," Holly called out as her girl disappeared around the corner.

Her husband came barreling through a moment later. He paused to plant a kiss on her cheek, then let out a pretend bellow and galloped after Joannie, whose shrieks of delight reached deafening levels. A moment later, the girl tore through the kitchen again, sliding before she rounded the corner.

Holly sighed. One of these days, her daughter would listen to her. Maybe.

She opened the oven, calling out, "No running, oven open!"

Joannie peeked her head in, and Holly felt the girl's gaze on her back as she loaded in the last tray of cookies. She glanced over her shoulder and caught Joannie sneaking another cookie. Holly arched an eyebrow in the classic Mommy Look, and the girl had the decency to look embarrassed.

"No more," Holly said, wagging a finger.

"Sorry, Mama."

"Our little girl was sneaking cookies?"

George's voice startled Holly; she hadn't heard him approach. She flashed him a quick smile, was about to remark on Joan's poor sneaking skills when she saw the hint of Shadow in his eyes.

"It's fine, sweetheart," she said, smiling to show that it really was all right. "She knows the rules. She knows she's not supposed to have any more. Right, Joannie?"

But their daughter had already charged away, still intent on playing Bad Guys. "Come find me, Papa!"

"It's fine," she said again with a laugh. "Our Joan is a good girl."

"She is," George said, smiling proudly. Then he called out, "Here I come, Joannie!" And he ran out of the kitchen.

Holly started thinking about what to make for dinner. Sure,

she could have the Runners fetch stuff, but she enjoyed doing the domestic thing. And George preferred it. Maybe something fun, like tacos . . . She looked at the comlink on the wall, right next to the bright red Panic Button there for emergencies. Maybe she'd call in Mexican after all. Why make a mess and clean it up when it could all be done for them?

She saw Joannie return, stealing glances at the cookies on the racks. Holly smiled, shaking her head. Really, her child had a hopeless sweet tooth.

Joannie's hand darted out, snatched another cookie.

"Joan."

That was George, standing behind Holly. No, not George— that was Blackout's voice, low and filled with menace. Holly whirled, saw her husband standing in the kitchen doorway, black rivers swimming over his arms, in his eyes. His voice silky and dark, he said, "You broke the rules, Joannie."

"Sweetheart," Holly said, "really. It's okay."

"It's *not* okay. How's she ever going to be a good Squadron soldier if she breaks the rules? Good girls don't break the rules, Joannie!"

Behind Holly, her daughter let out a frightened sob.

"George," Holly snapped. "Stop it. You're scaring her."

"She *should* be scared. She broke the rules. Crumbs all over the floor!"

Holly smiled, a tentative thing filled with fear, and she reached out to her husband even as she reached inside of herself and *pushed* Light into him, soothing him, calming him.

He grinned—a hungry, ugly grin that froze her heart.

"Oh, Holly," he said. "You really *do* care, don't you? They made you perfect, didn't they? My perfect . . . little . . . wife."

Oh Jehovah, he sounds insane.

"Yes," Blackout said softly, almost thoughtfully. "They gave me *exactly* what the doctor ordered." He laughed, and the sound was filled with madness.

Holly whispered, "George?"

"Come here, Holly. Give me a hug."

And then the Shadow reached for her.

She didn't cry out, not at first. The black bands chilled her as they wrapped around her body, sucking out her warmth. Her breath frosted and her lips cracked, and still she smiled, showing George that she loved him, that she knew he'd never hurt her, not really. Not on purpose.

And then the Shadow squeezed.

Surprise was the first thing that registered as her ribs cracked. And then, as the snakelike black bands tightened even more, the pain hit.

Holly panicked, lashing out with her power and her body. Neither made a difference.

Blackout giggled.

"Joan," Holly choked out, blood spilling from her mouth, "emergency!"

She heard her little girl cry, thought she heard Joannie run.

The last gift she gave her daughter was distraction. Holly Owens Greene threw the last of her Light at Blackout, forced him to keep his attention on her for just another moment.

A Klaxon sounded—Joannie had hit the Panic Button.

"Good girl," Holly said, or tried to say. But it was lost in a river of blood.

As she died, Holly's last thoughts, surprisingly, were of Hal. He was holding her close, whispering that it was okay.

It was a lie, of course. But Holly died believing it, her bloody mouth fixed in a gentle smile.

CHAPTER 46
LUSTER

Instances of violence among what Corp is calling "extrahumans" is nearly 33 percent higher than that of the general population. Suicide, depression, schizophrenia, and a host of other disorders . . . all off the charts. Nobody listens. Nobody ever listens to me.

—Matthew Icarus, diary entry dated 2020

You're in the chocolate river, Dad."

Lester blinked and focused on the shimmering holo board in front of him. "So I am, darling."

Callie fidgeted in her seat. "Candyland is boring. Can we turn on the 3-D unit and play Killer Commando?"

"Absolutely not," said Valerie, from where she was going over that week's press with Yuriko. "Les, I told you that game would give her nightmares."

"I like shooting mutants in the face!" Callie insisted. "Their brains go everywhere."

"*Les.*" Val said with a sigh in the tone that let him know he wouldn't be getting any that evening. Nothing to take the edge off what tomorrow would bring.

Lester wished in that moment, truly, that he drank.

"All right, all right," he said. "Callie, we'll finish the game, then you can have one hour of cartoons before bed. Fair?"

Callie furrowed her brow and nodded. She had her mother's height, and a certain elfin quality to her features, but she had his eyes and thick black hair. No one could ever deny they were father and daughter. "Dad, you're smiling weird," Callie said as she rolled the dice. Lester ruffled her hair.

"It's only because I love you so very much, girl. Now make your move so we can get to those cartoons."

Callie's holographic piece slid along the board, then suddenly the game vanished, replaced by a flashing red signal.

"Priority one alert," said the holo station. "Vista Villa apartments, penthouse suite."

Valerie shot up from the sofa. "That's Holly and George."

"I know." Lester was already reaching for his uniform. Ignore the plummeting sensation in his chest. Ignore the spike of panic. *Uniform belt boots GO*, the training turning him into an automaton.

Valerie started to strip off her sweat suit to her costume beneath, but Lester shook his head. "Someone has to stay with Callie."

"Yuriko can . . ."

Lester held up his hand. "If this goes badly, someone needs to be there for Callie."

Valerie drew back like he'd slapped her in the face. "Les, don't even talk about that."

"My little girl won't be an orphan, Val. Watch her." He reached out and kissed his wife, hard and quick. "I'll be home soon."

Vista Villa was far more posh than Lester's own apartment. Not that he couldn't afford something just as opulent, but Callie needed a university fund if she chose not to attend the Academy. He and Valerie needed a retirement plan that didn't involve Corp.

George and Holly clearly had no such compunctions.

Two Beta Team heroes were at the door, pounding with the

flat of their fists. "Blackout! Angelica! The distress signal went off—please respond!"

"Out of the way," Lester ordered them. He had the sick falling feeling in his stomach again, one he'd thought he'd finally erased when he joined the Squadron, saved people from people like his father.

But it returned now, nearly spinning him around as he pressed his ear against the Greenes' front door.

He could hear crying, just barely. Crying, then screaming.

"Joannie! You can't hide from your papa!"

Lester jerked away from the door like it was a hot skillet. "Oh . . . fuck."

"What's the situation?" Night's face appeared beside him, blank and featureless under his cowl.

"It's happened," Lester said softly. Inside the apartment, the screaming got louder. "Get out of the way."

Night tensed, and for a moment Lester thought that the bigger man was going to hit him, wrap him in cold Shadow and smother him. Then Night nodded and stepped aside with a sweep of cloak. "Velocity, Senator—with me. Luster has the lead."

Lester grew a strobe in his hands, white-hot, and threw it at the door. It exploded inward, flying clean off the hinges, and Lester ran in. He ignored procedure, didn't cover his corners, just bolted into the apartment, praying that he wasn't too late.

He saw it all through a fractured lens, everything too bright and too loud, jagged and screaming.

A scattering of cookies and crumbs on the kitchen floor.

An overturned table in the living room.

A body on the floor of the hallway.

Not a body.

Holly.

The blood was too dark. It didn't look real, sunk into the oatmeal-colored rug that probably cost more than all of the furniture in his and Valerie's apartment. It looked black, like blood in old flattie movies. Black and thick, like the chocolate syrup Bela Lugosi had sucked down in *Dracula.*

Holly was on her back, her body twisted like a pretzel, arms stretched in supplication.

It was freezing in the apartment. Lester could see his own breath, feel the blood slowing all through him as Shadow crept over everything.

Cold, so cold, cold as a grave . . .

"Luster, move!" Night snapped, and powerful hands pushed him out of the way of a Shadow creeper.

Lester regained his balance, looked through the open doorway to a bedroom—a little girl's pink bedroom. George Greene crouched by the closet, blood gushing from his nose.

"GET OUT!" he bellowed, as Shadow writhed all around like a nightmare garden.

"You two," Night jerked his head at Velocity and Senator. "Take point."

The Betas followed instructions, then Night focused on Blackout. "George," he said, his voice calm. "Whatever's wrong, we can fix it."

"I don't think so, mate," Lester whispered. He looked back and down, saw that Holly's eyes were open. Blood had spattered across her face, a trail of fairy kisses etched in red.

Blackout screamed.

Lester heard the man lashing out as Night approached. Lester kept looking at Holly. Blackout's fight would be futile; when Night wanted you subdued, he would bring you down, no matter the cost.

And in a moment, Blackout was down, whimpering.

In the open silence after, Lester heard crying. Not Blackout's whimpering sobs—this was softer, higher. Lester tore his gaze from Holly's body, following the sobs.

They came from the closet.

He stepped over Blackout, who was curled on his side as Night slapped stun-cuffs on him. "Hello," Lester said, opening the door cautiously. "Anyone . . ."

A tendril of Shadow snapped out, almost smothering Lester's face.

He created a strobe, set it to floating. The sparking ball kept the Shadow at bay—and revealed a tiny, thin face surrounded by a cloud of corn silk hair. The gold was spattered with Shadows.

"Well, hello, Joan," Lester said softly. "I see you there. You don't have to be scared."

"I'm not coming out!" She crouched back, away from the light. "Can't make me!"

"And I wouldn't dream of trying," Lester said, giving the little girl a smile. "It's quite roomy in here, really. For a flat in the city, you're lucky to get this much square footage."

Her brow crinkled.

"You know me, Joan, don't you?" He extended a hand. "Callie's my little girl."

"Callie's nice."

"How about this, Joan . . . if you want to come out of there, you can come home with me, and you and Callie can have a sleepover tonight."

Joan regarded him with her impossibly wide eyes, then took his hand. "My mommy is sick," she said softly. "Papa said she's sleeping."

"I know he did, luv," Lester whispered, moving the girl's hair out of her face. "Now, can you grab onto me and hold very tightly?"

Joan jumped into his arms.

"Shut your eyes," Lester said as he backed out of the closet. "Just shut your eyes, darling, and think of nice bright things." He cradled her head against his chest and sidestepped, shielding her from Blackout, then, down the hall, from Holly's body.

"You're safe now," he crooned, stroking Joan's hair. "We're going to keep you safe."

"Go," Night murmured to him. "We've got this under control."

Lester walked out to the waiting ambulance, for once not surrounded by a storm of press. Wouldn't do for Corp to have one of its families spattered across the evening news.

Joan's family.

Lester heard the voice, his own voice, inside his head as the hover glided over the city, over its mess and disorder and ugliness.

This is my fault.

He'd told George the truth years ago, when Luster had been

lost in grief over Valerie's miscarriage. And the truth had broken him. The guilt ate Lester. Consumed faster than fire. Lester slipped off his mask, loosened his gloves and his cape and the straps on his boots. He wanted to set the whole thing aflame.

He would never be Luster again. Not after tonight.

He had to get his own family away from this, this great spreading stain of madness and secrecy that turned good men into murderers and little girls into orphans.

Had to, before he caused another Blackout and Angelica.

CHAPTER 47

NIGHT

Observing the remnants of Team Alpha going through the grieving process is better than anything on the vids. If they weren't extrahuman freaks, I might even feel sorry for them.

—From the journal of Martin Moore, entry #188

Night was silent during Blackout's sentencing. He did his duty, of course, giving his full report of what had happened that fateful afternoon—down to how the little girl, a Shadow power, had been saved. But other than that, he said nothing as the proceedings went on—not to Luster, next to him in a civilian suit and muttering under his breath; not to Blackout, doped up, stun-cuffs covering his wrists; certainly not to the press. Night's face was an impassive mask, one devoid of emotion.

His thoughts, though, churned through his mind, Shadow-chased and cold.

Weak, he thought. Blackout had been weak. He'd given in to the Shadow instead of controlling it. For that, the man deserved death. He wouldn't be killed, though; Corp-Co didn't sanction capital punishment, which meant that neither did the government. No, they'd lock him away in Blackbird, medicated and insensible, in a cell in Maxi. Maybe even next to Doctor Hypnotic. For all intents, Blackout would be dead anyway.

Just like the wife. Angelica had deserved death for coddling Blackout instead of helping him fight against the Shadow.

Everyone who encouraged weakness was, in turn, weak. And everyone who was weak deserved death. Simple, really.

Night could give them death so very easily. His mastery of Shadow was specific: He repelled light. And people, whether human or extrahuman, at their core were made of light.

He could take that light away with a thought.

Next to him, Luster growled something and glared hatefully at Blackout, who didn't notice.

Luster wasn't weak. That was comforting, Night decided. There were so few people he could count on to remain strong in the face of the enemy—especially when the enemy changed masks so easily. Luster was steadfast.

And he'd saved the little Shadow.

A smile quirked his lips as he thought of the little girl Luster had coaxed out of the closet. She'd been surrounded by Shadow, using it to camouflage herself when her father had been looking to kill her. So early for such an ability. But then, stress tended to bring out the best in extrahumans. Unless it made them go crazy or killed them, of course.

The girl would be an asset.

He remembered the shocked look on her face, her dark eyes terrified, her mouth set in a silent scream as Luster had hugged her, telling her that she was safe now, that they were going to keep her safe.

But Luster was a Lighter. What did he know of Shadow?

No, that would be up to Night. He was practically the girl's parent now; the two of them were the only Shadow powers on this side of the world. He couldn't raise her, of course—she was already in the Orphanage wing of the Academy, surrounded by Runners and Therapists and others trying to help her adjust.

And keep her calm, of course. She was a little Shadow, which meant she was unpredictable.

Clearly, Night would have to become an instructor at the

Academy in time to teach the girl. He had to; she had no one else to turn to for help with the Shadow.

He smiled grimly. Oh, he'd help the girl. He'd train her, make her the perfect Shadow power. And in turn, she'd help him rid the world of weakness.

Simple, really.

That was the moment the judge sentenced Blackout to life at Blackbird Penitentiary, no parole.

Next to Night, Luster muttered, "Better than the bastard deserves."

"We all get what we deserve in the end," Night replied.

Interlude

It occurs to Garth that there's more to heroing than wearing a costume. He has this epiphany as he dodges Elephant Man's tusks.

The deadly points arc past him, almost close enough to nick his whiskers. He falls backward, hitting the ground hard on his left shoulder, using the momentum to tuck into a roll. Somehow he gets onto his feet and scrambles out of the way as the Ram charges past.

Thankfully, the Ram has one direction: forward.

Garth, panting, stands in a loose ready position, elbows in by his ribs, legs bent as he faces Elephant Man. The massive extrahuman isn't bothering to run at him again; instead, he's picking up the two cartons he'd removed from Morse's Pawn Shop.

"You're under arrest," Garth shouts out. "Put your hands up!"

Elephant Man rumbles a derisive laugh. "Whatever you say, mouse." He hefts the two cartons onto his massive shoulders.

"Hey! Stop—" Garth's about to add the classic "In the name of the law" line when the Ram crashes into him from behind. Now Garth is airborne, in massive pain, and feeling incredibly stupid for forgetting about the other former hero. Elephant Man is kind enough to stop his flight with a body block. Garth bounces off the marble-hard hide and slides down to the ground, dazed. And seriously rethinking the hero thing.

"You heard the wannabe," the Ram snorts. "Put 'em down."

"Get scorched. I was here first."

"Oh yeah. I'm impressed." The Ram laughs. "You were a

second-stringer in the Squadron, and now you're just a pathetic Earther in serious need of braces."

Insults fly. And soon the cartons come crashing down as Elephant Man and the Ram fight tusk and horn.

Garth slowly picks himself up, shakes his head to clear it, and blinks as he sees the two rabids pounding each other into tenderized steak. This isn't the plan, but then, he didn't really have a plan going into this; he'd sort of stumbled onto the robbery in progress. So . . . time to improvise.

He sidles his way to one of the fallen cartons. Tries to move it. Nearly gives himself a hernia. Right. Bad plan. Next?

Garth spies the open store door and makes a gimpy dash for it. Once inside, he sees the broken counter glass, the goods scattered on the floor, and the man lying on the ground. Garth limps over and puts a hand on the man's neck. A pulse. Good. The man groans. Better. "Sir, can you move?"

The man says something, either a prayer or a curse, then rolls over to look at Garth. And then he lets out a girlish scream.

It takes a moment for Garth to remember that he's wearing a black trencher and black ski mask, probably looking more like a criminal than a wannabe hero. Maybe he'll rethink the costume idea. "Sir, I'm here to help. Do you need an ambulance?"

The man considers his wounds, then shakes his head. "Did you stop him? Elephant Man?"

"He's outside."

"Tied up? Unconscious?"

"Well. No. Not exactly. He's sort of fighting another former hero for your stuff."

The man lets out a truly impressive curse.

"Sorry," Garth says. "It's my first fight."

"You should reconsider the day job." The man tries to get up, then groans and lies back down.

"I'll call the police," Garth says. "Phone?"

The man weakly motions to the broken counter.

Garth hobbles over, picking his way around the broken

glass. Spying the phone, he reaches down for it . . . and sees the baseball bat half-buried in the debris on the floor.

Oh yeah.

Walking out of the pawnshop, Garth tosses the phone to the battered man and tells him to call nine-one-one. Outside, the two rabids are still trading blows. They've drawn a cautious crowd of onlookers, all of whom look ready to bolt in a heartbeat. None of them are trying to step in or look in on the man whose store was being robbed. Garth isn't really surprised. Elephant Man and the Ram are pretty damn frightening. Each time a punch connects is like a small peal of thunder.

He creeps forward, quiet as the mouse Elephant Man had called him. He brings up the bat. And he actually grins. Maybe he is just an extrahuman wannabe. But he'd been the home-run king for the Middlewood Hornets junior and senior year.

It occurs to him, as he takes the first swing, that a real hero wouldn't hit someone from behind.

But then, he's no hero.

Final score: Garth 2, rabids 0.

He doesn't stick around for the official collar. But when he gets back to the apartment, Terry and the others throw an impromptu party. And when they get the news that finally, *finally,* some of the Latents are coming through and making their way to New Chicago to help, then Garth allows himself to get good and drunk.

No, they have no idea what they're doing. But hell, doing something is worlds better than doing nothing.

NOW

CHAPTER 48

JET

Hypnotic's power is more insidious than the other Mental-ists'. Or perhaps it is not the ability but the skill behind it. Other Mentalists are grade-schoolers with scissors; he is a surgeon—focused, precise, and, at times, surprisingly cre-ative. Aaron and I both are certain his is the power we need to mimic if we're ever to get the Squadron under control.
—From the journal of Martin Moore, entry #57

Two big differences from when Jet had approached Hyp-notic's hideout a few days earlier: one, this time there were about a hundred people standing outside of the aban-doned building, staring blankly, unmoving. And two: Jet was waiting until she and the others were in place before going in, no matter how worried she was about Iridium.

Jet and Frostbite touched down simultaneously. As she ab-sorbed the Shadow floater, he walked up to the nearest civilian and waved a hand in front of the woman's eyes. No reaction. He snapped his fingers, but still nothing.

"No one's home," he said.

"Look at them all." Jet stared at a group of entranced nor-mals, some in business suits, some in more relaxed garb, a few in workout clothing. "They couldn't have all just been walking here when they fell under his power."

"Think Hypnotic summoned them?"

"Maybe. Snared them with his mental mojo, then directed them here."

"To do what? Be lawn gnomes?"

Looking at a young girl, frozen hand in hand with a woman in a professional unisuit, Jet sighed. "Hostages."

"We can get EMTs here to clear them out."

"And what if his Mental wave or however his power works broadcasts again and they get snared also? More hostages." She navigated her way through the living statues, but once she was within three meters of the door, the zombies lurched forward.

Jet halted, her arms out, ready to call up a graymatter shield. But there was no need; as soon as she stopped heading toward the entrance, the normals stood still, their arms loose at their sides, their eyes white.

"Creepy," said Frostbite. "A living motion detector."

"Better than trip wires."

"Not really. I can make an ice bridge over trip wires."

"So make an ice bridge onto the roof," a man's voice called out from above. "See if they secretly have ice picks up their sleeves."

Jet looked up to frown at Taser, seated on his hover. Steele rode behind him, her arms loosely draped around his waist.

"About time," Jet said.

"Hey, I'm impressed you actually waited, honey. Usually it's the guy who shoots off too fast, but you superdames are more cocksure than a locker room full of wrestlers. By the way, I love the new look. It's sexy."

And damn it all to Darkness if Jet didn't feel her cheeks heat.

"Are you going to banter all day," Steele said sharply, "or are you going to park this thing so we can help?"

"Oh look, a spot." Taser gunned the engine before he parked the hover directly across the street from Hypnotic's lair.

Frostbite shook his head as Steele and Taser walked over to him and Jet. "You worried the meter maid's gonna ticket you?"

"I don't fancy zombies scratching my paint job."

Jet tuned them out as she tapped Ops on her earpiece and

let Meteorite know that the four of them were gathered and would be entering the building. "I'll keep the channel open so you can hear what's happening. From what I've seen, his power is based on both sight and proximity. You'll be safe."

"Good luck," Meteorite replied, her voice stripped of her usual snark.

"Thanks." She turned to face the others. "Frostbite, you can clear us a path to the door. Once we're inside, keep your eyes covered. He likes to use light to capture your attention. We'll go in, get Iridium and the others, and get out."

"We have to take him out," Steele said gruffly, staring past the bespelled citizens, her gaze boring a hole through the door.

"We don't want a repeat of the Manhattan Siege," Frostbite said. "I'm with Jet. In and out. Rescue our own, regroup."

Steele tightened her jaw. "He can't be allowed to stay free. He's too dangerous."

"He let us go last time," Taser said. "Doubt we'll be so fortunate the second time."

The large woman stared at the mercenary, her eyes glittering. Then she went metal, her flesh transforming into living steel. "Fine," she grunted, turning back to the door. "Let's do this."

Jet and Frostbite exchanged a look. He mouthed: I've got her back. Jet nodded once.

"Okay," Frostbite said. "One ice tunnel coming up."

He squatted down, placing one hand on the sidewalk. Ice spread from his fingers, stretching its way toward the front door, sliding under the humans. Once it touched the door, it slowly expanded outward, gently pushing people out of its way as it formed a covered path. None of the zombies reacted. Jet assumed they'd been programmed to block the door to prevent only uninvited guests from entering.

Jet noticed the sweat beading on Frostbite's brow, saw the small tremor in his fingers. He'd been out of the field too long; before this week, the most he'd used his power in six years was to make homemade Slushies. The ice path gleamed in the morning light, beautiful and fragile as a rose in winter.

Come on, Derek the Dork. You can do it. Get us in there to save Callie.

Frostbite was sweating freely now, his brow furrowed in concentration. The walls of the covered path thickened, and thickened again. More zombies were nudged aside.

"Just a little more," Jet said.

He grunted, perhaps agreeing with her or telling her to fuck off.

"Jet."

She glanced over at Steele. "Yes?"

"Where's Firebug?"

Jet considered lying, something small and harmless, like she'd overdone the croissants and was doubled over on the can. But Jet was a horrible liar; Iridium had always been the one who could smoothly talk her way out of anything.

Almost anything, Jet thought, sliding a glance at the nearest zombie. Was Callie like that, standing like a child's doll, waiting to be used? Jet's lips pressed together tightly as she imagined Iri reduced to a mindless puppet. Was she unconscious? Hurt?

Worse?

The sound of Hornblower's agonized scream reverberated in Jet's mind, his leg pulled off at the knee.

"She's back at headquarters," Jet replied coldly.

Confusion in her eyes, Steele asked, "Was she hurt?"

"No."

Comprehension dawned on her metallic face. Her eyes wounded, she turned away from Jet.

Another minute, then Frostbite was done. He sat down hard on his ass and mopped his blue hair from his eyes with a shaking hand.

"Nice job," Taser said, whistling. "You make sculptures for weddings?"

"Frostbite, stay here to guard our flank," Jet said crisply. "Steele, you take the door. Let's go."

"Good plan," Frostbite said, smiling briefly. "Scream if you need me."

The three of them walked down the ice path, Steele leading

the way, Jet behind her, and Taser bringing up the rear. Peripherally, Jet saw the normals launching themselves at the tunnel, then sliding down the walls to the ground. Some of them beat at the ice with their hands and arms, but Frostbite had done his job well: The tunnel stood, and the three of them made it to the door without having to fight any of the innocents.

Steele grabbed the door handle and turned it. When nothing happened, she grunted, took a step back, and then leveled a kick at the door. It slammed open.

The three heroes entered Hypnotic's lair . . . and saw dozens of costumed extrahumans standing like discarded toy soldiers, their eyes blank. Jet's gaze roamed over them, identifying numerous Squadron soldiers and a handful of known villains.

There, off to the right: a tall man, radiating confidence to the point of arrogance, even with his eyes blinded by Hypnotic's power. Arclight.

And by his side stood his only child, her stance as arrogant as his—her eyes also white on white, lost in Hypnotic's spell.

Iridium.

Jet took a step toward them, Iri's name on her lips.

"Why, Joan, how lovely it is to see you again."

She spun left, and there he was, still in his prison grays: Doctor Hypnotic, smiling benignly.

"And look, you brought guests. Children," he said loudly, "go play." He snapped his fingers.

And that was when all the entranced extrahumans attacked.

CHAPTER 49

IRIDIUM

*Out of all of the children I've created, the only ones who
scare me—really terrify me—are the Mental powers. If they
realized their abilities . . . who knows what they could do?*
                              —Matthew Icarus, diary entry, undated

She had saved another hostage, beaten another villain. People were cheering and Bruce was waiting with open arms. Bruce was always there, but lately Iridium had felt alone even when he was with her.

Even when she was in a crowd of admirers, lining up to see the Hero of New Chicago.

Iridium knew that she didn't have any friends besides her husband. Her loving husband. Who'd been talking about kids.

Iridium put him off, though. She couldn't tell anyone, least of all her perfect husband, about the voices.

How they whispered, anytime she was in the dark.

Dimly, Iridium recalled that she'd had a friend who was afraid of the Dark.

Then the thought slipped away from her, like it always did.

The thoughts about her father, about the Darkness, about friends she'd never known.

This was what she wanted, underneath everything. The thing she'd never gotten the chance to be with Corp—a hero. A real one.

Iridium shivered as she stepped away from the crowd. The sun was coming down, but she was freezing. Freezing cold. Her friend had always been cold.

Jet. Her name was Jet.

"Jet," Iridium whispered.

Bruce cocked his head. "What was that, sweetie?"

Jet and Bruce. Together. Kissing.

"You . . . you slept with her," Iridium gasped. Once she'd remembered the name, it was like a dam burst inside her skull, thoughts slipping and tumbling over her all at once.

She was cold. So cold.

"You had a mask," Iridium whispered. "You had a mask and a different name."

"Sweetie, you're not making any sense." Bruce frowned. "What will the press think? What will your father say?"

Lester behind a mug slate on the front page of every newspaper in New Chicago.

ARCLIGHT CAPTURED, CITY SAFE

"My father isn't real," Iridium choked. She couldn't breathe, couldn't think.

Bruce's face was hard, cold, a shell with nothing behind it. The buildings were flimsy, and everything was going dark as the street faded around her . . .

"Iri!"

A hand pulled her to her feet. Small and cold. Not Bruce.

"Iri, wake up!"

Her eyes flew open to blackness, blackness that retreated like the sun rising through the cold of space.

Jet let go of her and cocked her head. "Are you with us?"

Iridium tried to answer but her teeth were chattering. "What . . . what . . ."

"Hypnotic," Jet said. "He got you. I had to blanket you in

Shadow just to make you stop strobing me. You were screaming something about hostages."

"Oh, Christo . . ." Iridium clapped her hands over her mouth. "Jet, I couldn't fight it . . . he made me see what I really wanted . . ."

From somewhere, she heard shouting.

"Later," Jet said. "We can apologize later. Steele and Taser are getting the others. We have to go."

"No," Iridium said, her eyes wide and shocked. "My dad . . ."

"Callie," Jet said, gripping her shoulder. "Your dad is being rescued."

The building shuddered, and a strobe sailed past Jet, splashing burns on the wall behind Iridium's head.

Lester stood behind her, strobes ready in both hands. His eyes were white, vacant.

Enslaved.

Iridium's heart fluttered with panic. "My dad is right behind you."

CHAPTER 50

IRIDIUM AND JET

I never wanted to hurt them. But it was the only way to save the rest of us.

—Matthew Icarus, internal report filed
with Executive Committee regarding radical lobotomy
of Subject 7789, code name "Dreamer"

Executive Committee gave Therapy stamp of approval. They had to. Kane and the others know what happens when Squadron members reach their "extracritical" points. Now we don't need to decommission them—just erase the bad, emphasize the good, and force them to obey. Everyone wins. Except the Squadron, I suppose. But they're only extrahuman.

—From the journal of Martin Moore, entry #65

IRIDIUM

Jet whirled, throwing Shadows. Iridium saw her father dodge, his hands glowing.

"Go!" Iridium shouted, hurling a strobe at Lester, arcing just over his face. "Get Hypnotic! I'll take care of Arclight!"

"Don't get killed." Then Jet was gone, swallowed in Shadow.

Iridium strobed again, fast and furious, then dove behind the lobby's abandoned security desk, trusting that between her power and the sounds of battle erupting around them, her father couldn't pinpoint where she'd gone off to.

"You can't beat me, girl." Lester's voice was low, snarling, foreign to Iridium's ears. Crouched as she was behind the ancient desk, she concentrated on keeping herself in as small a ball as possible.

Her father couldn't strobe what he couldn't see.

At least, she hoped not.

"Give up, Callie!" Lester shouted. Another strobe rocked her cover. "I don't want to hurt you. I love you—you know that!"

"You're not my father!" Iridium screamed. If he just got close enough, she could knock him out without hurting him. "Let go of him and face me yourself, you pissant coward!"

She thought she could knock Lester out. Probably. Maybe.

"You're fighting the wrong man, Calista." The strobes were definitely closer. "You should be fighting our common enemy. Who is really the one who caused this?"

Iridium knew the answer. *Corp.*

"Give it up, Hypnotic!" she called. "You're not any more interested in stopping Corp than you are in taking up ballet!" Keep him talking, that was the trick. Jet said Steele and Taser were getting the others out. She had to keep Lester focused on her to keep the others safe.

Iridium risked peering around the side of the desk, saw Lester advancing on her with strobes and those cold, dead eyes.

"You'd leave your own father to rot in jail and the men who put him there walking free?" Another strobe. "I should have had a son. *He'd* do what was needed."

Iridium flinched at that. Lester had always treated her like a tomboy, but she'd never imagined he'd really wanted a *son* . . .

Stop that. Her mind was still cloudy from Hypnotic's influence. The words spouting out of Lester's mouth were just lies, designed by the mind-reading madman himself to throw her off-balance.

"If you wanted a son so bad, I guess you were lying all of those times you said you were proud of me! That you loved me and Mom!" she called, scrambling to the other side.

"I was."

The quiet in Lester's tone was what stunned Iridium. He wasn't ranting any longer. He was standing there, surrounded by a constellation of strobes, his face harder than tilithium. Gone was every trace of her father's warmth. There was no Lester.

There was only Arclight.

JET

"Hypnotic!" Jet called out.

He appeared from nowhere, ducking his head in a mocking bow, then disappeared around a corner.

She followed, leaving the sounds of battle behind her. Her goggles firmly in place over her eyes, she picked up the pace. Up ahead, she heard a door slam.

"Jet," Meteorite hissed in her ear. "Don't be an idiot! You've got Iridium. Get out of there!"

Jet turned her comlink off.

She navigated another corner and paused to scan ahead. Long, narrow hallway with sickly yellow walls and a thin dark carpet; eight forest-green doors, three on either side and two at the end, facing her.

"No games, Hal," she shouted.

Nothing.

Fine. The hard way, then.

She approached the first door on the left, placed her ear to it and listened. A muffled scraping from within. Jet turned the handle, and the door swung wide, revealing a small room filled with roses.

"Flowers?" she called out. "Are you asking me out, Hal?" No response. "For the record, I don't like flowers."

The next room was filled with dust and nothing else. Cute. "Hal," she said, her voice low and reasonable. "Come out. Talk to me."

The third: mirrors. In each mirror, Doctor Hypnotic stood behind Jet.

She whirled around, saw nothing.

From the mirrors: "You want to talk, Joan? Then let's talk."

IRIDIUM

"I gave up my whole life for you, so you could do something great with yours. And what do you do? You crawl back to Corp in the end." Arclight's tone was sharper than a blade.

Iridium held her head. How she wanted to block him out— but she had to listen, to judge how close he was.

"I gave you a normal life, a life of privilege, and look how you throw it back in my face." Arclight advanced, throwing a strobe for every sentence that bored into Iridium like a surgical drill. "Expelled from the Academy." *Flash*. "A fugitive." *Flash*. "A *weakling*."

"*A normal life?*" Iridium screamed. She stood up, hurling a strobe of her own at her father. He batted it aside, hissing as it burned his hand.

She could do the same to his strobes. They'd be at this until one of them got tired. Or died.

STOP it!

"You call the life you gave me normal?" she shouted. It was more than distraction, now. What Lester had said was too close to the bone to be only Hypnotic's doing. "I had a father I never saw, a father who got himself carted away to prison when I was a tiny girl and left me with nothing but the *privilege* of being the daughter of a rabid! You left me *alone*, Dad! You *left* me!"

She flung another strobe, and Lester didn't bat this one away. He sat down hard, blinking the stars from his eyes.

"Yeah, you gave me everything a daughter could ask for," Iridium snarled. "Thanks for fucking nothing, *Daddy*."

Lester could have blocked her final strobe, but he didn't. He just stared at her, the pain in his face nearly crumbling the wall around Iridium's heart. For a moment, she thought Hypnotic's hold had loosened. But then his expression twisted.

"You never did know your place, girl."

Iridium didn't reply. She released her strobe, and Arclight fell back, unconscious.

She swiped away her tears before anyone saw, pretended they were only from the unbearable brightness of her power and not for her father, lying cold and still on the floor.

JET

Jet turned again, slowly this time, her hands twitching. From elsewhere in the building, something crashed heavily to the floor. She tensed, debating whether to go back to help the others. In the mirrors, Doctor Hypnotic had put his hands on her shoulders. Jet couldn't tell if she really felt gentle pressure near her neck, massaging away the tension, or if it was all in her mind.

"Please," he said. "Come in."

Lifting her chin, she stepped into the room. As soon as she cleared the door, it shut behind her, locking with a soft *click*. "Nice trick," she said, keeping her panic at bay. She still didn't see him.

"Once my power touches you," he said, "you're mine anytime I wish it. You're under my power, Joan. You have been since we first talked all those days ago."

"That sounds like something out of a cheesy suspense vid." Iri would have been proud of her quip.

The lighting dimmed so that all she could see were the dozens of mirrors, all of them reflecting her and Hypnotic . . . whose hands were moving lower on her body.

"Stop that," Jet said, resisting the urge to slap at her breasts. His hands weren't really on her. They weren't.

"Of course," he murmured in her ear.

She refused to react to his presumed nearness. Either he was there or he wasn't. She smelled a whiff of musk and sweat, a completely masculine smell that made her light-headed.

In the mirrors, his hands went back to her shoulders. Possessive. "I love what you've done to your hair," he said, sounding pleased. His reflection stroked the loose tail of her blond hair, his long fingers entwining strands of gold.

Not real, she told herself. Speaking to the mirror directly before her, she said, "You don't have to do this."

"Do what?"

"Entrance innocents, putting them in hospitals."

"But Joan, that had been your idea."

The audacity of his words hit her like ice water.

"Don't you remember? You said I could help make a difference." His reflection smiled broadly. It was a good smile. "And so I have. I send my power out, and it gives each mind it touches its own version of paradise. Those people aren't unhappy, Joan. Far from it."

"No, they're just stripped of their free will."

"A small price to pay for paradise."

She wanted to tell him he was wrong, that the price was much too great. But that wouldn't reach him. So instead, she fed his ego. "How are you doing it? A device to amplify your ability?"

The smile gave way to bemused laughter. "No, Joan. That's just me. Oh," he said, perhaps in answer to Jet's gasp of surprise, "even I'm not strong enough to broadcast widely for very long. And then it takes me the better part of a day to recharge enough to send out another signal. The mind is willing," he said, grinning, "but the body is weak. For now. After I rest, my strength will be greater. And then I can travel the Americas, giving everyone, human and extrahuman alike, their own personal utopia. Think of it, Joan!"

She did, and it made her want to vomit.

"But don't you see?" she said, a note of desperation in her voice. "It's not utopia. You're stealing their lives. You're making it impossible for them to make this world, the real world, a better place."

"Because they've done such a marvelous job of it already," he said, his mouth twisting into a sneer. "They pollute the sky and land. They attack each other with words and fists. I may be stealing their lives, Joan, but they've been stealing from one another for centuries! Money. Power. Love," he said, his voice breaking. "They steal, and they don't care who they hurt."

"That's not everyone," she said. "Some, yes. But not all."

"There are only two kinds of people, Joan. Those who steal from others, and those who've had things, people, stolen from them. They stole your mother, Joan."

In the mirror, Jet and Hypnotic disappeared. In their place was a woman a little smaller than Jet, wearing a sparkling white skinsuit and flowing cape, her sunlit hair playful around her face. She had a breathtaking smile.

Her mother.

No. Jet's fists clenched so hard her hands shook. *Not real.*

"They stole your love."

Next to Angelica, Samson appeared, so big and broad and full of life.

Jet squeezed her eyes closed, turned her head away. "Stop it."

"I didn't take them from you," Hypnotic said. "But I can give them back to you. Why wouldn't you want that?"

Her voice a whisper, she said, "Because it's not real."

Hands on her shoulders, turning her around slowly. "Honey," a silky voice said, one that made her tingle, "I can make it so real that you'd never know there'd been anything else."

She opened her eyes and saw Bruce Hunter standing before her, hugging her, his bright blue eyes wicked, his sensual lips set in a hungry smile. His hands flowed over her back, pulled her close.

"Holly," he murmured, leaning down as if to kiss her. "I've missed you so."

No.

Her power sprang to life, flowing through her and around him, wrapping him in a lover's embrace. She squirmed out of his grip and stepped backward, watching as the Shadow lulled him. She raised a shaking hand to her mouth. Her mother and Sam were dead, and Light, she missed them so. But having Bruce—not Taser with his smug, hidden grins and cocksure attitude, but Bruce Hunter, the man she'd taken to her bed—so close to her had almost been her undoing.

Hormones really were going to be the death of her.

The Shadow-wrapped man collapsed to his knees and slowly fell to the floor. She called her power back, touching one of her belt pouches to take out a pair of stun-cuffs.

As the Shadow seeped into her, she realized that she hadn't felt Hal's light—that she'd blanketed him, but she hadn't sensed the man beneath the Shadow.

A crushing pain in her back, a blow that sent her to her knees.

"That," Doctor Hypnotic said, "was incredibly rude. And after I've done such nice things for you."

She rolled and came up on her feet, her power pulsing through her. "I told you before, Hypnotic. I'm duty-bound to this world. The real world. You can't buy me with your version of paradise."

A smile crept over his mouth. "Maybe I should unlock the Shadow voices once more. Let them whisper to you and steal your soul."

She froze.

"What do you say, Jet? Shall I let you go crazy again?"

She allowed herself a moment to enjoy the feeling of the Shadow working its way through her without the struggle to hold on to her sanity. "So be it," she whispered.

And then she leveled a Shadowbolt at him, hitting him square in the chest. He flew backward and hit the wall—went *through* the wall, stopping only when he hit another wall, one Jet hadn't been able to see until just now. They'd been in the front lobby the entire time, somehow avoiding the other extrahumans in their duels and battles. Even now, the others didn't seem real—they were ghostlike, walking dreams that warred with one another.

Nice trick.

Hypnotic was already pulling himself up, still smiling at her. "Your mother would be proud of you, Jet. And so would your father."

In her mind, the cell holding the Shadow voices evaporated. And the Shadow let out an ecstatic roar.

little girl little Joan missed you missed you so very much . . .

Adrenaline and rage and fear warring within her, Jet snarled as she hit him with another burst of Shadow.

IRIDIUM

After she'd given herself a few seconds to collect her emotions, cage them up, and tamp them down, Iridium turned to help Taser. He and a rabid—Gaslight, Iridium thought—were circling each other warily, until finally the petite heroine blinked. "Dude. Who the hell are you, and why do you have on that stupid mask?"

"Taser, is she . . ."

"She's in her right mind." Behind her, someone put a massive hand on Iridium's shoulder. She turned to see Protean looming there, smiling. "As are we all."

Iridium felt herself physically sag with relief. Protean gripped her, holding her up. In her ear, he murmured, "See to your father."

"We still got a problem here," Taser said. He ducked a cloud of noxious poison from Gaslight. "These guys aren't our friends!"

"Burn in hell, Corp puppets!" Gaslight screamed. The dozen other rabids in the room all turned on the small knot of allies.

"Oh, bollocks," Kindle said.

Peripherally, Iridium saw Nevermore take flight, saw Lionheart shift into his cat form. Next to her, Protean curled his fists.

"Everyone take a rabid," Iridium barked. "Subdue, don't kill."

"Speak for yourself, Princess!" Nevermore screeched. She and Freefall were engaged in a midair tussle, Freefall's antigravity field making Nevermore sway drunkenly as she fought to keep aloft.

Iridium herself went to ground under the onslaught of Knife, his steel fingernails slashing the air where her face had been.

Protean grabbed him and flung him into the far wall, but the Judge swung his massive gavel. Protean joined Iridium on the ground, dodging the blow.

"Get your father to safety," he said, pointing to where Arclight lay in the midst of the tussling extrahumans.

Before Iridium could move, Sonic Scream opened his mouth and unleashed a wave of sound. Iridium hit the ground for a second time, cradling her head in her arms to keep her eardrums from rupturing.

"This isn't working!" she screamed at Protean.

He just shook his head . . . he couldn't hear anything in the onslaught of sound.

Well, the douche bag had to run out of breath sometime.

Iridium tossed a strobe at a lizardlike rabid who was sneaking up on Lionheart, then another at Freefall as he and Nevermore tumbled back to ground.

The rabids shied away from her strobes, gathering like a Roman legion in the corner of the lobby.

Iridium grabbed Kindle by the shoulder. "I have an idea!" she shouted, hoping he could read lips. She snapped a finger at the rabids, used her other hand to shape a cage.

Kindle nodded and pantomimed getting the rabids closer together.

"Lionheart! Protean!" she bellowed, flinging another strobe as Creeper started to stretch out and sneak toward her from the group.

The heroes caught on, and Lionheart bounded around the group, nipping at their heels. Protean simply picked up anyone not already in the corner and threw them like they were luggage on an international flight.

Dry heat swept Iridium's face as all of the moisture evaporated from the air, the precursor to Kindle's pyrokinesis. The Irishman furrowed his brow, and a spot of flame appeared, hanging in midair like a tiny sun.

Sonic Scream's sound wall fell as Protean punched him in the gut.

"Get clear!" Iridium shouted in the silence. "Get out of the way!"

With a *whoosh* and a roar of displaced oxygen, Kindle's fire cage sprang into being, like a vision or a mirage of the most beautiful oasis Iridium had ever seen.

She rubbed her pounding head. "Thank Christo for small favors."

Protean, Lionheart, and Nevermore formed up around Kindle as he stood with his hands out, sweat beading on his forehead. "You all right?" Nevermore said. She actually sounded like she cared.

Well, Kindle was sort of cute. If you were into old guys.

"Be fine," he gritted. "Just don't break me concentration."

Iridium knelt next to Lester and slapped his face gently. "Dad."

After a moment he opened his eyes, and groaned. "Bloody hell, Calista. You strobed me."

"I had to," Iridium said crisply. "Only way to break Hypnotic's hold."

"Callie." He caught her hand. "You have to know I had no control over what I was saying. Seeing. You have to know I didn't mean any of it, girl."

Iridium looked at his hand on hers, his eyes, which were clear and warm once again. But those words were still there, ugly, hanging over her head.

"Bloody hell, Callie. Say something."

"You already said it." Iridium pulled away and helped him up. "We need containment, backup, and crowd control before—"

There was a massive crash, scattering the group of Blackbird inmates.

From nowhere, Doctor Hypnotic suddenly appeared, groaning as he sat up. Iridium saw Jet nearby, her fists clenched, Shadows leaking between her fingers.

Protean, Lionheart, and Nevermore scattered from Hypnotic like he was radioactive. As they scampered, Jet slowly approached him, Shadows writhing around her.

"Impressive, Joan," Hypnotic slurred. He pulled himself up, swaying like a drunk, and a deep gash in his forehead spoke to a concussion. "But can you keep the whispers away long enough to finish me?"

Jet hesitated.

"Just what I thought." Hypnotic purred. "You can't do it. You know what's inside you and you'll never let it out. The Darkness has its teeth in you, Joan, and it's consuming."

Jet's forehead furrowed. "Don't make me hurt you."

Iridium stepped up beside Jet. "What are you waiting for?" she murmured. "Finish him off."

"He . . ." Jet let her hand drop. "He took away my Shadow. It was . . . it was . . ."

"Wonderful," Hypnotic purred.

Iridium felt a strobe grow reflexively. "You shut up."

"I don't have to say a thing," Hal said. "Joan's a prisoner of her power."

Iridium looked away from him, trying to block out that smooth tone, that seductive voice that could give her anything she ever wanted. "No, Joan," she said softly. "He's lying to you."

Twin tears worked their way down Jet's face. "We can't beat him."

"I can't," Iridium said softly. She put her hand on Joan's shoulder. "But you can."

Jet shivered under her touch.

Iridium put a little light heat into her grip. "You don't have darkness inside you, Joannie," she whispered. "You have bright, beautiful things. I know."

Jet sniffed hard. "How do you know?"

Iridium sensed Hypnotic looming closer, and she tightened her grip. "Because I know you, Joan. I know you."

Iridium turned, and before she even thought about it, she released the heat in the hand that had been holding Jet. Jet's creeper hit Hypnotic at the same time.

"You think that'll stop me?" he bellowed, staggering. "Nothing stops me! I'm Doctor Hypnotic!"

Iridium strobed him again, and Jet's Shadow creepers grew ravenous.

"Christo," Jet said tiredly. "Shut up, will you?"

Hypnotic crumpled to the ground.

Iridium kept strobing him, and realized she was screaming. She didn't care, didn't stop hurting the monster who'd taken her mind and now her family from her.

Gloved hands pulled her away and Taser wrapped his arms around her, making her still.

"It's over," Taser whispered. "Callie, stop."

Iridium felt his heart beating under his Kevlar, the rapid rhythm in time with her own.

"Callie? Can I let you go?"

Iridium forced herself to breathe. She looked at Hypnotic's bloody, still form on the floor and nodded, slowly and shakily. "It's over."

JET

Sighing, Jet stared at the fallen man. Doctor Hypnotic looked so old, lying there on the floor. So helpless. Difficult to imagine he'd entranced hundreds of people . . . or that decades ago, he'd caused the deaths of hundreds more, scarred the minds of thousands.

scars and screams and sweet sweet sounds . . .

She clenched her fist. *Shut up!*

The voices giggled, and receded. For now.

"Well," Taser said. "That's a big win, yeah?"

Someone brushed past Jet, nearly pushing her off her feet. Rubbing her bruised arm, Jet glowered at Arclight, who knelt and inspected Hypnotic's face. He was silent for a long moment, then he spat on the unconscious man's cheek.

"Hey," Jet said, affronted.

"Don't you 'Hey' me, little girl. You don't know what he made me see." Arclight sneered at Hypnotic's crumpled form before he pulled himself up to his full height.

"He's sick," Jet said quietly, only somewhat surprised that she was making excuses for one of the most feared supervillains in recent history. "He needs help."

Arclight laughed, the sound harsh and cruel. "He needs a bullet through the brain."

"Seconded," said a rabid Jet didn't recognize, a thin Goth girl who clung to a light fixture on the ceiling. Upside down, she pulled out a Hogan cutter from her sleeve.

"Put it away, girl," Steele growled.

"Yeah? You going to make me, Tin Can?"

Steele glared up at the girl on the ceiling, her metallic fists gleaming.

"Enough." Jet's voice echoed in the hallway.

For a moment, there was only the sound of the fire cage crackling and the mutters of the captured rabids. Then Arclight said, "Of course. We shouldn't be arguing. We're all on the same team after all." That last made the Goth girl giggle.

Ignoring them, Jet took out a pair of stun-cuffs and slapped them over Hypnotic's wrists. Her chest felt too tight, and behind her optiframes, tears stung her eyes. Well, enough of that too. The voices were back already, but hopefully she wouldn't start getting the headaches again. Or at least, not until tomorrow. "He's going back to Blackbird, as are you."

Now the Goth girl chortled.

"Not going back there," said one of her cohorts, a big man with oversized muscles. Protean, Jet recalled. Sent away seven years ago for smashing through the vaults of First National with his fists. How did they all escape prison in the first place? "You can't put me back there. They junk me up so much I can't think."

"My team and I aren't going back," Arclight said, smiling as if he'd just won the national lottery. "We have a free pass, you see."

Jet arched a brow. *"Really."*

"Really really," Iridium said, her voice flat. When Jet turned to face her, Iri sighed. "Signed and sealed. The five of them are free, and so am I, as long as we report to our boss and do what we're told, like good doggies."

Dreading the answer, Jet asked, "And who would that boss be?"

"Why, dear girl, don't you know?" Arclight grinned. "Corp-Co."

Steele said, "You must be joking."

"No joke," Iridium replied. "It's all aboveboard."

Jet opened her mouth to argue, to deny what father and daughter were insisting, but at that moment something slammed into the building with a thunderous crash. Losing her balance, Jet toppled into Protean, who helped her to her feet.

Light, did he have to be chivalrous when he was also a villain? That wasn't fair at all.

At the window near the front door, Taser said, "Uh-oh."

Iridium stumbled over to him. "Uh-oh what?"

"Uh-oh that."

Iridium looked, and then she let out a curse that made Jet's ears bleed.

"What?" she asked, really not wanting to know.

"You remember those sewer mutants?" Iri said, her voice too high. "Looks like they're back."

"And this time," Taser added, "they brought a hundred or so of their friends with them."

CHAPTER 51

IRIDIUM

*I have no illusion that I'm in control. I'm the figurehead,
the man who unlocked the door to the age of the extrahuman. But Corp is the master of their fate. Those poor children. I should have never tried to save them.*

—Matthew Icarus, diary entry dated 2018

W e should get out there." Jet shoved past Iridium and
started for the front door. "There are innocent civilians."

"Fuck that," Nevermore said. "Look at the size of those monsters."

"You *criminals* are welcome to do whatever you want," Jet
snapped. "I have a job to protect these people."

"Who do you think just saved your ass?" Nevermore demanded. "The Tooth Fairy?"

"Everybody shut it!" Iridium bellowed, as she saw the Blackbird fugitives and the Squadron begin to divide into sides, sides
that would no doubt erupt into another superhuman slap fight.

Jet flicked her the patronizing, annoyed glance that she'd
learned from Night before he went nuts. "Something to add,
Iridium?"

Iridium pointed at the street outside, where the mutants

milled among the humans, grumbling or crying or laughing to themselves. "They don't seem all that interested in plain old humans. I don't think getting yourself turned into Jet pâté will be a huge help at this point."

"I can't leave them to rampage!"

"Just leave them alone," Iridium gritted, "and they'll leave us alone."

"And if you're wrong?" Jet shook her head. "We can't risk that."

Iridium sighed. She was exhausted, her head was throbbing again. "Fine. Do whatever you want, Joan."

"Fine. I will."

"You should listen to my daughter, girl." Lester spoke from the back of the group, where he and Protean were watching Hypnotic.

Jet blinked at him, then turned to face Steele. "What do you think, Harriet?"

"I think we have a prisoner," Steele said, "and he should be in lockdown yesterday. Hypnotic is the priority."

Taser pointed at the street. "Something's got them stirred up."

First one mutant, then another turned its swollen eyes to the north, and as one they lumbered up the street, occasionally knocking over a frozen civilian. A shine glinted in the weak sunlight, and Iridium caught a glimpse of blue hair. "It's Derek," she said.

"And they are on him like fat kids on cake," Taser said.

"They're clearly attracted to extrahumans," Lester said. "Must be something in the way we smell."

"Terrific," Iridium muttered. "Dad, Taser, come with me. We've got to clear a path for him. The rest of you, stay here and watch the rabids."

Jet sighed dramatically, but she didn't argue with Iridium's orders. That was a nice change.

Iridium ran into the street, throwing a strobe not at the mutants but at the pavement in front of them, exploding concrete and gravel. "Run, Derek!" she screamed.

Frostbite froze the first giant hand that reached for him,

dodged the second, then fell under the third pair. He rolled out of the way and came up while Lester used the refracted light in the air to create a dazzling envelopment of prisms around the mutant who'd been about to squish him.

Taser scooped Frostbite up and handed him off to Iridium. "Go," the merc said. "I'll cover the retreat."

"Your six!" Frostbite shouted, freezing the feet of a mutant who'd been about to snatch Taser and snap him in half. The mutant swayed and fell with a crash like a tree trunk.

Iridium tugged at Frostbite. "Come on. We've got to get back inside before they realize it's an all-you-can-smash extrahuman buffet in there."

They ran, Iridium's heart pounding like it had only a few times before. As soon as they were inside the apartment building, Lester slammed the door shut. Iridium swallowed, tried to get her pulse back under control. "You okay, Derek?"

"Fine," he said. "I was waiting for the emergency responders when Meteorite commed me." He rubbed the shoulder he'd landed on. "Our bloaty pals out there are not the only mutants running loose. Everyman has released a pack of them into the Downtown Grid."

Iridium sighed. "Of course they have." She'd beaten Doctor Hypnotic—wasn't that enough for one day?

"How many is a pack?" Jet asked quietly.

Derek grimaced. "Enough to put it in the We're All Doomed, Doomed I Say column."

"Okay," Iridium said, thinking quickly. "Jet, you and I and anyone else with long-range powers should get down there. Where's Firebug?"

"Back at HQ," Jet gritted. "She couldn't face Hypnotic."

"Well, I hope mutants are more to her liking."

Before Jet could open her mouth to argue, there was a scream from behind.

Iridium spun to see Kindle lying on his back, wheezing for breath, the Judge's gavel lying near him on the ground.

Knife grinned as the fire cage faded. "Feeding time at the zoo, boys and girls. And what a spread we've got today."

Before Iridium could react, an ice wall appeared in front of the Squadron and the Blackbird fugitives, separating them from the rabids.

Frostbite lowered his hands. "What now?"

"Now?" Iridium peered around the shield at the advancing rabids. "We end this once and for all." She pointed at Kindle's prone form. "Get him help. The rest of you, pick your nutjob ex-hero and get to punching."

The Squadron and the Blackbird contingent spread out in a loose formation. *Amazing how well you could work with people you despised when your ass was on the line,* Iridium thought. She picked out Sonic Scream, the wanker who'd caused all of the trouble in Round One.

He went down with one hard strobe, but that left her with Creeper, who tangled her in his rubbery arms and sent her down, hard. Something in Iridium's arm gave.

"Remind me," she said through clenched teeth, summoning up radiant light-heat. "What temperature does rubber melt at?"

Sweat worked down Creeper's face while he tried to squeeze the life from her. "How much pressure does it take to break a mouthy Lighter's back?"

She could burn him badly enough that he let go, or he could crush her unconscious. It all came down to willpower.

Finally, Creeper released her as he fell to the ground, screaming. "My hands!" He writhed on the floor, holding his smoking hands away from his body. "It hurts!"

"Tip for next time," Iridium gasped. "Human flesh melts faster." The sound of electric charges made her turn to the left, and she saw Taser unleash a stream of electric bolts. Three rabids dropped.

Iridium smirked. "Show-off."

"Only for you," he said, and she knew he was winking under the goggles.

Jet, fighting with Knife, threw Taser a pained look before she dodged the rabid's steel-tipped claws.

"Keep your head in the game," Iridium snapped at Taser, frowning for Jet's benefit. Why, she had no idea. "This isn't over until the fat rabid sings."

"Yes, ma'am," Taser said, still with that infuriating grin

underneath his mask. He turned back to the battle, and Iridium followed him, taking note of the fights around her.

Lester and Steele worked together to bring down the lizard creature that Iridium didn't recognize.

Nevermore broke Freefall's arm and his concentration with it, destroying his gravity well.

Lionheart, elephant-sized, took out two more rabids by sitting on them.

Iridium herself strobed the Judge and his partner Gaslight, and when she looked up, it was over.

Lester approached her hesitantly. "You did well, girl."

Iridium mopped sweat from the back of her neck and managed a small, stiff smile. "You too, Dad."

"And your new friends aren't half-bad in a scrap," Lester said. "Perhaps there's a future in pooling our resources. Things change, after all."

"Yeah," Iridium said, looking to where Protean was helping Jet up from the floor. "They sure do."

CHAPTER 52

JET

Abducted by Shadow freak. Forced to show her lab rat. End result was both gratifying and disappointing. Serum worked exceedingly well. Hoped rat would be harder to kill. Almost ready to begin Project Sunstroke.

—From the journal of Martin Moore, entry #290

Someone was offering her a hand. Jet, still shaking off Knife's attack, accepted. She was surprised to see it was Protean, still gallant after taking down the rabid. "Thanks," she murmured.

"Sure."

"This is what, an even dozen of rabids?" Iridium let out a laugh. "The press is going to love it." She held up her hands, as if imagining the headline. "New Squadron Takes Down Dirty Dozen. Yeah, that has a nice ring to it."

"Deadly," said the Goth girl—Nevermind, or something like that.

Jet frowned as she looked at the unconscious rabids. Something nagged at her. She counted, blinked, then looked around.

Next to her, Steele said, "What?"

"Nothing. I guess I miscounted. Thought there were

thirteen all told, including Hypnotic." The man of the hour was still out cold, his hands cuffed behind his back. Turning to Arclight, she was suddenly taken aback, seeing him standing there, his skinsuit torn in numerous places, his white cloak covered in dust.

She remembered the night he had saved her life. He'd seemed so big, larger than life, as he'd reached for her, promising her that now it was safe, that everything would be all right.

That had been a lie. But it had been a pretty one. And the five-year-old girl she'd been had needed to hear it.

Her voice firm, she said, "I suppose now we're even."

Something passed behind Arclight's eyes—remembered pain, perhaps, or the ghosts of old friends. "Never even, little girl. We were too late to save your mum."

Yes. And Light, how that still hurt.

Jet approached Arclight, reached out to take his hand. "He would have killed me too," she said, her voice breaking. And he would have. Blackout had been insane, lost to the Shadow voices. He'd been coming to kill Jet just as he'd murdered Angelica. Jet remembered trembling alone in the dark, hiding in the closet, the Shadow first whispering to her then, promising to make her one of them.

She still had the nightmares. Sometimes.

"Even so, I wish it could've been different." Arclight paused, a glitter of emotion behind his eyes. "So many things I wish could have been different."

"As touching as this Hallmark Moment is," Taser said, "we sort of have a situation outside. Oof."

"Shut it, Bruce." That was Iri. "You have the soul of a used-hover salesman."

"Christo, woman, do you sharpen your elbows? I'll have a bruise under my ribs now."

"Quit your crying."

Jet squeezed Arclight's hand once more, then let go. "No, he's right," she said, turning to the others. "The people outside, the ones Hypnotic entranced. They need to get to a hospital."

"I can make a sled out of ice," Frostbite said. "Not the most pleasant thing for them to touch, but they're all zombied out anyway and won't feel the cold."

"Hook it up to me," said Lionheart, his human voice sounding monstrous coming from his lion's throat. "I'll haul them over to Cook County."

Jet frowned. "The mutants will charge you."

His fangs flashed as he managed a feline grin. "They can try. At this size, I've been clocked at twenty-four kilometers per hour."

"Good," Jet said, nodding. She still didn't trust the former Blackbird inmates, but as long as they were here and helping, she'd use them. To Frostbite she said, "Can you make a special delivery to Blackbird?" She motioned to the unconscious rabids littering the ground.

"Sure thing. I'll have Meteorite call ahead so they'll be expecting the care package."

"Excellent." That would not only get the rabids out of the way; it would also take Frostbite out of the scrimmage. He was paler than usual, and purple smudges bruised the skin beneath his eyes. He'd need rest, and a lot of it. Getting him out of the fighting was a good start—and it was the fastest way to get the rabids locked up.

Arclight said to Lionheart, "You'll come back after you drop off the invalids, yes?"

"'Course." He transformed back to his human shape. "Don't want my special pass all torn up."

Arclight slapped the other man's shoulder, then Lionheart headed for the door. "Come on, Ice Man."

"Frostbite," Frostbite growled.

"Whatever."

The two headed outside to load up the civilians. "Steele," Jet said, "watch their backs. Any mutants get close, push them back. Defense only."

"On it," the other woman said.

"Protean, help her," said Arclight. The huge man nodded in agreement, and the two joined Frostbite and Lionheart outside.

Jet slid Iridium a look. "This proves we can't just leave the mutants to run through the city. With all the rabids and rogues still making trouble, the mutants are sure to attack. Civilians could get hurt."

Iridium sighed, rolling her eyes. "Fine, fine. You've made your point. The evil sewer mutants from hell must be stopped."

"They're civilians too. Everyman junked them up with a serum that turned them into those monstrosities."

"Right, right, no taking out our frustrations on the sewer mutants," Iridium said with a huff.

"They won't think twice about ripping you apart," Jet said, thinking of Hornblower. "And they're fast."

"So we need to tranq them," Arclight said.

Kindle, looking outside, let out a whistle. "That's a lot of tranqs."

"We don't have those sorts of resources," Jet admitted. "Maybe we could approach the military . . ."

"I can hook us up," Taser said. When Jet looked at him, he said, "What, you think I've just been working the Runners? I'm still a merc, honey. I've got access to a lot of equipment. You'd be amazed how easy it is to just knock out targets instead of fighting them."

"No," Jet said dryly, "I'm pretty sure I have a good idea." Next to her, Iridium snorted.

Around his hidden mouth, Taser's mask pulled into a grin. "Don't worry. I'll be sure to charge for supplies as well as labor."

"You do that," Jet said, her voice clipped. "Just get the tranquilizers. Fast."

"Rush delivery's extra."

"Of course." Well, until Corp froze those accounts, they'd be able to pay whatever the mercenary demanded. And then some.

"While you're at it," said Iridium, peering outside, "tell the Runners to start working the press. Get the media on our side for a change."

Taser was already pulling out a handheld from a pouch on his belt. He started tapping keys. "What should they tell the newsies?"

"They should clear the streets while we clean up Everyman's mess," Jet said. "Maybe Lee will listen to good old human Runners—he sure won't listen to us. And make sure Wagner gets that message as well."

"Ooh. Idea." Iridium smiled wickedly—a smile Jet remembered all too well from the Academy. "Make sure to also tell them that Hypnotic had attacked the Squadron when he first escaped from Blackbird."

Jet frowned at her.

"That's why the extrahumans had gone crazy," Iridium said, winking at Jet. "It was Hypnotic's fault. You see? It's *perfect*. The media will eat it up and beg for more."

And it got Corp off the hook. Jet's frown increased.

"And now that we've captured him," said Arclight, getting into it, "the Squadron, along with Blackbird Special Forces trained to go after Hypnotic—led by me, of course—is confident that things will return to normal soon."

Jet sighed, picturing all the press conferences and exclusive interviews that would come out of this. Based on the gleam in Arclight's eye, he was already there.

"And," Arclight added, grinning hugely, "all damages to the city and to individuals should be sent to Corp-Co."

Jet actually smiled at that.

"Ooh," Iri crowed. "Gordon's going to love that! Brilliant!"

Jet had no idea who Gordon was, but she nodded anyway. The plan was far from perfect. And it still begged the question of why just about all the extrahumans had, indeed, gone crazy once Corp had stopped brainwashing them—whether they really were damaged goods that Corp had been trying to control.

But for now, it would do.

Interlude

"Terry, you see this?"

"Copy. Ugly fuckers, aren't they?"

Garth makes a face at the handheld. Next to him, Mary Janice covers a frightened giggle. "Well and good," he says. "What're we supposed to do, offer them a day trip to a beauty salon?"

The handheld spits out a burst of static. Then: "Any chance they're an illusion? Some of Hypnotic's work?"

"Fuck if I know. They look pretty damn real to me."

"Hang on, Jose's saying something." The connection clicks off.

Garth mutters, "Yeah, okay, we'll just stand here with our dicks in our hand while a bevy of beasties crash down the street . . ."

"You've the soul of a poet," says Mary Janice, sounding all of sixteen and trying not to scream. She's staring wide-eyed at the three enormous humanoid creatures. "Holy Jehovah . . . I think the female one's wearing pearls. Isn't that wrong? Monsters shouldn't wear pearls."

"Neither should swine." Garth catches something peripherally, and he turns to see a familiar figure looming in the distance. "Terrific. Here comes Colossal Man."

"Well," Mary Janice says, "maybe he'll, you know, stop the monsters?"

Garth fingers the baseball bat, hanging from its belt holster. "With our luck, he'll probably join them." If that happens, he and Mary Janice are rabbiting right quick back to the apartment.

The communicator clicks on. "Listen, those things are flooding Third Street. Rough count is a hundred. Reports are, they go batshit when they come across the Squadron."

Garth watches Colossal Man stomp his way closer to the monsters in tattered suits. "Define *batshit.*"

"Attack the Squadron soldier and try to tear his fucking head off."

That sort of batshit. Good to know. "Is it the powers that gets their backs up? The costumes?"

"Could be their fucking horoscope for all we know. So far, none of those things have attacked our people or civvies. And they only seem to attack cops and soldiers if they're attacked first."

"Polite monsters prejudiced against the Squadron," Garth says. "I think I've heard everything now . . .'"

"Until we can figure this out, do not approach. Repeat: do not approach."

"Yeah," Garth says, wincing as one of the beasties lets out a teeth-rattling howl. "About that. Our three monsters just spotted Colossal Man."

A long pause, then Terry replies, "Well, let them do our work for us. Do not approach. I'll call it in."

"Might want to call the morgue. May have a faster response time."

"We take what we can get. Stay in the vicinity until the cops show. Do not reveal yourselves."

"Copy," Garth says. He tucks the handheld back into his pocket and watches as the three beasts tackle the giant extrahuman's legs. The man's huge hand comes down, swatting at them like mosquitoes. Contact—one monster goes flying, lands hard against some normal's car, which morphs into an accordion. *Well,* thinks Garth, *that'll teach the person to park streetside when there are rabids and beasties and gangs overflowing the streets.*

"Uh-oh," says Mary Janice.

Garth hears the bellow before he turns back to see the two remaining creatures savaging Colossal Man's leg. One gets in a massive blow, and the giant goes down.

Timberrrr!

The crash is still echoing as the two things pound the fallen rabid into pulp.

Garth and Mary Janice exchange a look.

"We have to do something," she says.

"Yeah." He pulls the bat from its homemade holster and tests the grip. *There are times,* he muses, *when seeing in the dark means exactly Jack Shite.* "You get just as close as you need to get in range. And then CO_2 them."

She bites her lip. "I sort of have to touch them for that."

"Of course you do." He closes his eyes and says a brief prayer. "Okay. I'll smash with the bat, and you grab on when they're down. Right?"

"Right."

Garth hears the terror in her voice. "It's okay, lass. We'll make a great team."

She flashes him a tight smile.

Thinking of Julie, he charges forward.

He's there before he knows it, deftly avoiding scattered piles of wreckage that once might have been cars or trees or street. The bat's part of his arm, so natural in his hands, and he brings it back as he imagines the windup, the pitch—

A solid *THWAK* as the wood connects against the monster's oversized noggin. The creature's already shaking it off and starting to turn as he swings the bat the other way, feels the impact explode along his arms and shoulders and back.

"Now!" he shouts, not stopping to see if Mary Janice does her part. Blind trust in your partner goes a long way in a fight. His back to the first creature, he shoves the tip of the bat into the second thing's bulging neck. He sees the string of pearls just as the wood hits home. If not for his momentum, he would have pulled the blow. Physics, happily, overcomes chivalry as his full weight goes into the strike. It doesn't crush the creature's throat, but it does make the thing stagger back, rasping for breath. Feeling like a heel, he hits the thing again, a home-run swing that sends the beast to its nyloned knees.

Garth turns back to Mary Janice, who's holding on to the first creature's leg in a white-knuckled grip. The beastie itself is slapping at its face, as if trying to shoo away a fly. But the arms are moving slowly, weakly, and now they're not moving at all. With a groan, the thing rolls up its eyes and crashes to the floor. Mary Janice lets go just in time.

"One more for you," Garth calls out, his gaze back on the wheezing oversized creature in the tattered yellow unisuit. It's scrabbling forward, not quite on its feet. "Now would be good!"

"Need . . . a second . . . catch . . . my breath."

Right. One second, coming up. Garth lunges forward, wielding the bat like a sword as he swipes at the monstrosity. The thing skitters back, just out of the bat's arc. It's peering at him with flat, black eyes, and it grins at him, showing off perfectly white teeth framed by a lipsticked mouth. Garth barely notices the creature's hungry growl; his gaze has fastened on the yellow sunburst patch, at first blending with the remains of the yellow suit the thing was wearing.

Fuck me, he thinks, *but I think that's an Everyman. Everymonster?*

It bellows a challenge just before it launches itself at him.

He gets the bat up and knocks the creature back, and that's when Mary Janice, bless her, clamps onto the Everything's massive neck. A minute later, the creature is on the ground, unconscious.

Garth leans against his bat and lets out a shaky laugh. "Not bad for a couple of extrahuman wannabes, eh?"

Sitting on her haunches, breathing heavily, she flicks him a smile.

Colossal Man's still doing his roadblock imitation across Third. Not like there's any traffic; most people have gotten the hell out of New Chicago days ago, once the Doctor Hypnotic jailbreak hit the news.

Garth stares at the massive belt around the giant's waist. He's moving before he can think twice about it.

"Garth?" Mary Janice calls out, her voice shaky. "What're you doing?"

He peers into the first of the belt pouches, doesn't see anything useful. The second, though, reveals a pair of stun-cuffs.

Giant-sized. Grinning, he pulls them out. "Just securing the situation."

By the time they hear the sirens, Colossal Man is cuffed.

"So," Garth says amiably to Mary Janice as they walk away. "Want to go monster hunting?"

THEN

CHAPTER 53
NIGHT

The Everyman Society has everything I need: like-minded people and an unlimited supply of potential lab rats.
—From the journal of Martin Moore, entry #260

Night hated being naked.

He sat in the coffee shop in Looptown Mall, drinking black coffee and wishing he were in uniform. But no; for this meeting, he had to be in civvies. He didn't even wear the comlink; he was officially off duty. It made him feel itchy, but whether that was from being in normal human clothing or from not having the earpiece soothing him, he couldn't say.

Well, sacrifices were to be expected; Night couldn't have Corp listening in on this meeting, and the person joining Night would have been offended by the costume. And Night didn't want to offend him. This meeting was an unexpected surprise—one that Night had decided to turn into an opportunity.

A hero needs a villain, after all.

While he waited, Night called up the latest edict from the

Corp-Co Executive Committee—distributed earlier that week—
and he reread it via his wristlet screen:

POLICY CHANGE #425-C

Effective this memo, all Squadron branch headquarters
throughout the Americas are hereby dismantled. While
the Executive Committee encourages Squadron members to mix with their fellow crimefighters when off
duty, this interaction should be limited to their individual Sponsored Housing Complexes throughout the
Americas or to the sole remaining Squadron Academy,
based in New Chicago. Should more than seven extrahumans, on duty or off duty, be found gathering in places
other than these Corp-Co-approved sites or other
preapproved locations, those Squadron members will
have their active duty immediately suspended. If there
are any questions about this policy change, contact
your local Corp-Co Extrahuman Resources representa-
tive.

Night snorted. He wouldn't miss the headquarters, Christo
knew. Always surrounded by other idiots blathering the Duty
First party line was enough to make him want to punch out
someone's teeth. But he chafed at being limited in his interac-
tions with other extrahumans. Granted, normals were sheep
and fodder, little more.

And yet, now he and his brethren had to devote more than
50 percent of their active duty time to their corporate sponsors.
Those sheep had certainly learned how to put on wolves'
clothing, he mused. The triple-header of Angelica's murder,
Blackout's sentencing, and Luster's defection all within a two-
month period had decimated the Squadron's reputation and, by
proxy, Corp-Co's stock prices had plummeted. Stockholders had
not been amused.

Extrahumans might be small gods compared to their human cousins, but money made even gods slaves.

Bradford must be laughing his ass off.

A man's voice called out, "Rick?"

Night planted a smile on his face and as he closed the report, he turned to face his brother.

Frank Wurtham looked good. He was a man now, not the obnoxious teen Night remembered. Well, it had been more than ten years since they'd last seen each other; there were bound to be changes.

But Night was counting on certain things to have remained exactly the same. He nodded. "Frank."

His brother offered a hand, and after a moment, Night took it. They shook, and Night was faintly bemused by both Frank's hesitation and then by his attempt to outsqueeze his brother's hand.

Frank eyed Night's coffee cup. "Need a refill?"

"No." Night kept his voice level. "Thank you."

His brother sat, and for a minute or so, the two men said nothing as they looked at each other. Night could almost see individual emotions flitting across Frank's eyes: worry, fear, excitement, hope. Finally, Frank said, "I've been reading about your exploits."

" 'Exploits'? Do you mean my work?"

"Your costumed adventures, yes." Frank took a deep breath. "Rick, you didn't want to hear me out years ago. I'm hoping you will now."

"Are you referring to the time when you called me a freak of nature? When you told me my kind were dangerous to all humanity, and we should be locked up for the good of the world?" Night smiled thinly. "I know, it's a shock to think I didn't want to be insulted by my little brother."

Frank's face reddened. At least he had the decency to be embarrassed. "I was a kid. I never should have said those things to you in that way."

"You mean like a jealous norm?"

His brother's eyes glinted, and for a second the old rage was there, stamped across his features, contorting his face into something ugly. Then his features smoothed, erasing the anger until Frank was left with an earnest expression. "I can see why it would look that way. It wasn't jealousy, Rick. It never was." He spread his hands wide, placating. "It was concern."

"For my well-being? I'm touched."

"You're my brother, and I love you. I want what's best for you." He paused, as if measuring his words. "Rick, I'm begging you: Stop using those abilities. Leave Corp."

"Why should I do either of those things?"

Frank took the easy one first. "Corp is nothing more than a megalomaniacal organization that will crush anyone, anything in its path."

"Just like any other corporation out there," Night commented.

"Other corporations don't have an army of freaks to do their bidding."

And there it was. " 'Freaks'? Some things will never change, little brother."

Frank flushed again, but he didn't back down. "It's the truth. You're monsters, with abilities no normal human should have."

"We're not human. We're extrahuman."

"You're unnatural." Frank took a deep breath and visibly tried to calm himself. "And you're being used. Don't you see that? You're out there, trying to do good things—yes, I see how you save people's lives and try to make the world safer, I do see that, Rick—but it's Corp taking all the credit. Corp is using you."

Night shrugged. "So?"

His brother gaped at him. "What do you mean, 'so'? So tell them enough! So walk away from them! Leave Corp, and leave your costume, and live a normal life!"

"I can't do that."

Frank's eyes narrowed. "You mean you *won't*. You like being their toy soldier, don't you? You like throwing your weight around and terrifying normal people. Admit it!"

Night chuckled, thinking, *Same old Frank.* He said, "And here I thought you were trying to save me."

"I'd hoped you'd want to be saved! But no, you're all too happy to do Corp's bidding, to use that unnatural ability of yours to help Corp squeeze this country so tight that our blood will water the streets!"

Ah. And there was the rant that Night had been waiting for.

He leaned in close. "Between you and me, little brother, you're right. Corp is dangerous."

Frank's eyes widened.

"And so are extrahumans." Night lowered his voice. "We live on the edge, use our powers to shove normal people around. We make the police irrelevant. We're celebrity heroes, and Corp gets fatter from our successes."

"Yes," Frank whispered, his eyes fevered. "Jehovah, man, you *do* see! You do understand!"

"But not enough people do." This was it; Night had to make it convincing. "You're just one man, Frank. And one man's voice gets lost in the din of the mindless masses. But you can't be alone. There have to be other people, everyday people, who feel the same way you do."

"Yes," Frank said, nodding, "I know I'm not the only one . . ."

"What the people need," said Night, "is a voice to help them oppose extrahuman control. They need someone to speak for every man."

The last words echoed, then silence hung between them as Frank considered. Night waited.

"Every man," Frank Wurtham repeated, looking thoughtful.

"You could be that person, Frank. You could be their voice."

Frank met his brother's gaze. "Do this with me, Rick."

"I can't. It has to be regular people. Normal people. I'm just a freak, remember?"

His brother looked abashed. "I didn't mean . . ."

"You did. And it's okay. Because you're right," Night said. "My place is with the other freaks. But your place is elsewhere. It's a good fight, Frank. Are you willing to fight? To let out a rallying cry? To be the leader people need?"

"I am," his brother replied.

They shook hands, and Frank nodded respectfully just before he left.

Night allowed himself a small smile, then finished his coffee. Yes, every hero needs a villain. And with Corp-Co growing ever more powerful in the media and the world, it needed an enemy.

It was Night's fervent wish that Frank Wurtham would be that enemy.

After all, what else were brothers good for?

One month after the Wurthams met over coffee, a small group of people gathered to talk about the extrahuman threat. The meeting went better than expected, and the following month, they more than doubled their numbers. A month after that, they needed to rent a hall to accommodate everyone.

Within six months, the Everyman Society had more than ten thousand members. And that was before Frank Wurtham began his national campaign.

Night, when he learned of Frank's ambition, thought only one thing: *Took him long enough.*

Corp-Co Chairman Stan Kane tapped his fingers on his desk as he considered Night's report. Night stood at attention, waiting for judgment.

Finally, Kane said, "You're sure Wurtham would agree to a meeting? That he doesn't believe his own propaganda?"

"Oh, he does, sir," said Night. "But he's also an opportunist. He'd understand that by working quietly with Corp, the Everyman Society could better achieve its aims." He let it go unsaid that the clandestine alliance would, of course, also help Corp. Night could easily see Stan Kane and Frank Wurtham—or maybe Frank's Number Two, a man called Gordon—sequestered in some remote location—Maui, perhaps—discussing how to leverage their organizations' strengths to better support their own goals of power and prestige. All for the cause, of course. Whatever cause that might be.

Heroes and villains. They were one and the same. Even the masks were interchangeable, Night mused. Bradford was proof of that.

"I appreciate your report," the chairman said. "It's good to know we have someone on the Squadron who appreciates the bigger picture."

Night smiled thinly.

"Keep this up," Kane added, "and you may find yourself on the Executive Committee one day."

Thinking of Blackout's little Shadow girl—due for Academy training in six short years—Night replied, "Actually, sir, there's something else I'd like."

Kane arched a brow. "Oh? Name it."

Night named it.

Kane smiled. "That's it? Well, consider it done."

This time, Night's smile was wide, but it still didn't reach his eyes.

"Do you like it, sir?"

Night settled back in his chair. It was oversized and pleather, and it had wheels on the bottom. Very business-retro. It was the most stylish thing about his office; the rest was extremely spartan. The desk had no 2-D photos or hols; no pictures adorned the bare walls. The floor was equally bare. His elbows on the armrests, Night steepled his fingers. "Thank you, Celestina. This will do nicely. Please give the superintendant my thanks."

"I will, sir." A heartbeat, and then she hit him with a stream of words: "We're all so excited that you're joining the staff, sir. Having an active hero as a teacher!" The girl blushed, and Night fancied he saw stars in those odd purple eyes.

"I'm sure that enthusiasm will die down once you and the others take my Street Fighting Techniques class." He smiled briefly. "I have a feeling I'll be a difficult instructor."

"Oh, sir," she said, giggling. "You're one of the best heroes ever! You were part of the Siege of Manhattan! You've taken down the Torrent Brothers! You were part of Team Alpha!" She prattled on, listing his accomplishments like a groupie. Then she added, "And I'm sure you'll capture Arclight and Glitter Vixen any day now."

That last irked him.

When she paused for breath, Night dismissed her curtly. Wouldn't do to have the girl getting used to running on at the mouth whenever she was around him. Celestina closed the door behind her when she left, still giggling like an idiot. Night frowned, listening to the last of those giggles play out and finally fade. The girl admired him, clearly. But she didn't fear him.

That would change.

He turned to his computer, bringing up the latest reports, columns, articles, and opinions about Arclight and Glitter Vixen. The mainstream media were still properly horrified over the Good Guys Gone Bad, and politicos on all sides of the spectrum continued to rally behind Corp-Co in its effort to smear the Bradfords as bad apples from the beginning—and never mind that Luster had been the official Hero of New Chicago. Mainstream media, it seemed, had a short-term memory.

But the underground newsies, they *loved* the Bradfords, called them the Squadron Bonnie and Clyde. One rag in particular, cleverly called *Underground* magazine, was utterly infatuated with Arclight. Picture after picture of the man as he entered New Chicago Savings, entertained everyone with jokes and banter as he and Glitter Vixen politely robbed them blind, as the two made their glamorous getaway in a waiting garbage hover. Night scanned the latest editorial, rolled his eyes over the inane purple prose scribed by someone named Lynda Kidder, then turned away from the computer. His gauntleted fingers drummed a beat on the desk as he mulled over the situation.

Lester Bradford. Certified genius. Master of Light. Traitor to Corp-Co.

A disappointment, certainly, but Night couldn't say he was truly surprised. Bradford, after all, was a Lighter, no matter what idiotic designation he used. He was still an arrogant son of a bitch. He thought he could thumb his nose at Corp-Co and take on the entire Squadron, one by one.

Of course, the problem was that, so far, Arclight had been doing just that. The police didn't want to go after an extrahuman—especially not after one who'd worked with them on so many collars in the past. And the handful of Squadron soldiers who'd tried to tag Arclight . . . well, Night was certain they'd be released from Medical anytime now.

He grimaced. Second-stringers, sent to do an Alpha's job. Ridiculous.

But there was no more Team Alpha, no more separation between the heroes. They were all part of the Squadron, getting their marching orders directly from the Executive Committee. And those orders were explicit: You went after only the rabid you were assigned to collar, unless you happened to catch one doing something illegal during your patrol. It was even in the new handbook.

Well, eventually, it would be Night's turn to have a go at his former teammate.

Night's grimace pulled into a tight smile. If he was exceptionally lucky, all it would take was a few more *Underground* articles, or perhaps just one more headline story in which Arclight boasted about being a modern-day Robin Hood to Corp's Prince John. More likely, it would take months, even years. Bureaucracy was a bitch, but it was the way of the world.

But eventually, Corp-Co would send Night after the Bradfords.

When that happened, Night would not be going up against a former colleague, a man whom he grudgingly respected. No, Luster was dead and gone, buried in the arrogance of Arclight. His wife was an afterthought.

On that day, Lester Bradford would learn what it meant to be afraid of the Dark.

Content for the moment, Night turned back to his computer and started the tedious process of pulling together a syllabus for his class. He hoped that there would be at least one Light power among the brats that were to be his students.

After all, he had a special place in his heart for Lighters.

CHAPTER 54

ARCLIGHT

"It was only a matter of time before you lost one of them. You can't show a starving man a meal and expect him not to gorge himself."

—Matthew Icarus, testifying before the
Executive Committee re the killing spree
of Subject 6524, code name "Razor"

It was another bank robbery, in a string of at least a dozen, pulled off with style and flair by Arclight, New Chicago's most dastardly villain.

It would also likely be the last. First Federal was one of the only banks in the city not to install heatproof vaults in the year Lester had been on the run from Corp.

Still, he didn't believe in looking gift horses—bank vaults?—in the mouth.

Shouldering one sack of digichips and one of bearer bonds, Arclight stepped from the vault, his black cape swirling around his ankles.

What if you get yourself killed? Valerie had demanded the first time he'd stepped out in his new costume.

Not a costume. A uniform, a symbol of the resistance. Of

the amends he was making to Holly Owens and her daughter Joan.

Haven't come close yet, he'd said, with perhaps more arrogance than was strictly necessary. He'd come home to Valerie in the small hours after he'd pulled George Greene's little daughter out of that closet, in that awful abattoir, and, instead of breaking down, all he'd felt in his chest was a steely resolve.

We're finished with Corp, and Corp's rules, and the heroes who abide by them and allow themselves to be prostituted and killed.

Valerie had agreed. They'd planned, all through George's trial. They'd waited for the right moment, for the furor and the press to die down. Luster had used the underworld contacts he'd developed from years on the street to procure new identities and secret bank accounts for the money he'd been funneling into Callie's college fund.

And then one morning, when nobody would miss them for a few days—no press conferences, no training—before Yuriko had brought them coffee and the day's correspondence, they'd woken up Callie and run.

It had been so easy once Lester had seen the truth. His family or Corp. One or the other would have to wither and die to allow the other to flourish.

It had been easy to stop being a hero.

It had been easier to start being a villain. All he needed to remember was Holly's body on the floor and the face of that little girl. And the consistent, ever-present reminder:

You set this in motion. George killed her, but you started it.

Valerie, after she stopped worrying about him dying at the hands of some second-rate Team Beta wannabe, got into the act. She liked Arclight. Every once in a while, she even joined him as the newly dubbed Glitter Vixen.

And the sex had never been better.

There were even hints from Val about a second child. Lester let that bring a smile to his lips as he stepped through the melted front door of First Federal and into an onslaught of press.

Some things never changed.

"Arclight! Do you really think you'll get away with this?"

Lester flashed his smile into the cameras—the smile Corp had taught him, charming and devoid of real feeling. "Abso-bloody-lutely."

A wail of sirens in the distance put him on to the appearance of New Chicago's Finest, which meant he had less than a minute before some hero or another showed up.

"Anything to say?" another reporter shouted. "Anything to say to Corp?"

Lester tipped a wink at the reporter, a petite blonde with an unfortunately nipped and tucked face.

"As a matter of fact, I do." He hefted his loot so that the First Federal logo would be sure to show up on the newsfeeds in a few hours.

"And what's that?" the reporter prompted.

Lester grinned. This time it was real. "Catch me if you can."

"Where have you been?" Valerie demanded as Lester stripped out of his cape and dumped the two bags into the floor safe in their closet. He kicked a pile of dirty laundry over the spot, and spun to face his wife, who handed him a shirt and tie with a frown on her face.

"Check the vid. You'll see."

"Did you forget that your daughter has a birthday party going on as we speak?"

Lester skinned into the shirt and tie—nothing he'd have been caught dead in, in his old life. But this wasn't life. This was a cover. Charlie Ryan wore poncey ties even at home, so Lester donned it without complaint.

"Of course not. I told you I'd make it in time, didn't I?" He smoothed down his hair in the mirror. Now that Corp had stopped demanding he dye it, there were a few streaks of white creeping into the black, premature reminders of the hard road he'd taken so far.

"Callie's been asking for you." Valerie wrapped her arms around his waist and kissed the top of his ear.

Lester turned so he could return the gesture. "I'm just relieved she hasn't accidentally strobed the clown unconscious."

"There *is* no clown." Valerie cocked her eyebrow. "He's late, and his comm goes straight to messaging."

"Bloody hell," Lester swore, disengaging from Valerie's arms. "For the amount of cash I gave that wanker, he should be turning backflips while he makes balloon animals and whistling 'God Save the Queen' to boot."

"Les." Valerie swallowed when he frowned and started again. "Charlie. I handled it. Go enjoy the party. And for Christo's sake, tell your daughter happy birthday."

Lester nodded tightly and went through the hallway into the living room, where nine sugar-injected seven-year-olds were alternately shrieking, jumping on the sofa, and stuffing their faces with more sugar.

"Where's my birthday girl?" Explaining to Callie why her father was sometimes British and sometimes not had been a trick, but she'd adapted.

"*Daddy!*" she shrieked, leaping from the sofa and into his arms. "Did you bring me a present?"

"Indeed, I did," he said. "But that will have to wait."

Callie squirmed free and went back to her game. She'd blossomed since they'd left Corp, even with the fake names and the anonymous suburban house. No Runners watching her every move, no Yuriko scolding her that she'd be too fat for Branding if she ate a candy bar.

No one spying on his little girl, waiting to see if she'd be fit fodder for Corp's hero machine.

"Daddy, did you see the cake Mommy baked?" Callie shouted. "It's this big." She spread her arms wide, fell off the sofa, and collapsed into a giggle fit on the floor with some of her little friends.

"Be careful," he said. "Can't have any cake if you've got a concussion."

The door chime sounded, and Lester muttered "Bloody finally." Those bastards at Party City were giving back every cent of his deposit.

Years later, Lester would remember that he didn't check the security camera before he opened the door. He had been distracted, irritated, and preoccupied, like any father of a small, excitable child. If he'd seen the static obscuring his state-of-the-art security system, he would be a free man, he'd think, time and time again.

But he opened the door, and instead of a clown there were six impassive faces in riot shields.

The leader raised his shock pistol. "Lester Bradford. You are hereby ordered to submit to the authority of Corp-Co and appear before the Executive Committee on charges of robbery, fraud, and assault. You have the right to remain silent."

Blind panic was not something Lester indulged in. He had one second of mild shock, one *Oh*.

"Who wants cake?" Valerie called from the kitchen. "Put your party hats on for the birthday song!"

Lester stared at the leader of the Corp Containment squad, and the leader stared at him.

"Well," Lester said, not bothering with the fake Chicago accent. "Boris, isn't it?"

The leader blinked in surprise, then nodded. "That's right, Bradford."

"Boris, my daughter's in the kitchen having a birthday party. If you'd be so good as to have your gents come in, I'd prefer she didn't see this."

Boris peered in to check that Lester was really alone, then nodded.

"All right. For the kid's sake, Bradford."

Lester stepped aside, fingers digging divots out of the front door as his palms heated.

Boris held his shock pistol in Lester's face while his unit filed in and took up defensive positions. "This isn't personal, Bradford. You know that."

Lester shut the door and turned the dead bolt home with a soft *click*. Couldn't beat a good old-fashioned bolt.

"I know, Boris. Neither is this."

He released the energy he'd stored up in the minute since the Containment squad appeared on his stoop.

Boris, blinded, staggered and raised his shock pistol. Lester grabbed it, twisted his wrist, disarmed him.

In the kitchen, the kids and Valerie started singing "Happy Birthday."

"Charlie! You're missing the big moment!" Valerie called. "Hurry before she blows out the candles!"

The next Corp thug went down with a shock blast at point-blank range, his vest absorbing the small sound of the pistol. The third got an elbow to the throat, the fourth and fifth a broken ankle and wrist, respectively.

Lester didn't need his power when he had to be quiet. He'd learned how to inflict quick, subtle pain long before Corp. All it took was a cigarette butt, a blow to the soft tissue that wouldn't bruise, a hand on your throat, choking off your air.

The last squad member dropped. Valerie's tidy front hall looked like Jonestown.

Boris moaned in his sleep, and Lester took a moment to get his heart rate under control. All six were subdued, but they'd found him. Found Valerie.

Found Callie.

And there was no hero with the unit, which was against Corp guidelines as he knew them. Extrahumans for extrahumans. People like Boris couldn't be expected to take on Arclight with some shock pistols and body armor.

Someone had called off the hero.

Lester knew only one man with the clout and the single-minded arrogance to think he could take on the former Hero of New Chicago, defeater of the Ominous Eight, capturer of Doctor Hypnotic, protector of the people, alone.

He smoothed down his hair, not that it did any good coupled with his flushed face, skinned knuckles and torn shirt, and stepped into the kitchen.

Callie held out a piece of cake to him. "I made a wish, but I can't tell you what it was, because then I will have wasted it," she said solemnly. "But you can have the first piece."

"No, no," Lester said. "That's for you, birthday girl. All for you."

"Mister Ryan," said Callie's little friend—Tiffany or Swarovski or some ridiculous designer name—with a frown, "your accent is weird."

Valerie gave him a drill-bit look over the heads of the children.

"I've got some bad news, kids." His voice cracked, but at least it sounded closer to his cover of Charlie Ryan, lifelong resident of New Chicago. *Get it together. Breathe, refocus, and get it together, Lester.* "I've got an important meeting, so it looks like the party is over."

"Whyyyy?" Callie demanded with a whine. "I want to open presents!"

"Honey," said Valerie sharply, "don't talk back to your father." She gathered coats and party favors. "Come on, girls. Let's get you ready."

"You take them home," Lester said. "No need to call their parents."

Valerie stopped helping Tiffany-or-Swarovski into her shoes. "What are you doing?" she whispered.

Lester took her hand, which was cold and shaky. "What I have to."

"No." Valerie's eyes filled, not with tears but with fear. "I can't do this without you."

"Yes, you can. You're my Valentine. You're the strongest person I know."

"Come with us," Valerie begged. "Right now. The passports are under the front seat . . . we don't have to come back."

"You know there's no time." Lester smiled softly at her. She was the best thing that had ever happened to him.

But all good things ended, crumbled to dust.

Valerie grabbed him in a tight, fierce kiss. "Mom, Dad," Callie complained. "Gross."

"Take good care of her," Lester whispered against his wife's mouth. "And for Christo's sake, woman. Run."

Valerie let go of him, got the children in a line and out to the hover pad. She only looked back once.

When the shrieks and giggles had faded and the hover lifted off with a hum, Lester stood in the silent kitchen, listening to the cooling unit tick and the whisper of the house bots as they went about their tasks.

He took off his wedding ring, and set it on the kitchen table next to the remains of Callie's birthday cake. He took off the ridiculous tie, and slung it over the back of a chair.

In the drawer by the sink were a few knives, small ones for when Valerie felt like cooking rather than having a bot do it, or for making Callie a snack.

Lester shoved them into his waistband, leaving his shirt untucked.

He didn't know if the blades were to avoid being taken, or to avoid being taken alive. But their weight was a cold comfort as he walked down the hall of the stuffy little prefab house, stepping over the unconscious Containment officers, and opening the door to chill, crisp air.

Lester stopped on the stoop and looked at the figure on the walkway. A slow wind ruffled the black cloak and cowl.

"Hello, Arclight," Night said.

CHAPTER 55

NIGHT

Vids showed Night on the way to Blackbird. Tried to destroy the world. Can't wait any longer. Will roll out phase 1 of Project Sunstroke tonight. Sheer numbers will make up for whatever failings remain in the formula.

—From the journal of Martin Moore, entry #293

Standing in the doorway, Bradford smiled at Night, a perfunctory flash of teeth.

"Night," his former teammate said. "If I'd known you were coming, I'd have baked you a cake. Oh, wait." He snapped his fingers, and a light strobe popped.

Night's opiframes irised, canceling out the blinding flash. Automatic response. Night didn't move.

"I did bake a cake," Bradford said, stepping forward. "My daughter's birthday cake, to be precise."

"How is Calista?"

"Disappointed. Her birthday party was ruined when Corp rent-a-cops decided to crash it." He was out of the doorway now, standing on the top step of the front stoop. Free to move. "Do you have any idea how long we've planned this for her?"

"I know you placed the order for the clown a month ago. I know all the guests invited were normals, their parents in the dark as to who you really are."

"Been stalking us?" Bradford laughed, bemused. "How long've you known where we were before your masters allowed you to come play fetch?"

Nine months. Nine tedious months of waiting for the paperwork to play out, of waiting so very patiently for Corp to finally assign him to the Bradfords—specifically, to Arclight. Glitter Vixen was camera fodder, but Lester Bradford was truly dangerous. Nine months after pinpointing Arclight's secret civilian identity, Night was finally allowed to bring him in.

Nine fucking months.

But Night kept that to himself—that would be something for him to hang over Corp's collective heads, leverage for him to move up from instructor to proctor at the Academy. Instead, he hit Bradford where it hurt most: his pride and joy. "I know Calista's been giving her first-grade teacher fits because she's too smart for her own good." Night smiled, showing teeth. "I know she loves the spotlight. Wonder which parent she gets that from?"

Bradford's face hardened. "My little girl has nothing to do with this. This is between me and Corp."

"The girl's part of Corp," Night said, twisting the knife. "You and Vixen might as well have signed up for the breeding program. They've already slated a spot for Calista in the Academy once she turns twelve."

"Over my dead body."

"Melodramatic." Night sighed. "But then, you're a Lighter." With that, Night released the Shadow.

Bradford threw himself to the left just before the blast smashed through the front door. Night pivoted and the Shadow arced with him, hammering bullets of Darkness against the side of the house. Bradford was on his feet, hands out in a shooting motion, glowing white-hot. With a flicker of thought, Night had a Shadowshield before him. The Light missile bounced off, harmless. As did the second, third, and fourth.

"I repel light, Lester," Night taunted. If he got the man mad enough, he'd expend his energy that much sooner. "Your fireworks can't hurt me."

"No, but they do a fine job distracting you." Bradford pulled something from behind his back and hurled it—a knife, point gleaming.

Shadow could stop flying blades, but Night had to see them coming.

He saw the first knife. And the second. But after another burst of Light—a rat-a-tatting of strobes that went nova a second after Bradford released them—Night missed the third. It landed solidly in the meat of his left shoulder. He went down on one knee, grunting from the pain.

Bradford was on him in a shot, two kicks to Night's face. He went down heavily on his good arm, his jaw stinging, his left shoulder on fire.

"You should have left us alone." Another kick, this one to his gut. "I never would have come after you. You were practically family."

Snarling, Night lifted his face to glare at Bradford, who was standing over him like some warrior prince with a knife in each hand. "You think you were family? You think you could handle the Shadow swimming inside you?" He grinned suddenly, overcome by the image of Lester as one with the Dark. "Try it on for size. See if it fits."

And the Shadow poured out of him, leeching onto Bradford's face.

Night felt the sweat stinging his eyes, the pulsing agony in his shoulder. He ignored them as best he could, gritting his teeth as Bradford screamed. *Come on,* he thought. *Come on.*

Whether he was silently urging Lester Bradford to yield or the Shadow to eat Bradford's soul, he couldn't say.

With a roar to rock the heavens, Bradford grabbed the shifting black mass on his face and pushed strobe after strobe into it. The Shadow repelled the Light, but with every blow its grip on Bradford's face weakened until finally, the Shadow slipped off, twitching. His face frostbite yellow and streaked red with sunburn, Bradford slammed a bolt of light into the blot of Darkness. The Shadow, crippled, slunk back to its master and sank into his skin.

Shaking, Night forced himself to stand even as Bradford swayed heavily on his feet. Both men were panting, and staring at each other with equal parts hatred and respect.

"It doesn't have to be like this," Bradford said, rasping.

"It does. You're a criminal. I have to bring you in."

"You hate them just as much as I do." Bradford's eyes shone as if backlit by his power. "Be more than Corp's lapdog, man!"

Night smiled grimly. "Even lapdogs have been known to bite the hand that feeds them."

"Do it," Bradford urged. "Walk away from them. They don't deserve you."

"They don't." Night almost shrugged. "But they're what I've got. And you're under arrest, Lester."

Bradford stood straighter, a small smile playing on his lips. "You'll have to drag me in, kicking and screaming."

They circled, slowly, dance partners familiar with the steps but not the music.

"You had to go and taunt them, didn't you?" Night shook his head. "You couldn't just stay in the background. Always have to be in front of the vids, on the tongues of all the reporters and congressmen."

"You expect a Lighter to stay in the shadows?" Bradford actually laughed. "Corp's nothing but a bunch of wankers. They used us, made us their puppets. And when we break, they sweep us under the rug. Fuck them."

"We're not broken."

"What do you call what happened to Hypnotic, then? To Blackout? To poor Angelica?" Bradford was shouting now, and his hands glowed. "That was all on Corp's watch!"

"Hypnotic made his own choices," Night said coldly. "Poor choices. And Blackout was weak."

"Weak?" Bradford choked out a laugh. "I swear to Jehovah, you are an insensitive prick."

"Charlie?"

The sound came from behind Night—a man's voice, questioning and scared. Night didn't dare to take his gaze off Bradford . . . who had tamped down his power so that his hands looked normal.

"Get back in your house, Jack." Bradford's accent magically evaporated, replaced with the flat cadence of New Chicago. "Everything's fine."

Night took a step to the left, and then another; Bradford went to his own left, and again. Circling like sharks. Now Night could see the man Jack, tall and gangly, uncertain.

Enough.

Night lunged right and got Jack in a headlock. The man was too surprised to struggle; he flopped like a landed fish as Night tightened the hold.

"Night. Let him go."

"This man, who impeded an arrest? I don't think so."

"You're not going to hurt him," Bradford said impatiently. "You might as well—"

"Are you afraid of the Dark?" Night asked Jack. He lifted his free hand over Jack's sweating face, let the Shadow dance along his knuckles. "Want me to show you what's really in the heart of darkness?" He slowly lowered his hand, coming to a halt just over the man's eyes.

Jack whimpered, squeezed his eyes closed. Night smelled the ammonia stench of urine. Jack, apparently, was a bit of a coward. Perfect.

"Rick, don't do this," Bradford pleaded. "You're one of the good guys."

"Even good guys have to improvise sometimes." Night smiled grimly as he fished inside his belt pouch. "You want me to let him go? Put these on." He tossed the stun-cuffs to his former teammate.

The metal bands landed at Bradford's feet.

"What's it going to be, Bradford?" He tightened his grip on Jack's neck, and his hostage let out a pitiful gasp.

Bradford picked up the cuffs. Staring bloody murder at Night, Arclight growled, "You're no better than the criminals you're supposed to be fighting."

For a moment, Night heard himself telling Blackout that he was no better than the criminals. Blackout had just broken Calendar Man's back, and all he'd said about it was that crippling them made it less likely they'd come back for more.

Night had to admit that Blackout had a point.

"When a hero like you becomes a criminal," Night said, "it takes another criminal to stop him. Put them on, Lester, or I'll give this man nightmares to last a lifetime."

Bradford said, "Let my girl go."

"I can't do that, Lester."

The other man's eyes narrowed. "Good luck getting her away from Valerie."

"Thanks. Put them on, Lester. Now."

With a heavy sigh, Bradford snapped the cuffs home. As soon as they closed on his wrists, he lost his balance and fell hard on his ass. The power inhibitor in the stun-cuffs wreaked havoc with an extrahuman's balance.

Night loosened his hold on the hapless Jack. "Citizen, your role in assisting me with the capture of the dangerous criminal Arclight will certainly be reported."

Jack, free, stepped backward, his hands fluttering by his neck. "Arc . . . Arclight?"

Night walked over to Bradford and yanked him to his feet. "Lester Bradford, aka Charlie Ryan, aka Arclight. Wanted for robbery, assault, and a host of other crimes."

"Oh." Jack's voice was very small. "I'll, uh, I'll be calling the police then . . ."

"You do that." Night dragged Bradford up the steps and tossed him into the house. He landed heavily next to one of the unconscious Containment officers. Night looked around the living room and sighed, shaking his head. Really, Bradford was such a drama king. He touched his comlink.

"Ops," said a voice in his ear, so very different from the voices that whispered in his head.

"This is Night. I have Arclight. Send another Containment unit to the Ryan house. And send an ambulance." He glanced around the room again and said, "Better make it two."

Glitter Vixen and the so-called Code-Red Villainesses got busted robbing FreeMarket Financial Co. not even three months later. Night wasn't on that collar. Valerie Bradford was sentenced to Blackbird, same as her husband. Her sentence, though, was significantly shorter. Night wondered if she'd seduced the judge to make that happen.

Calista Bradford couldn't go in the Orphanage wing of the Academy; her parents were both alive, if rabid. Instead, she was placed in the foster care program, and one of the Academy Support workers, Abby Underwood, took her in.

No one took in Joan Greene. Night made sure of that. When the little Shadow came to the Academy to study, he didn't want anyone else to have a place in her heart.

Night never visited Arclight, Blackout, or Doctor Hypnotic at Blackbird. Really, there was nothing to say.

He saw Valerie Bradford exactly once, just before he became a proctor at the Academy. She no longer went by either her married or her maiden name. She had turned her back on her past and had become a respectable citizen—at least, on paper. As for what she did quietly, behind closed doors, Night couldn't prove and didn't care to pursue. Valerie Vincent Bradford was no more. Night wondered if Arclight knew.

The two of them talked for a long time. It was an uncomfortable conversation, but in the end, he agreed to her request. When the time came, he would recommend that her daughter and Angelica's daughter be roommates. He knew that Joan Greene wouldn't remember her childhood friend; the little Shadow had been so emotionally scarred she was lucky she remembered her own name. And whether the Bradford girl recalled Blackout's daughter from days past, well, that didn't concern Night. The girls could become roommates. It was a small thing, one that wouldn't change his plans in the long run. And if the two became friends, well, he would just have to use that to his advantage.

As far as Night knew, the woman who had been Vixen never did another thing for her daughter. Not that Night cared.

When Calista Bradford officially registered with the Academy on her twelfth birthday, Night was surprised by how much she favored her father in appearance. Maybe without Lester's influence, Calista would grow up to be a by-the-book superhero.

But Night sincerely doubted it.

Interlude

Panting, Garth rushes forward and jumps on the back of the hulking beast in the tattered remains of an expensive unisuit. He hooks his arms around the thing's neck and shouts, "Now!"

Mary Janice snakes a hand out and latches onto the creature's pant leg. Her lips peel back as she grunts.

The monster beneath Garth lurches forward, its hands clawing at its neck. Or it would be doing that, if its hands could get close—but something invisible blocks its way. Frantic, it starts bucking. Garth hangs on for dear life.

Slowly, the creature stops fighting. Its hands drop, and it crashes to its knees. Garth hops off before the monster falls prone.

Mary Janice keeps her carbon dioxide bubble in place for another thirty seconds before she lets it pop. Then she sways drunkenly. Garth catches her before she falls.

"Deadly, MJ," he says, hugging her. "That was positively deadly!"

Exhausted, she flits him a smile. "Any more?"

"Not that I can see." He flips open his radio and pings Terry at Command Center, otherwise known as the back room of Jose's store. "Old man, tell Toni we need one more set of steel cuffs."

"Scorch me, what's that make—twenty-two?"

"Something like that." Actually, it was twenty-six. He'd been counting. But he doesn't bother correcting Terry.

"Where are you?"

"Corner of Third and Obama."

"Toni'll be there in ten."

"So hey," Garth says, still keyed up from the fighting. "You give any more thought to my proposal?"

"Absolutely."

He doesn't want to get his hopes up, but his stomach flutters all the same. "And?"

"And it's going up for an official vote at the next meeting."

Garth, elated, spins Mary Janice in a circle and gives her a hug.

"What is it?" she asks, breathless.

"We're voting on it next meeting."

She grins. "It's crazy. I shouldn't want it to happen, but I do, you know? After everything we've been doing . . . I want it to happen." The grin melts, and she twists her finger around a lock of her blond hair. "Do you . . . do you think it'll happen?"

"Oh yeah," he says, feeling like he could fly. "I surely do."

NOW

CHAPTER 56

JET

Phase 2 of Project Sunstroke under way. Ninety-eight volunteers this time. Have to start planning phase 3. Wonder if I can get into the city's water supply.
—From the journal of Martin Moore, entry #299

This is the last of them," Protean shouted. With a grunt, he tossed four unconscious mutants onto the ground.

"Careful," Jet said. "Don't hurt them."

"*Them?* Christo, I think I wrenched my back . . ."

"Take a pill," Iridium said, dusting off her hands. "Not like you've got sewer-mutant stink in your hover or anything . . ."

Between the Squadron, the Blackbird group, and Taser leading the Runners, they'd scoured New Chicago, tranq-gunning every serum-warped person they could find. Those who flew had taken to the skies, raining down sleep like a gentle god. Not including Nevermore, who'd cackled every time another mutant went down. "Like shooting babies," she'd crowed. Jet had sincerely hoped the girl was exaggerating.

The rest had grabbed hovers and land cars, patrolling the

streets and air in search of the oversized, overmuscled creatures.

They'd even taken down a handful of Squadron rabids,
which was quite the nice bonus. Jet winced over how much
Taser would be charging for those extra bags and tags, but then
she decided it wasn't her problem. It was Corp's.

The thought made her smile. She still couldn't say anything
negative about Corp-Co without her brain catching fire,
couldn't even really think anything negative. But she could picture the administrative nightmare Corp's Executive Committee
would have explaining all the charges from the Squadron to the
chairman. Stan Kane might even have a heart attack, the poor
man. Well, luckily, Corp offered an excellent medical plan.

Now Jet and the Blackbirders were outside of the Illinois
State Prison, in front of the reinforced and electrified gates
(which would have done nothing against anyone who could
fly), waiting on the Containment crew to load up their newest
arrivals. Frostbite and Steele had headed back to HQ , stuffed in
the back of a Runner's van—the blue-haired Water power had
been swaying on his feet from exhaustion, and Steele had said
she needed to have words with Firebug. Alone.

Jet thought that boded ill for Kai.

Taser, too, had taken off, saying he had other jobs on his
docket for the day, but he'd be in touch, with his bill. He'd
blown Iri a kiss, which had pissed off Jet immensely. And then
he'd turned to her and done the same. Which had also pissed
her off.

Why did the man have to have such amazing lips?

Once the other Squadron members had left, Jet contacted
Meteorite, confirming that Ops had called everything into ISP
and had kept Commissioner Wagner in the loop. Meteorite had
laughed, promising Jet that she knew how to do her job.

"You really need to unwind," she'd told Jet. "Maybe borrow
Taser for a few hours."

Light, the woman was incorrigible. It didn't help that part of
Jet had thought that was a terrific idea. She tapped off her comlink, then put on the white-noise setting. She knew it wouldn't

do much to keep the Shadow voices at bay, but every little bit would help.

Light, please don't let me go crazy too soon.

"Getting twitchy?" Iri asked her. She must have noticed Jet tapping her ear.

"Just sick of listening to white noise."

"Yeah, waterfalls are boring. Maybe try some classic rock."

Jet grinned. "You remember the talent show from First Year?"

"Oh Jehovah," Iri groaned, laughing. "When Dawnlighter got onstage and sang that song . . . what was it?"

" 'Stairway to Heaven.' "

"Hah! Right! Took me days of cranking Led Zeppelin to get her wailing out of my ears."

They shared a laugh, and it felt so very right. Then Iri *beeped*. Or, more accurately, the handheld she pulled out of a pocket *beeped*. She grimaced as she scanned the message, then she groaned. "Oh goody. Gordon's got a bug up his ass."

"What's our illustrious leader want now?" asked her father.

"Us. Now. My place."

"Well then. Let's not keep the bloke waiting, shall we?" He turned to Jet and smiled. "I trust I'll be seeing you again."

"I'm sure." She just didn't know whether it would be in a Containment cell at Blackbird or not.

She watched Arclight, Lionheart, Kindle, and Nevermore herd into two hovers. Their strongman, Protean, waved shyly before he got into the vehicle.

He was sort of nice. For a villain.

Iri loitered. "What're you doing after this?"

"Heading back to HQ. Splurging on a hot shower. Why?"

Iridium smiled as she watched her father and the other Blackbirds zoom away. "I was thinking of getting some Mexican. Tacos, maybe. And a big, fat margarita."

Jet laughed softly. "That sounds divine."

Iri glanced at her, the smile still in place. "Want to join me?"

They shared a look, and finally Jet smiled. "Love to."

"I'll swing by after we're done getting berated." She hopped into Boxer's hover, and the two criminals—former criminals?—took off, leaving Jet alone to wait for Commissioner Wagner to give an official statement, or for the Containment unit to finally haul the mutants off, whichever happened first.

She stared at the enormous pile of slumbering warped people. There were well over fifty of them lying there, and probably close to a hundred. Anger stirred deep within her, heating her blood. Everyman had a lot to answer for.

Martin Moore had even more.

Now that all the Corp files had been downloaded and they had a ton of Runners helping with decryption, Jet fervently hoped there'd be something that incriminated Moore and, better, connected Everyman to—

A throbbing between her eyes, subtle, promising pain.

Jet blew out a sigh. Well, the process had begun. She thought of Lynda Kidder, a woman driven to find the truth—a truth that had consigned her to an early grave. *There will be justice done,* she promised Lynda silently. *Your death won't have been in vain.*

It was twenty minutes before the Containment crew opened the gates and came out of ISP. The team leader, a young man who was huge and bald, had gaped at the pile of mutants for a solid minute before he barked out orders. His crew was organized; it took them less than ten minutes to get all of their new charges inside.

Wagner arrived just before the last group of mutants were carted away. "Holy Jehovah in a minihover," he said, eyeballing the creatures. "Those things are even bigger and uglier than I'd been told."

"They're just people," Jet said tiredly. "Normal civilians, mutated by a serum. The Squadron's researching a cure." Translation: Frostbite and the Runners were scouring the decrypted Corp files for any information that would lead to such a cure.

Wagner frowned at her. "And you know this how?"

"My source is very believable." Inspired, she added, "If you're taking official statements, let it be known that the Squadron invites Everyman to help us find a cure for these human casualties."

His gaze hardened. "You're saying Everyman had something to do with this?"

"We have no proof that Everyman created a serum to warp humans into those creatures to go and attack extrahumans," said Jet, the epitome of professionalism. "Or that a man named Martin Moore may have been responsible for Lynda Kidder's death and the distribution of such a hypothetical serum."

He pulled out a digipad and jotted something down. "M-O-R-E?"

"M-O-O-R-E. Even though we have no proof that Everyman was involved in such a horrific act, the invitation for Everyman to join us in finding a cure for these poor, afflicted humans is sincere." She even smiled. "I'm certain Frank Wurtham will have a comment at the ready."

"Doesn't he always?" Wagner excused himself to speak briefly to the Containment captain.

Jet sighed, closed her eyes. Light, she was tired. But finally, after a week of utter insanity, she felt like she could breathe. There was still work to do, of course—far too many of the Squadron were still running around, junked up on their new-found freedom from Corp or maddened from the release of their mental shackles. But it no longer seemed like cleaning up New Chicago and the Americas was an insurmountable task. A long way to the top, to be sure, but at least the top was in sight.

She decided that she was going to thoroughly enjoy that margarita.

Wagner returned, pulling her aside.

"You should know that the wire's abuzz with how Hypnotic has been behind the Squadron going nuts," he said.

"Word travels fast."

"Very. Lee's doing a press conference in the next couple hours to officially acknowledge the work you and the others have done to try to rein in the chaos." Wagner smiled grimly. "Word is, he's going to not only thank you all by name, he's going to admonish Corp-Co for not keeping him and other government officials in the loop. Because obviously, Hypnotic's attack on the Squadron had to be on the QT to avoid widespread panic."

"Obviously," Jet said, impressed by how quickly Lee had moved to take advantage of the situation. You have to love election years.

Wagner looked at her, thoughts flashing behind his eyes, mouth pressed into a thin line. It was the look of a man with something important on his mind.

Patience was one of those traits the Academy had drilled into Jet. She waited.

And soon, Wagner told her, very quietly, what he was thinking about.

Jet had to bite her lip to keep from cheering. Smiling hugely, she told him that she'd let the others know. And then they shook on it.

CHAPTER 57

IRIDIUM

Corp-Co has built its empire on the broken backs of my children. I pity them. They have no idea the storm they've started brewing.

—Matthew Icarus, diary entry dated 2020

At the warehouse, which Iridium felt like she hadn't seen in weeks, Gordon waited in precisely the spot she'd left him. Tapping his toe. Looking at his watch.

"Waiting for a bus?" she said. "Those stop at the corner."

"On the contrary," Gordon said. "After your display in Looptown, I find I'll be staying here for quite some time."

"What are you on about?" Lester said.

Gordon produced a sheaf of old-fashioned paper files, passed them out to each of the rabids, including Iridium. "Your records are hereby expunged, and Corp has instructed me to offer its gratitude and support. You are all heroes again. As long as you work for us."

"Excuse me?" Nevermore said. "We're not still in your pocket. We did what you said."

"Right," Kindle agreed. "We even helped the heroes clean up Hypnotic's and Everyman's mess."

"If you have compunctions about returning to the fold . . ." Gordon patted his tie. "Remember who it is holding the keys to your cage."

"I'd sooner be six feet in the ground than working for Corp again," Kindle spat. He tore his file in half and threw the pieces at Gordon's feet. "Lock me up again, if you will. I'm nobody's dog."

Gordon's mouth crimped. "That's unfortunate." He drew his plasgun and pulled the trigger.

Kindle dropped, a leaking hole in the front of his jumpsuit. Protean cried out, dropping to the ground to try to stop the bleeding.

"It's not as simple as reincarceration," Gordon said. "You all now know far too much about Corp's . . . shall we say, private face. You work for us. Or you are a corpse. I hope that's sufficiently clear."

"I'll speak out," Iridium said. Her eyes darted from Kindle, with Protean cradling his head in enormous hands, back to Gordon. "I'll tell everyone exactly what Corp has been doing since the disaster. Recruiting felons, letting that nutcase Moore run loose. Brainwashing heroes. I'll tell the whole world what goes on behind that shiny corporate face and they'll believe me." She folded her arms. "After all, you made me a hero."

"Even you aren't that stupid," Gordon sneered. "Take the deal, Iridium."

Iridium started for him, her only thought to make him stop smirking at her, when she felt a hand on her wrist.

"Callie, that's enough." Lester looked Gordon in the eye. "You heard the man. Our records are clean as of this moment." His gaze slid left. "Lionheart. If you please."

Gordon had time to say "What?" before Lionheart streaked through the space left by Kindle and took him down. Lionheart's jaws closed around Gordon's neck, but there was no garish spray of blood. Very little leaked onto the warehouse floor.

With little sound and no fanfare, Gordon died. Lionheart sat on his haunches and licked his chops.

"But . . ." Iridium looked at her father. Just looked at him, trying to see some trace of the man she knew. But there was none.

This wasn't the same thing as suggesting they kill Doctor Hypnotic to save New Chicago. This had been an execution.

"We could have done what I wanted," she said. "We could have gone public and gotten rid of all of Corp, not just him."

Lester rubbed between his eyes. The lines on his face and the gray in his hair were very prominent, stark signs that Arclight was no longer the unstoppable villain he'd once been.

"Callie, I've learned some things since you were a girl. The most important: there will always be a Corp."

"Dad . . ." Callie started, but the sight of Gordon's blood spreading down like a halo around his head stole her voice. She glanced at the others, but Nevermore, Protean, and Lionheart simply looked between the body and Iridium, waiting to see what the outcome of the father/daughter battle would be.

"You know it's true," Lester said. "I tried to destroy Corp, and look what we wrought. Things are the worst that they've ever been. Yes, we're free." He gestured at the warehouse. "But this is the price. Destruction and loss and chaos. A world of anarchy. And Corp still exists."

Iridium rubbed her forehead. "So you're giving up, Dad? You're saying you'd live under Corp's thumb after what they did to you?"

"I'm an old man, Callie." Lester took his pardon from the folder and carefully made it into a small square, tucking it into his boot. "And I'm very tired."

"I guess you're not the hero Gordon thought you were," Iridium whispered.

"Far from it," Lester said. "I'm only extrahuman, Callie. As are we all, heroes and villains alike. The day will come when you must choose between heroics and your life. And I am choosing to end it."

"Where will you go?" Iridium asked him. She felt a sudden,

panicky emptiness inside her. Absent or present, Lester had always been her rock, her guidance system for right and wrong.

"Switzerland, probably. Your mother set up accounts there before she was arrested that Corp never found. Europe is lovely. It's been far too long since I traveled." He looked at Nevermore, Lionheart, and Protean. "You lot are welcome, of course. Couldn't have done it without you."

"Count me in, Pops," Nevermore said immediately.

Lionheart shifted back to his human form. There was blood down the front of his shirt, like a birthmark. "Yeah, me too," he rumbled. "No future in this city."

"Callie?" Lester raised his eyebrow, his expression telling her exactly what her answer would be.

"I'm staying," she said.

"To play the hero," Lester scoffed.

Iridium gritted her teeth. "If you wanted a supervillain daughter, you shouldn't have taught me so well, Dad. You showed me how to be a hero. Nobody else to blame."

Lester sighed, then turned to Protean. "What about you, big man?"

Protean stepped closer to Iridium. "I'm staying too. I like it here."

A smile quirked Lester's face. "So be it. I'll watch for you in the vids." He turned with a swirl of his black cape and started to leave.

"Dad!" Callie cried. She might never see him again, and he was just leaving? Lester turned back, and Callie pulled up short. "I just wanted to say . . . um. Have a safe trip."

She let out a surprised squeak when Lester swept her into a tight embrace. "I'm proud of you, Calista my girl," he whispered. "Don't forget it. You *be* the hero I never was."

Iridium blinked away the sting in her eyes. "Yes, sir."

Lester pulled away, and almost as an afterthought, took off his cape and handed it to Callie. "Take care of it, daughter."

Arclight walked out of the warehouse, head high and back straight as always, and Iridium stayed where she was, feeling fledgling and fragile as she had on her first patrol.

Protean nudged her. "What say you put that thing on and we go fight some crime for the greater good?"

Iridium slung the cape around her shoulders. It settled, not heavy. Just . . . present.

She flashed Protean a grin. "Yeah. Let's go kick some ass."

CHAPTER 58

JET

First day at the job. I'd never admit this to Aaron, but I'm eager for this opportunity. Working for the Squadron is exciting—and we have the chance to help them help the world.

—From the journal of Martin Moore, entry #2

When Jet arrived at the old Wrigley Field headquarters, she hadn't expected to see Taser there, chatting up a group of female Runners. The man was worse than Lady Killer. But at least he didn't wear nearly as much cologne.

"Ah, just the woman I was looking for." Taser walked over to her, arms wide, his mouth clearly grinning even behind the ski mask. Hooking one arm over Jet's shoulder, he said, "We should have a little talk."

Jet stiffened. Part of her wanted to knee him in the balls. The rest of her wanted to hug him. Light, she was hopeless. Jet ducked out from Taser and stood in front of him, hands on her hips as she glared at him. "I can't think of what I'd possibly want to talk about with you."

"A business proposition," he said.

Jet frowned at him. "Does it include kidnapping me and delivering me to a psychotic former hero? If so, pass."

As she turned to walk away, Taser said, "I promise you, Jet, this is something you're going to want to hear."

"Fine," she muttered. "Come on."

On the way to her quarters, a Runner tried to get her attention, but Jet was in a foul place and chose to ignore the woman instead of possibly bite her head off. Or worse; the Shadow had grown . . . unpredictable.

Once Jet and Taser were alone, she sat at the edge of her cot, arms tucked around her knees. "Well?" she said. "What's this business proposition?"

Taser leaned against the wall, his arms casually crossed over his chest. "I think we have us an unprecedented situation. Corp's going to want to take credit for Hypnotic's capture, and I'm sure they'll manipulate things so they'll have been behind you guys reining in the poor, sweet sewer mutants."

"Your point?"

"They can't brainwash you and the others anymore. That cat's out of the bag. You have that over their heads. You're in a position to make demands, and they'll have to listen."

Jet couldn't say anything about it. But Light knew, Iri could. And Frostbite. And Hornblower, still in the hospital, his leg gone. Oh yes, Jet thought, her eyes glittering, they certainly could say things. Horrible things.

True things.

"I've been talking to the Runners," Taser said. "Getting them pumped up. They liked getting out there, tranqing the mutants, getting into the thick of it. They want to do more than be your Stepin Fetchits, Jet. They want to actively help the Squadron, not just run their errands and pick up their dry cleaning."

Her own words, from just a week ago: *Maybe it's time for us to reach out to the citizens of New Chicago, work with them now more than ever before. Build goodwill.*

Yes, Jet thought, a smile playing on her face as she remembered Wagner's offer. *Yes.* The Runners could be their civilian counterparts, working actively with the police and Lee's office.

Branching out from New Chicago to expand the network throughout the Americas.

"What about . . ." Damn it to Darkness, she still couldn't say *Corp*. It made her want to scream.

Taser understood. "What about them? They can't tell you no, not anymore. Don't you see, Jet? For the first time, you and the Squadron are in control."

She frowned up at him. "You said this was a business proposition. What's your role in this?"

"Me? I'll be your friendly local mercenary, ready to do the dirty deeds you good-guy heroes aren't allowed to do. Consider me the ultimate negotiator."

"For a price," she said, "of course."

He shrugged. "Of course. A boy's got to eat."

"I'll talk to the others." She stretched, then began to massage her left shoulder—her weak spot, ever since she'd first dislocated it Fourth Year.

When she felt his hands on her shoulders, she stiffened. "What are you doing?"

"I'm still trained in massage," he murmured. "Among other things."

She slid out from his hands and pivoted to face him. "No."

"No?"

"No."

He cocked his head, looking her up and down, his hidden gaze lingering on her chest. "You still want me, Joan. Don't try to deny it."

She swallowed thickly. "I don't deny it."

"So?" He leaned forward, reaching out to her, stroking her cheek. "What's the problem?"

She wanted to lean into his touch. Instead she shrugged away. "The problem, Bruce, is the last time I trusted you like this, you betrayed me the next day."

"That was just a job."

Hugging herself, she got off her cot, showing him her back. "Yes, it was. I get that. But that was also the last time you'll ever get me."

He chuckled softly. "We'll see."

"Don't you have to go find Iridium and hit on her? Or maybe one of the dozens of female Runners you keep tucked around you?"

"Thanks for the permission." A pause, and then, "Be seeing you, Joan."

She stayed with her arms wrapped around herself for a long time after he left. And then, finally, she went to shower.

CHAPTER 59

IRIDIUM

The horror is, I can pinpoint exactly how it came to this. How I changed the world. I wanted to save my daughter. I doomed the world instead. I doomed it to Corp, and to their Squadron of thugs. I opened a floodgate, and the tide has drowned me.

—Matthew Icarus, diary entry dated 2020

By the time old Wrigley Field hove into view, Iridium was feeling decidedly less chipper.

The day she'd avoided at age seven, when Night had merely captured her father instead of killing him, was happening now. She was, for all intents and purposes, an orphan.

Would the Squadron even want her, now that they weren't up to their asses in sewer mutants?

Would anyone even care that Iridium, no longer a villain, was still breathing?

"Everyone," she said when she stepped into the ready room. "This is Protean. Protean, that's Firebug and Meteorite. You know Taser."

"Hey, man," Taser said, shaking his hand. "Glad you decided to stick around."

Protean nodded, smiling mutely.

"I'm Kai," Firebug said, extending her hand. "Welcome aboard." She left it at that, and quickly pretended to be busy at a console. *She should be uncomfortable,* Iridium thought. Hypnotic wasn't the only boogeyman out there. Kai might not last if she was that easily rattled.

"It's good to have you," Meteorite said, and Iridium was shocked to see an actual smile creep across the former Weather power's face. It looked like it hurt her a little. "We can always use another hand."

"And I can see I'm in fine hands, myself," Protean said, bowing over Meteorite's grasp. The Ops controller turned pink.

Iridium rolled her eyes. *Ah, young love.* "Where's Joan?" she asked Meteorite, before she got lost in Protean's eyes.

"In the briefing room," Meteorite said, "going over the sifted data. Trying to sniff out information on Moore. Doesn't want to be disturbed."

"Of course she doesn't," Iridium said, and went down the curve of the corridor and ducked into the small room that housed mounds of data printouts. Jet, her back to Iridium, was hunched over the desk, scanning what looked to be a kilometer's worth of reports. "Hey," Iridium called out. "Meteorite said you were hiding out in here."

Jet turned, and Iridium was momentarily at a loss. She couldn't remember a time she'd *ever* seen Jet in civvies—even at the Academy, Joan had always been in one uniform or another. Not to mention with her hair down in loose waves, and a smile on her face. And no optiframes.

It was official. The world had, indeed, been turned inside out.

"Iri!" Jet's face fell as she stared at Iridium. "Callie, you look terrible. Did something happen?"

"My . . . my dad left," Iridium blurted.

"Left?"

"Took off. Gone. Vamoosed. Protean stayed behind, with me. I came by to drop him off with you heroes." She made a move to step back. The corridor suddenly seemed very close.

"Wait." Jet pressed a button on a pager, and when a man's voice answered, she said, "Lowell, Iridium needs a change of clothes, please. Do you mind?"

"Sure thing," came the reply. "Seven all right?"

Numbly, Iridium nodded.

"Perfect," Jet said. "Thanks." She took in Iridium's disheveled appearance and added, "Oh, could you also bring a hairbrush? And a full can of hairspray?"

"Screw you, Jetster." Iridium actually managed a half smile.

"Go shower, get clean," Jet said. "Then we can get some food and talk. About your dad. About everything."

"I don't really want to talk," Iridium protested. "I just wanted to make sure the big lug was going to be safe with you supertypes."

"Well, I want to talk," Jet said. "Besides, I believe you said something before about margaritas."

"There's something I can't figure out," Jet said.

Iridium downed her second margarita. At least now she didn't feel empty. Just numb and slightly buzzed. Taking a guess, she said, "How Hypnotic escaped from Blackbird?"

Jet raised an eyebrow. "I hate it when you do that."

"Eh, you're easy. What else does an OCD superheroine think about in her free time?"

Jet smiled as she took a bite of enchilada. "Well?" she asked around the cheese.

"Radar," Iridium replied. "He pretended to be an inmate named Radar. Mind control, from the very beginning. If that guy didn't have puppets to string along, he'd be useless." She sneered, trying to be tough and pretend Hypnotic hadn't gotten to her, but the memory flashed all the same.

Bruce, the smiling crowd, her father free and happy and by her side.

"Son of a bitch." Iridium frowned at her empty glass. "I'm glad he got what he deserves."

"Me too," Jet said absently, staring at the fish tank in the corner of the restaurant. A lionfish floated alone among the coral, fins flicking sadly.

"Well, this has been fun and all, but I should be getting back." Iridium signaled for the check. The restaurant had human waiters, another plus. She'd been around far too many extrahumans lately. "Wreck City isn't going to clean itself up."

"Iri, wait." Jet downed the dregs of her margarita. "There's something else we need to talk about."

Iridium shook her head at the waiter. "Cancel that. Bring me another one of these." She waved her glass, and the man retreated.

Jet told Iridium about Taser's plan, the blackmail . . . and the founding of an independent superteam, one that went beyond the extrahumans.

Iridium snorted. "So Taser is what, now . . . Superconsultant?"

"If we did form a new team," Jet said hesitantly, "I'd want you to be a part of it."

Iridium choked on her first sip of new margarita. "Excuse me?"

"Say yes, Iri."

Iridium wrinkled her brow. "For Christo's sake . . . why? Why do you want me?"

"What happened during Fifth Year . . . that's behind us. You got a raw deal. You didn't get a chance to work with the Squadron until this week. You're good, Iri. Damn good. And I miss you. I miss my old partner." She bit her lip. "I miss my friend."

"What is this," Iri muttered, "Extrahuman Confessions?"

Jet waved a hand. "Never mind, Callie. I can see you're not comfortable with the idea. Forget I said anything."

"Are you kidding? I'd be happy to be part of the team." To be wanted. Needed.

To have her friend back.

Jet grinned at Iridium. "Together again. Just like old times."

Iridium took a gulp of margarita and grinned back. "Christo, I hope not."

CHAPTER 60

JET

Received Matthew Icarus's original notes after Aunt Sarah's funeral. Spent the weekend reading. Everything I'd thought about extrahumans was wrong.
—From the journal of Martin Moore, entry #48

Excuse me, ma'am?"

Jet looked up from the mounds and mounds of raw data. "Please, Tara," she said tiredly. "Just call me Jet."

The Runner blushed. "Sorry, ma'am. Um, Jet. Here." She handed Jet a memory stick.

Jet blinked at it, and said, "For me?"

"That's what was in the post-office box. You know, the one in Old Chicago?" She nibbled her lip. "I've been trying to give it to you, but you've been busy . . ." The Runner's voice trailed off.

"It's all right," Jet said, her mind already flashing to another memory stick, one she had found back at Lynda Kidder's apartment all those weeks ago. "I should have made myself more accessible. Did you see what's on this?"

The Runner looked abashed. "Of course not!"

Jet flicked a smile. "Thank you, Tara."

"Glad to help, ma'am."

Jet sighed as Tara scooted away. "Ma'am" made her feel much older than twenty-two. She pushed away the piles of decrypted information and inserted the memory stick into her computer.

There were three files on it. One was labeled READ ME FIRST. Another was called ICARUS PROJECT. And the last was simply MM.

Go save the world somewhere else, the teenage girl snarled at Jet, her eyes telling a different, desperate story.

Jet opened the READ ME file.

My parents are card-carrying members of Everyman. Me, I'm the afterthought daughter. I'm also a thief. A good one.

I stole the two files you're about to read.

They're copies of the original journals—written the old-fashioned way, on paper—that I borrowed from Martin Moore. Couldn't keep those, because if he discovered they were missing, he'd probably do something crazy. Because he is crazy, you know.

The first file is a copy of Matthew Icarus's journal, back from the 1980s.

The second file is Martin Moore's personal journal. (Sort of ironic: He writes at one point that he finds hand-writing to be much safer than keeping an electronic log, which anyone could steal.)

There's interesting stuff in there. Thought you should know.

I may be a thief, but I also know the difference between right and wrong.

What they did was wrong.

What he's doing is wrong.

Good luck, Squadron. You're going to need it.

—Kylee Selene

Jet's heart pounded in her chest as she reread the file. Then she opened up the ICARUS PROJECT.

Two hours later, with a trembling hand she opened up the MM file.

When she was done, she asked Meteorite to come into the room.

Soon the Weather power was reading, and Jet was trying to keep her brain from exploding. She sat, curled in a fetal position, chanting aloud how Corp was good, knowing full well that it was all bullshit.

Corp was despicable.

The thought brought fresh fire to her head, and so Jet bit back a scream and rocked and tried to tell herself again that Corp stood for justice, that Corp had the best interests of humanity at heart.

A heart that was black and rotten.

When Meteorite was done, she said nothing for a long time. Finally, she asked Jet if she should bring the others in for an urgent meeting.

Jet agreed.

"This . . ." Meteorite swallowed. "This is it. We can finally bring Corp down. Can't we?"

Jet didn't know. "Call the others," she whispered.

Soon they sat in the main room: Steele, Firebug, Frostbite, Meteorite, Taser, Iridium, and Protean. Boxer was in the hospital, visiting Hornblower, and he wouldn't leave his nephew's side for anything short of "a minor or major Apocalypse."

One of Meteorite's numerous computers had Kylee Selene's files uploaded. Jet began talking. At points when the pain overwhelmed her, Meteorite spoke for her.

And this is the story they told.

Martin Moore and his twin brother Aaron are descendants of Dr. Matthew Icarus, the founder of a New Jersey-based fertility clinic—which was open from 1988 until 1991—and the creator of the Icarus Method: a gene-therapy treatment that stimulated fertility in women and allowed them to conceive naturally. This part about Icarus Biological was well-known. So was the fact that Corp-Co bought Icarus, which was completely absorbed into Corp's biological sciences division in 2018.

What was less known was that Corp-Co had also bought disease-control centers in Mumbai and Hong Kong—which were also absorbed into the organization's bio-sci division.

What was not known at all was that Corp had not merely *bought* the troubled facility, which had been plagued with lawsuits from former patients as well as a fire that had all but destroyed the original clinic. Corp had actually funded Icarus's gene-therapy research.

According to Matthew Icarus, Corp-Co was looking to create a breed of programmable soldiers that would replace the armed forces and the police alike—superior fighters who would obey commands instantly, without question.

The experiment went awry. The majority of children born as a result of the Icarus Method had horrific birth defects or mental disorders. A number of children were tested and found to be clean, with no measurable side effects. And a handful of children were born with extraordinary abilities. They were the initial extrahuman generation.

Corp-Co oversaw those extrahuman children's education and training. When those children were adults, Corp created the Squadron.

And then Corp expunged all records of its involvement in the genetics program. Matthew Icarus himself stayed with Corp, developing many tools and measures to train the Squadron and to oversee the next generation of extrahumans.

One thing became clear to Icarus: There was a basic flaw in the extrahumans' genetic code. This flaw invariably led to various disorders and pathologies, including but not limited to suicidal tendencies, mood disorders, schizophrenia, and dementia. Some extrahumans' conditions were mild; others were severe. Still others were incredibly dangerous, to themselves and everyone around them. Because of this, Corp-Co insisted on medicating the Squadron to lessen the severity of what CEO Sebastian Lister called "going extracritical." Thus began the practice of lacing the extrahumans' food and drink, to help keep them stable for as long as possible.

This was all in Matthew Icarus's journal—which had fallen into the hands of Aaron and Martin Moore twenty-five years ago.

And then there were the revelations of Martin Moore's log.

The Moores were both scientists on Corp's payroll when

they discovered the truth of the extrahumans' origin and their liabilities. The brothers decided to use Icarus's notes to create tools and methods that would better control the Squadron. The Executive Committee gave them its blessing.

The two most prominent items in the Moore brothers' legacy were the comlink and Therapy.

Because they were interested in mind control, the Moores studied Doctor Hypnotic and the other Mental powers closely— including Angelica, who they had determined was a Mental power and not a Lighter. After much trial and error, they successfully created the comlink. Through this earpiece, a signal was sent out to all extrahumans, one that would effectively keep the Squadron loyal to Corp-Co—and to the Moores themselves.

As for Therapy, Aaron Moore created the technique as a permanent solution to what he'd dubbed "The Extrahuman Question." The first extrahuman patients unfortunately were lobotomized. But over a period of eighteen months, Aaron Moore perfected the procedure. Now, as Squadron members reached their "extracritical" points, they underwent Therapy. The result, according to Martin Moore, was beneficial to everyone.

But the tone of Moore's journal changed after his brother was killed by Doctor Hypnotic. It became darker and more vengeful, with Martin blaming the Squadron and Corp for Aaron's death. One thing became clear: Extrahumans were ticking time bombs, and it was Martin Moore's mission to destroy them before they went insane and annihilated everything in their path.

Moore stayed on in Corp's employ, lying low as a computer technician while he quietly worked to sanitize his records and expunge all mentions of himself and his brother from Corp's files. On the side, Moore began experimenting to create a serum that would mutate normal humans into powerful beings that would be completely devoted to Moore, and programmed to destroy extrahumans. Lynda Kidder was the prototype. Moore expressed disappointment that Kidder had been defeated so easily by "the Shadow freak," and said his goal now was to unleash a horde of mutants to keep the Squadron busy, while he worked to perfect the serum and create a new breed of creature that would not stop until the Squadron was destroyed.

Where did he get the resources for such experiments? The Everyman Society. When he joined, he quickly became close with a core group of people who felt the same way he did about the extrahumans: "Put them down like the rabid dogs they are." Moore's involvement with Everyman, he admitted, was just a means of obtaining a steady supply of fanatical volunteers who were devoted to the pretense of making everyday people as powerful as the extrahumans.

His last entry was after the Ops signal had been cut off, thus freeing the Squadron from the brainwashing frequency fed through the comlink. In this entry, Moore was furious over Frank Wurtham's cutting off Moore's funding. The chairman had discovered that Moore was a Corp employee. This prompted Moore to hire Bombshell to blow up the New Chicago Everyman branch office, and to firebomb City Hall to divert suspicion from himself.

As of now, Martin Moore was still at large.

But the Squadron has his journal, as well as Icarus's notes—both of which damned Corp for its role in engineering the extrahumans.

When Jet and Meteorite finished speaking, silence reigned. Everyone in the room sat, stunned and speechless, looking lost.

"We really are freaks," Firebug whispered.

"No," Jet said, her voice hollow. "We are what we are. Extrahuman."

"We're all going to go crazy!" Firebug's eyes were wide with fear. "Don't you see? We're broken!"

"Kai," Jet said, her voice sharp, "we're broken only if we say we're broken. Stop gibbering. You're a Squadron soldier."

Firebug's breath hitched. Steele put her arm around her shoulders, and Firebug sobbed quietly as her partner soothed her.

Weak, Jet thought coldly. And the Shadow voices agreed.

"We've got them," Frostbite said, slamming his fist on the counter. "We finally got them. We're going to the press!"

"Which accomplishes what?" Protean asked. "Other than causing worldwide panic over how extrahumans are wired to explode?"

That shut Frostbite up.

"Frankly," Iridium said, "I think this is a load of cowcrap." She turned to Frostbite. "You haven't gone crazy, even after what they did to you. I haven't gone crazy. None of us have." She looked pointedly at Jet, who managed not to flinch.

"Corp lies," Frostbite said, nodding, clearly willing to believe Iridium's words. Jet thought Iri would make a terrific politician. Frostbite said, "This is all probably just one big wad of bullshit."

"Hear, hear," Taser said, lifting an imaginary glass in a toast.

Meteorite looked green. "What if it's not?"

"It is," Iridium said firmly. "My dad may have been a criminal, but he was never crazy." Her gaze slid to Jet. "Unlike some of our former mentors."

Jet ignored the Shadow voices whispering in her mind. She was too busy taking in the other extrahumans' responses. Iri clearly would be fine. So would Frostbite and Taser, who looked bored. Protean seemed to accept Iridium's words as a small truth, if not complete gospel. Steele was unbendable; no matter what, she would fight the good fight. As for Firebug, well, she would have to make it through this.

As would Jet. Maybe the Icarus journal was nothing more than one man's speculation and oddly wishful thinking. Maybe it was all lies, and Martin Moore decided to believe those lies.

It didn't matter. They were heroes.

Duty first.

Always.

"So what next?" Jet asked. "Do we pretend nothing has changed?"

"Go to the press," insisted Frostbite. "Corp's got to pay."

"I have a better idea," Iridium said slowly, a smile blooming on her face. "Let's blackmail the hell out of those sons of bitches."

CHAPTER 61

IRIDIUM

I cannot fight the future. I only hope my children will.

—Matthew Icarus, in his suicide note dated 2020

TWO WEEKS LATER

Iridium looked at the loose knot of heroes waiting on the debris of the old playing field. "I don't like it. They're just . . . standing there."

Taser shrugged. "No law against standing."

"I don't like it, either," said Frostbite, frowning at the costumed strangers. "Who asked them here?"

"Corp," Iridium said. "Looks like Squadron: India finally got an offer they could agree to. Bet you an E they've come to clean up Corp's mess and make sure we're not fomenting revolution."

Frostbite folded his arms. "My point exactly. I say we tell them to screw off. Possibly with fireballs."

Firebug rolled her eyes. "Don't volunteer me just yet. We should at least talk to them first."

"They haven't made a hostile move," Steele said, backing up her partner.

"True," Jet said. "Iridium, Frostbite, come with me. Taser, stay close in case the situation degenerates."

Iridium rolled her eyes and followed Jet down the bleacher steps, Frostbite bringing up the rear. In the past two weeks, Jet had become positively unbearable in her role of Fearless Leader.

The problem was, Iridium had to admit she was pretty good at it.

The three of them approached the onetime pitcher's mound, where the five costumed strangers waited. "Hello, fellow heroes," Jet called out.

Then again, Iridium thought, there were moments like this.

"Jet." One of the men, presumably the team leader, nodded. He was tall, dressed all in black, and had curly dark hair that wanted a trim. He carried himself like Taser—that loose, catlike posture that spoiled for a fight no matter what the situation.

Iridium narrowed her eyes. "Something we can help you boys and girls with?"

"I'm Deathdealer," the man said, holding out a hand. "Leader of Team *Aik*." He pronounced the word *Ek*. Hindi for *one*. "Squadron: India sends its regards. And us." He spoke English with a trace of Brit, and Iridium felt inexplicably comfortable with him.

That made her frown deeply. She never felt inexplicably comfortable with *anyone*.

Jet solemnly shook his hand. "A pleasure to meet you."

Iridium stared at the woman standing next to Deathdealer—her hand was pressed to her forehead, as if she were fighting off a migraine. Iridium, who knew when she was being vibed by an empath, popped a strobe. "Stop that," she warned. "We learned to sense emotional tampering back at the Academy." Celestina had been a particularly effective instructor. It had been one of the few classes Iridium had bothered to pay attention in.

The empath glared at her, but she lowered her hand. The good vibes stopped.

"No disrespect intended," said Deathdealer. "Merely attempting to avoid a confrontation."

"Here's how you do that," Frostbite piped up. "Get back in your hover, point it east, and fly until you get home. We don't want Corp's help."

"You've made that abundantly clear," said Deathdealer. He turned and spoke to his team in Hindi, and as one they drew back.

Iridium and the others waited.

Deathdealer smiled politely. "It is also clear that your resources are thinned, and that you're desperate enough to take on criminals." That last was clearly meant for Iridium.

She decided he'd be nice-looking if he didn't have such a hard-assed expression on his face. "*Former* criminal," she returned. "I was pardoned."

"Team *Aik* is willing to offer its services until such a time as you can repopulate your ranks," Deathdealer said to Jet.

Frostbite snorted. "And in return, you spy on us for Corp."

"But of course," Deathdealer said, arching a brow. "I would have thought that was obvious."

Iridium snickered. Oh, she liked him. "What's your power, Deathdealer?"

"I slow the biological function of the body, impeding cellular reproduction and inducing cell mortality."

Iridium whistled in appreciation. "The touch of death?"

He nodded, and a tiny twitch in his cheeks stood in for a smile.

"Cool with me," she said. "You know, Jetster, we can't really turn him down."

"Excuse us," Jet said, then grabbed Iridium by the wrist and dragged her off to the side. Frostbite, humming, followed. When the three of them were alone, Jet hissed, "You don't make decisions for the entire team, Callie."

"Of course not. But can you really turn the guy down, considering how many rabids are still out there?" Iridium ticked off the points on her fingers. "Hornblower's still in physical therapy, Moore is still loose, the rest of us are exhausted . . ."

"And besides," Frostbite added, "that man is incredibly hot."

Iridium chuckled.

"Seriously, Iri's right. We're stretched way too thin. And what better way to give Corp disinformation than to feed it to their spies directly?"

"The enemy you know," Iridium said cheerfully. "And yeah, Deathdealer is too hot for his own good."

"Fine!" Jet huffed, holding up her hands in surrender.

Iridium grinned as she and Frostbite followed Jet back to the Squadron: India reps.

"Deathdealer, Team *Aik,* we are happy to accept your generous offer," Jet said magnanimously. "Welcome to New Chicago. When we're out of the field, I'm Joan Greene." The show of ultimate trust: the offering of one's nondesignation name.

"My name is Sunil Patel," Deathdealer said.

"I'm Calista," Iridium said. "But you can call me Callie." Next to her, Frostbite *harrumphed.*

Deathdealer cocked one eyebrow, then slowly looked her up and down. He didn't bother trying to hide his appraisal of her body. Iridium decided she liked that. A lot. "Very well, Callie. Please call me Jay."

Iridium's mouth quirked. "You ever been to New Chicago?"

"I have not."

She offered her elbow. "Wait until I show you Wreck City."

She walked with Jay back toward the clubhouse, tailing Jet and Derek, leaving the others in Team *Aik* to follow.

It wasn't the warehouse, and being a superhero rather than fighting with them still sat strangely with her, but Iridium couldn't deny that if this was being a hero, she liked it.

CHAPTER 62

JET

While we can control them for now, it begs the question of what will happen when they are no longer subject to our will. What would the Squadron, freed of its Corp-Co messaging, choose to do with its power? Would it serve mankind . . . or demand to be served?

—From the journal of Martin Moore, entry #98

Jet kept the smile painted on her face and pretended all the hundreds of people in the crowd outside of City Hall wouldn't be looking at her when she took the microphone in a few minutes. In front of her, blathering for all the vids, Mayor Lee droned on. And on.

"Babe," Meteorite said in her ear, "your BP is skyrocketing. Calm down. It's just a press conference."

"I know," she replied, using the old trick of not moving her lips. Can't have the Shadow power talking to herself, now, can we? We don't want people thinking she might be just a wee bit soft upstairs—especially now that she was hearing Shadow voices almost all the time.

Light, she hated public speaking.

"You want to know what your favorability rating is?"

"No."

"Want to know how many people want to sleep with you?"

"No!" she hissed, stretching her smile wide, wide, wide.

Meteorite chuckled. "More than 64 percent. That's higher than it ever was pre-Hypnotic." That's how they were dividing history now: pre-Hypnotic, when they were all slaves to Corp-Co, and post-Hypnotic.

Jet couldn't quite bite back a groan.

Standing next to her, Iridium leaned over to whisper: "Picture him naked."

Ew.

"Wow, she *can* smile without looking like she's screaming," Iri mused. "Who knew?"

"Shhh!"

"Please. Like anyone's going to care about us girls chatting behind the mayor's back."

The mayor, pompous as ever, loudly and proudly announced how thrilled he was to have the Squadron back, how extrahumans were once again the protectors of their human cousins, how he had no doubt that New Chicago would once more rise up to be one of the jewels of the United and Canadian States of America, et cetera.

And the crowd ate it up. The Runner network had been doing its job better than Jet had anticipated—they were proving themselves to be the exemplars of public relations, far better than Corp had ever done. Bruce had known what he was doing when he'd gathered them together during the crisis.

Damn him, anyhow.

"By the way," Iri whispered, "I like the new look."

Jet tried not to blush. "It's not that different." She still wore the black leather–Kevlar blended skinsuit, which covered her from neck to wrists to ankles. The boots, gloves, and utility belt were the same. Her optiframes were in place, as always. But no cloak, no cowl. Her golden hair hung in a thick braid down her back.

"You don't look like a female Night anymore. It's good."

Jet smiled, even though she was now blushing madly.

"She's right," Meteorite chimed in. "If I swung that way, I'd do you."

Jet choked, then covered with a polite cough and thought of the many different ways she'd love to kill the Ops coordinator.

Finally, the mayor introduced Jet, once again the official Hero of New Chicago, their own Lady of Shadows.

The crowd, as they say, went wild.

Trying not to panic, Jet stepped forward and shook the mayor's hand. He was smiling for the cameras and staring bloody murder at her, warning her silently that if she even thought of skipping off now to do anything short of saving the world from exploding, he'd personally chop off her head.

She stepped up to the podium and smiled at everyone standing on the steps outside of City Hall, cheering for her. Cheering for New Chicago. Jet took a deep breath, then she spoke.

"Thank you, Mr. Mayor, and thank you, New Chicago." She paused to let the audience settle down. "When Doctor Hypnotic broke out of Blackbird a little more than two weeks ago, it felt like the End Times were upon us. Hero turned against hero; extrahuman turned against human. People were hurt. Property was destroyed. All on the whim of a man who would have bent all of our minds, forced us to live in the world of his creation."

She hated the lie. But this was the compromise. And the good part was yet to come.

"Doctor Hypnotic is once again in Blackbird. And that wouldn't have happened without the work of human and extrahuman, of heroes and former villains." Jet looked to Iri, who stepped forward and—*ack*—waved, grinning like a fool.

Flashes and pops of cameras and vids as Iridium made her public debut.

"This is Iridium. She works with light. She's one of a number of people who have set aside their differences to come together for the common good. Get a good look," Jet said, smiling warmly. "You'll be seeing a lot of Iridium."

Iri's hands sparkled, and the media ate it up.

Jet waited until the crowd's roar of appreciation died down. Then she said, "We're only two of many extrahumans who have been fighting to protect New Chicago and her citizens." She looked to her right, bowing her head to Commissioner Wagner, standing next to the mayor. "But we have done nothing more than New Chicago's Finest, those brave men and women who constantly put their lives on the line to serve and protect all citizens who call New Chicago their home."

A large burst of applause. Wagner nodded at her, acknowledging her words.

"We may be extrahuman," Jet continued, "but we couldn't do our jobs without the help of a very human group of individuals who have been with us from the beginning, running errands and messages, supporting us. Helping us to help you."

More applause, this time more hesitant.

"Doctor Hypnotic may be once again behind bars," she said, "but that doesn't negate the damage he's done. Many extrahumans who had fallen under his control are still fighting to free themselves from his influence. And there are others whose minds were horribly shattered." She paused, allowing her somber words to sink in. "We will do everything we can to help our brothers and sisters to heal. But our first priority, as always, are the citizens of New Chicago and of the Americas. Duty first."

The vids whirled.

"Along with extrahumans," she said, "many humans have been hurt by Doctor Hypnotic. We've been told that these victims of the so-called zombie plague are starting to wake up from their trances. Confused, to be certain, but healthy."

She was interrupted by massive applause, and was only just able to hear Meteorite say, "Man, Lee is *pissed* you scooped him on that. Heh."

Jet smiled broadly. "The doctors and nurses and paramedics who have been working nonstop to help these victims are also heroes, and we are grateful to them all."

More cheers, well deserved.

Okay, she thought. *This is it.* "Mr. Mayor, you introduced me as the Hero of New Chicago. But that title truly belongs to everyone who's been fighting to keep the people of this amazing city safe, both human and extrahuman. And this is why we are no longer a Squadron of extrahuman soldiers, working with a corporation to be textbook heroes."

Utter silence.

"We are human and extrahuman," she said, and both Iridium and Commissioner Wagner stepped forward on cue. "The police and the Squadron from this moment on will work together as the Protectors of New Chicago, and of the United and Canadian States of America."

Now the crowd was ecstatic, the roars of approval deafening.

"We will no longer be bound to corporate sponsorships," she shouted over their cheers. "We stand before you today, human and extrahuman Protectors, to promise you all that your safety, our citizens' safety, will be first and foremost of our priorities. Thank you, Mr. Mayor. And thank you, New Chicago."

Thunderous applause.

The mayor, looking shell-shocked, shook Jet's hand again. Based on the crowd, it would be a while before he came down on extrahumans again. Can't go on the record being opposed to something the constituents love—not with elections right around the corner.

"This," Iri said, waving, "is really freaking cool."

And it was.

Jet, smiling, also waved—and way in the back, on the tail end of the crowd, she thought she saw a tall boy, his Earth-power physique all too clear, his light hair shining as brightly as his smile.

Samson smiled, his eyes full of love and pride.

Tears stung her eyes, but her optiframes masked them. She blew a kiss to the ghost of her love. That night, the media would tear itself into a frenzy over who the intended recipient of that kiss was.

Jet, doomed to go insane, allowed herself to put aside her fear of the Dark and simply enjoy the moment.

At least, for a little while.

And in the End...

Julie McFarlane opens her eyes for the first time since falling victim to the zombie plague, and Garth is right by her side. His smile is blinding, and tears of relief slide down beneath his sunglasses.

When they kiss, she accidentally blinks off the hospital room's overhead lights. Neither Garth nor Julie notices.

EPILOGUE

This time, when Jet and Iri visited Hornblower in rehab, he didn't toss them out right away. He let them stay long enough to tell him how the move to the new building was progressing before he threatened to blow them out the window.

"Well," Iri said, "that could have been worse. At least he didn't throw anything this time."

Jet was depressed, so Iridium insisted on Mexican.

The quesadillas were sinfully good. Jet took another bite and sighed blissfully as her taste buds cheered.

"My goodness, I think Jettikins just had a minor orgasm."

Jet laughed, and quesadilla nearly ran down her chin. "I don't know how I'm going to survive having the Plaza across the street from the best Mexican restaurant in the city."

"In the country," Iri insisted. "Yeah. We'll get fat as whales. Good thing we've also got the best training wing since the Academy."

Jet nodded, swallowed. "Can you believe the size of the pool?"

"Pool, nothing. Can you believe the size of the hot tub?" Iridium punctuated that with a bite of taco.

"Almost too good to be true."

The two shared a sober look, then tucked into their meal.

Corp-Co's donating Protector Plaza to them wasn't the weirdest thing that had happened since Iridium and Taser had taken down Ops almost three months ago and had inadvertently started an extrahuman revolution. But it was weird enough that Jet, Iri, Frostbite, Taser, and Commissioner Wagner—the unofficial executive branch of the Protectors—had hired a lawyer to review the contract.

Everything came back clean: Corp-Co, as a sign of goodwill (at least, publicly), had donated 1600 Obama Avenue to the Protectors, formerly the Squadron, which Corp-Co officially recognized as an independent entity, etc. etc. And Corp didn't get anything in return, except for a huge tax write-off.

The extrahumans in the Protectors knew this was only part of Corp's paying them for their ongoing silence about Corp's involvement in the Icarus Project. None of them said anything about it to Wagner.

The timing of the new headquarters worked out well. The Protectors had needed a place to hang their hats (or capes), and a good chunk of former Squadron soldiers had come to their senses over the past few weeks—nowhere close to the original four-hundred-plus active Squadron members, granted, but enough so that onetime baseball bars were nowhere near large enough to accommodate everyone.

And more than that, they had all the Academy students and staff as well. The day after the first Protectors press conference in front of City Hall, Wagner had gotten a call from Celestina. She and Stretch, another proctor from the Academy, had ushered the students and staff out of the building when all the chaos had ensued and had taken them to Northern Illinois University as part of an "unexpected field trip." When everything got sewered in New Chicago, the two proctors led the Academy refugees to Lake Wissota State Park, Wisconsin. The students and staff had been roughing it outdoors while Celestina and Stretch kept tabs on the extrahuman situation. The press conference had convinced Celestina and Stretch that it was finally safe for them to bring the students back to New Chicago.

That was another four-hundred-plus people. Including all the Runners and the extrahumans who'd come back to the heroing side of things, that put them just over six hundred people. Corp's gift had been too good to pass up.

So they'd cautiously accepted the new headquarters, which they had taken to calling Protector Plaza. Cheesy, yes. But it wasn't like there was a huge P at the top of the building.

Before they signed on the dotted line, they had an engineer come to scour the place and make sure there were no surprises. That scan, too, came back clean. They charged the review to Corp-Co for good measure.

The lawyer who'd overseen everything, a young woman named Jeri Thomas, offered her services as legal counsel to the Protectors. Her great-grandmother's brother had been Squadron, and her dad was a cop. The Protectors council agreed that it couldn't hurt to have their own Legal Department.

And they needed to start classes for the students.

And they had to create duty rosters.

And then there was Meteorite pushing for PR control.

And there was Squadron: India, still involved, even though the Protectors' ranks had filled up. Corp still wanted its spies in place, and the Protectors council wanted their enemy where they could see them. Besides, Iridium was dating Deathdealer.

And Martin Moore was still out there, somewhere, perhaps with more of that serum. The mutated normals were all doing well at ISP, according to Wagner, but they needed to be cured, not contained. If only the Innovator wasn't still rabid . . .

Jet sighed. The logistics of actually launching the Protectors was enough to make her head spin. Life had been simpler when she'd been Corp's puppet and just went out fighting crime and doing photo ops. Maybe Meteorite would be the chief operating officer and oversee all of the day-to-day stuff . . .

"You've got that look," Iri said.

Jet blinked, looked up at the dark-haired woman. "What look?"

"The business look. Christo, Joannie, let yourself be on break for a day. Hell, an *hour*."

"There's just so much to do . . ."

"It'll keep," Iridium said. "For once, let yourself come first."

"But—"

"I promise, the city will still need saving, even after you've had time off. Waitress, please bring this woman a desperately needed margarita."

"It's not even noon," Jet said, abashed.

Iri winked. "Live a little, Joannie."

So Jet drank the margarita.

"Where do you want these?"

Jet glanced up from her wristlet. The Runner floor captain was holding a carton labeled BOOKS. Jet motioned to the back corner of her room, near her bed. "The back corner, please. Thanks, Lowell." She sounded distracted, even to her own ears. But then, she had reason.

Lowell left, and she went back to her black wristlet, a holdover from Academy days. It still served as portable data storage and was the tool of choice when someone wanted to send an untraceable instant message—one way only.

Police Commissioner Wagner had just sent such a message.

HG OUT. QT.

She stared long and hard at the message. Doctor Hypnotic had gotten away, and Wagner was keeping it out of the press.

How had he done it? Had one of the guards at Blackbird slipped and forgotten to medicate him one morning? Had it been an inside job?

She remembered how, on the day she and the others had defeated Hypnotic, she had thought there were supposed to be thirteen prisoners, not twelve.

Had Hypnotic even made it into Blackbird in the first place?

Jet rubbed her eyes. The how didn't matter. Doctor Hypnotic had escaped.

And part of her—the part that listened to the Shadow and basked in the dark—was glad. Before she could fret about her reaction, her comlink chimed softly in her ear. "Excuse me, Ms. Jet?"

She sighed. For the millionth time, she told the Ops trainee: "Please, Tara. Just Jet."

"Sorry, ma'am. Um, Ms. Iridium says you need to come to Reception. Um, she says, right now. She actually said a curse word in there, too, but I'd rather not repeat that."

"Is everything all right?"

"Um. Yes?"

There was a vote of confidence. "On my way."

She got down to Reception, expecting to see Iri and maybe a few others. She hadn't expected to see roughly fifty people crammed into the waiting area.

"Jet," Iridium said, grinning hugely, "wait until you hear this. Go ahead, Mr. McFarlane."

A tall redhead in sunglasses stepped forward, offering his hand. Jet shook it cautiously.

"My name is Garth McFarlane," he said, the kiss of a brogue in his voice, "and I'm an extrahuman."

Jet blinked. "Oh?"

"We all are," he said, motioning to the crowd of people in Reception. "We call ourselves the Latent Network, because our abilities were always small enough to stay off Corp's radar."

"Ah," she said, glancing at Iridium, who was still grinning like a child locked in a candy shop.

"When the Squadron went berserk, we knew we couldn't stay hidden. We couldn't help you with Hypnotic, but a group of us did help with those beasties that had been rampaging along Third Street."

"Really?"

"We took down twenty-six of them," he said proudly. "Some rabids too. And that's when we decided that we were joining you."

"You . . . what?"

"Voted on it, and everything. It was unanimous."

"Um. Mr. McFarlane . . ."

"We know we'll need training," he said. "Most of us don't know the first thing about fighting. And our powers are small. But we're extrahumans, and we want to help. We're joining the Protectors. Only sixty-two of us were able to get to New Chicago so far, but we're all excited about this."

Only sixty-two? "How many of there are you?"

"One thousand, five hundred and twenty-six."

Jet's mouth opened, then closed with a *snap*.

Next to her, Iridium grinned. "Bet you didn't see this one coming."

"Not in a million years," Jet said, a smile blooming on her face. "I think we need bigger headquarters."

ABOUT THE AUTHORS

JACKIE KESSLER (Jet, Angelica, Night, Garth) learned everything she needed to know about Good versus Evil from reading comic books. When not writing about superheroes and the villains who beat the snot out of them, she likes to write about demons, angels, and the hapless humans caught between them. In addition, she has a pseudosecret identity as a novelist for teens. For more about Jackie, visit her website: www.jackiekessler.com.

CAITLIN KITTREDGE (Iridium, Vixen, Luster/Arclight) is a lifelong lover of superheroes. Growing up homeschooled in a rural area, her best friends were Batman, Spider-Man, and Wolverine. In addition to collaborating on the Icarus Project, she writes two bestselling urban fantasy series, the Nocturne City and Black London novels, as well as steampunk stories for young adults. She lives in Massachusetts with two cats, her Cobra Commander action figures, and more comic books than she can count. For more about Caitlin, visit her website: www.caitlinkittredge.com.